At The Going Down Of The Sun

By

G.M.Hague

G.M.Hague

AT THE GOING DOWN OF THE SUN

by GRAEME HAGUE
First published in 2014
This edition published in November 2022

Copyright for all editions owned by G.M.Hague.

Contents:

G.M.Hague

At The Going Down of the Sun.

Three and a half thousand Australian airmen lost their lives during the Allied effort to bomb Germany out of the war from the beginning of 1942 through to the end of hostilities in Europe in 1945. All aircrew apart from members of the Pathfinder squadrons were expected to complete thirty operations over enemy territory to reach the end of a tour. The highly trained Pathfinders had to finish forty operations.

The chance of surviving those thirty missions was less than two percent. Almost from the moment they took off, the bombers were over the unforgiving ocean or the enemy-held continent. If the men weren't killed by their aircraft being destroyed around them, they risked drowning in the freezing northern oceans or execution on the ground. The lucky ones were taken prisoner.

They flew mostly at night, and for most of the war didn't have any protection provided by Fighter Command. Hundreds were shot down by German night fighters guided by radar, or they were blown out of the sky by the accurate anti-aircraft or "flak" gun batteries surrounding every target.

Some men were more skilled at their trade, others made up for any shortcomings with sheer courage. No one was immune to the spectre of bad luck, or the unpredictable circumstances that put your plane in the wrong place at the wrong time—in the gun sights of the enemy. And the more the bomber crews flew, the higher the odds stacked against them.

Yet amazingly some men survived and even signed up for a second tour, convinced that their fate wasn't to be killed over Germany. It was always going to be someone else. For the price of the enormous risks they took, they lived in comparative comfort in Britain within reach of good food, drink and their wives and sweethearts.

RAF Bomber Command suffered the highest rate of casualties than any other service.

One

Waddington, England. March 1944.

'This is silly. We're going to freeze to death out here.' Susan's voice was sullen, and she sniffed wetly to make her point. Her WAAF uniform was hidden beneath a bulky overcoat, and she wore a wide, blue and black football scarf that almost came to the bottom of her cap. Hunching her shoulders helped to close the gap. As a result, Susan's pale face was a white blob among her dark clothing. Only a few wisps of red hair escaped to touch her cheeks. She sat uncomfortably on a camp chair, her figure a resentful mound watching her friend standing beside her. The damp grass came up to their knees.

'The sun is shining. It's quite warm, really—it's spring, don't forget.' Dianne had already heard one plea from Susan about returning to their quarters and a hot cup of tea. She kept gazing across the green countryside towards a rumbling, pulsating noise coming from beyond the runways. She was dressed the same, except she didn't have a scarf and had to make do with turning up the collar of her coat against the chill morning breeze.

'Tell me again why we're doing this?' Susan knew the answer. She was only hoping to expose the madness of it all. They were waiting at the end of the main airstrip. It was a popular place. The rickety camp chairs lived permanently there for anyone who visited.

'I promised we'd wave him off—we promised, remember? It'll bring him good luck.'

'For goodness' sake, it's a damned training flight. They're only going to fly a few circuits around the airfield so they know how to take off and what the ruddy place looks like from the air, and that's it. Back in time for morning tea—' Susan shook away the thought of her hands wrapped

5

around a steaming mug. 'That short chap, the one who tried to tell me he was a pilot, but he's just a gunner—the lying sod—he told me.' She pulled a gloved hand from where she hugged it under her armpit to point at Dianne. 'It only goes to prove you can't trust Australians. My mother told me that when she heard they were coming. Gave us all sorts of grief during the last war, she says.'

Dianne replied absently, 'They would have been soldiers. There's a difference. These fellows are air force, obviously. And they're not all Australians, don't forget. There's all sorts.'

'Canadians and New Zealanders too,' Susan said mournfully, as if that were worse. 'But mostly Australians. I don't think my mother's opinion is good about any of them.'

'Your mother doesn't like anyone who might like you. Her precious virginal, God-fearing daughter who would do no wrong—'

'All right, all right—I know, I must have a chat with her sometime.'

'The disappointment will kill her,' Dianne murmured.

She tried to stand on tip-toe and see further, but it wasn't any good. The sea of long grass rippled as the breeze gusted and she nearly toppled over, caught off balance. Susan let out an unlady-like curse as she was buffeted by the wind too. She swayed alarmingly on her chair, the legs sinking into the soft ground.

'Damned weather.' She stood to reset the chair, giving it an annoyed shake.

'Charming language,' Dianne laughed, turning to watch. 'Where did you learn that?'

'Where do you bloody think?'

'You need to put on a bit of fat. That'll keep you anchored to the ground and put your mother's mind at ease. Not so attractive, see?'

'And give you first chop at all the lads? Not likely.'

Both the girls were slim and slightly built, the rationing of wartime Britain making sure they stayed that way. Their heavy coats and thick uniforms felt ungainly. The regulation shoes weren't coping well with the open ground.

***

The night before, in a warm pub and with most of their extra clothing draped across the furniture, the two WAAFs had found themselves the centre of attention when the room filled with noisy, boisterous aircrew. Another squadron had been assigned to their station. Despite a drunken farewell two nights before to the departing squadron, it had always been a plan between the girls to be there that night as well, knowing the newcomers would head into town for drinks in the evening. You never knew who you might meet. Susan had been a little reluctant. She was having a tenuous relationship with a fighter pilot based in Plymouth. Despite the regular endearing letters from him, it was clearly not going to last much longer. She saw him too little. But her guilt still nagged, since she hadn't told him how she felt.

The girls raised their eyebrows and shared a smile when the lounge got loud with a chorus of strange, harsh accents and quite a lot of profanity. One dark-skinned, serious man sat in a corner close by and watched everyone silently as he sipped on a pint.

'Hello, he's an aboriginal, you know,' someone quietly told Dianne, using it as an excuse to squat uninvited beside her. 'We use 'em as trackers back home. To find lost kids and stuff in the bush. Dangerous place, the Aussie bush. Full of deadly snakes, spiders—you name it. That's where I live, by the way. Still…' he let out a dramatic sigh. 'You learn to be careful.'

Dianne was about to give her grudging admiration when the supposed native twisted to show the Canadian flashes on his shoulders and he called through the noise, 'My grandmother was a Seneca Indian from the Great Lakes region. I can't find my socks most mornings, let alone these missing babies that Australians regularly misplace. Please don't be impressed by William's fanciful stories.'

'You have to spoil everything, don't you?' William told him without rancour. 'I was doing bloody well until you opened your gob.'

The Canadian didn't reply, pointedly hiding his expression behind the pint glass.

Dianne said mildly to William, 'You weren't doing anything at all, actually. Aren't you uncomfortable down there? Wouldn't you be happier standing at the bar?'

'Good-oh,' he smiled, pleased with himself. 'We can go to the bar if you like.'

'No, I meant just you. I'm happy right here.'

'Oh... all right. Worth a shot, I suppose.'

The girls used similar tactics to discourage a queue of hopeful suitors. Susan's conscience gladly rebuffed each one, but Dianne was enjoying herself. Besides, no one really struck her fancy. Until they were approached by a shy-looking man called Daniel.

'I'm afraid that I'm the only one in our group who hasn't asked if you'd like a drink,' he admitted to Dianne, shuffling awkwardly next to her chair. 'So they've insisted I try. I can't be much cleverer than that.'

'Then I'll have a gin and tonic,' Susan said quickly, cutting Dianne off. She gave him an encouraging smile that somehow removed Dianne from the room.

He frowned at her, but he was smiling. 'Your hair is so incredibly red. Everyone is commenting on it.'

Susan blushed and was lost for an answer, long enough to give Dianne a chance. Unconsciously fingering her own brunette curls, she said, 'I'll have the same, thanks. This is Susan DeCourt. My name's Dianne Parker.'

'And I'm Daniel Young,' he said, unexpectedly offering each in turn his hand. Amused, they shook it. He had dark hair, thicker and longer than regulations allowed and was clean-shaven. Most of the men had grown the thin, fashionable moustaches. His cap was stuffed into a pocket. 'May I join you for these drinks?'

'Well—of course.' Dianne was surprised. 'You're buying.'

***

It was an hour later as they were leaving, after Dianne had clearly gotten the ascendancy for Daniel's interest, that part of their farewells became a promise to wave at the bomber's departure from the end of the airfield the next morning. They could have gone to the dispersal point, but these were scattered far and wide across the aerodrome and Daniel's was one of the furthest. Trapped by Daniel's grateful enthusiasm, Susan could hardly say she wouldn't be there too.

The growling of the Lancaster's engines filled the morning air, beating at them in deafening surges of sound.

'Here they come,' Dianne announced, ending any chance of Susan slipping away.

She groaned, 'Have you any idea how long it takes a squadron of bombers to take off? We could be here all day. We're supposed to be on duty in twenty minutes.'

'Of course I do. We'll wait that long, or until we see Daniel's plane. Cheer up, it might be the very first.'

'He is not the squadron leader, no matter what he might have told you.'

The thunderous roar grew impossibly louder as the leading Lancaster bomber turned off the last section of taxiway and onto the landing strip. Sunlight gleamed in the arcs of the four spinning propellers and glinted off the Perspex cockpit.

Dianne waved madly with both arms above her head. 'Have a good flight!' she yelled, the words hopelessly lost in the noise.

Then it pulled away, moving ponderously at first, until it was speeding down the tarmac to lift itself from the ground.

Susan yelled as the next bomber got close. 'Was that him? How do you know?'

'No, it was the wrong letters on the fuselage. Theirs is D-Delta—like D for Daniel, that's how I remembered easily.'

'Then why did you wave?'

'Have a heart, Susan. Why not?'

'Are you going to go stupid at all of them? Your arms will fall off.'

'Oh, don't be so grumpy. You should do it as well. It'll warm you up.'

Susan got up slowly and stood beside Dianne. 'Don't tell my mother I wished good luck to any Australians, all right—'

She stopped talking to break into wild waving with Dianne as the next aircraft started to accelerate away. The two girls collapsed into laughter when it had gone.

'I'm exhausted already,' Susan cried, pretending to mop at her brow.

Daniel's plane was the fourth to take off. Nobody waved back at the girls, although it was difficult to tell. Dianne half-imagined one of the heads in the cockpit turned their way and belatedly lifted a glove. She wasn't certain.

'Did you see that?' she asked Susan excitedly. 'I think the pilot saw us.'

Susan was panting and holding her sides. 'Isn't Daniel the upper gunner?'

'That's right, I forgot. Was anybody in the turret?'

'I didn't look. I was too busy waving.'

'Damn it, what was I thinking?' Dianne stared after the vanishing aircraft. Susan tugged at her sleeve.

'Can we go back now? We might squeeze in a cuppa, if we're quick.'

'Next time I'll watch the turret.'

'Next time, you're on your own.' Susan tried to reorganise the camp chair and swore again when it unexpectedly folded and crushed one of her fingers.

Two

'Did you see that?' Captain Alec Branner called on the intercom as the Lancaster settled into a steady climb. 'There were a couple of girls waving near the end of the runway. They must be balmy. It's bloody freezing out there.'

'That'll be for our boy, Daniel,' Bruce Flanders answered sourly. 'They didn't want to talk with me, the stuck-up tarts. English roses my arse, sitting there like—'

'Hey, hey,' Daniel cut him off from where he sat perched on an ammunition box near his turret. His intercom lead trailed up into the gun. Too late, he'd realised he wouldn't be able to see if the girls had kept their promise. The business of getting ready for the flight made him forget. 'They're actually very nice girls who don't want to associate with any riff-raff like yourselves.'

'They knocked me back too,' Charlie Wills called from the rear turret. 'That's not my idea of nice.'

'You told them you were a bloody pilot and they saw through you straight away. What do you expect?'

'It was on the spur of the moment. A bad idea,' Wills grumbled.

From Wills' perfect viewpoint at the rear of the bomber the ground below was already a patchwork of green cultivated fields. It was like every square inch of England that wasn't an airfield or training area was being turned into farming land. He kicked at the controls of the turret making it jerk left, then right. The hydraulics whined satisfactorily. Like Daniel, there was little need for Wills to be at his guns, but his turret was hard to get into and almost all rear gunners opted to man their position on take-off and stay there for the entire operation. Plus, he was very keen to shoot down his first German fighter. He figured there was always a chance a Messerschmitt 109 or Focke Wulf fitted with long-range tanks could be sneaking around, looking for a surprise attack, and Charlie could save the day. Heroes who shot down German fighters surely had a better chance with the girls.

'How's the rest of them going?' Branner asked to stop the chatter.

'Give me a second.' They could hear Wills counting under his breath. 'There's still nine on the ground and two more up behind us. I think that's P for Peter right up close, with those repairs on her wingtip... I'll give 'em a wave.'

'For Christ's sake, this isn't a bloody bus trip.' Branner said, but he hadn't pressed his intercom switch. His engineer, Dave Sexton, sitting on a canvas chair beside him, could guess what Branner had said. Sexton gave a wry grin and rolled his eyes.

Wills reported, 'He didn't wave back, the bastard.'

The bombardier, Geoff Barrymore, replied, 'That's because the bastard you're referring to is an officer, and you're a sergeant.' He was also the nose gunner when it was called for. 'Officers don't wave to idiotic, sergeant tail-gunners. Whereas with important people, like bomb aimers, perhaps he'll consider it.'

'That'll do,' Branner tried again to shut them up. 'Stop nattering so I can work out what the hell I'm supposed to be doing. What is that exactly, Bruce?'

'Going around in circles, skipper.' At his navigator's table, Flanders grinned to himself.

They could all hear the deliberate breath Branner took as he got annoyed. A commissioned flying officer and their "skipper", plus at twenty-four years of age the oldest among them, Branner expected his authority to be taken seriously when it counted. Often his crew didn't seem to pick those moments and continued to play the fool. Sometimes he worried they would never respect him.

Flanders sensed he had been too glib and quickly said, 'I mean it. We've got a circuit or two yet, before everyone gets off the ground.'

Branner wasn't mollified. 'After that, I'm talking about.'

'Course is zero-fifteen degrees for thirty miles. Apparently, there's a cathedral spire that you can't miss. Then it's a turn to course two-sixty degrees towards sunny Wales for another forty miles. They don't want us straying too near the Channel while we're still in our knickerbockers.'

'We could handle anything,' Wills put in. 'Let's go east instead.'

Branner said, 'Charlie, you are an idiot. I'll be happy if we never see a German fighter for the entire war. We're in Bomber Command, not with the glamour boys in their bloody Spitfires. Leave that up to them.'

Morgan Baxter, the Radio Operator, rarely took part in any of these conversations. Baxter was shy, lacked confidence with his eighteen years, and used the radio headphones as his excuse not to chat with the others. Instead, he listened avidly to what was happening around him, brought by the staccato rattle of Morse code in five letter groups. Nonsense to anyone else, to Baxter was all the latest news

The Lancaster also had a short-range VHF radio which Branner used from his pilot's seat. 'We've got a bunch of Hurricanes somewhere near,' he reported to everyone. 'I can hear them talking about us, yabbering away. They're thinking of doing a practice attack, I reckon. Anybody see them? I want to make sure everyone knows who's friendly and who isn't.' He reached out and flicked a switch that put the VHF through the intercom for the crew to hear.

'They'll be too busy combing their hair and trimming their damned moustaches,' Flanders growled, getting a laugh from somewhere.

'They might be out here for a reason. Maybe some Jerries are doing a fighter sweep too, and they've been scrambled. Have you jokers thought of that?'

There was a silence.

'Hang on,' Daniel pulled a face and climbed into his turret. As he strapped himself in, he could almost hear Branner's growing impatience. He looked up into the clear blue sky. There was a wink of silver and some fading contrails. 'I've got something dead above, skipper. Very high. You wouldn't think they'd bother. It'll take them all day to get back up there again.'

'That's what Fighter Control just told them,' Baxter reported. He was good at picking important bits out of the babble of radio that could fill the air over Britain. 'They want them to stay up there. Didn't mention any Jerries though.'

Branner just nodded, his face set. Sexton gave him a thumbs-up to mollify him, but Branner didn't seem to see it.

The bomber was a trembling, loud machine around them. Having a conversation without the intercom was almost impossible, unless you were close enough to yell in the other person's face, like Sexton and Branner. The crew had learned to chat over the intercom. Even Wills and Barrymore, isolated in their respective turrets and separated by the length of the plane, could talk naturally and trade insults as if they were standing beside each other in a bar.

The plane's heater was working hard, but Branner was climbing fast too. The heating didn't go beyond the mid-section and Wills started to feel the chill seep into his clothing. When he'd boarded the bomber, he was sweating badly in the spring sunshine, but hadn't taken anything off. Even with these short training flights he had learned that staying warm wasn't easy, although today he had foregone the usual electrically heated suit he would wear on missions. It was the one thing he really dreaded, looking ahead to their first operation and the long hours he'd be at the guns. Trying to stay warm at the freezing heights they would fly. With thirty missions to complete before he had an option to quit, Wills figured he'd better learn to get used to it.

Five minutes later Baxter said, 'Everybody's up. We're ordered to get on course at 8000 feet and head for the first waypoint.'

The squadron of bombers began to "stream" on the same course, each plane close behind the next as if they were flying down a narrow corridor, however with every aircraft at a different height. This was the crucial element to avoiding collisions, especially in the night-time operations they were training for.

'Everything going all right?' Branner asked Sexton.

'So far,' Sexton nodded at some instruments. As the engineer, he kept the gauges under close scrutiny, allowing Branner to concentrate on flying the plane. 'It's a bloody big thing to keep in the air. Lots of things to go wrong. Christ, imagine if we had a full bomb load. They must be a right bastard to get off the ground.'

'They say the B-17's even bigger. And it's got guns sticking out of it like quills on a ruddy porcupine. Trust the Yanks to make a plane like a flying battleship.'

'Makes sense. The more guns, the better, I say.'

Flanders broke in, 'I can't see a bloody thing back here, don't forget. Isn't Barra supposed to learn the local landmarks?'

Branner thumbed the intercom. 'Bombardier, that's right. Anything of significance, tell Flanders about it. Navigator, make notes.'

It sounded awkward and unworkable. Flanders' opinion was clear in his reply. 'All right... but how shall I code them?'

'What?' Branner frowned at Dave Sexton, who shrugged silently back.

'How shall I code the notes? What if we get shot down over Germany and the Jerries find my diary? It might tell them where our airfield is.'

'Navigator, do you know how to do your bloody job or not?'

'Just double-checking, skipper. I'll think of something.' Again there was that trace of mockery. Was Flanders really concerned about encoding his notes, or was he just trying to be too clever? Branner grimaced at his own doubts and called, 'Is everyone else keeping their eyes peeled?'

'All clear, skipper,' Daniel answered. 'No one we don't know, anyway.'

'Same here,' Wills added.

'Nothing, skipper,' Barrymore said from the nose turret now.

'That turn west must be coming up soon, skipper,' Flanders called. 'I don't suppose Geoff has even seen a church. We didn't think of that.'

'And I suppose you were a choir boy?' Barrymore shot back.

'Shut up and get your minds on the job,' Branner said tightly.

Barrymore sighted the spire. Picking his moment, Branner brought the aircraft around to port, turning on an imaginary point in the sky with the church steeple below.

Twenty minutes later it was starting to get boring. The further they moved away from the coast, it lessened the chance of encountering any German fighter sweeps. It became an exercise only for Branner and his flying skills, keeping his place in the stream.

For the others, the Lancaster offered little in the way of something to do. The fuselage was a narrow space that wasn't quite wide enough for a man to stretch his arms. The curved walls were covered with the aircraft's internal workings such as racks, electrical cabling and hydraulics lines.

Each crewman was almost trapped at their position in the plane. There was little point in moving around.

'We're turning to go home,' Branner announced finally. The cheers of the crew were unheard, but he could imagine them.

As they drew close to the airfield the gunners, including Daniel, all came alert. Although it was daylight, German night fighters had been lurking near airstrips and gunning down bombers during their final approaches, when the plane was committed to a straight path. The Germans would flee before anyone could react and move to another unsuspecting airfield.

As the black strip of the runway filled Branner's windscreen he wiggled his toes nervously, as if he might stretch his boot down to feel that first, reassuring contact with the earth. He was concentrating so hard it needed Baxter's voice coming urgently, before Branner realised a radio call was for them.

'Did you get that, skipper? They want us to abort the landing.'

'What? I bloody can't now. What the hell are they talking about?' Branner switched the VHF out of the intercom and curtly replied to the flight controller. Turning away wasn't a choice. If need be, he could try a "touch and go"—land the Lancaster, keep the power on and take off again. But he hadn't bothered to aim for the beginning of the strip and there was a risk he would run out of runway before getting airborne again.

The control tower changed their orders.

Branner explained to his crew, 'Now they're saying we're to get out the way quick smart the best way we can. There's a shot-up Halifax looking for an emergency landing. Everybody behind us has been turned away. We're the last in and this bloke's going to be hot on our tail.'

'I can see him,' Wills said excitedly. 'He just slid in behind us from nowhere. Christ, he's got smoke pouring out from all over the place and bits falling off... he's in a bad way.' The Halifax was a large four-engine bomber like the Lancaster. Wills could see only two of the propellers were spinning.

'All right, Charlie. Keep an eye on him,' Branner said through gritted teeth. 'Stay alert, you blokes. The poor bastard might have been jumped by a Jerry fighter over here, or he wouldn't be this far inland trying to get down. The bloody German might still be around.'

This galvanised the turret gunners who started staring earnestly at the sky, swinging their guns to and fro.

Branner told them all, 'We're going to land and dodge into the first taxiway we can, even if it doesn't take us back to the dispersals.'

Wills said worriedly, 'Honest, this bloke is coming in fast, skipper. He's going to come right up our arse, if we don't get out the way.'

Sexton glanced at Branner and saw he was too preoccupied in forcing the bomber down quickly to reply. He asked, 'Can you see an undercarriage, Charlie?'

'I was just about to tell you, he's only got one leg. I wonder if he knows—why isn't he heading for the grass, the bloody idiot?'

D-Delta slammed down onto the runway, changing Wills' report into a shout of surprise. Even amid the roar of the engines they could hear the superstructure groan with the unexpected weight. Branner was stabbing at the wheel brakes as much as he dared, trying to slow them down.

'Are you aiming for that?' Sexton said doubtfully, pointing at a taxiway approaching fast.

'I'm hoping,' Branner grunted.

'Christ, there's not much room.'

'Skipper...' Wills called with a rising panic. The crippled Halifax was filling his Perspex window. He could see the strained face of the pilot staring at them.

Branner nearly didn't turn, they were still rolling too quickly. Wills' alarm convinced him to try.

He swung the Lancaster to port, belatedly yelling, 'Hang on everybody!' over the intercom. Wills cried out as the tail whipped around so quickly he was thrown sideways by the force. The few loose things in the fuselage crashed about. A box of ammunition for Daniel's guns flipped onto its side spilling out the belts of cartridges like an escaping snake. All of Flanders' books and charts cascaded off his small table and onto his lap.

Branner didn't quite make the turn. He cut into the corner too early and one of their wheels dropped off into the soft grass, bogging down. It had the effect of accentuating their motion, bringing the Lancaster to an abrupt halt on the port side and sending the tail slewing out further. When they were completely stopped, the last twenty-five feet of the Lancaster was still sticking out over the edge of the runway.

'Oh shit,' Wills muttered. He had a clear view of the Halifax bearing down on him. If it had been an undamaged aircraft under full control the danger would have been slight. Any pilot could edge over to miss the stranded Lancaster suddenly in front.

But the Halifax might go in any direction once it hit. This was going to be more of a crash, than a landing.

'Get the hell out if you can,' Branner called, swiping at the switches, turning everything off. Sexton was trying to help, and their hands got in each others way. 'Get moving, Dave. Don't worry about me, I'm right bloody behind you.' The Merlin engines were winding down to a halt. In the comparative silence of the stalled aircraft they could hear Barrymore cursing in the front, trying to release himself and get out too.

A quick look out the cockpit window showed Branner there was no chance of them leaving the Lancaster before the Halifax reached them. Seeming to hover crookedly above the runway, it was about to touch down.

Wills had decided the same thing and was making no attempt to move. With their engines stopped he had no hydraulic power to swing the turret, or he might have turned it all the way to the stops and rolled out the open rear door, as if he was bailing out. Now his only escape was to crawl out of the turret into the fuselage and to the main door. It would take too long, so he chose to stay put and see his fate coming.

Strangely calm, Wills thought, If I survive, it might be worth a few drinks in the mess. Absently he released his harnesses and intercom cable.

Daniel, Flanders and Morgan Baxter were able to escape. Daniel wrenched at the door and shoved it wide. He hesitated, seeing he would be dropping onto the hard tarmac. Normally they would use a ladder, but there was no time for that. The height was about five feet.

'For God's sake, get going,' Flanders snarled, giving Daniel a shove.

'Hey, watch out you stupid bastard.' Wind-milling his arms, Daniel pitched forward. He managed to tuck his legs under him, rolling as he hit the ground to end up sprawled on his side. Flanders thudded down beside him, then so did Baxter.

'Jesus, look at this,' Baxter said in awe, staring towards the runway.

They were transfixed by the sight of the Halifax landing.

Trailing two thick streamers of smoke, one from each outer engine, the single undercarriage leg touched the tarmac. It didn't offer any resistance and buckled immediately. The Halifax flew just above the ground dragging the wrecked wheel, the spinning arcs of the remaining engines just barely inches from the bitumen. Then abruptly the bomber flopped to the earth with a grinding crash and the squeal of tortured metal. With their propellers instantly snapped off the engines were howling unhindered at maximum revolutions. Flame licked around the cowlings of the two smoking motors. A spectacular shower of sparks sprayed out from the belly.

It slid straight along the runway with pieces of the plane flying off in all directions. The wreck bore down on the crew of D-Delta to slide past with only ten feet separating the wingtip from Wills' turret. They felt a blast of heat from the nearest burning engine and had to clamp their hands over their ears at the dreadful screeching of the steel underbelly on the tarmac.

As Daniel and the others turned away and choked on the fumes and cloud of debris, the Halifax drifted off the runway and lurched to a stop about two hundred yards away. The engines screamed in protest for a few seconds longer, and then cut out.

It seemed eerily silent afterwards, despite the throbbing of the remaining Lancasters circling above. And from the distance, clamouring bells announced that ambulances and fire crews were racing across from the hangers.

'Come on, all of you. We'd better lend a hand.' Branner had dropped out of the Lancaster and slapped Daniel on the shoulder as he ran past. Everyone followed, sprinting across the runway through the clearing smoke. Behind them, Wills was the last to get out of D-Delta, finally rolling over the lip of the doorway to fall awkwardly down.

'Hey, wait for me,' he yelled, waddling in his heavy clothing and flying boots. Barrymore was closest, but he ignored him.

The main door on the Halifax's fuselage had burst open. Branner reached it first with Daniel close behind. The wrecked plane stank of leaking oils, petrol and burning smells like melting rubber and hot metal.

'Bloody hell, skipper,' Daniel put a hand on Branner's arm as he was about to step inside. 'This thing could burst into flames any second.'

'Then we'd better be quick.' Branner took an instant to stare wildly at Daniel.

With the aircraft flattened to the ground, it was strange to just step over the coaming. Inside, it was gloomy and filled with smoke, shot through with bright bars of sunlight coming from hundreds of bullet holes in the fuselage. They could hear flames ominously crackling somewhere and the ticking, creaking noises of the ruined plane settling. Undecided, Branner stood still and looked around. It took a second for them to comprehend a pair of limp legs hanging from the mid-upper turret. They dripped something from the tip of one boot. A figure loomed out of the shadows.

'Help us get Bill out of the fucking cockpit.' The man sounded shocked and utterly exhausted. He turned away without waiting for a reply. By now, Flanders and Baxter had crowded inside too. There was no room for Sexton, who lingered anxiously outside and waited for Barrymore and Wills to catch up. The four crew of D-Delta tried to follow the man through the unfamiliar plane, not looking at the bloodied corpse in the upper turret. Branner climbed over something. Daniel lost his balance and planted his foot firmly down on a yielding, soft thing. Bending down he saw a man's body, barely recognisable in the dark and with the shapeless flying suit.

'Oh shit, I just walked on—'

'Don't worry about him,' the voice ahead snapped. 'He can wait.'

Now they could see forward. Bathed in cheerful sunlight streaming through the cockpit canopy, another of the Halifax crew was straining to pull the pilot from his seat and haul him towards the main fuselage. Brunner turned and said quietly to Daniel, 'Go back and drag that other poor sod to the door and out the way. It's going to be hard enough getting this bastard out as it is.'

Daniel nodded dumbly and motioned at Flanders to help.

Outside, Wills had reached the Halifax and stumbled through the ploughed grass to the tail section. With the sunlight, smoke and glare he couldn't see clearly inside the rear turret. A lot of it was starred by bullet holes. One section had a large puncture the size of a teacup.

'Are you all right in there?' Wills shouted, making out a slumped form behind the gun. He leaned close and cupped his hands against an unbroken part of the Perspex to see. Then he saw something was smeared all over it and he pulled back hurriedly before realising it was on the inside anyway. Finally, he saw it was blood—a lot of it. Between the rivulets, Wills picked out the white face and open, staring eyes of the dead gunner looking back at him. The man's chest was a messy pulp where he'd taken a direct hit, probably from a cannon shell that had made the largest hole.

'Oh Jesus,' Wills rocked backwards, sickened. He lost his footing and sat abruptly on the ground. He couldn't take his gaze off the pale blob behind the shattered glass. 'Oh Jesus,' he said again hoarsely. 'God, don't let that happen to me... fuck, that is not going to happen to me.'

***

Wills didn't register the racket of the ambulance and fire trucks arriving. Suddenly the Halifax was surrounded by emergency crews. Water sprayed everywhere as they worked to dowse the threatening fires. A minute later, someone helped Wills to his feet and led him to an open lorry. The rest of D-Delta were there sitting forlornly on the wooden benches. For all their efforts to help and despite having been inside the aircraft trying to lift the wounded pilot through the fuselage, they had been immediately ordered back out and bustled onto the truck.

No one thanked them for the attempts. One of the fire crew had angrily told Sexton, 'Get out the bloody way.'

'Where the bloody hell have you been, Charlie?' Barrymore asked. 'Sneaking a fag?' It was a poor attempt at a joke and he knew it, grimacing.

Wills didn't reply, silently finding a space to sit down. He opened his mouth to tell them about the rear turret gunner and found he couldn't say anything.

Three

Outside it was raining and cold, the winter season stubbornly hanging on. Inside the same hotel, the smell of damp woollen uniforms competed with the odours of stale beer, tobacco and a fire struggling with wet wood.

'I know you're supposed to be shy, but not this much.' Dianne raised her eyebrows at Daniel, who sat opposite her at the small table. In the crowded room it was incredibly lucky to have some space for themselves and Dianne doubted their good fortune would last much longer. Daniel's friends were gathering purposefully in the corner and glancing their way often. It was like they were planning to give Daniel only a certain amount of time before they came over to try their own luck. Susan was due to arrive soon too.

'Sorry, I've got some things on my mind,' Daniel said, pulling a face.

'You mean that Halifax today?'

'You know it was a Halifax?' He looked impressed. She wasn't pleased.

She said icily, 'After the first few hundred raids we all get quite good at aircraft recognition. It's helpful to know if the planes are going to drop incendiary bombs or invitations to dinner.'

'I'm sorry, I keep forgetting you've all been putting up with this for a lot longer. The Blitz and everything, I mean.'

'Plus I am in the air force, just like you. We have had some training, other than how to make cups of tea. Some people even think the WAAFs are quite useful—'

'Please, I did say sorry.'

Dianne pressed her lips together and let her annoyance linger a few seconds longer, and then let it go with a shrug. 'Yes, you did. So I'm sorry too.'

Daniel asked carefully, 'How on earth have you put up with it for so long? Worrying about if your blokes in the bombers will come back?'

23

She was drinking a gin and tonic, which she stirred absently with a stick, poking at a slice of lemon. 'Well, we don't worry about it. What's the point?'

He frowned. 'Surely you must get a bit concerned about... close friends or relatives. I mean, have you lost anyone you really cared for? Not that it's any of my business, of course,' he added hastily.

Dianne knew he was fishing for details of her personal life. Amused at his clumsy attempts, but wistful, she said, 'There was a fellow who flew Blenheims. For a while we were putting up everything that had wings to drop mines in the Channel. He went missing late in 1941— somewhere over the coast, I was told. We haven't heard a word since.'

'That's bad luck. It's even worse getting no news, I suppose. If he was a prisoner of war, you should have heard by now. It's been years after all... I mean—' Daniel stopped himself. He wanted to look her in the eye and show he was genuinely remorseful, but a faint gleam of satisfaction could betray him. The Blenheim pilot's loss was his gain—so far.

She nodded once. 'He's been officially listed as missing, presumed killed. I've accepted that he's most likely dead.'

'Were you very close?'

Dianne looked at him a long time. 'I'm trying to explain to you, you don't get close to anyone these days for exactly that reason. Otherwise, you'd be worried sick all the time.'

'I see.'

After a brief silence he tried, 'I suppose it's hard for a chap to compete with all these Americans everywhere. They've got money to burn, and pockets filled with all kinds of stuff. Like chocolate and nylon stockings. I'll bet you get plenty.'

'Yes, they often think we can be bought quite cheaply too,' Diane said tightly. Daniel missed her edgy tone, encouraged by Dianne's lack of endorsement for Americans.

She added, 'Anyway, all they ever talk about is home. You can't help feeling that at the drop of a hat they'll jump back on board their ships and sail off over the horizon. They'll leave behind a lot of broken hearts, believe me, when they do go. And that won't be all,' Diane added meaningfully.

'Oh? Oh—you mean babies and all that.' Daniel sucked his lip disapprovingly.

'Yes, unwanted children and all that.'

Daniel bought some time by fidgeting with his glass, then after a moment said, 'So... I suppose then, if you decided you liked me a bit, that you still wouldn't worry much?'

She let out an impatient sigh, making sure he heard it. 'I don't know. I haven't decided if I like you yet. I've only known you since last night and for one drink tonight. And even that's finished.'

'Fair enough.' His shoulders sagged until he took the hint. 'Oh, sorry—same again?'

'Yes, please.'

Daniel left the remains of his pint on the table as a sign to anyone else that Dianne wasn't alone. He shifted nervously at the bar as he waited for the drinks to come, glancing back at her to make sure nobody moved in. The room was filling impossibly with noisy drinkers, and it felt to Daniel they were all talking about Dianne sitting by herself, and what they should do about it. It was a relief to get back.

As he sat down, he began, 'But if you did like me, how—'

'Here we go again,' she cut him off. 'I doubt I could worry about someone who goes on like this. I think we should change the subject.'

'I was changing the subject.' He tried an earnest smile. 'Honest.'

She was suspicious. 'All right, go on.'

'If you did like... someone,' he judiciously made a small alteration. 'How far would you go with the war still on? I mean, would you get engaged, say?'

Dianne made a coughing sound, her eyes wide. 'Are you asking me if I'd marry you?'

'Good God, no! Damn, I mean—not that anyone wouldn't want to marry you. I'm asking if you'd consider taking the risk, if you liked them enough, despite the war...' He ended on a miserable note, wishing he could take it all back.

Daniel was saved any further pain by Susan arriving beside the table. 'Hello,' she said loudly. 'What do you two look so cheerful about?'

'Daniel's asking me to marry him,' Dianne told her. Daniel spilled some of the pint that was halfway to his lips.

Susan smiled at him sweetly. 'You don't want to marry her. She's very bossy and can't even cook. Whereas I can do wonders with one egg a week. Why don't you ask me?'

Tormented, he could only think to ask, 'Why on earth would you only use one egg a week?'

'That's all the civilians get, you know.' Susan frowned at his ignorance. 'With the rationing. You fellows might get a big, nosh-up breakfast every time you come back from a raid, but the rest of the country's on barely enough to feed a field mouse.'

'Oh? I didn't realise it was that bad.' Daniel couldn't have felt worse about how things were turning out this evening. He expected by now that Dianne was just waiting for the chance to get away from him.

'Well, now you know,' Susan said, unperturbed. 'Look, can you two join me at the bar with the rest of your crew? That rotten gunner has tricked me into letting him buy me a drink and I don't want to do it alone. Please.'

'Was it Charlie?' Daniel looked across and saw the hopeful expression on Wills' face. 'With his double-headed penny, I suppose.'

Susan's eyes glazed for a moment. 'Double-headed, is it? I see. He said that if it was tails, he wasn't ever going to ask me again—God, I knew there was a trick. Come on, we'll see who laughs last about this.'

Susan moved away, pushing through the crowd. Dianne stood up and read Daniel's expression.

She surprised him by leaning close and grasping his hand. 'We'd better go,' she said gently. 'Don't worry, I was only teasing about whether I like you or not. Of course I do.' She squeezed his fingers. 'But you shouldn't ask too much of people these days. No one likes to plan too far ahead anymore. It doesn't make much sense under the circumstances.'

Daniel let her pull him to his feet and they went to the bar, joining the crew. As he expected, they gathered hungrily around the two girls. Wills was in the process of vehemently denying the existence of his double-headed penny. All the men tried their luck chatting to Dianne, and Daniel didn't mind. He felt safe now. Sometimes she even looped her arm in his possessively for a few minutes. He couldn't be sure if she was being affectionate or using it to discourage the others. Daniel wasn't about to risk asking any more awkward questions.

***

Late in the evening, he walked Dianne back to her quarters. In front of them Susan was noisily surrounded by Wills, Barrymore and a sullen Flanders, who was upset he wasn't getting much of Susan's attention. Nobody worried about the drizzle still falling. Daniel walked slowly, Dianne's arm in his again as she pressed close to hide from the cold, and they deliberately let the others pull further ahead.

'What are you doing tomorrow night?' he asked her.

She shook her head, smiling in the dark. Her dark, curly hair brushed against his face. Whenever she could, Dianne avoided jamming it under her cap even though tonight it would get damp. 'Loose talk costs lives, remember?'

'Ah ha, do you know something we don't?'

'No, and I wouldn't tell you, if I did. Let's just say I can see the signs.'

A thrill went through him. 'Do you think we'll be doing an op' tomorrow night?'

'I told you, I can't say.'

'What if you're wrong and nobody's on duty?'

'There's a picture showing in the village I wanted to see—or I might just have an early night.'

'Can I take you?'

She stopped, pulling him up, and thought about it for a second. Spending three evenings with Daniel in a row was encouraging him too much. But she couldn't completely deny his hopeful look. 'All right, perhaps. Why don't you meet me here about sixish? Either way, I'll slip out and tell you what I've decided. As long as you promise not to get upset, if I don't want to go.'

'Of course not. I hope you will.'

They were still a distance from the WAAF quarters. It was as close as the men dared go. The billets were strictly off limits. Dianne looked across at the others and saw Wills trying to convince Susan to give him a goodnight kiss. Barrymore was arguing she should kiss all of them. Susan was happily attempting not to oblige anyone and enjoying the fight.

Dianne quickly kissed Daniel on the cheek, taking him by surprise for the second time that night. 'It's my bedtime, and I'd better rescue Susan—although I'm not sure she wants to be saved.'

Daniel fingered where her lips had touched, watching her walk away. 'So I'll see you tomorrow?'

She gave him a final wave and called back, exasperated, 'Perhaps. We'll see what tomorrow brings. Goodnight, Daniel.'

Four

The next morning Dianne was shaken awake by a young WAAF who said she was to report immediately to the Operations Room. The girl moved on through the house stirring everyone still asleep. Finally, just for good measure as she left without closing the front door, she also flicked on all the lights.

Susan's cot was empty. The house was bitterly cold, and it took a huge effort to crawl out of the blankets—which hadn't provided enough warmth anyway. A coke fire in the lounge, hardly capable of heating the room let alone the whole quarters, had long since died to cold metal. The meagre amount of fuel allowed, like always, had soon run out early in the night. Her billet was one of the old married quarters, a house now converted into separate rooms. At least they had more privacy and could share a small kitchen and bathroom.

Dianne had carefully hung her uniform the night before and although in the dull electric light it barely passed muster, she put it on, hoping that everyone had more important things to worry about than knife-edged creases in a blouse. Shivering at the chill, she used a hand mirror to hurriedly apply a thin gloss of lipstick, her breath steaming the glass. A busy day in Operations was hardly worth any expenditure of precious make-up, but the habit was impossible to break. Dianne could at least thank the gods she was blessed with clean, clear skin.

Hurrying through the door into the pre-dawn morning she nearly bumped into a friend, Narelle, who was likewise rushing with her head down. She fiercely chewed a piece of bread soaked in dripping and smiled a greeting with oily lips as they passed. Dianne could smell the hot fat. Narelle was dressed in heavy overalls, boots and a cap placed jauntily on her curly hair. She drove the small tractors that towed the trains of bomb loads out to the aircraft.

'Narelle,' Dianne called, almost too late. 'Do you know what you're loading yet? You are loading, aren't you?'

'Mines,' Narelle yelled back, walking backwards.

'All of them?'

'Just eight of the new ones. The fuel load isn't enough to wet a baby's arse.'

The women who had taken over from the men the dirtier and more demanding jobs had also adopted the language that went with it. No one complained. The amount of fuel was a clue about the target chosen. The bombers were only being given sufficient aviation petrol to complete their mission. A large load meant a dangerous journey deep into the heart of Germany. Small amounts meant one of the "milk runs"—a relatively easy trip—to a target just across the Channel.

So Dianne could safely guess the new Lancaster squadron, eight of them at least, were going to be blooded on a soft target—or "gardening", as laying sea mines was called. Starting this early in the morning almost certainly meant a daylight raid, which unfortunately increased the chances of losses due to enemy fighters.

Dianne knew all this because it was part of her job. A lot of things had to be decided before any bomber left the ground. She helped assign the crews to particular planes and chose the aircraft according to their availability—most crews did four or five missions before being given their own plane. When that was confirmed, she would write them up on the blackboards and fill out many of the required forms. Bomb loads had to be distributed, since not all planes might carry the same ordinance, and take-off times and heights were allocated.

Dianne played a large part in choosing who would go on the raid. It might even be up to her whether or not Daniel flew that day. Today, it would be unlikely that different crews would be assigned to unfamiliar aircraft. So if D-Delta was picked, Daniel would be flying. As she hurried in the gloom across the grounds towards the Operations Room, a frost crunching under her feet, Dianne hoped someone else would make that decision this morning.

Wing Commander Simmons ran the OR. He was a reservist before the war, a bank manager in his normal life, and he'd become as adept at the task of juggling all the variables of a bombing raid as he was balancing bank ledgers and shuffling pound notes. He was a small and dapper man who revelled in his chance to wear the uniform for real, including the obligatory pencil moustache, but he treated his subordinates with a civilian courtesy, rather than as a military captain. It made him popular with the women, many of whom were also volunteers for the war and never comfortable with the discipline expected by the regular air force officers.

'Good morning, Sergeant Parker,' he called happily from his desk cramped into the corner of the main room. He was in his element, surrounded by loose sheets of paper and open books that needed bringing into order. As if Dianne had a choice, he added, 'Thank you for coming in so early. Have you had some breakfast?'

'Good morning, Wingco. No, not yet, sir. I'll grab something later.'

'Good girl. Find a cuppa and come and help me here, will you?'

Dianne went to an urn and made herself a strong, black tea. As usual, there was no milk or sugar left, so she was teaching herself to like it this way. Several other staff were at their posts, and they called greetings as she passed. Everyone was cheerful, although they looked tired and drawn. It was normal. Dianne went to stand by Simmons, who nodded at the blank blackboard.

He said, 'We need eight to go on a gardening trip to the Frisians this afternoon with a group of Wellingtons from 4 Group. With a bit of luck they'll have a fighter sweep happening at the same time keeping the Jerries busy, so it should be a safe-ish trip. Bomber Command wants to send some of those new Lancaster crews that arrived the other day. Do you know of any lame ducks that can't go? They did a training flight yesterday, didn't they?'

Dianne had worked on the reports written by the pilots and engineers after their flights. She hesitated a moment. Just mentioning Daniel's plane might be enough to put it into Simmons' mind to be chosen. Then she berated herself for even thinking that way. It wasn't right, and it wasn't fair on all the other crews. She simply had to do her job properly.

'D-Delta got stuck in the mud after avoiding that crashed Halifax, sir. It had to be towed out, but the ground crew chief has given it the all-clear. No damage done.'

'The pilot needs driving lessons, hey?' Simmons smiled at his own joke.

31

'He should check his mirrors,' Dianne joined in weakly to please him. 'Actually, I've heard he did a very good job of getting out the way.'

'Yes, good show, I suppose,' Simmons said, staring at the blackboard as if the blank spaces might give him some inspiration. 'All right, let's use the first eight, then. Same crews as yesterday. Let's not make things hard for ourselves.'

He meant alphabetically the first eight planes in the squadron. They were all identified by a letter.

'Fair enough, sir,' Dianne nodded, inwardly sighing that Daniel's plane was going. 'I'll pass the word to the ground crews, then make up the boards.'

Simmons yanked a sheet of paper from his desk and scribbled his signature across it. 'Get the word to the refuelers and armourers which planes we want. They already know the loading. Six mines each to everyone, they tell me. Nice and simple.'

'Yes, sir.'

It was simple—simple decisions and a single piece of paper to make it all happen. It would be the catalyst for hours of work by the ground crews to make sure the Lancasters were ready.

***

The crew of D-Delta had been told to stay on base until Battle Orders were posted. It was one small step towards a possible operation that got their nerves tingling, but nothing was certain yet. At a loss what to do, Daniel grabbed a bicycle and rode out to D-Delta. He took his time, pedalling slowly and taking in the open countryside. Most of the bombers were on dispersals that had natural shelter from tree lines or a rise in the ground. The dispersal itself was a circle of concrete large enough for the aircraft to be turned around. This was also room for fuel tankers and bombing trains to drive around the back and come underneath the plane. Many had a roughly made hut for the ground crew, known universally in all their trades as "Erks", where they stored tools and, most vital of all, brewed endless mugs of tea.

He found the ground crew fussing around the Lancaster. They thought of the aeroplane as their own even more so than the people who flew it. The crew chief, a long-serving air force sergeant called Granger, hovered around his charge like a protective dog. Frequently he darted in and helped someone else, tightening a bolt here or checking a screw there, before moving on. Granger chewed on a small, straight pipe even when he talked, and smoked if there was no danger from refuelling, even though it wasn't allowed any time on the dispersal point. He squinted at Daniel through a curl of illicit blue smoke.

'Morning to you, Sergeant Young,' Granger doffed his greasy cap after eyeing Daniel's name badge to remind him.

'Same to you, Sergeant Granger,' Daniel said. He peered up at a mechanic perched high on a rickety ladder to work on the starboard inner engine. 'Thought I'd come out for a look—we're stuck on base. Is everything fine?'

Granger tapped his teeth on the pipe stem. 'In tip-top shape, despite your little adventure yesterday.'

'Well, that could hardly be helped.'

'No, I suppose not.' Granger seemed content with his mild rebuke. He nodded toward a ramshackle hut, little bigger than a gardening shed. 'You'll find a pot brewing in there and a spare mug. Help yourself. Honey to sweeten it, if you like. No milk, though.'

'Thanks, I will.'

Granger followed him over and they cramped inside the hut, making the tea, before re-emerging to stand and look at the bomber while they carefully sipped the scalding brew. Granger started to relight his pipe and Daniel offered him a cigarette, which he took, in turn cupping a match towards Daniel.

Their attention was caught by a distant growling and they peered upwards, searching the sky.

'There,' Granger grunted, pointing. From behind a line of clouds a large formation of glittering pin-pricks emerged to slide across the deeper blue. They were United States Army Air Force B-17 bombers heading out on a daylight raid.

'Rather them, than me,' Granger said. 'Poor bastards.'

'They're bloody high already,' Daniel said.

'And they'll get even higher, not that it'll help them much.'

'Why don't they raid at night, like us?'

'The Yanks reckon it's better to fly high and be able to see who's shooting at you, so you can shoot back, even if it does attract a swarm of Jerry fighters.' At Daniel's doubtful expression he added, 'Don't worry, they think we're just as crazy buggering about in the dark at low altitudes.'

'Who do you think is right?'

Granger let out a scornful laugh. 'They can do it their way and we do it ours. Saves a lot arguing.'

The bomber formation was moving close to the sun and Daniel put up his spread fingers to shield his eyes from the glare. 'Have you worked on a B-17? Are they any good?'

'Never laid a spanner on one myself, but I hear they're good. The Yanks call 'em ships. Mind you, they're so weighed down by armour, guns and ammunition that the payload they can carry is hardly worth the trip to bloody Germany. All that effort just to drop a half-dozen bombs.'

'It does seem rather a waste of time,' Daniel said, thinking the USAAF crews doubtless wouldn't agree about having too much protection and fire power. 'Anyway, I hear that the lads in the last squadron were a good bunch of chaps. I hope we can keep up the good reputation.'

Granger tipped his head. 'I hardly got to know any of them. You're our third crew in four weeks since we got transferred over from a Halifax mob. The first one was lost over Bremen. Nobody got out of that one—a direct hit by a flak gun. The second got shot down by fighters over Holland. A few 'chutes popped out of that one, they told us, but it's hard to be certain when the Jerries are dropping them like flies. There weren't many left from that squadron to transfer away when you think about it.' He added without much conviction, 'Maybe you blokes will have a better run of it?'

Daniel's smile was strained. 'Yes, third time lucky, I hope.'

'Aye, always look on the bright side,' Granger agreed thoughtfully. He chomped on his pipe stem and didn't offer anything more.

'Do you think something's on tonight?'

'Today, if at all, with this early start.'

'How do you know?'

'Oh, you know... You get the odd hint that an op' might be on and we make sure everything's ready. It doesn't harm to check again. You're the mid-upper gunner, right?'

'Yes, that's right.' Daniel thought Granger was going to give him a piece of advice. He tried to look keenly attentive.

'I'll bet you wish they'd move that thing a few feet forward or back.' Granger pointed at the large blue and red roundel that identified all Royal Air Force aircraft. They were painted on the wings, and unfortunately for Daniel, on the main fuselage almost directly below his turret. Like a practice target, it was a popular aiming point for the German fighters.

'Ah, yes,' Daniel said, unhappily reminded. 'Sometimes I don't know why we need them at all. It's obviously a bloody Lancaster and the Germans don't have anything looking remotely the same.'

'They can still come in handy. Just ask the Yanks.' Granger let out a bark of laughter. American aircraft had suffered being shot down by their own anti-aircraft guns.

They were interrupted by a staff car grinding noisily towards them across the grass, taking a short-cut rather than staying on the hard runway. It was labouring, mud spraying out from the spinning rear wheels. It wove a path until it reached the dispersal and stopped in front of the hut. A young WAAF opened the door and stood on the running board, grinning cheekily across the car's roof.

Before she could say anything, Granger called, 'You'll get stuck one day doing that, young Connie. And you'll be asking us to come and pull you out.'

'I'm too good for that, Jim,' she answered with a laugh and waved at the Lancaster. 'This one's going this afternoon. Armourers and fuel are on the way. You're about fourth in line.'

'Right-oh,' Granger lifted his hand. She ducked back into the car and with a clash of gears roared away. He said sombrely to Daniel, 'You'd better go and see if you're rostered to take her.'

Daniel had turned cold, his face draining of blood at the sudden nervous anticipation. 'I think I'm about to find out,' he said, seeing a bicycle rider appear from behind a distant bomber and pedalling furiously their way. He lit another cigarette from the butt of the first while the cyclist completed the journey. Granger moved quietly away.

It was Branner, flushed and exhausted from the ride. 'There you are. I've been looking all over the bloody place for you. Come on, they've posted the Battle Orders. We've got a sortie on this afternoon.'

'Are we taking D-Delta?'

'That's what I've been told,' Branner puffed.

Daniel caught Granger's eye across the distance, then went to get his bicycle.

On the ride back, Branner was hardly capable of speaking, he was too much out of breath, but Daniel had to ask.

'Do we know where we're going, skipper?'

Head down as he pushed against a breeze, Branner told him curtly, 'Of course not. It's all hush-hush and secret until the briefing at ten o'clock. They're loading mines, so it's a gardening trip. That's all I know.'

Daniel free-wheeled for a moment and looked around. The airfield appeared to be even busier than its usual hive of activity. 'I'll bet everyone else knows,' he grumbled.

***

Susan supervised equipping the crews for their missions. She organised sandwiches and hot drinks for the flights, and the ration packs for surviving after bailing out. Another task was overseeing packing the parachutes and helping some of the men strap them on.

That morning, with a half-dozen other girls, Susan worked at the long tables where the silk canopies and shrouds were meticulously sorted, folded and loaded into the packs. Everyone hated to think that a man might plunge to his death under a failed parachute because of an error by a packer. Even though the WAAFs chatted and appeared relaxed, they concentrated closely on their job.

One of her team sidled up close.

'Can I have a quiet word with you, Susan?'

'Of course, Jennifer,' Susan frowned at her seriousness. 'Is something wrong?'

Jennifer motioned with her head to move away from the table.

The two of them went to a desk that had no chair. Susan picked up a clipboard and idly flicked through its contents as a pretence.

'Well?'

'It's the new girl, Robyn. She started telling me something that I thought you should know.'

Susan raised her eyebrows. 'This is no time for gossip. Are you sure it's something worth starting—'

'It's nothing like that.'

'Oh, then what is it?'

'You know when we help the lads put on their 'chutes and some of them make... jokes, when you do up the crutch straps?'

Susan smiled. 'I'm waiting to hear something new. They all say, "Not too tight, love. My family's future is down there," or "Make sure you don't tighten the wrong thing". God, it's like they teach them the same old jokes in flying school—'

'It doesn't worry me either,' Jennifer said. 'Or you, obviously. But Robyn felt offended the first time and says she's thinking about complaining. It seems the more she's asked the boys to be good, the comments just get worse. It's like they don't realise she's really upset.'

'It's just a bit of fun.'

'We know that, but...'

Susan pinched her brow tiredly. 'Well, at least she'll have to speak with me first. I can sort her out then.'

Jennifer was shaking her head. 'You're forgetting her uncle's the station Warrant Officer for the RAFP. One word in his ear and he'll start a ruddy crusade. That's what she's saying.'

'Oh, damn.' Susan tossed the clipboard down. As the RAF's equivalent of the police, the Warrant Officer was a stickler for discipline and proper etiquette. He suffered a righteous outrage with the flood of what he considered shabby volunteers and reservists. 'We don't want him looking over our shoulders all the time. Neither do I want to write some foolish memo about it all, just because one of the women is a bit silly...' She bit her lip in thought. 'Look, try and keep her on the tea and sandwiches, instead of helping the lads strap up. It shouldn't be hard, if she's unhappy doing it.'

'That's another thing,' Jennifer screwed her face up knowing how Susan would react. 'She almost seems to ask for it. Robyn's the first to jump forward and help them out, and she goes for the blokes she knows will give her an earful of cheek.'

Carefully, Susan looked across at Robyn, who with her tongue poking out was determinedly folding a canopy exactly right. She had an appealing, pixie face and good figure. It wasn't surprising she attracted the attention.

'All right, Jennifer. Thanks for letting me know. I'll give it some thought. If she mentions it again to you, say something—any damned thing—about the Official Secrets Act. That usually shuts the new people up for a few days.'

Jennifer nodded, unsure if Susan was serious, and walked away.

Susan muttered, 'It would help if the silly little cow was a bit more plain-looking.'

***

The air in the Briefing Room was thick with tobacco smoke. No one seemed to mind, even though they all squinted at each other. The covered map on the small stage was obscured by the haze. Then the Intelligence Officer, called Harris, entered.

'Good God, someone open a bloody window,' he said, waving his hand in front of his face as he climbed onto the stage. Someone obliged, hurrying back to their seat. Harris gave them time to settle, but it was hardly necessary. Most members of all the crews were there, nervously waiting for all the information they could get on their first mission. He couldn't have had a more intent audience.

'All right, you're going gardening, as you'll probably have guessed from the armorers,' Harris said, turning to pull the cloth away from the map. 'To the Frisian Islands, which are to the north and northwest of Germany and the Netherlands.' He tapped the map perfunctorily. 'They're a chain of islands that lay across the entrance to several major canals and as such pose a bit of a navigational hazard for German maritime traffic. With a bit of careful mine-laying, we can make it a damned sight worse. We've already dropped hundreds of the things and it's usually a fairly easy trip. There aren't any anti-aircraft batteries to worry about, if you fly a straight course. Get lost and wander over Berlin and things might be a little different.' He let them laugh. It sounded hollow and forced.

'There might be fighters, of course. Hundreds of the buggers, if the Luftwaffe find out you're coming. However, your course should keep you well clear until the last moment and get you out again quickly. Also, Fighter Command is doing a sweep about sixty miles to the south of where you'll be most at risk. That will hopefully draw a response that will leave you all alone—which you aren't, by the way...' He consulted a note in the palm of his hand. 'A dozen Wellingtons are doing the same job. Watch out for them. First plane gets off the ground at fourteen hundred. You should be over the target in the late afternoon, when the Huns will be thinking their day's work is over. Everyone's back in time for a late supper. And one last thing. If you get into trouble and have to bail out, make sure your aircraft doesn't land in one piece without you. Lock them on a course to splash into the drink, if you must. We don't want the Germans getting a good look at the wizardry in these Lancasters before we even know how some of this equipment works. All very straightforward really. Any questions?'

It was a sobering end. As Harris waited for questions, none of which came, two other men filed in. One was the Station Navigator and he took Harris' place to explain their course and altitudes. Then it was the Meteorological Officer's turn.

'There's a bit of cloud about,' he explained, almost apologising. 'It will get worse as you get closer to the target area. It won't be so bad you can't see to drop and that's in your favour. Something to hide in, if the worst happens.' He went on with winds and expected temperatures.

Harris finished up. 'There's a meal being made for you now. Eat heartily, no matter how you feel. Then I suggest you get out to your aircraft early and check everything. The ground crews are excellent, but don't rely on them to think for you. They're not the ones waving their bums at Adolph.'

He got another laugh and hurried out during the noise.

'Shit, is that it?' Wills asked Daniel. They were sitting at the back.

'What else do you need to know?'

Wills thought about it. 'Buggered if I know.'

'That's right.' Daniel slapped him on the knee and stood up. 'You don't—and he does. I'm sure we've been told everything we need to know. So come on. We get a decent feed before a raid.'

'Like condemned men,' Wills said.

***

The blackboard for writing up the names of the crews was on a vertical sliding rail. To reach the highest rows, Dianne pulled the board downwards. For just eight Lancasters it wasn't a big task, but with seven men in each plane it was tricky to fit them all in. The rows and columns hadn't been designed for aircraft with such large crews.

As she started chalking in the first names, Dianne looked across at another WAAF working at her desk. 'Beatrice, please tell me there's no extra passengers going. There's hardly enough room as it is.'

'None that I know about, Dianne.'

'Thank goodness for that.'

When Dianne was writing in the list for D-Delta she tried to put faces to the names. It was hard, even though she met them only the night before. It reminded her of the days during the Battle of Britain, when Dianne had been posted to a fighter group, and too often men that she had met would be erased from the boards by the following evening. Back then, she taught herself not to get too close. Not to remember faces or voices intimately. It made things easier.

Simmons came behind her. 'First take-off is at 1400 hrs, Sergeant Parker. Space them thirty seconds apart. Expected return can be 1900 hrs.'

Her chalk scratched busily. 'Do they know where they're going yet, sir?'

'Briefing started at ten o'clock, so they should.'

Dianne finished and went to her desk, double-checking the flight crew lists. Around her, no one had time to chat. Weather updates were coming in continuously along with any reports of enemy activity, which had to be evaluated as the whether they might affect the mission.

Beatrice dropped a piece of paper on Dianne's blotter. 'This bloke's been pulled by his skipper. He's a mid-upper gunner. Sick with the colliwobbles or something.'

It wasn't Daniel, but a gunner on B-Bravo. 'All right, thank you.'

Dianne took the news over to Simmons. 'Replace the whole crew, sir? Or just the gunner?'

'Just the gunner,' he decided immediately. 'Take your pick from the next crew in line, or whoever you can get hold of the fastest.'

The thought struck Dianne again. What if D-Delta wasn't going, but they were the next plane on the list? Here she would have the perfect opportunity to pass over choosing Daniel and find someone else. Nobody would be any the wiser.

'I have to stop thinking like this,' she told herself aloud.

'Sorry?' Beatrice was close by.

'No, nothing. Just talking to myself.'

41

Dianne's phone rang and she snatched it up. Everyone felt the same sense of urgency, that each second counted and even a small delay picking up the telephone might make a difference. The voice on the other end squawked demandingly. 'All right, hold on a moment,' she told them, her eyes searching for Simmons. 'Sir? C-Charlie is requesting a test flight. They're fuelled but haven't seen the armorers yet.'

'Damn.' Simmons tapped at his desktop with a pen. Any problems with the aircraft had to be resolved with a test flight, before going on a mission. Would replacing the aircraft take more time than a quick test circuit? 'Tell them okay, but shake out the next reserve crew as well. Let's cover our bets.'

Dianne passed on the order, broke the connection and began making more calls, glancing at the large clock on the wall. The aircrews would be collecting their equipment and going to dinner. No rush for them, but not much time to bring in a new aircraft. Waiting for someone to answer at the other end of a call, Dianne dimly heard another WAAF, called Iris, with Simmons.

'Those met' reports aren't looking so promising anymore, sir. Cloud build-up over the target area may be more than we expected.'

'May be?'

'We don't have an awful lot to go on from that part of the continent. It could be the Meteorological lads are fudging the figures up, just in case.'

'Then we'll keep going. I need something more concrete than that before we pull the plug.'

Dianne got in a sigh before the telephone was answered and her mind was snapped back to other things.

***

The crew of D-Delta all sat at the same long table for their meal. The atmosphere was filled with an anxious anticipation. Everyone tapped their fingers or feet. Baxter whistled under his breath.

'Bacon and eggs for a meal in the middle of the day?' Wills grumbled, poking at his plate. 'A bit strange.'

'Ungrateful sod,' Daniel said, remembering the conversation with Dianne and Susan. 'We've got a whole village's rations on this table in one lot.'

'I don't know if I can eat,' Barrymore announced mournfully. 'It doesn't help that I keep thinking of those poor bastards in the Halifax.'

'Eat,' Branner told him firmly. 'It could be a long time before you get another decent feed.'

'That's cheerful,' Flanders pulled a face. 'A POW camp on our first 'op?'

'I'm talking about us sitting out at the dispersal and waiting for a go-ahead, then the mission, the debriefing... all the what-have-you,' Branner frowned at him.

The mess hall was filling with airmen looking for dinner. The crews heading out on the operation were distinctive in their full flying kit. No one gave them a second glance, it was so commonplace. There was no sense of occasion. Still, the D-Delta men felt self-conscious.

'We're making history, I suppose,' Sexton said.

'He's been listening to bloody Churchill's speeches again,' Wills said to Daniel quietly.

'No, you idiot,' Sexton threw a scrap of crust at him. 'This could be all over by Christmas. I read somewhere that the Jerries might sue for peace before they starve to death over winter.'

'I don't think that would be Hitler's idea,' Branner nodded, half agreeing. 'But it's possible.'

'Before the Russians get to Berlin, you mean? All of a sudden the Germans reckon we're quite nice chaps,' Barrymore said, still picking at his food. The egg was going cold and congealing, making it even less appealing. He wondered how he might get rid of it without Branner seeing.

'There is that,' Branner said. 'But don't expect to be asked in for dinner if you bail out and land on their roof. Especially after we've dropped a stick of bombs down their chimney.'

Flanders mused, 'Hmm, Barrymore... Barrymore—sounds almost Russian, doesn't it? You might want to sing "Rule Britannia" at the top of your lungs, Barra, as you parachute down. Just in case they mistake you for a Russian. The Jerries hate the Ruskies.'

'No one's going to be bailing out,' Branner said coldly.

'Just a bit of a joke, skipper.'

'Then try using the funny bit next time.'

This amused Wills, who choked a laugh on some food. He had turned his bacon and egg into a sandwich and stuffed most of it inside his mouth.

'Steady on,' Daniel told him, brushing crumbs off his sleeve.

'I'm going to risk another cuppa,' Sexton said. 'Anyone else?'

There was a silence while they all considered it. Flanders said for all of them, 'I don't want to be busting for a pee all the way to Germany and back.'

There was a basic toilet in the Lancaster. Most men tried not to use it to avoid undressing and exposing themselves to the cold. Branner had a hospital bottle next to his seat, so he wouldn't have to leave the controls.

'It's hours before we even get off the ground,' Sexton reminded them.

'About ninety minutes, actually,' Branner said, glancing at his watch. 'And we should be out at the plane soon to run checks. So make it quick, if you're going to.'

All of them trooped together over to the urn, except for Branner who gestured for Sexton to bring him a tea back.

A middle-aged WAAF wearing a permanent, discouraging scowl was standing beside the urn to ensure no one took more than their fair share of milk or sugar. 'Where are you blokes off to?' she asked without much interest, eyeing their flying gear. She had a thick, Liverpool accent that was almost incomprehensible to the Australians.

'Oh, just a gardening trip,' Wills said, as if he did it every day. 'A piece of cake.'

'Fair enough. Don't end up swimming home, then,' she said.

'No chance of that.' Wills gave her a wink, which made no impression. 'I can't bloody swim.'

Daniel was standing beside him, waiting for his turn at the tea, and he gave Wills a nudge. 'You're not supposed to talk about operations outside of the briefing. You'll get us all into strife.'

'That's right,' the WAAF replied for him, sounding bored. 'I'm really a Nazi spy who reports directly to Hitler himself. I've got his number right here,' she patted a pocket. 'He lets me call reverse charges all the way to Berlin.'

Daniel blushed with embarrassment and didn't know what to say. From behind him, Flanders said, 'We can drop Adolph off a package, if you like. One that makes a big bang when it lands in his letterbox. Save you giving him a ring.'

'Ooh aye,' the WAAF turned her attention to him. 'Maybe he'll send some sugar back, since your mate here with the sweet tooth is scoffing the bleeding lot.'

Baxter had been almost counting the grains of sugar on his spoon. He jumped guiltily and looked panicked.

'Just pulling your leg,' she said with the ghost of a smile.

Back at their table Branner seemed to regret allowing the last cup of tea and he noisily slurped his, motioning for the others to hurry. They stood around and did the same.

Between scalding gulps Daniel asked Wills, 'You can't swim? Not at all?'

Wills tried to dismiss it with a shrug. 'We used to muck around in the dam at home, where you could always touch the bottom. I never actually swam, I suppose.'

'What if we have to ditch?'

'We've got the Mae Wests.' As a tail gunner, Wills' inflatable life jacket was built into the heated suit. 'And the life-raft, anyway. Who needs to swim?'

'But you can't be certain—' Daniel stopped himself. There was no sense worrying about it now. A flicker of doubt on Wills' face told him he was all too aware of the dangers.

'Everyone ready?' Branner thumped down his cup.

They went outside to their bicycles. Hundreds were scattered everywhere, ridden by the crews at lunch or working nearby. The airmen of D-Delta would ride over to draw their Mae Wests, parachutes and other final pieces of survival gear, then carry on in the back of a lorry to the bomber.

**

'Any trouble?' Susan asked Jennifer as they watched the last of the aircrew, laden by their gear, waddle across the tarmac towards a waiting truck.

'She slipped past me to help one fellow and made a right fuss of him. Then I heard her complaining to Diedre about his rudeness and how she hardly knew how to put up with it.' Jennifer puffed angrily on her cigarette. 'I think she's a right tease, that one. That's all it is. But when trouble starts, she'll scream blue murder and her bloody uncle will make sure she comes out squeaky clean.'

'Maybe I can get her transferred to something where she doesn't have any chance to bugger things up?'

'Where there's no men?' Jennifer rolled her eyes. 'On an RAF Bomber base?'

'All right, perhaps somewhere she has to keep her hands to herself.'

'That's precisely why she'll complain, if you do. I can't see Robyn getting her hands too dirty.'

'You're not helping.' Susan tossed her butt into a tin of sand, then clicked her tongue and went over to make sure it was out.

'Write a report to Julie Giles. Pass the buck on and let her worry about it. That's what Warrant Officers are for. At least you'll have some sort of record about being concerned, if the pot starts boiling.'

'I'll think about it.' Susan lit another smoke without even thinking about it. 'I still hope a quiet word in Robyn's ear might be the best way.'

'Hah! Good luck.'

They waved at the truck as it drove a wide circle and headed towards the taxiways and distant dispersals. The back doors had been left open, swinging wildly and a little dangerously. Gloved hands and helmeted heads poked out to return the farewells, before pulling the doors shut with a slam. The women watched it drawing out of sight, staying out in the open despite the cold wind that had them wrapping their collars tight and hugging themselves between puffs on their cigarettes.

'Have you met that little bloke, the gunner, before?' Jennifer asked.

'Charlie Wills? At the pub,' Susan nodded. 'Not by choice, really. He sort of tricked me into having a drink with him. Turned out not a bad fellow, if a bit intense.'

'A virgin,' Jennifer said knowledgeably. 'Hoping to break his duck in case he gets the chop.'

'Jennifer! Really? What on earth do you mean, his duck?'

'Like in cricket. If you don't get any score at all, it's called a duck... understand?'

Susan groaned and shook her head. 'Anyway, Dianne Parker's keen on his friend, the quiet one that was next to him. Daniel's his name.'

'Then you're both mad. Getting chummy with aircrew, especially before they've even finished five ops.'

'Not me. It's Dianne, I told you.'

She knew Jennifer was right. There was a higher mortality rate among the bombers flown by crews on their first five operations. There wasn't much to explain it, other than experience providing the extra nerve when it counted.

***

There were plenty of last-minute checks to be done on the aircraft with the engines running, warming up and bringing power and hydraulics.

For Daniel, the moment when all doubt vanished about flying the mission came when the chocks were waved away and the Lancaster started moving. Until then, anything could happen to scrub the operation.

Daniel was in his turret, seated and ready for action with all his checks done.

Branner's voice crackled in his intercom. 'Pilot to crew, we're on our way.'

The engines surged and the bomber jerked forward.

As the bombers emerged from their dispersal points, they took a place in the line of aircraft filing along the narrow access roads. With only eight leaving this afternoon it wasn't so bad, but Branner was nervous while he was finding the right moment to move into their slot. The aircraft excelled in the air. On the ground crawling along at five miles per hour, it was an unwieldy beast.

The slow journey out to the end of the strip seemed to take an eternity. Then the final minutes, waiting for the aircraft in front of them to race away, took forever. There was no radio contact with the control tower. The Germans monitored the airwaves and might guess a raid was on their way. Aldis lamps with a red light operated by ground crew at the end of the runway made each bomber wait in turn. A change to green sent each aircraft at full throttle down the runway.

Sexton said, 'Skipper, I don't much like the look of that. What do you think?'

Branner had been intently watching the Aldis lamp holding the plane in front of them.

'What?' he almost snapped, frowning. He saw Sexton was gazing upwards through the canopy at thickening clouds.

'Do you reckon the Met' boys have got it right?'

'Does it really matter? It's here, isn't it?' Branner wasn't really interested. The Aldis had changed to green and the bomber before them was roaring away. He edged D-Delta forward to the line.

'Well, we'll cop it on the way back, I suppose,' Sexton murmured. Branner only shrugged.

Weather systems over Europe moved from west to east, giving the Allies an advantage in forecasting conditions over the enemy. It also meant, like now, that aircrew generally flew towards their target through weather they would encounter again on the way home.

'Here we go,' Branner said, nodding at the green light.

Sexton helped move the throttles forward to full, holding them there while Branner used all his skills to keep the bomber straight and on the strip. The Lancaster was only lightly loaded with the mines and soon raised its tail-skid, hurtling down the runway. Seconds later came a bump as the weight left the undercarriage. Immediately Sexton used one hand to retract the wheels. Some pilots lingered a few seconds before pulling up the undercarriage, as if to make sure they had definitely left the ground. Branner was the opposite. Besides, an aborted take-off most likely couldn't be saved with the wheels down. There was no room on the runway left to touch down again safely. A belly landing in the fields beyond was a better option.

The ground fell away and everyone let out a breath of relief they'd never admit to—not in front of Branner at least. Particularly Barrymore was pleased. With his spectacular view in the front nose turret, he often cursed his imagination. He could easily picture one of those lush, green fields imploding through his Perspex, smashing him utterly, as the aircraft nose-dived into the earth.

Now D-Delta would take around forty minutes to climb to their assigned altitude, make formation with the others of their flight, then turn towards the target, the northeast coast of Germany.

The first operation for Branner and his crew had begun.

Five

'Pilot to Rear Gunner, are you squeezing that tube?'

'Yes, skipper, I'm squeezing the ruddy tube,' Wills answered with barely concealed impatience. Branner had reminded him a half-dozen times since they'd reached altitude and been ordered to switch on oxygen through their masks. Condensation from Wills' own breath could freeze in the rubber tube, blocking his supply. Men in rear turrets of Halifaxes had been known to pass out, then asphyxiate. Crews returning safe from raids had found their rear gunner dead.

The answer was to constantly knead the rubber, breaking up any ice forming. Wills did this, frowning at the inconvenience. He had enough to worry about, he figured.

They were flying in formation with three other Lancasters. D-Delta was the end aircraft and furthest back in a finger-four shape, each aircraft positioned like the fingernails of a spread hand. Another four Lancasters were distant specks ahead, visible only to Branner, Barrymore and Sexton.

'Shouldn't we be closer to the chaps in front?' Sexton asked.

'It's not my decision,' Branner gestured at the leader of their flight. The four aircraft dipped and rose as if on a gentle sea. They were surrounded by clear, blue skies, but below them a carpet of dirty white was thickening. 'And you were at the briefing. The squadron leader didn't want all his eggs in one basket. Two separate flights, two minutes apart.'

'So if one gets attacked, the others can make a run for it?'

'Something like that.'

'Marvellous planning.'

'Navigator to Pilot, I make it three minutes to the French coast.'

'Thank you, Navigator.' Branner stared ahead. He couldn't sight any landfall.

In his front turret, Barrymore looked at the scudding clouds below and caught a glimpse of the English Channel beyond them. The ocean was a cold, uninviting grey and littered with lines of whitecaps. Barrymore realised that to see them so clearly from this height meant a strong swell. He shuddered, imagining having to ditch the Lancaster and the crew trying to escape into the dinghy. Even in good conditions, Barrymore didn't think the aircraft would float for long, if at all. Especially on the outward trip and fully loaded with bombs and fuel. And surely you wouldn't stay dry and simply step into the dinghy? Everyone would be soaking wet, freezing cold and possibly injured.

What hope did a man have of surviving that? He decided that bailing out over Occupied France was better. He'd take his chances with the Germans, rather than the sea.

Wills broke into his thoughts. 'Tail Gunner to Pilot, skipper—how are we supposed to eat these sandwiches and drink coffee, when we've got our oxygen masks on?'

In the cockpit Branner was annoyed. 'What? We've hardly got started.'

'I'm starving, skipper. Honest.'

Daniel broke in, 'It's supposed to be bad luck, Charlie. A Kiwi pilot I met in the pub told me no one ever eats or drinks anything until they're safe and almost home.'

'I could have fainted from hunger by then.'

'Pilot to Tail Gunner,' Branner took over harshly. 'Superstition or bloody not, I suggest you save it until later. There's a long way to go. And cut the damned chatter on the intercom. We're nearly over enemy territory. That means German fighters could bounce us anytime. Look sharp.'

'Navigator to Pilot, I say we are over France now. You should see a coastline below.' At his chart-table behind the cockpit, Flanders stood up awkwardly in the space and went to a small window in the fuselage. The view didn't give him any downward vision and showed him nothing except the blue sky and a hint of the clouds lower.

'Pilot to Nose Turret, have you got a visual confirmation?'

Barrymore had just decided that a darker grey-green below, edged by a continuous line of white, was the French coast with a beach.

'Just now, skipper. We're crossing at this very instant.'

'Pilot to everyone, did you all hear that? We are now definitely over enemy-held territory. Keep your eyes peeled and stop the chit-chat.'

It was a sobering moment and no one had a reply, funny or otherwise. The three gunners all swung their guns about, searching the sky for that first tell-tale speck that might turn into an enemy fighter within seconds. Glancing at the other planes as his turret swung fully forward, Daniel noticed their crews doing the same, scanning the air around them. Occasionally, lines of condensation streamed out from the bomber's wingtips leaving long white trails against the blue. It could give them away to the Germans. Daniel quietly cursed nature.

Sexton tugged at Branner's sleeve. 'Leader's signalling, skipper.' A portable Aldis lamp flashed from the upper turret of the lead bomber.

'Change of course—Navigator, what will be our new heading?'

'Zero-one-zero, skipper. A straight line to the target. We stay on this until the drop.'

'So, we all settle in and enjoy the ride,' Branner said, banking the aircraft into a turn. Sexton was grinning, giving him a thumbs-up. Branner shifted in his seat, his parachute already feeling like concrete under his rump. The silk canopy, rather than being soft, quickly compacted into a hard and uncomfortable lump.

***

Those first minutes over France were nerve-wracking to the novices in D-Delta, but it was difficult to keep up that intensity. As time slipped by, the Lancaster crew began to relax, telling themselves the sky was a big place and with care and vigilance, it was possible get home in one piece. Maybe they wouldn't see a single enemy? The gunners allowed themselves small luxuries, like stretching cramped limbs and rubbing at their eyes which ached from the bright sunlight.

'Fighters at five o'clock low!' Wills' voice cracked with excitement.

'How many?' Branner nearly shouted.

'Hard to tell, skipper. They're a long way off and skimming the cloud. Four—maybe five. They're cutting across our rear... damn. They've gone.'

He wasn't sure if they had dropped into the cloud, or he had lost track. His turret's Perspex was speckled with oil and mess thrown into the slipstream from the engines.

'Pilot to Tail Gunner, just how low were they?'

'Just above the clouds, skipper. They might even have ducked for cover.' Wills stared at the white below, willing the Germans to re-appear. He saw nothing.

'Pilot to crew, that's a fair way below us. It could take them fifteen minutes to climb up here and cause us trouble. Forget them. Watch for fighters up here with us.'

Branner was watching the closest Lancaster, deciding if he should try and report the sighting with their signal lamp. The rear turret of the leader was angled slightly off-axis, pointing towards where Wills said the fighters vanished. He guessed their rear gunner had seen the Germans too.

Baxter called in, 'Radio to Pilot, leader's sending a sighting report to base.'

Branner was amazed, as always, that Baxter had heard, understood and even decoded the rapid transmission of Morse all in his head. 'All right, Morgan.'

A strained quarter of an hour passed as everyone watched for attacking Germans. Flanders and Baxter could only stare at their instruments, waiting for an explosion of machine gun fire as their first sign of an attack. The Lancaster thundered around them, shaking itself as it touched on the turbulence caused by the other planes or hit a pocket of colder, harder air. It rattled the men's nerves too.

Twenty minutes later Branner allowed, 'Pilot to crew, looks like they couldn't be bothered. Perhaps they were low on fuel or had other things on their plate. Don't slack off though. The Luftwaffe have plenty more planes.'

Daniel uttered under his breath, 'Yes, yes... all right. For Christ's sake, do you think we're all going to have a bloody nap in the sun?' It was the sun giving Daniel the most trouble. It was getting low and perfect for a beam attack, and he was very tired from staring into the glare. It was the oldest trick in the book for one aircraft to attack another with the sun behind it, hiding in the blinding light. Below the cloud was a solid sheet of white reflecting the sunlight. It was a small comfort that any fighters underneath the Lancaster formation would clearly show silhouetted against the backdrop.

However, the clouds also meant the Lancasters couldn't see to drop their mines on the target. The bombers were carrying on now in the hope the sky above the target area was clearer.

***

'Navigator to Pilot.'

'What is it, Bruce?'

'I'm not lost... exactly. But I haven't got a bloody clue where we are.'

Branner sighed. 'All right, I doubt the flight leader is in any better shape.'

Between them and what was now the German coastline below was still a completely unbroken layer of cirrus, beautifully painted orange and red by a setting sun. The bombers were supposedly over the target, but nobody could see it. By dead-reckoning, navigation based on their course, speed and time in the air, Flanders believed the formation was over the Frisian Islands. Without any sort of landmark to confirm this, there was no point dropping the mines. The smallest change in weather might have pushed them too far off course and the mines might land harmlessly on land.

'Nose to Pilot, what happens now, skipper?' Barrymore was waiting to change to the bomb aimer's position.

'I'd say the flight leader will call it a no-show. We can't locate the damned target, so we'll turn around and go home. We haven't got the fuel to do much else.'

'No chance we'll drop down and have a look under the clouds?'

Branner was shaking his head. 'It's too likely they'll go all the way to the ground.'

Wills said, 'So we've come all this bloody way for nothing?'

'Pilot to Tail, if you like, you can bail out and annoy the bloody hell out of some Nazi storm troopers, instead of irritating me.'

'Sorry, skipper. It just seems so useless.'

'You think I don't know?'

'Looks like you're right, skipper,' Sexton said, pointing at the flight leader. A flashing signal was being repeated.

The mission had been scrubbed. The formation was being ordered to follow the leader in a turn towards home.

'What a bloody waste of time,' Branner called to Sexton.

Sexton ticked an imaginary blackboard with his gloved finger. 'Not completely. At least we get a trip marked up against our names.'

'Yes, with nothing to show for it.'

The journey back was an anti-climax with the formation edging further to the west and flying more over the sea. It lessened the risk of being intercepted and landmarks for navigation weren't so vital. The mines were dumped into the ocean without arming them. Darkness fell thirty minutes after they'd left the target area. Only once in the far distance they saw the flashing of gunfire flickering below the clouds. It was like far-off lightning.

'I wonder what they're shooting at,' Barrymore asked for all of them.

'The Wellingtons going home, maybe,' Flanders answered. No one else had thought of them before now.

Close to the English coast the flight leader deemed it safe to break VHF radio silence and asked for a navigation fix, which would tell the aircraft what part of the country they had made landfall. They proved close to the mark and the bombers easily made their way to the airfield to land with the aid of a flare path.

Although the raid had been uneventful and comparatively short, the men were exhausted from the constant tension and physical effort of keeping their positions in the cramped aircraft. Now came the standard routine of a full debriefing, gathering together around tables in turn with intelligence officers, technical staff and others who all wanted to know exactly how every minute of the mission had transpired.

Finally, late in the evening, the crew for D-Delta were waiting at the door for Branner to have a last word with a female WAAF intelligence clerk. Beyond them, the room was being tidied by a single kitchen hand tiredly straightening chairs and wiping the tables. Branner thanked the WAAF and joined them.

'You're not going to believe this,' he said bitterly, as they all turned to leave. 'The bloody Wellingtons found the target and laid their mines. Our group of eight were the only ones to scrub the op' and come home.'

'How the hell did they do that?' Barrymore asked among the curses of the others.

'I don't know. They just did, that's all.'

Branner strode away, his disappointment clear.

Six

Dianne took a train to London. She had just two days leave, which gave her a single night staying with her parents—and that was more than enough. It wasn't something she enjoyed. Besides, she couldn't stay a second night and be back in time for duty the following morning. There had been a few occasions she took a hotel room in Piccadilly and not even admitted to her mother she was in town. The subterfuge made her feel guilty, but it avoided the sense of being imprisoned in her family home with her mother's stifling presence.

She spent most of the journey with her nose buried in some sort of reading. There was a newspaper and a dog-eared novel she didn't particularly like, then in desperation a catalogue from Harrods filled with things no one could afford—if, indeed, they actually stocked them. Anything to focus Dianne's attention away from the other occupants of the carriage. Several servicemen were trying to catch her eye and find the slightest excuse to start a conversation. Dianne wasn't interested. If forced, she would take the road of least resistance and make empty promises, shake them off at Victoria Station, then never see them again.

It wasn't that she was vain or snobbish—it was practical. These days, she met so many people, especially young men, and too many of these friendships proved fleeting, ending with a death notice in the newspaper.

Some days, like today, she wanted to avoid the heartache and keep her privacy. Maintain some distance and limit the number of people she found herself promising to write, call or join for a drink. When her parents loomed at the end of the journey, Dianne didn't feel like good company anyway, although it was doubtful any of the soldiers, sailors and airmen eyeing her off right now cared about if she would be nice company.

The trip was slow and occasionally the train crawled at such a speed the soot and steam from the engine billowed around the carriages, seeping inside despite the closed windows. The pointed coughing and doleful glances were more opportunities to start chatting. Dianne kept her head down and silently rued the extra delay. No one would say why a train from Lincoln to London was made to wait by a war being fought everywhere except that part of the world, but "there's a war on" was the reason for all things late, lost or expensive. It was hardly worth complaining anymore.

She was glad to reach London, not just to escape the carriage. Dianne loved the city and would live there again, away from her parents, when the war ended and WAAF postings to distant airfields didn't matter. The people here were mostly stoically cheerful, still defiant after the months of the Blitz, and determined to make the best of a bad situation. No one mentioned the bombed-out buildings or the streets where gaps had appeared overnight, and entire families had vanished. Nobody even wondered if the war would be won. It was only a question of how long it might take.

Dianne had just the one bag slung over her shoulder and although she could transfer straight to a Tube connection to her parent's home, she decided to walk through the city awhile. She ambled along, keeping to one side so the people hurrying could pass. The shops were a sorry sight. The storefront displays were forlorn attempts to make something out of nothing. The windows had been criss-crossed with thick tape.

She hadn't bought a present for her mother yet. Dianne was paid better than her mother had ever been, and probably more than her father had too. He was an invalid on a pension these days. She wished her salary had never been known—she had announced it proudly one day and the news backfired. This on-going perception she was suddenly wealthy was another thorny point in Dianne's relationship with her mother, who bitterly resented the money Dianne made. Rather than ignore it, Dianne tried to smooth things over with gifts or rations beyond her mother's budget. Usually, she carried something all the way from the airbase, since it was easier to buy illicit cheese or a half-dozen eggs from the country.

This time, Dianne hadn't given it a thought, her mind frustratingly occupied with the idea she was going on leave without seeing Daniel beforehand.

It was none of his business, they hardly new each other. Still, Dianne felt disturbed she had left without telling Daniel she was going. No doubt Susan would let him know, if she saw him in the pub. That in itself was worrying. Giving Susan an evening's free access to Daniel wasn't a good thing either.

'I should have made her promise to behave,' Dianne told her reflection in a window.

Beyond the glass she saw a shawl. On impulse, it would do.

The girl behind the counter looked barely old enough to be out of school. She was thin and pale and couldn't help glancing at Dianne's uniform with undisguised envy.

'Are you working in King Charles Street, miss?' she asked in a rush, as she wrapped the shawl in green tissue paper and fumbled a piece of ribbon around it. King Charles Street was where the war cabinet bunker had been built.

'No,' Dianne smiled. 'I work at one of the bomber airbases in Lincoln. I'm only in London for the day.'

'Oh, I wouldn't want to be up there,' the girl said with surprising certainty, frowning with concentration as she tried to tie a bow in the ribbon. Dianne obliged by placing her finger on the knot.

'It's not that dangerous or anything,' Dianne said, and then felt an odd urge to add, 'I mean, we've been bombed, but they didn't get close.' It sounded lame. This girl was in more peril living in London with the German V1 bombs targeting the city.

With wide eyes the girl said, 'I'm talking about the Americans. There are still millions of them here even after the invasion started. I wouldn't want to miss out.'

Dianne pictured her still-childish face inexpertly made up with powder and garish lipstick. It made her feel sad and a little angry. 'Aren't you a bit young to be thinking about such things?'

The girl pouted, her mood quickly sour. 'I'll be seventeen next month.' She pushed the parcel across the counter.

'Then what about the local lads?' Dianne knew it was the wrong answer. No doubt, all the good ones had gone to the war. Besides, she should hardly be encouraging the girl's promiscuity.

'They don't have any money,' the girl said with a soft snort. 'How are you supposed to have a good time?' She took in Dianne's uniform with another look that said everything. It's all right for you. You're older and prettier, and you've got a good job earning plenty of money.

Dianne felt her cheeks start to burn and had no reply she liked. She wished the girl was one of her WAAF privates so she could tell her not to be silly, and to be careful—for what that might be worth, which was probably nothing.

Instead she said, annoyed as she picked up the parcel and turned to leave, 'Then I suggest you have a chat with your mother, before you get too excited. Even if you are turning all of seventeen next month, I'm sure there are still a few things you need to learn.'

The girl let her get to the door, before calling out sullenly, 'My mother was killed last month and my dad's in Africa—' she stopped, having never known how she would finish. Then she added shakily, 'I'm living with my aunty.'

With the door open, Dianne looked at her, the anger instantly dissolved and replaced with a heavy regret. She said softly, 'Then for God's sake, talk to your aunty—anyone. It's not that simple, you know. Going out with boys, I mean.'

'Of course, I know.' The girl was standing stiffly, waiting for Dianne to leave.

Dianne left, closing the door gently behind her.

Outside she took a deep breath and cursed herself. The brief confrontation felt like her fault, although that was stupid. Worse, it put her in no good state of mind to deal with her mother.

Clapham had been almost untouched by the bombing. There were no important targets within the area or even close by, which might have brought near-misses. Still, some bombs had landed here, and several streets had lost houses. The terrace buildings tended to collapse completely, creating the almost bizarre result of single homes disappearing completely while the properties on either side were apparently untouched. Only looking closer showed the windows were broken, the walls singed and the gardens blasted.

Dianne walked past one bomb site on her way from the Tube station to her parent's house. She paused to look, hoping no neighbours would be offended by her gawking. The home was now just a pile of rubble between the walls of the adjoining properties. Timber, steel and the remains of furniture poked out of the wreckage. There were no signs that someone had been killed or injured. It was possible there had been no casualties at all.

She was trying to get some feeling of what it was like to be on the other side. To be on the receiving end of all her work—a bombing raid flown from Waddington.

Dianne's mind stayed blank, disturbing her. She felt untouched by the scene and it made her feel guilty.

Her mother opened the door as Dianne walked up the path. Beryl Parker had been waiting at the window, the drapes discreetly to one side just a few inches.

'I thought you were never going to get here.' She gave Dianne a kiss on the cheek.

'The train from Lincoln was delayed.'

'Nothing runs on time anymore—well, come in, come in.'

The house smothered Dianne with its familiar smells and sights. Her father's tobacco hung in the air. It permeated the furnishings and carpets, the odour never going completely away. A stew was boiling in the kitchen, the meagre amount of meat probably rabbit, the strongest smell one of sour vegetables. Dianne actually liked the food mass-prepared at the airfield, because it was better than her mother's cooking even from before the war and rationing. The usual meal in the Parker household was always roasted, stewed or fried to tasteless extinction.

Her father sat at the kitchen table and tilted his head back to let Dianne kiss his forehead. 'Hello, girl. Back from the wars?' He said this every time.

'You might as well call it that, Dad.' She had dumped her bag in the hall and placed the wrapped present on the table.

'Giving bloody Hitler hell?'

'George!' His wife scolded him.

'Good God, I'm sure she's heard worse by now.'

'A damned sight worse,' Dianne told him, delighted to see her mother wince.

'Of course you have, girl. Of course, you have.'

Dianne accepted an offer of a cup of tea and sat opposite her father. As her mother fussed at the stove, chattering something about the neighbours, her father's eye began to stray back to the newspaper. Dianne soon felt the same resigned despair that she struggled to hide. She could have been away a day, a week or a whole year—she might have conquered the world—but her homecomings were always exactly the same. Nothing changed. The sense of duty that brought her back seemed pointless, and the amount of time and reason she was absent made no difference.

A question pierced her reverie. 'Have you made any new friends, love?'

'There's always new people, Mum. Some you meet, others you don't. It's a big place, don't forget.'

'You know what I mean...' It was Beryl Parker's metaphor for asking about Dianne's love life.

It sparked interest in her father. With a twinkle in his eye he added, 'Any lucky fellow got his slippers under your bed?'

'No, Dad. No one special. We're all far too busy for that sort of thing.'

Her father cleared his throat meaningfully, teasing her, but her mother was considering it seriously. Dianne remembered the conversation she'd had with Susan, standing at the end of the runway in the freezing morning to wave the bombers farewell. Dianne had mocked Susan for maintaining a myth with her own mother that her virginity, and therefore her dignity, was still intact. At least Susan's mother cared.

In truth, Dianne's parent knew little about their daughter anymore. Her introduction to sex, so long a sacred thing in Dianne's mind, was a discussion that had never taken place, and now was a private knowledge Dianne didn't want to share. Somehow, in the few years since it happened, everybody understood that Dianne had started sleeping with her male friends. Without fanfare or grief, it was accepted.

'What about that nice bloke from Ardent Street?' her mother was asking. 'I haven't seen his parents for a long time—she kept to herself anyway, mind you. He was a very pleasant fellow.'

Dianne sighed. 'How many times do I need to remind you, Mum? He was posted as missing after Dunkirk. If they've heard nothing by now, he won't be coming back.' His name drifted around the edge of her memory, but Dianne couldn't picture his face, like the dead pilots she had learned to forget. 'It's a good thing you haven't seen his mother. Imagine how upset she'd be—'

'Yes, yes,' Beryl dumped a cup of tea with a saucer quickly in front of Dianne, who was so used to enamel mugs it made her blink. 'I'm sorry, I must be thinking of someone else. I get them all mixed up.' It sounded as if hundreds of men circulated through Dianne's life.

They did, but Beryl Parker never met them. She probably couldn't imagine the vast force of service men that surrounded her daughter every day.

There was another not-so-subtle hint that Dianne resented. The reminder that ideally, she should meet and marry a man who lived only a few minutes away, such as in Ardent Street, within reach of Beryl Parker's needs. It was about family and tradition in her mother's mind. For Dianne, it would be like a long chain coupled to the odorous stove, snaking through the streets to where she would live nearby. In her mother's world, Dianne's proper fate was to cook her own scrawny rabbits in thin vegetable broth, so her own husband could read the newspaper forever.

Dianne tried to remind herself that she was being unfair, judging her mother on who she was now, instead who she had been. Did she deserve such unkind thoughts? Beryl Parker had the yellowish skin of a "canary", a woman who had worked long hours in the munitions factories during the Great War. It was an affliction that never left those workers, the chemicals from the millions of artillery shells painting their skin for life.

It was hard to imagine her mother as Dianne was today, young and wondering what the war and the world would bring. Looking for love and a magical future that had little to do with this grim reality.

'Where did the two of you meet again, Mum?' she asked, interrupting her mother's musings of who, exactly, she had mistaken the missing Dunkirk soldier for.

'Goodness—what?'

'Where did you and Dad first meet? Like when you knew you'd be seeing each other?'

Her mother was flustered, as if it was something she was embarrassed to remember. Her father gave a wry grin at a memory from a different time and place.

She said, 'It was in a pub in Norwich, after we all finished a shift. George, you kept buying me drinks and said you wouldn't stop until I promised to be there the next night. You were going to line them up on the bar, even if I didn't drink them. I couldn't stand to think of the waste.'

'We were all doing very nicely back then,' her father nodded. 'You could work seven days a week, if you liked. The guns on the Western Front could never get too many shells.'

'You didn't think of signing up to fight?' Dianne asked.

'I tried a few times. The boss wouldn't let me go. Very specialised, I was. Someone had to fight the war on the home front.'

Dianne sipped her tea. It was treacherous and cruel, but her father's words seemed to lack sincerity. She didn't like where these thoughts were taking her and she looked around for something to change the subject. The kitchen was filled with the memorabilia of nearly thirty years of marriage. Knick-knacks from the past. Some of the things had been in the same place for as long as Dianne could remember.

'Are you staying just the one night?' Her mother asked what she already knew.

'It's just a two-day pass, yes. There's a train at midday tomorrow.'

'You're hardly here, before you're gone again.'

Dianne gave her a wan smile. 'And I've got to nip down the pub after tea to see if a friend is there. I promised to check.'

'Anyone we know?'

'No, it's someone from the airfield who lives around here. They're on leave too.' It was a complete lie. Dianne was already feeling the need to get away. Before joining the WAAFs and the war, she wouldn't have dreamed of going to the local pub on her own. Tonight, there was no harm in having a quick drink and seeing if anybody interesting was there. She had done it before.

Her mother said, disappointed, 'I wanted to sort out those linen cupboards this evening. I need you to give me a hand. I can't reach the top shelves.'

'I'm sure Dad will help.'

'I'll what?' Her father came out of a daze.

'Never mind, George. I suppose I'll think of something.'

It was the last thing Dianne wanted to do, and in the morning she was counting on getting a sleep in. Still, she offered half-heartedly, 'Maybe tomorrow, before I go back?'

'Don't worry about it, dear.' The set of her mother's shoulders, where she stood at the stove again, showed her disapproval. Her father had packed his pipe and lit up, so Dianne took it as all right to light a cigarette. He gave her a conspirator's wink, seeing his wife stiffen even more.

After another half hour of halting conversation, Dianne decided she would go upstairs for a nap until tea. Again, it was more an excuse, but when she lay fully clothed on her old bed she was asleep within seconds.

The next thing she knew was a call to come for supper. When she got back downstairs her mother had opened the present and was wearing the shawl. With a hint of disappointment she thanked Dianne, wondering aloud if she had anything at all to match the colours. The meal coincided with a news bulletin on the radio that her father insisted on hearing. So they ate the stew and dipped bread into the broth in silence, listening to explanations of the battles beyond the Normandy beaches and convoy losses in the North Atlantic. It sounded like Hitler was still getting the worst of it in Russia, despite advancing within sight of Moscow the previous year. No one in England was going to complain if the German army battered itself to death against the Russians and a lingering East European winter. It kept enemy troops away from France.

Afterwards, Dianne helped with the dishes and made sure there was nothing else, apart from the dreaded linen cupboard, to be done. Then, in the hallway she shrugged into her coat and gloves, and put on her cap.

She called, 'I won't be that long. Maybe I'll be back in time for a game of whist or something?'

Her mother's voice echoed from the kitchen. 'There's not much good the three of us playing.'

'No, I suppose not...' Dianne stood helplessly for a moment, then shook off her guilt and slipped out the door.

***

The local pub was called "The Iron Horse". Three streets away, it presented a small challenge in the blackout. Dianne carried a torch which she flashed at intervals, looking for broken paving or anything that could turn her ankle. She was glad when the familiar place loomed out of the darkness.

The pub was noisy, thick with smoke and almost full with patrons who all wore some kind of uniform. The mood was merry. The people of London had money to spend and seemed determined to enjoy doing it. Everyone was earning a wage. If you weren't in the armed forces, you were a part of the huge workforce needed to keep the country at war. Against one wall of the hotel, staking their claim as regulars, were tables of young women—factory workers who had taken the place of men gone to fight and now enjoyed a new status.

Dianne fought her way to the bar and found herself being served by the landlord himself. He had a large and jovial face covered in broken blood vessels, a man who consumed a lot of his own produce. And he wasn't someone to forget a pretty girl.

'Young Dianne Parker,' he boomed as he pulled a pint. 'You're back in the big town.'

'Just for a night, Norm. Can I have a gin and tonic?'

'Who's paying?' He gave her a lecherous grin.

'I'm on my own.'

He raised his eyebrows disbelievingly. 'Then I'll buy this one since you're giving Hitler hell for us. Don't tell the missus.'

'Thanks, Norm. I won't.'

There were no tables free, so Dianne stayed at the bar, nursing her drink and staring around for a friendly face. There were some she knew vaguely, nobody she wanted to chat with now. Other eyes watched her surreptitiously, trying to decide if Dianne was on her own or waiting for a partner. She kept them guessing, looking nonchalant and at ease, and unapproachable. However, she didn't want to do this for long. Wasting an hour or so by herself didn't appeal, even though the alternative was going home to her mother's linen cupboard.

When she put a second cigarette to her lips the rasp of a lighter came from nearby.

'Allow me.'

Dianne turned to see a young pilot—very young, she figured immediately —bravely holding out a flame, trying not to show his nervousness.

'Thank you,' she lit the smoke.

'Can I buy you a drink?'

He was eighteen, she decided. The minimum age, joining up on his birthday and now fresh out of training. Too young for her, but it wouldn't harm to pass some time instead of standing on her own any longer. His dark hair was slicked down with Brilliantine and he had long, girlish eyelashes his mother would adore. The remains of adolescent acne spotted his brow and chin.

'If you like,' Diane said slowly, giving him every indication this was only a temporary situation.

He edged close to the bar, using it as an excuse to press a little against Dianne. She moved back, breaking the contact. There was a too-long silence as he tried to catch a barman's eye.

'My name's Harry—Harry Chambers,' he said suddenly, putting his face uncomfortably near hers.

'Harry,' she nodded. 'I'm Dianne.'

'Ah, like the Roman goddess of love.' He tried a smile. It trembled and he could feel it, so he quickly covered it by puffing his cigarette.

'She was the Greek goddess, actually. Anyway, I was named after my great aunt who was a spinster, and a miserable old sod who wouldn't know love from a bar of soap.'

'Oh?' Chambers wasn't sure if she was serious. He was saved by Norm appearing. 'Ah—same again, thanks. And here, too.' He flipped a finger at Dianne's empty glass.

Norm studied the gesture a moment, then looked at him deadpan. 'Sorry, lad. I can't recall what you're drinking again. Lemonade, was it?'

'No, of course not.' Chambers flushed. Dianne was glad to see it was more with anger than embarrassment. He had some spirit. 'It's a pint of bitter.'

'Aye, that was it,' Norm said knowingly. 'A pint of bitter indeed.' Dianne shot him a reproving look and he returned it with a wink. She felt a little sorry for Chambers, who didn't see he'd irked the publican.

To help him get his composure back, she said, 'So, you're a pilot?'

'Yes—well, of course you'd know.' He pointed at her uniform.

'Where are you based?'

'Tangmere. I've got a few days leave to visit my mum and dad.'

'A fighter pilot, then?'

'That's right.' He looked pleased. 'Hurricanes at the moment. Probably change to Spitfires soon, I suspect.'

'I see.' Dianne had guessed Chambers flew fighters. It's what gave him the courage to approach her. Most fighter pilots believed a set of wings on their chest and a seat in a Spitfire or Hurricane made them irresistible to women.

'Where are you posted?' he was asking.

'Waddington, up near Lincoln. It's a bomber squadron.'

'Bombers?' He gave a small shrug as he accepted the drinks from Norm and deftly passed back a pound note held between his fingers, like it was a conjuring trick. 'I suppose someone's got to do it. Can't be very much fun though.'

'Fun?' Dianne frowned. 'I didn't know any of it was supposed to be fun.'

He back-pedalled. 'No, I just meant flying those big buggers around—sorry. I mean flying multies, like the four-engine jobs. Even two is a bit like driving a bus, they say.'

Dianne took a large sip of her drink. It had become a bad idea encouraging Chambers after all and she wanted to move on. She could excuse him being pretentious because of his youth. It didn't make him any more appealing.

'How many sorties have you flown?' she said, watching him closely, knowing he wouldn't like answering.

'Oh... a half dozen.' He offered Dianne another cigarette, which she automatically took and lit again from his lighter. He waved the smoke away. 'Not many, I know. I only got my posting a week or so ago.'

'And have you shot down any German bombers?' She knew it was next to impossible. Daylight raids were unknown now.

'Well no, not yet, but I hope to bag one soon.' Hearing himself, Chambers sensed his credibility was falling. He added, to explain his failure, 'They don't come over in daylight too often anymore. We're more likely to find a brace of ME 109s doing a fighter sweep, or perhaps a one-one-oh. They're quick blighters with those twin engines. Not easy to catch.'

Dianne cursed herself for breaking a golden rule. Never give pilots, especially fighter pilots, a chance to chatter about aircraft or flying them. They could talk for hours. Before long, Chambers would be describing dog-fighting tactics to her, waving his hands in the air in a parody of two airplanes duelling in the sky.

She said with a thin smile, 'Not my department, I'm afraid. Means nothing to me so—' she put up a hand, stopping Chambers as he opened his mouth. 'And I don't want to understand, thank you. You won't ever get me up there.' This wasn't true. Dianne had taken several ferry flights and thoroughly enjoyed them.

'You never know. You might like it.' He glanced at her drink, hoping it would disappear faster and he could buy another one. Supplying cigarettes and alcohol seemed to be his best chance.

'Is that the right time?' she asked, peering through the smoke at a clock.

'Close enough,' Chambers looked and reluctantly agreed. 'Are you meeting someone?'

'I might be—it depends if they get here.' This was getting tricky.

'You don't mind if we chat until... they arrive?'

'Actually, there could be a scene.' Dianne looked thoughtful about that. In reality, she was considering how much compounding the lies would hurt and where it was going to lead.

Chambers fidgeted with his pint glass. 'Oh? The jealous type?'

'I don't know—'

Dianne was cut off by the distant wailing of an air-raid siren, which was quickly joined by others. A mixed chorus of groans and wry cheers came from the customers. Norm bustled out from behind the bar, pushing his way through.

He called, 'All right, all right—check the blackout curtains. You all know the bloody drill.'

She downed her drink in one go, made sure her purse was still in the same coat pocket, then calmly waited to file outside towards a bomb shelter. Thankfully, Chambers had melted away to find his own greatcoat, although she figured he would probably return. He would be feeling even more heroic and protective now.

After a minute, Dianne was surprised to realise nobody was leaving. Norm was back behind the bar and serving out a sudden spate of drinks orders apparently necessary to survive a bombing raid.

'Shouldn't we be going to a shelter?' she called to him as he drifted close. He put another gin and tonic in front of Dianne.

'That's on the house too,' he said quietly. 'If you leave, half the blokes sitting in the corner over there will go home as well. They all fancy their chances. Any chance you could look a bit more lonely like?'

'Norm, what about the air raid?'

He touched his nose. 'We made a deal with the Luftwaffe. They don't bomb us, and we won't send 'em any watered-down beer.' When he saw Dianne wasn't happy, he said seriously, 'The nearest public shelter is the Tube station ten minutes away. These days, by the time you get there, it's all over. We've got a bunker out the back if you want. The wife will take you. You shouldn't worry, there's nothing around here they want to bomb. If we were near the docks or something, it'd be different. It's not like the Blitz anymore, love.'

From outside an ominous hum from the bomber's engines was getting louder than the sirens. The noise of conversation and laughter in the bar lifted to compensate. An anti-aircraft battery opened up somewhere, too far away to be anything but distant cracking. Dianne watched everyone nearby and decided, against her instincts, they all knew better than her. Actual bomber raids on London had become sporadic and aimed at specific targets, rather than the indiscriminate bombing of civilians that occurred during the Blitz. More recently, it was the pilot-less V1 rockets that arrived out of nowhere. Looking around, she couldn't bring herself to scuttle into the publican's shelter on her own, or with his wife. Some of it was courage born from the gin and tonics, and some of it was, she feared, sheer stupidity.

Chambers hadn't come back, which was surprising.

A sound like falling hail came from the street and hotel roof. The anti-aircraft fire had moved overhead, the bombers passing directly above, and the expended shrapnel was dropping down. Dianne consoled herself it was a good time not to be hurrying along the footpath towards a shelter after all. Not without wearing a helmet.

The whistle of an approaching bomb gave the patrons of the Iron Horse enough time to exchange shocked glances—a cheated look that said, *this one's coming close,* as if the Germans were playing a game unfairly.

It exploded with a deafening noise and the windows of the pub blew inwards in a shower of glass. Women screamed and men cried out, with everyone falling to the floor. Someone cannoned into Dianne's back and sent her sprawling, a body crushing her, pressing her face against the sticky, smelling carpet. In the distance, bricks and timber collapsed and more glass shattered musically. The roar of the explosion seemed to echo for an eternity and it was a long time before Dianne realised much of the noise was inside her head, her ears ringing.

The weight on her shifted and somebody grunted an apology, before a hand under her arm helped Dianne to her feet. The electricity was still on and she found herself thanking a civilian, an older man who looked embarrassed to have possibly hurt her. She assured him it wasn't so, although she felt shaken and winded. Staring around, she saw most of the room was undamaged except for tipped chairs and scattered belongings, and the broken glass from the windows littering the tables and floor. It appeared no one was seriously hurt.

The relief lasted only a second.

She joined an exodus of people rushing to the door. Outside, lit by flickering fires, the building opposite was a jumbled mess of smashed masonry as if a giant's hand had scooped away the front half of the place, creating a ruined doll's house for everyone to see inside. Living quarters were upstairs. A floor that had separated the two levels hung shredded towards the road and furniture still on the upper half was balanced precariously. Already, figures were clambering across the wreckage, tossing pieces aside and shouting for a response from within the rubble. A single bed dangling from the upstairs was small. It had been a child's bedroom.

Dianne was about to join the rescuers, unsure what she could do except dig at the ruins too, then it struck her that George, the publican, would know who they might be looking for. She turned against the tide of customers leaving the pub and fought a passage through. George was comforting a woman who had been injured by flying glass. She seemed quite cheerful that a gash on her forehead was worth a very large glass of rum.

'George, it's the fish and chip shop across the street,' Dianne said urgently, squatting next to him. 'Who lives there? What should they be looking for?'

George understood, his face grim. 'Two women and the daughter of one of them,' he said. 'Both the husbands are off fighting, so it's just the three of them if they're all home.' He glanced towards the clock on the wall, now hanging crookedly. 'The girls were probably downstairs cleaning up at this time of night.'

'I'd better tell someone,' she said, getting up to hurry back outside.

Dianne saw the air raid was still going on, although it had moved on like a storm sweeping across the city. To the west the anti-aircraft fire stabbed at the sky, and searchlight beams probed high, sometimes revealing an enemy bomber as a silvery, moth-like shape. Jangling bells in the distance heralded a fire brigade rushing to the scene. Dianne spotted a man wearing an Air Raid Warden's helmet. He was standing close to the wreckage and urging people to be careful.

Dianne grabbed his elbow. 'There should be three women in there. Two adults and a young girl—'

'I know, miss,' he cut her off impatiently.

She felt silly. Of course, these are all local people. 'What can I do to help?'

He said curtly, glancing at her, 'Nothing, miss. Not in those shoes, and with those hands. You'd be useless and it's best to leave it up to the men.' He leaned sideways to see past her, dismissing Dianne.

Dianne felt a flush of anger, offended and astounded that her help had been refused—especially as the factory girls from the pub were among those pulling at the rubble. Apparently, her dress uniform made her otherwise useless apart from shuffling files. The warden looked to be a middle-aged man, too old for military service and now, she decided, enjoying his moment of glory.

'I'm sure I can bloody do something,' she snapped, dragging his attention back. Both their faces were streaking with dust and smoke from the fires. Dianne's eyes chose this moment to water at the fumes.

'I know who's in that building,' he repeated harshly. 'I've known them all my bloody life. If you don't know what you're doing, you can bring the rest of it down on our heads.'

A fire engine pulled to a stop. Dianne had to back away as the men rushed past. The warden strode off without another word. She retreated to the footpath outside the Iron Horse and watched. She did feel useless. Amidst the carnage of the bombing, the noise of the rescuers and the air raid still going on in the distance, Dianne could only stand and stare. Dianne hadn't been in London during the Blitz and had no experience of bombings in the city. She remembered only earlier that day, standing in front of the old bomb site and trying to imagine what it was like. Now she knew.

'Over here, Nick,' someone called hoarsely. They had pulled aside a slab of concrete. Underneath a small, pale hand protruded from between more bricks.

The rescuers worked feverishly. The hand belonged to the young daughter.

Gently placing her body on a stretcher, an ambulance attendant covered the girl with a blanket and they maneuvered her off the wreckage. They paused beside a man who briefly checked her condition. Dianne's heart stopped seeing them raise the blanket further, placing it over her face. The pathetic mound she made under the cloth had a tragic finality of its own, more disturbing than the body itself.

Somebody nearby said sombrely, 'If the young girl's there, the women will be under that pile too.'

The amount of volunteers had grown. Chains of men were passing the broken bricks and timber away from the impact point. Dianne didn't think there would be any survivors and she suddenly felt ashamed, a morbid spectator.

Feeling empty and inadequate, Dianne headed home.

Her mother was distraught and her father tried to be angry. Both of them had been panicking that Dianne had been hurt in the bombing and it took a while to calm them down. Dianne only cared about getting to her bed and it was hard to be patient with her parents. Finally, she begged that she was exhausted and went upstairs, leaving her mother looking dissatisfied that enough fuss had been made. Dianne hastily washed her face in the bathroom, afraid her mother might follow and start crying again.

Lying in bed with the lights out, Dianne stared up at the dark ceiling. The room spun a little. Images of the girl's blanket-covered body kept filling her mind. Dianne felt the same as everyone—she hated the

Germans and everything they did. All that they stood for. It was only right since they had started this whole damned thing. But she couldn't say the same for the war itself because it had brought Dianne freedom, money and excitement—the last not being something to admit too readily. It was true, though, for many people.

All sorts of unwanted thoughts haunted her now. The raids she helped plan and execute—everyone believed the British bombs crashed into factories and ammunition dumps. They destroyed tanks and sank submarines. It was all about smashing Hitler's weaponry and industrial machine to win the war. But it was also well known, though rarely discussed, that not all the bombs hit their mark. A large percentage missed altogether. No one said anything about killing innocent women and their daughters or spoke about little German girls being carried lifeless from a shattered fish and chip shop in Berlin or Stuttgardt.

As the things chased maddeningly around in Dianne's head she began to fear it wasn't so straightforward just who was good, and who was bad. It was frightening to ask, whose side would God really be on? Did the end justify the means?

It abruptly got too much to think about and she felt ill.

'God, how the hell would I know?' she asked the darkness, giving in.

***

The following morning, Dianne had a hangover, which was unusual for her. The gin and tonics had been large, and it probably explained the tormented soul-searching before falling asleep. She stayed in bed as long as possible, ignoring her mother pointedly banging pots and pans downstairs in an attempt to rouse her.

Finally, Dianne washed and dressed herself in full uniform ready to travel and packed her bags. When she came into the kitchen her parents, in their usual places like the night hadn't happened, looked surprised but took the hint.

'You're going already?' Her mother clicked her tongue.

'I'm sorry, I don't want such a long train ride back, and that raid last night might be making things worse.'

75

'When will you be on leave again?'

'You know I can't answer that. I have no idea.'

Her father grunted from his newspaper, 'Send someone to go and bomb the buggers who were here last night.'

'Maybe we can.' Dianne gave him a quick hug in his chair.

Her mother tried one last time, 'What about breakfast? Do you want some?'

'You keep your jam and butter. I'll get something at the station.'

The farewells at the door were brief with Dianne hurrying as if the train was leaving in front of them, but once she had rounded a corner and was out of sight Dianne considered detouring back to the pub and asking about the rest of the women in the bombed house.

She decided against it. Chances were the news would be bad.

It was a cold, fine day and walking in the bright sunshine to the Tube cleared the hangover fuzz from her mind. At Victoria Station, as Dianne suspected she always would, she changed her mind and checked her bag into a cloakroom. There was a later train she could take. The next few hours she spent browsing the shops and looking for something small to buy Susan. Dianne even had a few drinks of wine with her lunch in a bar.

By the time she was on her way back to Lincoln the alcohol was making her sleepy. Dianne put her bunched-up coat beside her head as a pillow, leaned against the carriage window and closed her eyes.

It was like sleep was her nemesis. More disturbing ideas from the night before trickled through her mind again, at least this time not so torturous. It was something she wanted to understand better. Dianne decided that when the moment was right, she'd ask others about civilian casualties in Germany from bombing. Did anyone know, or even care?

'Excuse me, is anyone sitting here?'

Dianne looked up to see a naval officer politely standing next to her, gesturing at the empty seat beside her.

'No, you can have it.'

'I'm sorry, I was hoping you weren't quite asleep yet.'

'I was just dozing. It's all right.' The coat slipped from the window, waking her further. She couldn't help a momentary frown.

'Oh dear, now I've done it,' he said, sitting down. 'Would you like a cigarette? I'll tell you what—' he smiled slyly and pulled a silver hip flask from his pocket. 'How about a nip of this? Navy rum. It'll put you to sleep in no time.'

No one else was in the four-seat cabin. Dianne gave him a pointed sigh to show her disapproval, then softened it with a smile of her own.

'I suppose you'll think I'm rude, if I don't.'

'Never dream of it,' he grinned, expertly flicking open a cigarette case and producing a lighter.

Seven

'We've been chosen for a special operation,' Daniel told Dianne with a hushed excitement. 'We have to start some sort of training.' It was late afternoon and the sun was low. They were braving the tiny, back garden of the pub. The metal furniture was chilled and uncomfortable. Neither of them wanted to admit it.

'I know,' she said. 'D-Delta has been pulled from the mission roster.'

'I forget you know things before I do.' He pulled a face, his news spoiled.

'Do you know what you're training for?'

'No, do you?'

'No, and I—'

'Wouldn't tell me if you did,' he finished for her. 'You're worse than those spy blokes, keeping secrets.'

'They say,' she raised her eyebrows at him. 'The girls behind the bar here will pass on information. For a price.'

'What? They're Nazi spies?' He nearly laughed, and a memory of the WAAF beside the tea urn didn't help.

Dianne explained, 'No, they just make a few quid passing on gossip.'

'To who?'

'To someone else who makes a few quid—just passing on gossip. That's how it works. They all think it's just harmless rubbish that someone is silly enough to pay for, but it all adds up.'

'Ah, I see now. You actually listen to those lectures?'

She frowned at him. 'Excuse me, it's not your country they wanted to invade.'

He dropped his head and looked comically apologetic. 'Fair enough. You're absolutely right.'

She ran her finger through a rivulet of water on the table and flicked it at him. 'Don't be a pain in the neck.'

'I mean it.'

'Like hell you do. Have you got a cigarette?' When it was lit, she asked, 'What's the training, do you know?'

'Low-level flying, the skipper says. Cross country.'

'Under the German's radar then,' she mused. 'Right into their back yard, I'd say.'

'Berlin itself, you think?'

'Something like that. You shouldn't sound so keen, you know.'

'I'm not. I'm bloody terrified.'

'That's more like it.' Dianne studied him as Daniel sipped his pint and his attention was momentarily drawn away by a rowdy group of airmen passing the fence. 'Danny, I can't help thinking we shouldn't get too... attached. Do you know what I mean?'

'Not really,' he pretended, putting his glass down carefully.

Dianne struggled for the right words and wasn't even sure she wanted to say them. 'I don't think this is the time and place to get involved with someone.' She saw his face starting fall, despite that he tried to hide it. 'Don't get me wrong—I like you and it's nice seeing you like this. But I don't want you expecting me not to see other fellows as well.'

It wasn't quite what she meant. Dianne was thinking to build some sort of a barrier between them for her own sake, so her feelings for Daniel wouldn't grow out of hand. If she was honest with herself, she had been undecided before now about taking a risk with her heart. The news of his special training abruptly changed things. A low-level mission deep into enemy territory meant it would be exceptionally dangerous. Daniel's chances of surviving his first five missions, let alone the remainder of the entire thirty required, had suddenly dropped.

'I'm not stopping you seeing other blokes,' he said unconvincingly. 'I'm sorry if you thought that.'

Dianne took a deep breath and admitted, 'Oh, it's not that so much.' There was a small silence as she stabbed out her cigarette. Staring at the ashtray, she said, 'My mum wanted me to go out with a soldier who lived just around the corner. Keep me nice and handy, more than anything.' She smiled without any humour. 'It doesn't matter now because he didn't get out of Dunkirk.'

Daniel nodded knowingly, surprising her. 'And now you reckon I might get knocked off too, just when you're starting to like me?'

'It's not a nice thing to think about, but there's times when we need to face reality.' Dianne dared to raise her eyes and saw Daniel grinning crookedly at her.

'That's a bit pessimistic, isn't it?' he said.

'No, it's being sensible.'

'Are you worried about this special op'?'

'I worry about every operation. For everybody's sake, by the way, not just people I know.'

'Well, you don't have to fuss about me. I've got a feeling I'll be seeing the whole war through.' He shrugged. 'I can't explain it.'

'You all have that feeling,' she said softly. 'Everyone believes it'll be the other fellow who gets shot down or has to bail out. No one thinks it'll be them.'

'No, I know—but I'm serious. I told you, I can't explain it properly.'

'All right.' It wasn't worth arguing. She shivered. The sun was losing its last warmth rapidly and she thought about moving inside. Dianne discovered she was reluctant to break this small moment together.

Daniel leaned forward and took her hand, which had been absently drawing circles in the spilled water. Her fingers were cold, so he covered them with his other hand. 'I'll tell you what, let's make a deal.'

Dianne had been startled by his touch. 'A deal? What sort of deal?'

'If I come back from this special operation, will you go out with me— just me, I mean? I'm not saying you couldn't still go out and have a laugh with other blokes and that, but... you know.' His words trailed off as Daniel lost his confidence.

'Goodness,' Dianne blinked at him. Then, ignoring a funny warmth in her stomach she said, 'Haven't you been listening to a thing I've said?'

'Fair's fair, right? If I get through this tough one, I'll probably come back from anything.'

'That doesn't make any sense at all. It will only be your second raid, remember? You'll still have twenty-eight to go and chances are—'

Dianne stopped herself. 'I'm sorry, that wasn't a clever thing to say, but you know what I mean. God, the war could go on forever.'

'That's exactly why you shouldn't be saying things like you are. Live for today, I reckon. Let the future take care of itself.'

'That's all right for you to say.' Her fingers were comfortably heated now, and Dianne thought about sliding her other hand in between his, but the intimacy would contradict what she was trying to say. 'You're not the one left behind, crying in your pillow all night.'

He looked pleased. 'Would you do that? Cry all night if I got shot down?'

Dianne said firmly, 'This is starting to get far too serious.' She shuddered again with a chill touching the back of her neck. Seeing it, Daniel guessed she'd want to move inside very soon. The rest of D-Delta's crew along with Susan and a few other girls were in the pub, having denounced any notion of fresh air as only for the foolish.

'So, what about our deal?' Daniel asked anxiously. 'Do you agree? We'll most likely be training for a few weeks yet. You could even see as many fellows as you like, until we go. To sort of help you make up your mind about me, if you know what I mean.'

'You're so obliging, a real gentleman,' Dianne said wryly. It was lost on him.

'So you will do it?'

'For pity's sake...' Dianne looked at his desperate expression and couldn't deny him. 'Let's say you can ask me again when you come back, all right? I'll think about it in the meantime and I'll be able to give you an honest answer when you're home safe.' A small voice inside Dianne's head scolded her. Suggesting a closer relationship wasn't a good idea. She knew that.

Daniel sensed a win and was satisfied. He couldn't help a silly grin as he pulled Dianne to her feet. 'That's good enough for me. Come on, we'd better get inside and make sure those stupid bastards haven't gotten into any trouble. We shouldn't leave them alone like that, you know. They're just like kids.'

Dianne nearly replied, We are all still just kids, really. Instead she told him, 'Susan will keep them in line.'

'Are you mad? She's the worst of the lot.'

He slipped his arm around her waist as they moved to the door, the first time Daniel had done something like that. Dianne didn't complain. It felt nice and she figured it could hardly do any more harm than she'd already done in the last five minutes.

Eight

'During all training flights we want you to fly at three hundred feet, nothing more and certainly nothing less,' an Intelligence major told the assembled airmen. 'Unless otherwise told.' His name was Sanders and he cultivated an aura of knowing many dark and desperate secrets. Chain-smoking, he walked up and down the small stage in front of the crews like a nervous cat waiting for someone to open a window so it could escape. He went on, 'Your navigators will have to be particularly on the ball, since landmarks and what-have-you will come and go before you know it at that height.'

As usual, the room was choked with cigarette smoke. They squinted at Sanders hopefully, waiting to hear more that might offer a clue as to the target when the mission came.

Flanders tentatively put his hand up. 'Ah, how will we see them anyway... sir?'

Sanders looked at him as if he were being stupid. 'This will be a daylight raid, obviously. We'd hardly expect you to fly low-level at night, would we?'

As a collective sigh went through the crews, Flanders replied quietly, 'No, of course not. Silly me.'

Wills nudged him and spoke close to his ear. 'Cheer up. You always wanted to see Germany. You'll be able to peek down their bloody chimneys and see what they're having for breakfast.'

Sanders overheard and said sternly, 'Who said anything about Germany? We'll tell you what the actual target is when the time is right for you to know. In the meantime, don't assume anything, and don't chatter about it in the pub either.'

Sitting with the others, Daniel immediately thought, Too late. Oh well, never mind. Still, surely Dianne doesn't count.

Someone asked, 'Do we know how long until the real thing?'

After a brief hesitation Sanders said, 'HQ want the whole thing sorted out within ten days. The quicker you chaps learn the ropes, the sooner you'll go. You'll start your first training flights... ah, this afternoon, Squadron Leader Eagleton?' Sanders turned to their squadron commander, who was sitting apart from the rest at the front of the room.

Eagleton nodded. 'There's a gardening trip going off at 1300. As soon as they're clear, you blokes will go. At the moment we're saying 1330 take off for you. Briefings will be before an early lunch at 1130—so let's say eleven for the briefing will do? There's not that much to say. It's in the gym hall away from everyone else. Tight security, all right? All your briefings will be there from now on, unless you're told otherwise. Keep that to yourselves too.'

That impressed them and the men exchanged looks. Six crews were in the room. No one knew how or why they were chosen. It was guessed they'd been drawn in some sort of ballot.

'Off you go now,' Eagleton said, standing. 'Oh, and by the way. Your training flights will be fully bombed-up for the weight, but naturally they won't be fused in case of accidents.'

'Oh, good,' Branner groaned. Flying at low altitude could be thrilling. With a full load of bombs, it wasn't so appealing.

As they filed noisily out into the morning sunshine, Wills pressed close behind Daniel.

'Hey, Daniel,' he whispered urgently. 'Low level in broad daylight— the Jerry fighters will be all over us like flies. We could bag a handful each.'

Daniel answered over his shoulder, 'I can't believe you see this as a good thing. Bloody hell, I'm with the skipper on this one. I hope I never have to pull the trigger of my guns for the entire war.'

'Bullshit, you don't mean that.'

'Maybe, maybe not.' Daniel was being honest. One part of him would give just about anything to shoot down a German fighter. He'd pictured the moment in his mind a hundred times and felt the savage triumph. He could also imagine the odds of a lone bomber taking on a Messerschmitt 109, perhaps the best fighter in the world despite all the legend surrounding the Spitfire. And the Germans would be over their own country with plenty of fuel and time to stalk them, attacking at the right moment. During the Battle of Britain, the Messerschmitts had barely enough time to start a fight before they had to turn tail and run for home with no fuel left.

'Well, I can tell you no bastard Jerry's going to get near our tail,' Wills slapped him on the back. 'At least, not until I've shot him full of holes.'

'Good for you, Charlie. We won't have to worry about a thing then.'

'That's right,' Wills snorted, but he wasn't sure Daniel was being serious.

***

'I didn't know willow trees grew to three hundred feet, skipper,' Barrymore called. 'We just passed one on the port side, in case you didn't notice.'

His shaky voice came from the bomb aimer's position below the front turret. With the countryside hurtling towards him like this, he didn't know if he should be exhilarated or terrified. The latter reaction, he worried, was getting the best of him. His stomach was churning with anxiety.

Branner tried to reply calmly, 'If we learn to fly this low and get used to it, then three hundred feet should be a breeze.'

'Didn't the boss say not to fly under three hundred?' This was Flanders, who suddenly didn't sound too happy either. Blind to the outside world in his navigator's seat, he wasn't aware until now what was happening.

'We're not allowed to fly that low, so he had to say that. You have to read between the lines, boys. The lower we go, the safer we'll be—hang on, fellows!'

The Lancaster lurched upwards as Branner decided there wasn't enough room between two tall trees and he should fly above them. The fuselage rang loudly with an abrupt bang, as if someone had slapped it with large stick.

'Everything all right?' Branner asked Sexton, who was instantly checking his gauges.

'I think so. What about you?'

Branner waggled the controls slightly. 'Seems fine.'

Daniel's morose call came on the intercom, 'We just did a bit of pruning, skipper. There's branches and leaves stuck on the port inner cowling. Sergeant Granger's not going to be pleased.'

That brought a shrill laugh from Wills, who with his perspective of the ground rushing away from him wasn't so alarmed. He was enjoying himself.

'Be buggered to Sergeant Granger,' Branner said. 'He's not the one going to bomb Adolf himself.' This was a fantasy they'd agreed upon as they'd waited in the Lancaster, doing their final checks before take off. The top-secret operation would be an attempt to bomb Hitler in one of his hideaways.

'Cattle ahead,' Barrymore reported hastily, seeing they were sinking closer to the earth again. 'We're definitely not allowed to spook any livestock, remember?'

Instead of climbing, Branner banked the plane left bringing the port wingtip alarmingly close to the ground. Even Daniel, who had faith in his skipper's flying, opened his mouth to say something, then wisely stopped himself.

Flanders couldn't keep quiet. He was looking out his tiny observation window and had caught a glimpse of the ground streaking past 'I thought the idea was to sneak under the Jerry's radar, not their bloody washing lines,' he grumbled.

Rather than be annoyed, Branner sounded delighted his flying was scaring them. 'I'm just warming up,' he said. 'I can get a little lower, if you like.' In truth, he was frightening himself and only the comments from the crew were keeping up his bravado.

The weather was an unending sheet of grey clouds above, with a few hundred feet below that, long banks of darker storm fronts with showers and sharp gusts of swirling wind. Branner was smart enough not to fly too adventurously when they neared these squalls. All the same, when the Lancaster was buffeted by a wind the crew had their hearts in their mouths for a moment, praying it was still just wind turbulence and not a wingtip brushing the ground or the plane's underbelly striking a tree.

The bomber completed a lazy 'S' around the paddock of cows and straightened up.

'Can you see the next mark, Geoff?' Branner asked. Again, it was a church spire and Barrymore's reply wasn't unreasonable.

'There's a flamin' church every half mile in this country. Why do they keep using spires for navigational marks? Something a little less common would help.'

'Can you see the bloody thing?' Flanders put in. It was going to be his navigation skills under scrutiny.

'Off to port at around ten o'clock—see it, skipper? Maybe five miles head. Looks like a tower of some kind.'

'Are you sure? Come on, you won't get to muck around like this on the way to Berlin.'

Wills said, 'I could hop out and ask directions, if you like, skipper. We're low enough.'

'Shut up, Charlie. Geoff, pull your bloody finger out. Is that the place or not?'

'It's the mark, skipper,' Barrymore told him, mustering all the confidence he could. He added with an inspiration, 'That weave around the cows threw my bearings for a moment.'

Branner had already edged the plane towards the tower. 'And what happens when we get there?'

They could hear the rustle of a map as Flanders checked his bearings in the cramped space. 'Turn east to course 280.'

They thundered over the top of the small hamlet, bringing people pouring out of their houses to look and wave. Wills swivelled his guns from side to side and was sorely tempted to let off a burst. That would get him into more trouble than he'd care to imagine.

Flanders told Branner, 'There's a river about five minutes ahead. Follow it to the north until the double-span bridge.'

'Hey, it's like a paper trail, when we were kids,' Baxter said with a rare, unprompted comment on the intercom. It made Sexton widen his eyes at Branner with mock amazement.

When the Lancaster banked to trace the river's course Daniel couldn't see the water below. The turret's upper position prevented it. He could imagine what it was like and he substituted the foul weather for a perfect, sunny day and a mild breeze. The river would be blue, reflecting the sky, he decided. He and Dianne were floating along in a rowboat, cuddled comfortably together, whispering sweet things to each other, their hands straying to places…

'Is everyone keeping an eye out?' Branner barked, startling him. 'I don't want to get bounced by any fighters, even friendlies having a practice.'

Wills called back, 'Eyes peeled, skipper.' They heard him biting into an apple before he switched his microphone off.

Daniel thought, It can't be done in a bloody rowing boat anyway, I suspect. It'd be too damned uncomfortable. He swung his turret around in a token gesture and ended up facing aft, peering for the next aircraft doing the same exercise. He didn't see anything. Eagleton had spaced them far enough apart so everyone had to rely on their own navigators rather than follow the bomber ahead.

'Have a bloody good look at this bridge, you blokes,' Branner said. 'I don't want to go around again.'

They'd been told that "something" had been placed on the bridge and everyone was expected to report back what it was—a test to make sure no one cheated or cut corners of the route.

Flanders called, 'I'll wager anybody a pint that someone sees it before Barra.'

'You're on, and I can taste it already,' Barrymore replied instantly.

It ended up being a large red flag and Branner recognised it at the same time as both Sexton and Barrymore. He had to stop the squabbling between Flanders and Barrymore about who owed the other a pint.

On Flanders' instructions the bomber swung east again.

'Look at that, skipper. Sexton pointed at a huge pile of leaves and broken branches on the edge of a field. Some farm workers were clearing away a large briar patch and stacking the rubbish for burning later. Sexton was sitting on his fold-down canvas seat beside Branner, enjoying the ride. 'And a bunch of land army girls working on it, I'd say.' This obviously interested him more. His grin and raised eyebrows dared Branner, who was about to edge the plane away. The slipstream could cause havoc. 'Come on, skipper. It can't be all work and no play, you know. Let's have a bit of fun.'

'This isn't supposed to be fun, Dave.'

'It can't be bloody doom and gloom all the time either. We'll go mad. Let's give the lads a laugh.'

Inadvertently, Sexton touched on Branner's weakness—his insecurity over the crew respecting his authority and taking him seriously. Sometimes he wasn't even sure they liked him.

'What the hell, why not?'

Before Sexton could answer he flipped the Lancaster into a steep turn to bring them back over the field. Everyone was taken by surprise. In the bomb aimer's position Barrymore tumbled over, crushing his notes.

He called, annoyed as he rubbed a sore elbow, 'Bloody hell—ah, skipper? Have we got our wires crossed somewhere? This is not on my flight plan.'

'A small detour everyone,' Branner replied with a humourless smile.

For Barrymore the reason became delightfully obvious as the Lancaster bore directly down on the pile of leaves. The two rear gunners had no idea, while neither Flanders nor Baxter cared, since they couldn't see. Baxter was grumpily searching around his feet for a dropped pencil.

The land army girls in front of them stood their ground, hands defiantly on their hips as if they might protect the stack, but they finally broke and scattered as the bomber roared over them.

Branner climbed a little as they passed, directing the full force of the slipstream onto the rubbish which exploded in all directions, showering around the running women. Wills whooped loudly with joy seeing what they'd done and even Daniel let out a cheer and laughed. The girls were shaking their fists after the Lancaster. Daniel would swear he saw the white teeth of wide, gleeful smiles on some of them.

'That's the spirit, skipper,' Wills yelled, a little loud for the intercom and making the others curse. 'I'll bet those girls would love to get their hands on you.'

'Not for the sorts of reasons you'd like either,' Flanders added chuckling, although he wasn't entirely sure what had happened.

'All right, lads. Back on the job,' Branner said weakly. Already he was worrying about someone complaining. It had been a silly thing to do.

Flanders told him cheerfully, 'Course 195, skipper. Twenty-five miles to the next mark. We've got some time to relax.'

***

'Some fool has upset the Land Army,' Eagleton announced at their debriefing. He seemed more concerned at the inconvenience of the trouble caused, rather than the crime itself. 'I'm not interested in identifying the culprit, since I'm sure all of you are quite capable of giving in to the urge for some high jinks if the opportunity presents itself. Take this as a reprimand to you all. This is very serious training for a vital mission. There will be no more skylarking, understand?'

The gathered crews murmured their assent with an appropriate amount of remorse. Wills asked from the back.

'What did they do, sir?'

'Ruined many hours of work, I'm told.'

'The rotten sods, sir. Those girls work damned hard, I know.'

Eagleton narrowed his eyes and searched for Wills' rank. 'The Land Army isn't entirely composed of women, sergeant. How do you know there were ladies involved?'

There was a small silence.

'No, sir. That's right,' Wills tried. 'I was just assuming it was women. It normally is these days...'

'What I do care about,' Eagleton cut him off. 'Is this aircraft was clearly under the three hundred foot minimum height you were given. So

90

was just about every other Lancaster, according to the observation teams on the bridge.'

A groan went through the men as they realised their mistake. No one had figured they might be being watched during the flight.

'Tomorrow morning you'll be doing a similar type of flight on a completely different course. Same rules, with the same signs to identify as you go. Briefing is here at 0830. You take off at 1000. Dismissed, gentlemen.'

Eagleton strode from the hall. Everyone waited until he was gone, a courtesy towards his rank, and it saved the bother of endless salutes if he'd been caught up in the mass exit.

Still sitting, Sexton offered Branner a cigarette. 'See? No problems at all.'

Branner shrugged. 'I was worried for a moment there.'

'It was well worth the laugh, skipper. Even with Granger ticked off about that shrubbery in the engine cowling. You know, I think you're right about that three-hundred-foot business. The old eagle didn't really tell us off. I reckon he might be happy if we hedge-hopped all the way to Berlin.'

'A scary thought,' Branner said quietly. 'Let's see where they put that flag—or whatever—tomorrow. We'll pop up to three hundred for that bit and stay lower for the rest. Sergeant Granger will just have to get himself some gardening shears.'

Nine

Dianne and Susan had made an arrangement to help wash each other's hair when they could. It was no simple thing, requiring the girls to heat several pails of water in the kitchen and carry them to their quarters, where they tipped it into a steel baby bath. Most of the warmth was lost during the journey and it was hard work lugging the heavy buckets without spilling too much. Asking one of the men to help would only cause trouble. No excuse was accepted for being found in any WAAF quarters.

Tonight it was Dianne's turn to go first. It was debatable what was better. The water was hotter, but she had to finish quickly for Susan's sake. Susan then had to use the dirty, lukewarm water next at least with the luxury of taking her time and enjoying it more.

Susan compensated for this rare off-duty evening where they didn't spend at least some time in one of the local pubs by producing a bottle of sherry.

With her head over the steaming bath while Susan poured water onto her hair, Dianne groped blindly at the table beside her. 'Light a smoke for me, will you?'

'Don't be silly, it'd be a waste. You've got your head in a bucket of water, for goodness' sake.'

'I've got plenty. My secret supplier delivered today.'

'Where the hell did you find an airman who doesn't smoke? What do you pay him for his ration anyway?'

'I don't. He gives them to me.'

'Greedy cow,' Susan said amiably. She looked helplessly at her wet hands, shook them dry and wiped them on her skirt, then carefully pulled out two cigarettes from the packet. Lighting both, she put one on an ashtray and the other between Dianne's fingers. Dianne did an impressive job of manoeuvring it into the bathtub to her lips. Cigarette smoked mixed with the steam.

'You must be giving him something,' Susan insisted, kneading Susan's hair again. It was hard to make any lather with the carbolic soap.

'Not even a peck on the cheek,' Dianne's voice echoed from within the tub. 'I don't want to start something I can't finish.'

'Do you think they'll ever issue fags to us? Some days I'm so desperate I reckon I'd go bombing the Jerrys for a packet of Players a day.'

'We may be in the same air force as the crews, my dear, but we will forever be women in a men's world. You'll just have to get your own smokes.'

'It's so unfair.'

'So is the pay, the food, the hours we work and the thanks we get. Keep washing, girl. This water's getting chillier by the second.'

Susan concentrated on her task for a few minutes, pausing only for the both of them to smoke and sip the sherry. Then idly she asked, 'You and Daniel are getting pretty close?'

'Ah, at last... I've been waiting days for you to start asking. I can't believe you've managed to contain yourself this long.'

'I thought you would have told me by now,' Susan said petulantly. 'I'm your friend. I shouldn't have to ask these things.' She dug her fingers into Dianne's scalp and got a satisfying yelp.

'There's no need to pull my hair out by the roots. What about you and Charlie, anyway?'

'No, you first.'

Reluctantly, Dianne recounted her conversation with Daniel in the hotel beer garden. It wasn't that she didn't want Susan to know. She dreaded her reaction.

'He's a very nice fellow and all that,' Susan said carefully. 'Rather good-looking. I'd be the first to jump into your shoes given half a chance. But isn't that a little... optimistic to promise him something more long term?'

'I tried to tell him—oh damn.' Dianne had dropped the last of her cigarette into the water.

Screwing her face up, Susan plucked it out and put the soggy butt in the ashtray. 'Hey, I've got to wash in that.'

'Sorry.'

'Too late now. So?'

'So what?'

'So Daniel.'

'Oh, well—what else can I say? I think he's very sweet too. I didn't want to ruin everything, and it was impossible to get him to ease off a bit.'

'It doesn't sound like you tried very hard.'

Dianne's silence was her answer. She changed the subject.

'And what about Charlie?'

'Oh, bugger Charlie. I'm just having some fun with all of them and a few others besides, while you and Daniel moon at each other in the shadows. Charlie just thinks he's got his nose in front of the pack after he bought me those drinks. Close your eyes, it's rinse time.'

Susan was using a small jug to tip water over Dianne's hair. Dianne murmured in appreciation while the soap was flushed warmly away. The pleasure was short-lived as she raised her head and droplets made instantly cold by the chill air fell on her neck. She dried most of the damp out and wrapped the towel around her head.

'Your turn,' she said unwillingly.

'Just a minute while I get another towel.' Susan went out to her own room.

Dianne snatched the opportunity to light another cigarette and topped up their glasses. She called, 'You're really not that keen on Charlie?'

'He's sweet, but he won't take no for an answer and it's easier to just let him keep trying.'

'And buying.'

'I never ask him for anything. I've even tried sending him away and he just keeps coming back.' Susan took her place at the table in front of the bathtub. As she was about to lean forward, she asked, 'Speaking of coming back, what's due this evening? We didn't send anyone out today. Can you hear that?'

It was the low rumble of approaching aircraft. 'No, no ops today,' Dianne agreed. 'Somebody must have been diverted here. The lads will have to get the flare path up quick smart. It's pitch black with that cloud still hanging around.'

Susan still didn't bend her head into the tub. Something felt wrong and she gave Dianne a strange look. 'It's been so quiet out there. You'd think we would have heard something if a diversion was coming. Let's have a look.'

She stood and headed for the door.

'Hey,' Dianne pointed at the tub. 'It's going to waste. I should be having my turn—'

'I'm just having a look from the front door. I won't be a moment.'

Dianne joined her outside, hastily closing the door to complete the blackout which enveloped them like cloak. 'We can't see a bloody thing, of course,' she grumbled, feeling a cold wind cut straight through the damp towel on her head and make her scalp tingle.

But they could hear something. The night was filled with the unsteady roar of a four-engine aircraft overhead. Their billets, the old married quarters, were close to the runway, offices and hangers. In peace time it allowed the men to go home to their wives for meals without traveling too far—and in those days the air traffic was light. Now with war being waged it meant the NCO WAAFs were disturbed by every take-off and landing, dozens of them each day, while the male officers got a good night's sleep, safely, some distance away.

'She's not in very good shape,' Susan said, staring upwards.

'No, you can hear it. She might even be down an engine. Look at that.'

She pointed at small wavering lights in the direction of the hangers. Crash teams in trucks were on the move, the vehicle's headlights reduced to slits by black tape. The noise of the aeroplane drowned out the truck motors.

Susan said grimly, 'They must be close. Where's the damned flare path?'

The long line of red and green lights that marked the runway suddenly lit up the night. The cloud was low enough to offer a soft reflection back, and against that backdrop both the girls spotted the stricken plane. It was to the west and almost directly above. They could see it had to fly away again from the airfield to make its landing approach.

'I don't know if I can watch this,' Dianne said. 'It sounds like it might fall out of the sky at any moment.'

'It's a Halifax,' Susan decided. 'There go the ambulances. They must have radioed in wounded.' The ambulance's bells cut through the night.

As they watched over the next few minutes several people ran or recklessly rode bicycles in the darkness past them.

'Here it comes,' Susan breathed.

With the approach of the Halifax the rumble of its motor had grown again to fill the air. Dianne could feel the noise throbbing against her cheeks. Her wet hair was forgotten, the butt of her cigarette dropped heedlessly to the ground. Beside her, Susan was hugging herself. The aircraft had come in too high and was clearly visible above the runway lights, close to stalling.

'Get down,' Dianne said aloud, voicing the thoughts of everyone all over the airbase anxiously watching.

The Halifax dropped but still didn't land, skimming the tarmac with uncertain dips.

Then the runway exploded with such a blast the girls screamed with the unexpectedness of it. Before they could comprehend what was happening, the struggling Halifax flew through the falling debris, attempting to land.

'What the hell?' Dianne cried, looking around. Susan was the same.

Another eruption came, then a third that tipped the Halifax up onto one wing, far enough to bury the other into the ground and send the aircraft into a spinning crash.

The noise of the engines didn't stop. Another plane was somewhere above. A fourth and fifth bomb burst deafeningly on the runway. Adding to the chaos came the wail of an air raid alarm, its tone rising as the operator cranked with all his might to be noticed among everything else.

A Bofors anti-aircraft gun beyond the hangers began sending a brilliant stream of tracers into the sky.

'Bloody hell, it's a Jerry bomber,' Susan yelled. 'He's followed the Halifax in.'

Dianne could only stare at the flaming wreck of the Halifax. They had gotten so close to safety and the crew must have believed they were going to make it.

The whole airbase had broken into furious activity. People were emerging in panic from their quarters and places they'd been working. Now Dianne and Susan were dimly lit by the burning aircraft, and as someone ran past they shouted angrily.

'Get into your slit trench, you damned fools! It's not bloody Guy Faulks night. Can't you hear the siren?'

'Yes—yes, sir,' Dianne called back without a clue who the man was. She grabbed Susan's sleeve and dragged her away from the porch. 'Come on!'

'Our slit trench?' Susan asked, stumbling. 'We've got our own trench?'

'You should take more bloody notice during the drills.'

Both of them were only wearing slippers and Susan lost one in a patch of mud. She didn't stop and hobbled gamely on. Dianne wasn't sure how to find the trench in the dark, heading in the general direction and hoping for the best. It suddenly appeared as an even darker, square hole in the otherwise black ground and they both teetered on the edge before tumbling to land in an inch of cold slime.

'Stay down,' Dianne gasped, grasping Susan's skirt as she tried to stand. 'It's not deep enough to stand up.'

'I want to see what's going on.'

'You don't need to, and you might get your head knocked off by a German bomb.'

'I haven't heard any more, have you?'

'That's not the point.'

They crouched at the bottom of the trench, keeping their rumps off the water, knees close to their chest and backs against the walls. Dianne felt a sticky dampness seeping through her blouse. It made her realise how cold she felt. For a moment she was puzzled why the same sensation didn't touch her head, then remembered the towel wrapped around her hair. She vaguely thought that, if she were careful, it might not need washing again, before the notion struck her as absurd in the circumstances

Above them, the Bofors still fired intermittently at the sky. Just when it seemed the gun had stopped for good another burst would rattle the air. It was shooting at shadows, since no aircraft could be heard anymore, although it was a possibility a wily German raider would glide back in for another bombing run. The siren kept up its mournful warning too. The rest of the noise came from grinding truck motors, shouting men and the ambulances and fire tenders.

Dianne tried to look towards each end of the trench. 'Is anyone else in here?' she called. It was only a short space and she couldn't see anybody.

'Don't be silly,' Susan growled. 'Everyone else is at the damned pub.'

***

Ten minutes later, which had felt like an eternity, the air raid siren droned down into silence. As the girls shifted stiffly and contemplated getting to their feet, a torch shone briefly down into their eyes. It was snapped off again. They saw a figure silhouetted against the glow of the burning Halifax.

'It's safe to come out now, ladies,' a man said gruffly. 'The siren's stopped.'

'Thank you,' Dianne said, trying to push herself up.

The torch flashed at them again. 'Where's your helmets? And your gas masks?'

'Our what?' Susan asked, disbelievingly.

'Your helmet and your gas masks, ma'am. You're supposed to carry them at all times or keep 'em nice and 'andy. You know the regulations.'

'They are nice and 'andy,' Susan managed to mock him. 'Next to our beds. We were too busy running for this trench.'

'I could put you on a charge, you know.' He was growing bolder.

Now Susan was getting angry. 'For God's sake, haven't you got something better to do? There's been a bloody air raid, or didn't you notice?'

There was a small hesitation and he replied, 'Good evening, ladies. Mind yourselves getting out.' His figure vanished.

The girls clambered to their feet and took stock of their situation.

Susan muttered, 'I don't care if that was Churchill himself. If I find out who that officious little prat was, I'll kick him in the teeth.' She glumly put the flat of her hand on the lip of the trench. It came up to their chins.

Dianne said, 'I'd have preferred you had waited until he showed us how to get out of this thing before you scared him away.'

***

Back at their quarters they stumbled gratefully through the front door. There was nothing to be done even though the airfield was still a hive of activity everywhere. The bombs had fallen on the runway itself and there was no damage control Dianne and Susan might help with carrying out.

Dianne sat heavily down on a chair at the table. She suddenly felt utterly exhausted. Susan stood close and ran the tip of her finger through the bathtub. A dirty scum had formed on top and the water was cold.

'Bastards,' Susan said quietly. 'They knew exactly when to attack. Right when I was going to get my hair washed.'

'There are spies everywhere,' Dianne said with her eyes closed. 'Did the sherry survive?'

'Better than those poor lads in the Halifax, I'd say.' There was a clink of glass as Susan poured drinks.

Without opening her eyes, Dianne held out her hand for a sherry. 'I was trying not to think about them.'

***

'The filthy, cheating bastards,' decided Flying Officer Munk. He was a South African and had a heavy Afrikaans accent that brought him endless teasing. Everyone accused him of being a German spy.

He was standing with most of D-Delta's crew near the WAAF's quarters. Daniel was watching hopefully for a glimpse of Dianne. The others were surveying the damage to the runway and the smouldering wreckage of the Halifax.

'What are you complaining about?' Flanders asked Munk, winking at the rest. 'You would have whistled them in. They say you've got a short-wave radio hidden under your mattress.'

'This isn't funny,' Munk told him. 'Those Kraut sods are not playing fair.'

No one could tell if he was being serious. Barrymore said, 'I suppose it is a bit below the belt. Is it against the Geneva Convention?'

Flanders said, 'This weather's against the bloody Geneva Convention.' He hunched his shoulders to make his point.

Overnight, the cloud had dropped even lower and brought gusts of freezing rain. It was like winter was coming, not giving in to spring. All flights were cancelled for the day. Besides, the German raider had crippled the runway needed for take off and landings with this wind blowing.

At breakfast, Branner had told everyone they would go to the morning briefing anyway, since they were training for a special operation. They shouldn't assume anything. Halfway to the hall they'd met Munk, the pilot of another aircraft. He had already discovered no activity at the supposed briefing.

'You blokes stay here,' Branner said. 'I'll try and find Eagleton and see what's going on.'

'All right, good idea,' Munk said, leading everyone into the lee of a parked lorry. Branner scowled and trudged away. He had expected at least Munk to accompany him. The South African traded cigarettes with Wills and started voicing his thoughts on the night's bombing.

'Why didn't the ack-ack boys get the bastard?' Barrymore asked.

'And the Coast Watch,' Flanders nodded. 'They must have been asleep. An all-round bad show by everybody concerned, I'd say. If it was up to us, this sort of thing would never happen.'

Sexton poked at Daniel at nodded. 'Look out, there's Dianne.'

She had emerged carrying a kitbag from her quarters. Seeing Daniel she detoured over, clutching the bag tightly to herself to ward off the wind.

'Hello,' Daniel said cheerfully. 'What are you up to?'

'Moving house.' She dumped the bag down gratefully before smiling a greeting to the others. 'Things got a bit too close for comfort last night and the powers-that-be have ordered us to move somewhere a little safer.' She jerked her head. 'The Nissan huts near the parachute shed.'

'No more penthouse suite then?'

'No more separate rooms, no.' She grimaced and shrugged. 'Not for a while anyway.'

'It must have been very frightening for you. Last night, I mean.'

'Oh, we know the drill,' Dianne said blithely. 'Nobody panicked. Susan and I thought we'd better take cover, so we waited in a slit trench for the All Clear. Bit of a nuisance more than anything. What about you?'

'We had to take shelter in the pub's cellar. It took the landlord ages to get us out again.'

'I thought you were looking a bit squiffy-eyed.'

'My wallet took the worst of it. No one said you have to pay for your booze during an air raid. They might have warned us.'

'I could have told you that.' Dianne looked at everyone. Munk was trying to smile invitingly, and she purposely didn't meet his eye. 'What are you all doing now? There's no flying.'

'We don't know—waiting for the skipper to find out.'

'The Met boys don't think this is going away. We might all get a day off...' Dianne raised her eyebrows suggestively.

'You think so? Flanno, you owe me a few quid—'

Daniel was cut off by Branner appearing from the other side of the truck. 'Right lads, it's full flying kit without 'chutes—oh, hello Dianne. Nice to see you. Just us, Monkey. Your crew get to do what you like.'

Branner's announcement brought a chorus of swearing.

'We can't be flying, skipper. Not in this muck,' Wills said.

Branner clapped his hands together. 'We're not, it's training at the pool. Bring your bucket and spade. You've got twenty minutes.' He walked away without waiting to see their reaction.

'Oh sod it,' Flanders snarled. 'If I fall in and get soaked, I'm going to be very, very upset.'

The concrete pool was a wide, circular water trough built above the ground. It was less than three feet deep and big enough to float a rubber dinghy. Enthusiastic crews could paddle in tiny circles. It was used to practice escaping a ditched aircraft in the ocean—albeit a very calm sea—and for this purpose narrow scaffolding had been built beside the pool. The catwalk was supposed to represent the width of a bomber and a square frame facing the water was a door. Aircrew had to rehearse boarding the dinghy from the platform. They were only allowed to pass through the frame as if they were abandoning a stricken plane.

The cold and blustery wind threatened a shower. With the men of D-Delta huddled miserably on the catwalk, staring at a bobbing dinghy, an air force gunnery sergeant began explaining how they couldn't cheat.

'You must exit through the door,' he yelled, making Daniel wince. His hangover was getting worse. 'If you enter the water, the exercise is void and we start again, since you can support your weight in this pool, but the English Channel is a little bit deeper.' He offered a grim smile. 'Once you are in the dinghy, any part of your body can touch the water as long as you don't reach the bottom. It is assumed here for the purpose of this training that the dinghy has been successfully launched from the wing and its integrity has not been compromised by enemy action.'

Wills asked the others quietly, 'It's what?'

Flanders told him sourly. 'It hasn't been shot to fucking pieces like the rest of the plane.'

'But isn't that a very good point? If the aircraft has been so buggered up we have to ditch, what are the chances of the bloody dinghy being all right?'

'Very slim, I'd say.' Flanders could see Wills wasn't happy with that and added gleefully, 'You'd better brush up on your long-distance swimming.'

'That'll do,' Branner told them from the head of the line. 'Okay, sergeant? Shall we start?'

'Board the dinghy, please gentlemen.' The sergeant pointedly took out a stopwatch and pressed a button.

Branner went first. The rubber boat skated alarmingly away from the frame as he stepped in, but once he was aboard it was easier for the rest of the crew after he grabbed an edge of the door and held the dinghy steady. It was a tight squeeze for seven men and the water came close to swamping them. How they were supposed to fare in any sort of swell was a mystery. Finally they were all perched on the inflated gunwales, each man facing the centre. It felt very unstable and liable to tip over at any time.

'Anybody bring any cards?' Flanders asked. 'I fancy a game of Bridge.'

'What now, sergeant?' Branner called.

The sergeant was inspecting his stopwatch. 'A little over six minutes, sir. I'm afraid that's not good enough. Our best information suggests you won't have more than four minutes before your aircraft sinks. We'd better do it again, and this time get a hurry on.'

Even Branner's enthusiasm took a dent. 'You could have mentioned that earlier, sergeant. Nobody said anything about time limits.'

'Didn't I, sir? My apologies.' His look of innocence was well rehearsed.

They discovered that leaving the dinghy without getting wet posed more of a challenge than getting into it. Clambering over the side of both the boat and the pool onto dry land presented a serious risk of falling in the water. To make matters worse, despite the weather, a small crowd of amused onlookers began to gather. As they escaped the pool, each of the

D-Delta crew lit a cigarette. The sergeant humoured them and used the opportunity to instruct them more.

'At best, you'll be able to climb out onto the wing of the aircraft, board the dinghy first, then launch it into the water. You won't even get your toes wet. Today you are practicing a worst-case situation. Remember that under real circumstances you are not to take anything with you that might be of value to the enemy. No maps, logbooks and flight plans. No code books. Also, unless your skipper is certain you will reach a landfall on enemy-held territory and they might be of use, do not take any weapons. They will be a hazard to yourself, your brothers-in-arms and the dinghy. Is that clear?'

'Yes, sergeant,' they answered like schoolchildren.

'Flying Officer Branner, can we try again?'

'Certainly, sergeant.'

Desperately dragging on the last of their smokes they lined up again on the platform.

Wills held his hand out, palm upwards, and said hopefully, 'I think it's going to rain, sergeant.'

'It's all right, son. It rains a lot in England. You'll get used to it.'

'I don't see any reason for us to really get wet—'

Flanders cut him off, raising his own hand tentatively. 'Sergeant, I've decided for the benefit of my fellow crewmen that I don't want to leave the aircraft. I'll sacrifice myself and go down with the ship, so to speak. That will leave more room in the dinghy and besides, I get seasick very easily...' He wilted under the sergeant's baleful glare.

Branner told them, 'Come on, you lot. The sooner we get this done, the quicker we finish up. Ready again, sergeant?'

This attempt was completed under the required four minutes. There were some smug grins aimed at the sergeant as he called out the result. Then he added, 'One more time, please sir.'

Branner couldn't refuse, so he stayed silent amidst his crew's complaining. The sergeant was in charge and would report back to Eagleton. It wasn't worth making any fuss.

Oddly, the audience got a little more animated. They knew something Branner and his crew didn't.

The sergeant reached out and tapped Flanders on the leg. 'This man has been wounded and is unconscious. Lie down, please. The rest of you will refuse to leave him behind since he is such an invaluable source of endless wit. You must pick him up and carry him into the dinghy. The same rules apply, and it must be achieved under four minutes. Be careful, this is where most people end up taken an unexpected bath and the water looks particularly cold today.' He smiled unpleasantly at Flanders, who with a murderous look was slowly lowering himself to lie down on the narrow planks. The onlookers let out a cheer of satisfaction.

'If you bastards drop me,' Flanders muttered, 'You'll all owe me a pint.'

'Like hell,' Sexton said. 'You'll be paying us as a thank you for keeping you dry. I haven't noticed before now what a fat, heavy bugger you are.'

They managed it with a comedy of errors that threatened to get everybody soaked, coming from a recklessness that was half-intended to fail and see their "wounded" man suffer a dunking—except he was too likely to take the others down with him. There was plenty of swearing and abuse aimed at Flanders, who for an unconscious man offered a lot of desperate advice when he felt their grasp on him slip. Eventually he lay spread-eagled on his back across the dinghy, deliberately taking up as much space as he could. Somehow, he had been able to light a cigarette. The others were too busy trying to stay seated around him.

'Very good, gentlemen,' the sergeant said reluctantly. The crowd shared his disappointment and were wandering away. 'You're expected to complete this exercise at least once a month.'

'Can I have this job every time?' Flanders asked Branner, luxuriously puffing on his smoke. The looks he got from everyone made Flanders add quickly, 'Just kidding lads—just kidding. Don't do anything silly now.'

***

G.M.Hague

The rest of the morning was spent in a small room practicing aircraft recognition. A frumpy-looking WAAF who seemed to have gone to an effort to appear unattractive determinedly showed them one silhouette after another, ignoring their growing boredom and insisting on answers for each shape which represented various aircraft seen from different angles. She didn't even crack a smile when Flanders decided one chart was really a pair of oversized knickers hanging from a flagpole in a stiff breeze.

'No, it's a Heinkel 111 seen from behind and below,' she crisply. 'Fair enough, that's one for the fighter boys really. What about this one?' She produced another picture from the back of the pile and placed it on the easel. No one answered because nobody really cared by now. 'Anyone? Flying Officer Branner, don't you think someone in your crew should recognise this?'

'Come on, chaps,' Branner said tiredly. 'I think I know. Anybody else?'

'It's another Focke Wulf,' Wills declared, frustrated. 'Trying unsuccessfully to dodge my Brownings, I might add. He's a goner. We can paint that blighter on the side of the Lanc' next to my turret.'

The WAAF frowned. 'Would you open fire at this distance if you saw this silhouette?'

'I would have shot him down from twice as far.' Wills grinned.

'Then you've just destroyed an American P-51D.'

That woke them out of their lethargy. 'You didn't say you were including Yankee aircraft,' Wills protested. 'That's cheating.'

'The United States Army Air Force has been providing long-range fighter protection for their bombers for over twelve months,' she replied primly, glad to have stirred some life out of them. 'You can expect to see them from here to Berlin and back again these days—at all altitudes,' she allowed with a tiny shrug.

'Why the hell don't we get that?' Wills looked at Branner.

'Probably something to do with it being pitch, bloody dark when we fly,' Branner said dryly. He still envied the idea of having fighters to protect them, however impractical it might be.

'Can't we put some driving lights on a Spitfire?' Flanders said, but everyone was having the same jealous thoughts and it didn't raise a laugh.

Branner swore under his breath. 'All right, so we have to worry about the Yanks as well. You'd better give us another look. What the hell is it again?'

***

At dinner, Branner made them all pay attention. The mess hall was nearly empty because so many people had been given twenty-four-hour leave passes with the bad weather. Branner suspected they were going to be given the rest of the day off as well. After lunch, he'd been summoned back to Eagleton's office to make a report and he'd had to be careful. It was just a matter of explaining how well they'd fared in their exercises that morning, but if the WAAF or Gunnery Sergeant had given them a bad marking, perhaps they'd have to do it all again this afternoon.

Eagleton had been blankly satisfied, and afraid to push his luck, Branner kept quiet and considered his crew fortunate.

'I wish you jokers would take things a bit more seriously,' he said, when they were huddled close over a table and listening.

'What do you mean, skipper?' Barrymore asked.

'You know what I'm talking about. We can't seem to do anything without somebody making a bloody game of it or saying some smart-arse comment. This isn't a game, all right?'

He had taken them by surprise. Sexton said, 'Calm down, skipper. We do take it seriously. Only there's no need to be so serious about it all the time, if you know what I mean.'

'Buggered if I do,' Branner wasn't going to be put off so easily. 'Being a funny bastard isn't going to help anyone when we're ditching in the North Sea.'

'Exactly,' Flanders put in quickly. 'I ask you, what was the point of all that mucking around this morning?'

'What do you mean? It was training, obviously. Even if you reckon you already know it, which we don't, you've still got to keep your hand in.'

Flanders snorted and said, 'I've heard stories from blokes on the North Atlantic convoys. The Jerry submarines are still sinking them like sitting ducks and when the poor bastards are in the water without a lifeboat, they're dead within a minute or two. You know why? Because it's so bloody cold. That's if they don't drown in a storm with snow and hail, and the twenty-foot waves.' Flanders pointed at a nearby window. 'What's the use in practicing how to ditch in that bloody duck pond? For Christ's sake, who believes for a moment that a Lancaster bomber shot to buggery is going to float for four seconds, let alone four minutes? Especially in any sort of swell.'

Branner glared at him. 'Don't be stupid. You won't be flying over the North Atlantic any time too soon. Not unless we decide to bomb bloody Canada. Everything's a bit far away in that direction, or haven't you looked at your maps lately?'

'North Sea—the North Atlantic—what's the difference? I'm just saying that paddling around in that pool is a waste of time if you think it's preparing us for the real thing.'

Daniel noticed Wills was uncomfortable and remembered he couldn't swim. 'Ignore Flanno. A plane will float for a while,' he told him quietly with more confidence than he felt. 'For a long time, if the petrol tanks aren't full. That's why they tell us to ditch in the ocean rather than bail out. You've got a better chance of surviving if you can get in the dinghy and stay dry. Your Mae West will keep you afloat for ages too, if that's the case. Plenty of fighter blokes came home all right after spending a night in the sea, back in 1940.'

'That's because they were floating just off Brighton Pier,' Flanders said dryly. He tapped the table with his fingertip. 'Look, don't get me wrong. I reckon we'll win the war and I also say we've got a chance of seeing the thing through. But if our luck runs out and we get shot down over the sea, we've got Buckley's chance and we shouldn't be fooling ourselves with rubbish like this morning. And that's another thing—' He spread his hands. 'It's all right to recognise a cardboard cut-out of an enemy fighter held up by some misery-guts WAAF. But up there, the buggers will come at us doing four hundred miles an hour, shoot us full of holes, and be home for beer and sausage before we know what happened. It all just seems a waste of time.'

'You're just a miserable sod,' Sexton said cheerfully to break the mood. 'I won't be lying down to die too quickly if we ditch. There's always a chance you'll get picked up by a submarine or some friendly navy chappies. Besides, who's to say we won't find ourselves splashing about just off the shore? How far is too far out?'

'Flanno doesn't like getting wet at all,' Barrymore said. 'You saw him this morning. He won't even take a bath. I can smell him from here.'

'Yeah—all right, all right...' Flanders put up his hands. 'It was just my tuppence worth, that's all.'

'I don't think it was even worth that,' Branner told him. 'Don't forget the air force is paying you to waste your time, if that's what they want. Listen, you blokes, like Bruce says, no one's going to get shot down and we're going to win the war. Simple as that. In the meantime we have to do training like everyone else. As you saw this morning, the sooner we get it right, the quicker you get to finish. So bear that in mind, understood? And let's get that bloody aircraft recognition up to scratch with the Yank planes. I don't think it will look too good painting a stars and stripes on the fuselage for our first kill.'

***

'You'll never guess what I've just done,' Daniel said to Dianne, sitting down at the table. It was that time of the evening in the pub when everyone seemed to peak at their loudest, the arguments raging, the jokes bringing raucous laughter, people shouting their conversation over their own noise.

'I know exactly what you've done,' she said, giving him a disapproving look.

'Really? How?'

'You've left me here for twenty minutes alone, fighting off every single bloke in the bar while you happily carried on with your mate over there.

No one wanted to believe we're supposed to be together, since you weren't taking a blind bit of notice of me. Including your South African friend I met today. He wouldn't take no for an answer.'

'Monkey? I saw you chatting. I thought you were getting on famously.'

'I had to tell him to bugger off.'

'Did you?' Daniel looked pleased. 'I wish I'd been here to see that.'

'I wish you'd been here too, so I wouldn't have had to do it in the first place.'

Daniel had brought Dianne a fresh drink and one for himself. He nudged hers closer. 'Don't be upset. I just bought a car.'

'A what? What sort of car?' Dianne was astonished.

'A Morris. He says it runs like clockwork and only wants thirty quid for it. He's got an overseas posting and he's desperate to get rid of it. I'm going to telegram my bank for the money.'

Dianne sipped her drink. The car was cheap, for certain, but it would still have been a major purchase for her even on the inflated war wages. It intrigued her that Daniel wasn't giving it a second thought.

'What's the point in having a car, if you can't get any petrol for it?'

'I'll get a ration like everyone else. There's a fellow close by who apparently doesn't mind looking after service types.'

Dianne pulled a face but didn't comment. The black market was thriving with the rationing, and everybody used it at some time. It was usually harmless, like a sly wink for an extra gallon of petrol. Nothing to get upset over. 'And where will you go in this marvellous vehicle?'

'I thought you and I could go for a drive tomorrow evening. Find a pub that's not filled with air force bods for a change.'

'No such thing. Not within range of a whole tank filled with petrol.'

'It might be fun looking. A nice drive in the country.'

She tipped her head. 'If this weather clears, I doubt I'll have tomorrow night off. They'll plan something to make up for lost time. The runway's repaired.'

Daniel tried his most charming smile. 'But if they don't, shall we do it?'

'I'll believe this car when I see it. Then I'll decide if I'm going anywhere in it. It could be an uncomfortable old wreck for all you know.'

'He says it's in very good nick.'

Dianne laughed at him. 'He's not going to tell you anything else, is he?'

'I'm sure he's being honest. It's just this posting and he needs to get rid of it in a hurry.'

'And where did he buy it?'

'From the graveyard, of course.'

Daniel said it lightly. It was the grim answer she expected. The graveyard was a pool of belongings that had been owned by men missing or confirmed killed. Many of these aircrew came from other countries and the logistics of returning many personal items were too difficult. So they were sold and the money sent instead. The prices paid were often a token amount.

'I thought as much,' she said. The practice of pouncing on the missing airmen's property was a little ghoulish to her, but it was another fact of war time life, like the black marketing.

'We won't go far, if you like,' Daniel pressed her.

'I told you, I want to see it first.'

'You'll be fine. I'll pick you up at six, at the main gate. Don't eat first, we'll find somewhere to have tea.'

'Do they have the word "no" in Australia?' she asked sweetly.

Daniel frowned. 'I can't remember it from school, now you mention it.'

***

The weather cleared over Britain very slowly and the Meteorological officers decided the heavy cloud would be covering most of Europe instead, obscuring any targets. D-Delta flew another low-level exercise in the morning, then the crew spent the afternoon in a lecture about what to do in the case of being shot down over enemy territory. No one made any jokes this time. The army captain speaking to them had been in

France and worked with the Resistance. He kept listing the many different ways escaping aircrew might meet an untimely death. Being shot was likely, but a hanging from a nearest tree was common too. It wasn't just the German armed forces—capture by enemy servicemen gave a better chance of survival. German civilians were known to take matters unpleasantly into their own hands, particularly in rural areas, while the French were considered unreliable.

'Like everywhere, there are good people and bad,' the captain told them as if to soften his dire warnings. 'The problem is the Russians are inflicting heavy casualties and a lot of ill-feeling is growing. In short, the Germans aren't so certain the war will end well for them, and some people are getting nasty about it. If you get caught and there's no hope of escape, insist on being handed over to the proper authorities and with luck you'll end up in a cushy little stalag until the end of the war. Get too smart-mouthed and you'll likely be taken to a wall somewhere and be shot.'

It was Baxter who put up his hand and asked, 'What about in France, sir?'

'Your chances are better for obvious reasons. The Resistance will help you get back to England, although some groups will treat you more as a nuisance than a hero. Beware many French civilians have been terrified by the German occupation and might hand you over, rather than take the risk of reprisals with D-Day landings looking so promising.' The captain shrugged. 'They've had a bad time and things are pretty tough in some parts.'

At the end of the lecture, the D-Delta crew gathered outside to await Branner's okay to finish for the day.

Flanders said darkly, 'That bloody dinghy's looking damned attractive right now. Never thought I'd say it, now I'm a big supporter of ditching anywhere we can and paddling all the way home. Bugger bailing out over Jerry land or risking the Froggies.'

'Cheer up,' Daniel told him. He was buoyed by the prospect of his drive with Dianne and couldn't be made despondent by anything. 'It will never happen. That's the idea, right?'

'Why are we suddenly getting all these instructions about ditching and escaping from enemy territory?'

'Everyone gets them.' Daniel looked at the others for support and got some reluctant nods. 'Particularly during bad weather when we can't do anything else.'

'It's this special operation,' Flanders said morosely. 'You think of the furthest, most heavily defended target in Germany. That's where we're going, I reckon.'

'You worry too much,' Daniel said. 'Where the hell's the skipper? I want to get going.'

***

Even Daniel was surprised at the good condition of the car. Still, he hurriedly cleaned it more and rubbed dubbing into the leather seats to make it smell new. He didn't really have the time and worked furiously. When he pulled up at the gate in front of Dianne, who was chatting to a guard, Daniel was still flustered from his haste and eager to impress her.

'What do you think?' he asked immediately, jumping out to open the door for her.

'Looks quite tidy,' the guard replied, disappointed that Dianne was leaving.

Dianne laughed at the expression on Daniel's face. 'Better than I expected,' she said, and waved at the guard. 'See you later, Doug. Don't let any Jerries sneak through.'

Sitting in the car, Daniel revved the motor before pulling way. 'Hear that? Sounds like it's in very good shape. Plenty of power.'

'Small, isn't it?' Dianne wrinkled her nose. 'It smells like a horse.'

'Ah, well—the leather has been treated to make it last. There's proper polish on the dashboard too and I think—'

'All right, I'm in the damned car. Where are we going?'

'I'll tell you in a minute.'

Daniel drove off, crunching the gears as he passed through the gate. He winced at the noise. 'The navigator from B-Bravo, Bluey they call him, he's given me a mud map to a watering hole he says serves brilliant fish and chips. It's not too far.'

Dianne shook away a painful memory of the bomb site in London and managed to say, 'That sounds like an adventure if nothing else. Is it easy to get to?'

Daniel patted the top pocket of his battle jacket. 'I can almost remember anyway. I've got the map just in case.'

'Perhaps we should have brought Bruce? He can be quite fun and he's good with maps, naturally.' Dianne said to tease him.

He didn't take her seriously. 'That miserable sod? Absolutely not.'

'Oh, I wouldn't say he's miserable. He just likes being grumpy.'

Daniel was about to tell her Flanders' gloomy prophecy about their secret bombing target and changed his mind so as not to spoil the mood.

The sun was getting low and Daniel had planned to find the hotel before it got dark. Also, he didn't want to be rushing around, looking for the way, and missing out on giving Dianne all his attention. The roads they drove were heavily wooded on the verges both sides and overhung by branches. Beyond the trees were fence lines for farming.

The two of them chatted happily, swapping stories of air force work. Dianne carefully explained how she might have excluded Daniel from a raid, if the circumstances were right. She made light of it and was glad to hear him say that special treatment wouldn't be fair, and she shouldn't ever think of it again.

The roads got narrow as Daniel took turns he figured were right. A small forest loomed ahead that would have looked peaceful and inviting in sunlight. Instead, with the evening closing in, the huddled trees appeared gloomy.

'Are we still heading the right direction?' Dianne dared to ask.

'Road signs would help,' Daniel admitted. 'I think so.'

'We took them all down when the Germans looked like invading. I don't suppose we'll put them back up again until after the war.'

'Fair enough, I wouldn't like them to find this pub either.' Daniel changed down a gear and slowed as they entered the woods.

Dianne said, 'It can't be in here surely?'

'Bluey didn't mention any forest, but let's press on for a bit and see. Besides, there's no room to turn around.' He tried to sound cheerful, but Daniel was worried their cosy, fireside evening in a quiet bar might be slipping through his fingers.

It wasn't long before Dianne said, 'This can't be right, Daniel. We're well into the backwoods of some farming land. This forest is like something out of Grimm's fairy tales.'

'I think you're right. I still can't turn even this little beast around. Look for a gate or something. Somewhere we can do a circle.'

'What's that through the trees? A shed or something? Maybe there's a gate to it.'

Daniel stopped the car and frowned through the windscreen. Then he abruptly got out and stood beside the car, staring across at the thing half hidden in the trees. 'Oh dear,' he said glumly. 'That looks a bit too familiar.'

'What do you mean?' Dianne bent her head to talk to him through the open door, then with a frustrated noise she got out and followed his line of sight.

'Do you think that's a rudder? A tail plane?' Daniel pointed. 'It seems like one. Like a plane's pranged into the trees, I mean.'

'It's grey, if it is,' Dianne agreed unhappily. Her instincts were prickling.

'A German, then—if we're right.' Daniel nodded with a heavy sigh. 'I reckon it's a Jerry bomber crashed over there.' After a reluctant, mental assessment of his duty he said, 'I suppose I'd better take a look before we lose the last of this daylight.'

'Daniel, are you sure it's worth it? Even if it is a Jerry bomber, someone else must know about it. It would have made a real racket landing in those trees.'

'Maybe not with the weather we've had. Perhaps it's the bugger who bombed our strip and the Halifax last night? The anti-aircraft lads might have got in a lucky shot.' As he spoke, Daniel began looking around for a walking stick or something he could take with him. It didn't make much sense, but he was going to feel happier with something in his hands. 'You'd better wait here,' he added absently. 'They might not have had a chance to... bail out. It could be a bit unpleasant.'

'Like hell,' Dianne surprised herself. 'What if they did? A couple of starving, desperate Germans might be watching from the bushes right now, just waiting for you to leave me alone. I'm coming with you.'

'All right, but not all the way.' Daniel gave in easily because he wasn't relishing the trip though the forbidding trees alone. 'What about the car? It's blocking the road.'

'Leave the keys.'

'What if the Germans steal it?'

She gave him such a look, he decided to keep his mouth shut.

They set off walking close, almost tripping each other up. The ground under the forest canopy was soft and pulling at their shoes like mud. Within moments, Dianne grabbed Daniel's arm for support, and he didn't complain. It wasn't romantic—he was in need of a little moral help himself, advancing carefully through the dark trees to what promised to be an ugly scene.

As they got closer, they could see the scars of white wood where bark had been ripped and torn away. A stench of aviation fuel and oil floated across. There had been no fire. Nothing they could smell, at least.

'He must have been trying to land,' Daniel said, whispering without knowing why. 'Found himself smacking into a forest. Unlucky bastard. He'd have thought his chances were good of finding open ground.'

'Why do you say that?' Dianne lowered her voice too.

'He would be spread all over this field, if he hit hard. Looks like he just sort of flopped into the trees instead.'

'Do you know what it is?'

'A Heinkel 111. They have two crew.'

Dianne gripped him harder. 'I'm coming right up close. You're not leaving me behind anywhere.'

Daniel didn't answer, squeezing her hand. A part of him pictured the German flyers lying wounded inside the fuselage, their minds filled with all the horror stories like Daniel had heard that day in the lecture. They would probably have a revolver each, loaded and prepared to shoot, ready to fight off enraged farmers with sharpened pitchforks and hoping to hang the Germans from the nearest tree.

'Steady on,' he muttered aloud.

'Why? What's wrong?'

'Nothing—sorry. I'm winding myself up.'

'Shouldn't we call out or something? We don't want to scare anybody into anything silly.'

'Good idea. I'm not feeling heroic.'

The Heinkel was lying broken-backed between the trees, the wings splayed out untidily like a fallen man with his arms spread. Most of the Plexiglass of the bomber's nose was smashed and scattered across the ground, glinting like jewels against the black soil. The fuselage was cracked open in several places offering glimpses into the dark interior. A rear door hung slightly open.

Daniel and Dianne stopped a few feet short of the wingtip. 'Hello?' he called out. 'Is anyone still in there?'

A rabbit was startled out of a shrub, the movement making both of them jump.

'Bloody hell,' Daniel breathed. Dianne let out a shaky sigh.

Only silence came from the aircraft.

'Stay here,' he told her, prising her hand off his arm.

He picked his way carefully over the strewn pieces of metal and glass to reach the door. Daniel called through the gap and shrugged back at Dianne when again no one answered. He gripped the edge of the hatch and hauled it aside. It came away with a loud squeal. After taking a deep breath, he climbed inside.

The stink of ruptured fuel and oils was much stronger, biting at the back of his throat. The light was poor, coming from the gaping hole of the missing nose. From what he could see, the inside at first looked familiar. Every inch was crammed with equipment, hydraulic lines and electrical cabling. When he looked closer Daniel noticed the German labelling on the instruments.

There was no sign of any crew.

He worked his way forward, placing each step slowly so he didn't twist an ankle or stab his foot on something unseen. It was getting so dark Daniel began thinking this was a bad idea. He didn't want to get trapped trying to fumble his way out. Then he realised it would be just as easy to step out the ruined front of the plane. In fact, he could have checked the pilot's position from outside.

'Idiot,' he told himself, but with the consoling thought he still would have searched the fuselage.

Both the cockpit seats were empty. Just as Daniel was about to call to Dianne that the crew must have bailed out, he looked out and saw her standing beyond the wreckage at the nose. She was watching for him.

'They're here,' she said in a dull voice. 'Both of them.'

Two crumpled shapes were on the ground near her.

'Oh, Christ.' Daniel scrambled to escape the Heinkel and get to Dianne. She didn't move when he put an arm around her shoulders. Dianne was staring at the bodies curled on the soil and half covered in leaves.

'They look like boys,' she said sadly 'Just a pair of lads.'

'They were quite happy to blow up that poor Halifax last night, if it was them,' Daniel said grimly. 'Anyway, they had been trying to bomb somebody.'

'I know,' Dianne nodded once.

'They must have been thrown forward through the nose by the impact. Hell of a bang to break their straps. These trees stopped them dead.'

'In more ways than one,' Dianne murmured.

Daniel went and examined them more closely. Both corpses had wide, staring eyes and there was no doubt they were dead—he was glad of that. He didn't want to be poking and prodding, looking for signs of life.

'That's it, then,' he said. 'There's nothing we can do here.'

'What shall we do? Go back to Waddington?'

'I'd say we'll find a telephone more quickly. Call the police and tell them. Not that I know where we are exactly.'

'I can't remember seeing one anywhere for miles. We'll have to try the first farm we see.'

'That might be a bit tricky with the blackout. You can't see anything off the road.'

Dianne held back a sudden urge to swear, loud and long, and very unladylike. Their pleasant evening drive had turned into an awful mess. She was trying hard not to think that this crashed German bomber with its dead occupants could easily be Daniel and his crew lying among trees on the other side of the English Channel, in enemy-held Europe.

'Come on,' Daniel grabbed her arm again. 'Help me turn the car around and we'll get moving.

They were both glad to get away from the wreckage. Dianne's skin crawled a little as she turned her back on the bodies. At the car, she guided Daniel in a tortuous about-turn making sure the wheels didn't drop into a ditch on each side. It took some time, the Morris edging around with Daniel hauling laboriously on the steering. In the near darkness the small slits allowed on the headlights were no help at all. Eventually they were driving back in the direction in which they came. Then at the first intersection Daniel swung the other way.

'Now what?' she asked.

'I'm feeling lucky. Let's see what's up here.'

'Feeling lucky? God, I'm feeling quite wretched.'

'I'm sorry this has turned out so rotten.'

If Daniel were honest, the fallen Heinkel with its dead crew made him feel slightly pleased. They were at war after all, and there were two less enemy he had to worry about when he was flying over Germany. That's what it was all about, right?

'It's not your fault,' Dianne told him. 'I suppose we should be glad the flak boys must have scored a hit, knocking down an enemy bomber and all that.' She didn't sound convincing. 'It was just seeing it in that gloomy forest, and the bodies.'

'They might have been bombing London for months, those two. Maybe they've dropped thousands of pounds down onto your heads.'

'I know, I should be thinking like that.'

Daniel didn't mention that the Heinkel had only three bomb symbols on its fuselage, indicating the aircraft with its young flyers was new and had done just three missions. Luckily, Dianne hadn't seen it.

The Morris gave a sudden cough, lurched unhappily for a few yards, then continued on—with an ominous sound coming from under the hood.

'Oh, damn.' Daniel peered at the gauges. The globes in them were very weak and he could hardly see. 'I think we're overheating.'

Dianne let out a long groan. 'I can't believe this. We're having just the worst luck. Are you going to stop?'

Outside the car, the countryside was dark and frightening.

'I'll risk it awhile and see how far the old girl can get us. The further we go, the less I might have to walk for help.'

'We might have to walk, you mean. You're not leaving me behind here either.'

'Cross your fingers and toes and maybe no one will have to walk anywhere.'

Daniel drove with his eyes more on the temperature gauge than the road. He willed the needle to stay below the red. Slowing down seemed to help and so did the fact that the sun was well and truly gone, chilling the air further. Dianne kept putting her head close to his shoulder to look at the gauge too. It felt nicely intimate, although he didn't dare say that.

They drove abruptly into a tiny village. With the town's blackout Dianne was startled to realise darkened buildings were sliding past the car.

'Hurray,' Daniel said, puffing his cheeks out with relief. 'We've made it somewhere.' He pulled over. 'You know, I have this strangest feeling... wait here a second.'

He got out and disappeared inside a doorway. The brief glimpse Dianne had of the inside told her it was a pub. Daniel took so long to re-emerge she began to believe he was having a quick drink without her, and she grew annoyed and considered going in after him. Then the door opened again and four figures came out. One of them came to her side of the car. It was Daniel.

'You won't believe it, Dianne. This is the pub we were trying to find all along. Our luck's changed. The local copper was in there having a pint. I told him about the downed Jerry. He and some lads are going out there with a lorry to—ah, pick up the crew. They've bought us drinks. The way they're carrying on, you'd think we had shot down the thing ourselves.'

Dianne was feeling guilty. Daniel was close enough that she could smell his breath, and he hadn't had a drink. She got out of the car and tugged at his jacket as Daniel turned to lead her inside.

She told him, 'This poor car has been wheezing and bubbling like an old kettle. What are we going to do?'

'It's not a good idea to have a look while it's still hot. Let's get a drink, have something to eat and perhaps it will have cooled down enough by then so I can stick my head under the bonnet.'

He didn't sound particularly worried. Dianne couldn't decide if that was a good sign or something new to be suspicious about.

Inside the pub it was wonderfully warm, thanks to a pile of blazing logs in a large hearth. There were advantages to living near forbidding forests. Ignoring some appreciative looks, Dianne went straight to the fire and toasted her hands for a while. The bar was small with around a dozen customers, only a few of them women, while the men were all mature-aged. Nobody else wore a military uniform, but one girl was in the Land Army. The men gave Dianne gruff, friendly greetings and one of them murmured, 'Well done, lass,' as she passed. It seemed Daniel hadn't been kidding when he'd said it was like they had shot down the Heinkel themselves. She offered back a grateful smile, which didn't make sense, but felt like the right thing to do.

Daniel was getting their drinks from the bar. Over her shoulder, she saw him chat to the publican, who in turn exchanged a few words with one of the customers. A wireless playing on a shelf smothered most of what they said. Dianne guessed it was about the car.

'I've ordered some of these famous fish and chips,' Daniel said, arriving with the drinks. 'There's a dining room through that door where we can sit down and eat, if you like. And that fellow's a bit of a mechanic. He'll have a look at the Morris after a while. Like I said, it's too hot at the moment.'

Dianne lowered her voice. 'I can't believe there's no other service personnel in here. It must be the only pub in all Lincolnshire not crowded with drunken, singing aircrew.'

'It's local's night, I'm told.'

'Local's night?'

'The publican has made it politely known around these parts that one night a week is supposed to be local's night—an evening where his regular customers can have a bit of peace and quiet. This is it, and fair enough too.'

'What about us?' Dianne sneaked a look around the bar, expecting to see veiled disapproval. She only saw exactly the opposite, for her at least. One man may even have winked.

'We're different.' Daniel raised his pint glass to her in a toast. 'You're an extremely attractive damsel in distress. It's against the law to refuse you. I'd better be on my best behaviour though. They'll kick me out into the street with the first excuse, so they can have you all to themselves.'

'That's enough flattery for one night,' she said, insincerely. 'Do you think he'll be able to fix the car?'

'I'm sure he'll tinker with something and get us going,' Daniel said offhandedly.

'What if he can't?'

'Let's worry about that when it happens.'

They ate the fish and chips in the dining room. The place wasn't heated, and the warmth of the bar didn't seep through. It was nice and private with nobody else in there, but Dianne was glad to return to the fire. The mechanic saw them come in and made a gesture towards the door.

'You might as well stay here in the warmth,' Daniel told Dianne. 'Hopefully it won't take too long.'

He bought her another drink before leaving. She nursed the gin and tonic beside the fire, half-hoping someone would come and chat with her. She watched the flames and wondered about what they'd do if the car wasn't repairable. First thing would be to telephone the airfield and let someone know they were in strife. It wouldn't do to be called AWOL—absent without leave—when it wasn't really their fault. Next, they'd probably have to pay someone to give them a lift back. It seemed unfair, dragging someone away from their nice, quiet night at the pub. Still, what else could they do?

Dianne was happy to wait for however long it took, enjoying the open fire while she could. It felt like a lifetime since she'd last done this.

Daniel came back looking uneasy. 'I've got good news and a bit of bad news. The old girl hasn't got a drop of oil in her. The sump plug must have dropped out. It doesn't look like any real damage has been done, so it's case of whacking something in the hole and scrounging some oil. That fellow says he can help us out with both.'

'All right, so which news is that? The good or the bad?'

'The good bit. Unfortunately, he can't do anything about it until the morning. He reckons just after sun-up is okay with him. We can be back at the airfield early enough to stay out of trouble.'

'Tomorrow morning? What are we supposed to do tonight?' It wasn't hard to guess. Dianne wanted to hear Daniel explain it with a straight face. She couldn't help thinking he'd be figuring his luck had definitely changed for the better.

'The publican said he's got a room upstairs we can rent cheap.'

'What luck,' she said dryly, then added in a sweet voice, 'Only the one room, I suppose?'

Daniel saw the look in her eye. 'I'm afraid so, but it's got separate beds. Look, I know what you're thinking. It's true about the car—you can ask the mechanic chap. I wouldn't try anything sneaky like this to... well, you know. It's not my style.'

She watched him steadily, sipping her drink without taking her gaze off him.

He sighed. 'I'll tell you what. I'll borrow some blankets and sleep in the car. You can have the room to yourself. I understand completely. It was a bit much to expect.'

'Hmm.' Dianne wasn't at all appeased by the offer. 'You should have at least asked me first.'

'I didn't think we had much choice.'

'That's not the point.'

There was an uncomfortable silence—for Daniel anyway. Dianne had gone back to watching the fire. He didn't know what to do or say.

Then, lowering her voice, she said firmly, 'If you even come near my side of the room, I'll break your nose and scream the roof down, is that absolutely clear?'

It took him a moment to understand and he gave her an awkward, grateful smile. 'Oh—absolutely. I promise not to do anything untoward. I won't even take any of my clobber off.'

'No, you certainly won't!'

'No, of course not. That's what I meant to do all along.'

She turned back around and fixed him with a grim stare. 'If I even think you've winked at any bloke in this bar during the remainder of the evening, I'll do you the same damage right here. In fact, I'll do more than break just your nose.'

'It's none of anyone else's business,' he nodded quickly.

'Don't even look pleased.'

'Why should I? It's rotten luck—it really is. We could get into serious trouble.'

'That's another thing.' Exasperated, Dianne looked to the ceiling for inspiration, but none came. 'No, there's nothing else for it. We'll have to borrow a telephone and call the guard room at the airfield. Tell them what's happened. I hope they believe us. I've never been on a charge before and I don't want to start now.'

'I could try calling the pub too,' Daniel said thoughtfully. 'That's where the skipper—or at least one of the lads will be. Susan too, most likely.'

'Give it shot before it gets too late.'

Daniel spent ten minutes on the publican's telephone. It was easy explaining to the guard room at the main gate at Waddington that they were stranded until morning. After calling the Saracen's Arms, Daniel was kept waiting for ages listening to the roar of the customers while the room was searched for D-Delta crew. Eventually Branner came to the phone. His skipper wasn't happy and couldn't be convinced that Daniel's return in the morning would be early enough to take his place on the flying roster.

'I'll get there, whatever it takes,' Daniel told him. 'Don't worry.'

'Make bloody sure you do,' Branner growled. 'I'll be covering your arse.'

Branner agreed to tell their tale to Susan, who was currently trying to avoid Wills' advances again. Susan would know what to do for Dianne's sake.

Daniel returned to Dianne, who had pounced on a pair of stuffed lounge chairs close to fire the moment the occupants looked like leaving.

'What a carry-on,' he said, blowing out his cheeks as he sat down. 'Still, I think everything is sorted out. The skipper's going to chat with Susan, if Charlie lets him get close enough.'

'Then we'll just have to make the best of things, won't we? Keep each other company.' Dianne smiled in such a way that he wasn't sure if she was still mocking him.

The evening passed pleasantly, better than Daniel had dare to hope. Without the bustle of their usual bar, surrounded by friends and colleagues from the airfield, Daniel was afraid Dianne might get bored. Instead, she seemed to relax more than he'd seen her do before. They talked about many things and avoided matters that might become too serious. It wasn't until late in the night, as other customers called their farewells to the publican and left, that a tension grew between them.

'I suppose we'd better find this room,' Daniel said, and drained his glass.

'I hope it's not too cold.'

They waited until the last drinker had gone and the publican could lock the door. Then he led them up a back staircase, through a musty hallway and to a room with a brass "2" screwed to the timber.

'My wife's parents are in number one,' he whispered. 'Lost their house in the Blitz. They'll be sound asleep by now, so don't worry about disturbing them. The bathroom's at the end of the hall. It's never locked.'

He showed them into the small room and left, closing the door behind him. Two beds on either side were split by a bedside cabinet with a window above. A radiator ticked and grumbled on one wall, working well enough to feel its warmth. Heavy blackout curtains were in place. Daniel twitched them aside a fraction and saw the sash could be opened.

'There's plenty of blankets. Do you want this up a little?'

'If you like. We can always close it again if it gets too chilly.'

They stood close between the beds. After a silence, Daniel raised his eyebrows and shrugged.

'What do you think?'

'I think you should go to the bathroom for a few minutes,' she said, pointedly.

'Oh, all right... I'll count to five hundred or something.'

'That will do.'

Daniel did just that, studying the tiling of the bathroom intently, shuffling his feet with his hands in his pockets to beat the cold because there was no heating in there. He forced himself to urinate, aware he had several pints of lager lurking in his system. Then with his heart fluttering he went back to the room.

Dianne was a mound under her bedding, lying with her face to the wall. She had turned on a small lamp. Her uniform was hung on the end of her bed. She said, 'You can turn off the light to get undressed and I'll keep my back turned.'

'Fine, thanks.' He didn't say anything about her change of mind about wearing all his clothing.

In darkness he stripped to his underwear and sat on the bed. It creaked alarmingly and promised to do it again with every move he made. 'This bed's very noisy,' he whispered.

'Then lay still.'

'I might have to get up in the night and go to the bathroom.'

'Then please do it quietly.'

'I'll try.'

He crawled under the blankets and got comfortable, wincing at every squeak and groan from the springs. When he was settled, he said quietly, 'Dianne, did you have a nice evening? I mean, apart from finding the dead Germans—and the car breaking down, and everything.'

'It was lovely, Daniel. Thank you.'

'I'm glad... goodnight, then.'

'Goodnight, Daniel.'

Dianne stayed with her face to the wall, her eyes wide open and staring, listening to Daniel's bed and for the first creaking indication he might be getting up and moving towards hers. She didn't know what to do if it happened. Dianne was feeling quite confused about how she felt, and what she wanted from him. Drinking gin and tonics all night wasn't helping now. Lying tense and expectant, her stomach fluttering, the minutes took an eternity to pass. The continuing silence from the other bed suggested he was going to behave himself—as she'd rather over-forcefully insisted upon.

He should at least have the decency to try something, she thought, her mood changing to annoyed disappointment and a little drunken self-doubt. Without the nervousness, she promptly fell asleep.

Daniel wasn't faring much better at understanding the situation. He kept himself absolutely still so the bedsprings didn't disturb Dianne, the effort a kind of torture. He also wasn't sure if he'd read her correctly. Would she be offended if he didn't make some sort of pass at her? After all, she had got undressed and allowed him to do the same. Was that a hint? Trying the wrong move might be an utter disaster—a complete cock-up.

In the darkness he smiled at his own pun and decided women were damned tricky creatures. They should come with proper instructions, like the machine guns in his turret. That last pint of lager was threatening to cause him trouble already too. Swelling his bladder a bit sooner than planned. Daniel decided he couldn't do anything about it in case Dianne thought he had other ideas. It was best to just sweat it out for a while and wait until she was asleep.

He dozed off, frowning with a half-formed strategy in his mind to turn an apology for his toilet trip into an invitation from Dianne to push the beds together. Carefully worded, it might work...

Ten

'I still don't bloody believe a word of it,' Flanders announced over the intercom as they taxied towards the start of the runway. The Lancasters were moving at their usual snail's pace along the perimeter roads and having four other aircraft in front of D-Delta meant there was time for a bit of chatter. Even Branner allowed himself a small grin at this latest challenge to Daniel's account of his night away. It had been a subject pursued relentlessly by the crew.

Flanders went on, 'Christ, I wouldn't have thought someone such as you would try a sly sod of a trick like that. Chuck a spanner in the works of the Morris when you're outside a convenient pub, then make the poor girl share a bedroom? A very cunning little plan. How much to bribe the publican did you reckon, Barra?'

'A fiver, at least,' Barrymore answered immediately, waiting for it. 'The landlord would want nothing less to diddle his books and say there weren't any other rooms.'

Branner blipped the port motor to get them around a sharp turn. Daniel waited until the noise dropped again to its normal roar. 'I'm a bit sick of this and I'd ignore you all except it's Dianne's reputation being slurred. I'll tell you one last time—nothing happened. We stayed in our own beds all night. Believe me, if things were any different, the smile on my face would be a dead giveaway. I couldn't help myself.'

'A very accomplished actor—we've got a real Chips Rafferty here,' Flanders said. 'There's a career for you on the silver screen, Daniel. After the war.'

'That'll damned well do. For Christ's sake we don't all have to ring bells and raise a flag every time we have a good night with a girl,' Daniel said, before realising it would undoubtedly be taken the wrong way. 'You're just jealous, if you ask me. I doubt you've ever even seen a girl undressed, Flanno, let alone stayed the night—unless she's your sister. Despite all those stories you tell us.'

Flanders said hotly, 'I've lost count of my women, I'll have you know. Cheeky swine.'

Wills chipped in, 'I've seen his sister starkers, by the way.'

'Like hell you have, you little bastard. I'd shoot you myself, if that was true.'

'Is she ugly, Charlie?' Daniel asked innocently.

'She looks like Bruce, but a bit more flat-chested. Make a handsome front row for Canterbury.'

'You wait until after this flight,' Flanders hissed. 'I'm going to break your neck.'

'Flanno's very touchy about his family, isn't he?'

Daniel answered, 'He's touchy about everything that isn't a joke he's making about somebody else.'

'All right, you blokes, a bit of quiet,' Branner said. 'We're coming up to the take-off line.'

In the cockpit, Branner was hoping they would obey. Small things like this are what preyed on his mind. Would they shut up? It was like having the last word in an argument. When after a few seconds the intercom stayed silent, Branner was just half-pleased. It had been mostly Daniel after all, and he was the best at discipline, while Flanders was probably sulking. At least Wills did as he was told for once.

D-Delta took off in a strong cross wind, the aircraft crabbing sideways the moment its wheels left the ground. Branner fought with the rudder while Sexton as usual looked after the throttles. When the Lancaster had settled on a course, nobody needed to see the grim look on Branner's face as he strained on the controls. They could feel the bomber was flying at odds with the wind, requiring Branner's full attention. It was going to be hard work for their pilot this morning.

Today they carried live ammunition with the fuses set. During their practice flight was a low-level bombing run on a marked target.

Barrymore had asked unhappily at the briefing, 'Will they have Spitfires doing mock runs at us too?'

'Not today,' Eagleton replied with a deadpan expression. 'Good idea, we'll look into some co-operation from a nearby Hurricane squadron for next time. They wouldn't be actually firing, of course.'

'Of course,' Barrymore murmured. 'They'd only get in the way.'

Eagleton heard him. 'Yes, that's exactly what we'd want them to do.'

Wills had leaned close and whispered at Barrymore, 'Will you shut the hell up and stop putting ideas in his head?'

Now Wills called over the intercom, 'Skipper, I reckon F-Freddy has stalled on the runway. She still hasn't budged from what I can see.'

Wills could see the Lancaster had failed to move from the take-off point. Something had gone wrong at the critical moment, and it was blocking the remaining bombers from leaving.

'All right, Tail,' Branner answered formally. He wasn't sure what would happen now. It hadn't been covered in the briefing, the possibility of half the squadron being stranded on the ground. Would they carry on, as they might in the real thing?

'They'll drag them out the way quick-smart,' Sexton offered a guess, seeing Branner's expression.

'Those lads will be ticked off,' Branner nodded. 'The rest will have to pull their fingers out to catch up too.'

'A balls-up before we even get started,' Flanders groaned. He was voicing everyone's thoughts. This training flight felt bad already.

Because of the tight security surrounding their mission all radio communication was done by morse code even this close to the airfield.

'Just received a message, skipper,' Baxter called in. 'Everyone is to proceed as planned.'

'There you go,' Sexton said with raised eyebrows. 'The poor buggers waiting for F-Freddy to get out the way will be expected to make up lost time. In this weather it won't be easy.'

Branner said, 'I suppose the war doesn't wait for the weather.' It struck him as a silly thing to say. Bad weather was the cause for many operations to be scrubbed. He was glad to hear no one contradict him.

The crew was too apprehensive about the coming bomb drop to appreciate the low-level flying today. It was more frightening than exhilarating anyway, since the racing ground below slewed sideways with the heavier wind gusts and showed them just how much the Lancaster was being pushed around by the crosswinds.

After Branner made another effort to correct for a wide drift, Sexton said, 'At least it doesn't make Geoff's job any harder. As long as you fly straight over the top of the target, he just has to push the teat. The bombs will hit before the wind has any chance to shove 'em anywhere.'

His mask unclipped, Branner nodded. He was well aware that accurate bombing from this height depended almost entirely on his flying the plane directly over the target. However, before that, they had to reach the practice bombing zone at the right time and from the correct direction.

'Navigator to Nose—Barra, we're looking for a wide river tributary with an arched stone bridge. Main road either side running close enough to north-south. Any minute now. If we're off-course, it'll be to starboard with these winds.'

'Right-ho, Bruce.'

Barrymore was anxiously watching the passing countryside. So far, Flander's navigation had been good on every flight. Barrymore worried about the day he might end up arguing over the intercom, insisting that a landmark that should be visible wasn't there and that Flanders was making a mistake. Branner and Sexton were an extra pair of eyes to back him up, but in flying conditions like these they were too busy.

He reported, 'No bridge yet. We're coming up on another Lanc though. See her skipper?'

'I've got her now. It must be C-Charlie,' Branner replied. 'She's slowed down a lot. They must be afraid they'll miss the navigation mark.' He frowned, deciding what to do. They needed to maintain a certain speed to finish the exercise within time, and D-Delta was doing all right. Over-hauling the aircraft in front of them might get awkward. 'Bugger it, let's back off a few revs, Dave.'

Sexton inched the throttles back until Branner nodded. After a minute, it was plain they were still gaining steadily on the other aircraft. A grey ribbon of water approached and they saw C-Charlie bank sharply over the expected bridge. Branner let Barrymore call the approaching landmark to Flanders before remarking, 'Maybe they'll get a hurry-on now.'

Flanders said, 'Skipper, turn to port when you get there. Course two-sixty for ten minutes or so.'

Branner asked sharply, 'Does that allow for this wind coming up our tail on that heading?'

'And our slowing down,' Flanders answered promptly with a hint of outrage the question was asked.

In the mid-upper turret Daniel was trying his hardest to remain vigilant, scanning the skies for fighters. It was highly unlikely, given the weather and the distance to the nearest German airfield. There was more chance that Eagleton had called in that favour to the Hurricane squadron after all to see if the Lancasters might be caught napping. That didn't seem worthwhile in these conditions either.

His mind kept slipping treacherously back to the evening before, wondering if he could—or should, more to the point—have done things any differently. Dianne had been fine in the morning, brisk and business-like about getting back to Waddington in plenty of time. There had been no joking or veiled references to having spent the night together, even innocently as they had. On the way home, after the Morris was coaxed into sluggish life, Dianne was in charge of a scribbled map given to them by the publican.

'It's the quickest way,' the landlord told her with a sly look. 'So don't let it fall into enemy hands.'

'I won't, I promise. Thank you again for everything.' Dianne leaned over the bar to give him a peck on the cheek.

Which, Daniel had observed wryly, was more than he had got.

Perhaps she liked her men more forceful? He imagined himself as some sort of Errol Flynn character, hauling Dianne to his chest and kissing her hard until her struggles melted into bliss.

'Then I'd let my guard down, so she can kick me hard in the shins,' he decided aloud, wincing at the thought. The sound of Branner talking to Sexton brought him back to reality.

Branner said, 'I suppose we should be glad now that F-Freddy blew a fuse. We'd have the rest of the damned squadron up our arse as well otherwise. I wish this joker would get a move on.'

Sexton gestured at C-Charlie in front of them and spoke of the pilot. 'Bill Parker's no fool. Maybe he's got mechanical problems?'

'Have you heard anything, Morgan?'

'Nothing like that, skipper. We're supposed to be keeping radio silence unless it's absolutely vital.'

'Let me know if you hear anything.'

'Yes, skipper.'

'Pilot to crew, we'll stick behind C-Charlie and provide support in case they're in strife, though there's not much we can do.'

Daniel's concentration wouldn't stick. He had asked to meet Dianne at the pub that evening, and she agreed. It was a good sign that she wasn't entirely upset with him. Now he was considering if she expected an apology, and he hadn't quite seen the clues. Things were so much easier when the girl was besotted with you, a luxury Daniel had enjoyed several times in his school days. They let you get away with murder then, he remembered, shrugging at the memory.

'I mean, it wasn't my fault the car stuffed itself, was it?' he told the dirty clouds streaking past his Perspex. 'Or those bloody Jerries getting themselves shot down. I was hoping to have a nice drive and few quiet drinks at the pub.'

Bloody hell, what was that?

Daniel had noticed that one of the specks of oil on his turret wasn't that at all—it was moving. A distant aircraft briefly glimpsed through the clouds. It had vanished already.

'Skipper, we've got an aircraft on our starboard quarter,' he called urgently. 'Miles away—and I only saw him for a moment. No idea who or what.' Daniel silently cursed himself. He might have seen more if he'd had his mind on the job.

Branner asked, 'Large or small, Daniel? Could it be another Lanc' off course?' Over the intercom you could sense the whole crew winding themselves up another nervous notch.

'Too small and too high for one of us. I didn't see it for long enough, skipper. I caught it out of the corner of my eye.' Daniel bit off an apology. That would hint of being to blame.

'Everyone keep their eyes peeled,' Branner ordered, adding, 'I doubt the Luftwaffe will be out for a ride so far from home today, but you never know. It's probably an RAF observer plane making sure we don't fudge on our course. We might be asked about it at the debriefing, so look out for any identification letters if it comes close.'

'Well spotted, Danny. Do you think we'll get a prize, skipper?' Wills asked.

'Shut up, Charlie. I've got enough on my plate without your damned jokes.'

'Navigator to Pilot,' Flanders drawled with exaggerated calm. 'Talking of which, we should be looking for a turn to course 190 around about now. Landmark is a small pair of hillocks like a camel's hump, so my notes tell me.'

'C-Charlie is swinging over them now,' Branner told him, ignoring the mild mockery. 'New course is a straight line to the target, yes?'

'Less than four minutes away, skipper.'

'Dave, open the bomb bay doors.'

The new heading brought the crosswind hard into their opposite side and Branner had his hands full even more. With the slower speed, still attempting to stay behind C-Charlie, the Lancaster seemed to wallow. The extra drag of the open bomb doors didn't help.

'Bill Parker's on his own after the drop,' Branner shouted at Sexton. 'Bugger this for a lark. Besides, he should make a bee-line for base and forget the exercise if he's really got troubles. We're supposed to continue south for a while yet.'

'You don't want to get much closer,' Sexton yelled back. The fuses on their bombs had delay timers so the aircraft dropping them wasn't caught in their own blast. Another plane following too closely behind might fly straight into the explosions in front.

They had the spectacle of watching C-Charlie do its bomb run. The target was a large, white oblong painted on the meadow with a circle in its centre. It was visible in the distance now, not much more than a thin line at this angle, rapidly growing. Branner supposed it was meant to represent the real target they were training for, which suggested a factory or specific building. Then again, it could be nothing like it—another piece of information purposely left out of the top security puzzle.

Branner whistled soundlessly as he saw how much C-Charlie was being bullied by the wind off her course only to be forced back again by Bill Parker. The Lancaster was blatantly yawing, her nose angled significantly from her course as the pilot tried to stay on line. Then at the last moment, as the watchers in D-Delta held their thumbs over the imaginary triggers of the other aircraft's bomb release, a fierce gust pushed C-Charlie sideways and the plane roared over unmarked ground, the target well beyond her wingtip.

'She didn't drop,' Branner called. 'I didn't see it. Did anyone see bombs falling?'

'I say she didn't,' Barrymore told him firmly. 'I saw nothing.'

Sexton tapped at Branner's elbow bringing his attention back from a glancing study of the gauges. 'Look. They're going around again.'

C-Charlie had banked into a steep turn to port. Whatever reasons they had for flying below the planned pace of the exercise, it wasn't stopping Parker from a second attempt at bombing his target. The manoeuvre looked so aggressively flown that Branner guessed the other pilot was annoyed at missing his bomb run after carefully nursing his aircraft to the target in the first place.

'Steady on, Bill,' he muttered. C-Charlie was cutting things fine.

What happened next occurred so quickly, it was over before anyone could react. Another strong gust hit C-Charlie as she turned. With her acute bank the wind lifted her upper wing higher, forcing the plane almost vertical. At higher altitudes any pilot might recover, but here she had no margin for error. The Lancaster side-slipped the last few feet of precious height and her port wingtip struck the ground. It had the instantaneous effect of tripping C-Charlie into a dramatic cartwheel, smashing pieces off the plane with every rotation until the entire remains of one wing was ripped away and that side of the fuselage slammed abruptly into the earth. Like a drowning man hold his hand above the water, the other wing stood poised straight up for a second, then flopped lifelessly over.

It was all in silence to the men in D-Delta, the noise of their own aircraft masking the tragedy in front of them. The shocked swearing of the three men who saw it, Branner, Sexton and Barrymore, wasn't enough to tell the others what they were witnessing.

Then Branner breathed over the intercom, 'Christ, her bombs will still be fused.'

C-Charlie's munitions exploded with a shattering roar, scattering what was left of her fuselage into a million flaming pieces. The blast punched D-Delta, making the aircraft shiver.

Wills yelled triumphantly from the tail gun. 'That's what I call fireworks, lads. Did they hit the target? Show 'em how it's done, Geoff-me-boy!'

Wills, like Daniel, Baxter and Flanders, had mistaken the explosion for C-Charlie's attempt to bomb the target. It made Barrymore remember the task they had and he asked in a shocked voice, as Branner was about to turn away from their run, 'What are we doing, skipper?'

Branner tweaked the controls, bringing the Lancaster back on line with the white square approaching fast. Hoarsely, he said, 'Take your shot, Geoff. That's what we're supposed to do.'

A few seconds later, with a lack of enthusiasm that surprised those men still ignorant of C-Charlie's fate, Barrymore announced, 'Bombs away.'

D-Delta lifted sharply, relieved of the weight and there was an anxious silence from the crew as they passed over the target. Then Wills let out a whoop of joy, seeing the flowers of dirt as the bombs buried themselves into the soil inside the target.

His cry was cut off as he got confused. 'Hang on—hey, what the hell is that?'

He was looking at the crater and debris that had been C-Charlie.

***

'What is the bloody use of practicing all this bailing out and ditching in the ocean rubbish, when you're flying at these altitudes?' Flanders asked everyone in disgust. They were crammed into the back of a canvas-topped lorry that was grinding its way back to the main buildings. A debriefing from Eagleton awaited them in the hall. When no one answered, he added, 'Bill Parker and his boys wouldn't have stood a chance. A parachute's no good if you get into the shit at that height. You need a fucking stepladder to get out of the plane.'

Sexton said tiredly, 'Don't start that rubbish again, Bruce. Obviously, we're not always going to be doing operations at tree-top level. This is something special.'

'Special? Suicidal, more like it.'

'That'll do, Bruce,' Branner said quickly. 'If you like, I can ask to have you put in another crew.'

'No, forget that...' Flanders angrily tossed his cigarette out past the flapping cover. 'I'm just so damned pissed off. What a waste of good blokes.'

'No one's arguing with you there, all right?'

The debriefing was strictly formal and dealt with C-Charlie's loss in clipped, official terms. Then as the men left the hall Eagleton said, 'A word with you, Alec.'

The rest of the D-Delta men lingered too and Eagleton looked about to send them away, then only waited until all the other crews had gone.

'All right, Alec. I'll be to the point. You get kudos for sticking to your bomb run and hitting the target, regardless of what was happening in front of you. That shows good discipline and good training. Spotting me in my Hurricane was well done. No one else did, because I was trying my damnedest to make sure you didn't.' His expression turned to a frown. 'But backing off and sticking with C-Charlie isn't on. We'll never know why Bill Parker was flying so slowly. We must assume he had problems and decided to finish the exercise. In the real thing, and not just this mission, one lame duck is one too many. Over enemy territory, what you did was make your aircraft just as vulnerable as his and risk the RAF losing two Lancasters and their trained crews, rather than one. A bombing raid is not an Atlantic convoy, matching the pace of the slowest ship. Speed and manoeuvrability are your best defences aside from your gunners. Anyone in trouble are on their own—you can do bugger all to help them, understand?'

'Yes, sir.' Branner was standing absolutely still in the face of Eagleton's disapproval. 'May I ask, what's the point of all our formation flying we learned?'

'A formation of undamaged aircraft has its obvious advantages. Quite plainly those same airplanes flying at half their speed to accommodate a cripple colleague will be over the wrong side of the Channel for twice as long, presenting German fighters with twice the opportunity to shoot the bloody lot of them down. Does that make it any clearer for you?'

'Yes sir, I just... yes, sir. Quite clear.'

Eagleton softened. 'We've learned to make some hard decisions since the war started. It doesn't mean we like them any more than you.' He dug into a pocket and produced a handful of crumpled pound notes. 'Any of you going to the pub tonight? I've got a damned meeting with some top brass from London. Can you put this on the bar for a toast to Parker and his crew?'

'I will, sir.' Branner took the money.

Eagleton nodded his thanks and left.

***

Barrymore, Sexton and Flanders had all drunk too much. Branner wasn't much better, his attempt at setting an example failing in the face of the drinks they kept buying him at the same time as their own. It didn't help that the four of them were feeling a little left out, despite their own company, and had made themselves a disgruntled island in the midst of the crowded bar with its packed, cheerfully shouting patrons. Daniel was tucked into a corner of the pub with Dianne, talking earnestly and she didn't seem to mind his close attention. Likewise Wills had Susan pinned against the fireplace. She didn't appear quite as pleased but wasn't making much of an attempt to escape him yet—although it looked likely to the keen observer who spotted her sighing and rolling eyes. To top things off, Baxter was doing surprisingly well in another corner with an attractive WAAF.

The remainder of D-Delta's crew were struggling to contain their collective jealousy.

'She's that damned cock-teaser from the parachute hanger,' Flanders finally remembered. He clicked his fingers, trying to bring back her name. 'Rob, Rob... Roberta? No, Robyn. That's her. Gorgeous, I must say. She looks like trouble. Come to think of it, I've heard a few stories about her.'

'Her old man's trouble, you mean,' Sexton said quietly, as if she might hear him above the roar of the hotel's customers. 'He's the RAFP Warrant Officer of the station. Touch her on the bum and you'll end up blindfolded and shot at dawn.'

'It could be almost worth it. Damned nice legs too.'

Barrymore gestured at her with his half-filled pint glass, slopping the contents. 'She'll spend all his money, smoke all his cigarettes, then leave him looking like a sheep standing all alone in a hundred-acre paddock.'

The others squinted at him, trying to imagine this. Branner gave up first.

'Anyway, don't be like that. Reputations can be very cruel, based on idle gossip. She's probably a very nice girl who needs a bit of advice on how to treat blokes, that's all.'

'I wish he'd bring her over here then,' Flanders growled. 'We could all teach her something. Morgan hasn't got a bloody clue, I'll bet.'

Branner shook his head. 'Don't include me in that sort of nonsense. I've got a girl waiting back home, remember.'

'What's her name again?' Flanders asked. 'You don't talk about her much. Are you sure she's real?'

'Real, and very pretty. Cheryl, her name is. We're not exactly engaged or anything, but you know...'

'And she's still waiting?' Flanders raised his eyebrows.

'Of course. She writes almost every week. Is that so strange?'

'From what I hear, it can't last for long. The bleeding Yanks are damned near invading all of Australia now, except they haven't got any guns. Their arms are filled with bloody chocolate, stockings, American fags... you name it. Sweeping the girls off their feet with kindness.'

Branner was uncomfortable. He couldn't tell if Flanders was teasing. 'Cheryl's not like that.'

'Everyone's like that, skipper. It's fine to stay faithful for a few weeks, then maybe a month or so. When it gets to be a year of more of being on your own and some other good-looking fellow is knocking on your door each night—well, you can't blame them, can you?'

They were interrupted by someone cannoning into them, the whole mass of customers swaying in unison around them. The D-Delta men snarled in dismay at the culprit. Flanders abruptly changed his tone.

'Johnno? It's you! Have you got that five shillings I lent you last week?'

Johnno, a thin and scruffy redhead, looked embarrassed. His hands were filled with cradling three full pints. 'Oh... Flanno. Didn't see you there. Sorry, these were with my last coins. Next pay, I promise.'

'What? Next pay? You might not be around by then.'

As Johnno blanched at the gallows humour and Flanders' colleagues dropped their smiles, Flanders added, 'I heard you blokes have been transferred to North Africa. Haven't you been told? No cold beer there, you know. Full of flies and camels, and girls who look like camels. Just your type.'

'Funny bastard,' Johnno said without a smile. 'Next pay, all right? And I'll buy you a pint.' He sidled away before Flanders could say more.

Unwittingly, Flanders' jibe had reminded them of C-Charlie's crash. The subject filled the silence now. Barrymore shrugged and said, 'Burial with full honours tomorrow. Coffins draped with flags and the whole works. They didn't even do the gardening trip to the Frisians. Dead and buried before their first op' and they get full honours.'

'In commemoration of a rather silly turn to port,' Flanders murmured.

'I wonder what they put in the coffins, or why they even bother?' Sexton said. 'It seems a bit of a waste. There can't have been much left of the poor buggers.'

'In the last war they used to fill them with sandbags,' Branner said with drunken authority. 'Even if they only found a hat or something. That's the whole idea. Nobody minds taking the risk of getting knocked off, but we all like to think it'll be nice and quick if it happens. And clean, of course. So we fill even the empty coffins with something and pretend the unfortunate fellow is all present and accounted for. All very civilised and it does wonders for the morale of the pall bearers.'

Flanders asked, 'What if he was a big, fat sod? Do they fill the coffin to the brim?'

'Do you take anything seriously?' Branner scowled at him.

'I take death very seriously. To the point of being quite fanatical about avoiding it. During my youth, at least.'

No one knew what to say next. In the silence, Barrymore changed the subject. 'Why do you think she puts up with him?' They saw him looking at Wills and Susan.

'She feels sorry for him, that's all,' Flanders said. 'Because he's so short.'

'She's like that girl with Bax,' Barrymore grumbled. 'As soon as Charlie stops buying her drinks and feeding her cigarettes, Susan will lose interest.'

'My, you have had your heart broken some time in your sordid past.' Flanders peered at him like a doctor examining a patient. 'Be fair, we know Susan's an all right sort. She just can't get past Charlie and come to chat with us.'

'Look out,' Sexton nodded at something across the room. 'Talking of which, Morgan's being attacked by a Hun from the rear.'

They turned to see the South African pilot, Munk, wearing a charming smile, joining Baxter and Robyn uninvited. The glare on Baxter's face was plain as he said something. Immediately, Munk made a small bow as if to apologise and backed away again. In turn, he didn't look pleased when his face was hidden from Baxter.

'Well done, Bax,' Barrymore clapped his hands gently and spilled more of his drink. 'Must have given Monkey both barrels at close range. The Hun's bailing out already.'

'I wouldn't have thought Morgan could hurt a fly. He certainly sent Munk packing, didn't he?' Flanders was impressed. 'Barra, are you still interested in drinking or do you prefer tossing that stuff all over me?'

'Whose shout is it?'

'Yours, actually.'

'Damn. All right, I'll be back in a second.' Barrymore finished off the last of his pint in one gulp and headed off towards the bar.

'Ah—not for me,' Branner called after him. Barrymore didn't seem to hear.

'Too late,' Sexton said. 'Never mind, one more won't kill you. Mind you, then it'll be your buy after this. You can't leave then.'

Flanders was shrewdly eyeing Daniel and Dianne in the distance. 'You know, if Daniel slips up for just a second, I'm going to be in there before you can say, "Tough luck, old chap". Dianne is rather a splendid girl and all's fair in love and war, right?'

'Then you'd be too slow,' Sexton said. 'Because I would be there first. What do you reckon, skipper?'

'I told you,' Branner said. 'I don't need to worry about that sort of thing.' He stared at Dianne for a moment. 'Bloody attractive though, isn't she?'

***

'I'm telling you,' Daniel was insisting. 'The whole crew is just waiting for me to get the measles or something and be sent away. You'd be smothered by the lot of them, all trying their luck.'

Dianne struggled to stop a pleased smile. 'You're very flattering, but I doubt it's quite like that. Is that why we're not drinking with them tonight?'

'No, I suppose I'm trying to make up for last night.'

'We spent all of last night together, alone.'

'Yes, but there was the car breaking down and the crashed Heinkel, and everything... well, never mind.' Daniel decided it wasn't a good topic. He just couldn't stop himself fishing for more clues about how he might have behaved differently that previous evening. It was so confusing. 'So, do you want to go and join the others?'

'Later perhaps,' Dianne smiled knowingly, as if she had guessed exactly what doubts were tormenting Daniel. 'Although I don't think we should have such a late night.'

'Oh? Can you give me a hint?'

Dianne sighed. 'Just because I suggest we shouldn't get blind, legless drunk again doesn't mean I know something. I haven't been chatting to Winston Churchill on the phone or anything.'

'I'm only joking. I know you can't say a word and I'm not really asking,' Daniel tried to be sincere and failed. 'We can't leave now, though. See? Morgan's heading off with that girl. He'll think we're spying on him or trying to follow, if we go as well.'

'I can go and you can stay, if you like,' Dianne said absently, watching Baxter and Robyn push their way to the front door.

'Absolutely not. I'll walk you back to your barracks any time you want. It's not safe for a pretty girl to be out alone.'

'Don't be silly. We couldn't be safer. Waddington isn't the middle of Soho, you know. Just one more drink then,' Dianne was still observing the departure of Robyn and Baxter. 'We'd better have a chat with the others or they'll get narky. Look, do you think Morgan knows what he's doing? He strikes me as a bit innocent and she's... well, Robyn can be sort of unpredictable.'

'That's a nice way of putting it.' He gave her a grin. 'Morgan's a big lad, but he won't learn not to play with poisonous snakes until he gets bitten, will he? Come on, I'll take the lead.' He grasped Dianne's hand and began shoving a way through the crowd.

Letting herself be towed along Dianne told him, 'You Australians do go on with a lot of rubbish about kangaroos and snakes, and things. And those bungyip things you were trying to frighten me with, for goodness sake. Who's on earth's going to be scared of something called a bungyip?'

***

Later, Daniel collapsed with a rueful sigh on his bunk bed and, as usual, reviewed the night's events and his progress with Dianne. If he was drunk enough, he could go over every detail of their conversations and see double meanings in everything. Tonight, despite a leisurely and pleasant walk back to the airfield, she had said goodnight with just a slightly lingering peck on the cheek and a squeeze of his hand. When Daniel had opened his mouth to ask for more, Dianne waved a finger in his face.

'We're not sweethearts or anything, remember? This was your idea. Until you come back from... you know. Even then, I might not agree,' she added, recalling her own uncertain side of the deal.

'Then I wish we could get it over with,' he'd said with a growl of frustration.

'It might be sooner than you think,' Dianne said meaningfully, then let go of his hand and set off for the Nissan Hut door. Daniel knew better than to call after her.

Staring at the darkness of his own blacked-out quarters, which Daniel shared with around thirty other NCO air crew, he pondered her last words. He guessed she didn't know anything for sure, but Daniel remembered that with her experience Dianne could see a mission approaching in the way things were being organised.

A door opened and a shuffling noise announced somebody trying to find their way to a bunk. A dull clunk and smothered curse heralded another shin had painfully found a bed-end in the dark, a common occurrence.

'Morgan, is that you?' Daniel whispered, recognising the swearing. 'Where have you been, you scoundrel? I saw you leaving well before us. Did you have a good time?'

Baxter's reply was slurred and halting. 'She's... she's a very nice girl, Daniel. Don't you let anyone else tell you different. She just likes to have a bit of fun, that's all. No harm done.'

'No, of course not.' Daniel figured Baxter sounded too drunk to be teased. 'Can you find your way?'

'As long as bloody Bruce doesn't try to give me directions. Useless sod of a navigator.' The sound of a body thumping heavily onto a bed told Daniel that Baxter had reached someone's bunk, at least.

'Goodnight, Bax.'

Baxter didn't answer, apparently already asleep.

***

Daniel awoke with a flashlight shining painfully into his eyes. Someone was shaking his shoulder and hissing in his ear.

'Sergeant Young? Daniel?'

'Yes—yes, that's me,' Daniel croaked.

'You're off on your mission this morning, sergeant. Get your flying gear and report directly to your own briefing hall. Everything will be brought to you there. Breakfast, parachutes—the lot. Absolute secrecy, sergeant. Don't go straying anywhere else.'

'What? Oh, right... shit. How about the others?' His stomach churning with nerves, Daniel tried to see with his ruined eyesight Baxter or any of the other D-Delta crew billeted in this hut. The darkness only showed him sparkling blotches left by the bright torch. The answer came from further away, in a loud whisper.

'You leave them up to me. Look after yourself. Good luck today, sergeant.'

'Thank you—hey! What the hell is the time?'

'Four in the morning,' the voice faded into the dark. 'The early bird catches the Jerry worm, they say.'

Daniel groaned, 'Bloody hell,' and let his aching eyes close for just a few grateful seconds. Alcohol was still dancing in his blood and his mouth tasted awful. He told the cold air, 'I have to say, it's rude to bomb even Hitler at this time of the morning.'

Eleven

It was only their second mission—cause to be nervous enough. The tense, expectant air coming from the commanding officers told the aircrews this was a special operation in other ways too. The low-level flights, the secrecy, the segregated briefings, it all indicated it was going to be different. Something out of the ordinary, if there was such a thing anymore.

Something dangerous.

***

The briefing came first and while the men waited for it to start, dire warnings were passed like a Chinese whisper about chatting to ground staff later. Outside the armorers and fitters were at the aircraft and labouring in the black, chilly morning.

Eagleton was standing at the front of the hall beside a covered map and talking to the Meteorological Officer. Their conversation was hidden in the murmur of the seated crews. Then, without fanfare Eagleton flipped a sheet back from the map, picked up a pointer and tapped it gently on the wooden frame. Everyone fell immediately silent.

He said, 'We're going to have a shot at the enemy's tanks, trains and U-boats all in one swoop, just to mention a few.' He paused, then used the stick to touch a dark stain on the map. 'This is Augsburg, and it's home to the Mann Diesel factory. You can imagine the logic for yourselves. Knock out the Hun's ability to make decent engines and none of their weapons of war can go anywhere. Diesel motors are a common denominator right across their manufacturing effort. It makes perfect sense and worth the risk. That risk, however, is considerable—let's not pretend otherwise. Augsburg, as you can see, is deep inside Germany. It's a round trip of over twelve hundred miles. No matter what flight plan we give you, it comes close to several large fighter groups. Avoid the Luftwaffe any further and you'll run out of fuel before you get home. I'm sure you'd all prefer to find your way back, am I right?'

The men chuckled weakly at his joke.

Eagleton put the stick under his arm and rubbed his hands together. He smiled at the men encouragingly. 'Quite simply, we expect you to sneak in and back out again before the Jerries know what hit them. That's what all this low-level stuff's been about. During the operation there'll be other RAF sorties being flown to keep the Huns busy. If they do get wind of you coming, with luck the fighters will already be running all over the sky. Anyway, you'll be down near the ground and hiding in the hedgerows.'

Flanders darted up a hand and said without thinking, 'For twelve hundred miles—ah, sir?' He stared at his own hand as if it had betrayed him. A few of the men laughed at him.

'It'll be tough on your pilots, but better than corkscrewing all the way to the English Channel. Any other general questions?'

No one said anything in the brief moment he gave them.

'All right, that's the gist of it. Let's get down to details.' Eagleton was obviously not keen on mulling over the dangers of such a long flight at low altitudes. They were plain enough.

***

As D-Delta roared and jerked forward onto the taxiway, Flanders was hunched at his table sorting out charts. In his mind he could still see his last glimpse of the outside world, the thinnest sliver of sunlight growing in the east.

He asked over the intercom, 'Why are we doing this in broad, bloody daylight?'

'It's all for your benefit,' Wills replied glumly. 'Even I can work out we'd never find the target at night. We need to see where we're going.'

Barrymore said, 'It's a big place, Augsburg. How can you miss it?'

'The factory, you idiot.' Wills sounded pleased to be the knowledgeable one for once. 'We have to pin-point those manufacturing sheds.'

Flanders grumbled, 'Then why don't we just bomb the whole damned lot? I'm sure I could find Augsburg in the dark. We'd be bound to hit the factory at some point.'

Listening in, Daniel asked, 'What about the civilians?'

'Jesus, Danny. They're only Germans,' Flanders seemed surprised. 'Does it matter?'

'It might, if you have to bail out.'

Flanders let out a harsh bark of laughter. 'At the heights we're flying, I left my 'chute in the truck. One less useless thing to carry.'

Branner spoke instantly, his voice sharp. 'You didn't, did you? You bloody better well not have.'

'Just joking, skipper,' Flanders sighed, rubbing at his eyes. He felt suddenly tired. 'You know me, always hoping to get a laugh out of the lads.'

In the cockpit, Branner gave Sexton a glance to share his annoyance. Flanders' sense of humour wasn't welcome right now. At the briefing, the operation had been given an extra ingredient they hadn't trained for. The Lancasters were flying in two loose formations of six. It made the low-level factor much more dangerous with other bombers just off your wingtips. Branner was in no mood for jokes or having to worry about his crew's discipline.

Sexton gave him a rueful grin. 'The lad's will be good, when it counts,' he yelled, giving Branner a thumbs-up in case he didn't hear.

Daniel was sitting in his turret and had his fingers on the triggers as he stared at the inky sky above, as if they were already over Germany and the air was filled with night-fighters. The full reality of their task was coming to him. Nervous butterflies jumped in his stomach and he wished the bombers were airborne. The canvas sling that served as his seat was cutting into his buttocks and he wondered how he was going to last the entire flight without going crazy with the discomfort. At least he was better off than Wills, who despite the plan to fly low was wearing the full, electrically heated suit and was now trapped inside his rear turret like a man crammed into a goldfish bowl.

D-Delta took off and circled twice until the twelve aircraft had formed into their two flights. The six bombers in each formation were in two flat vees of three, one behind the other, like two arrow heads without a shaft. Branner and his crew were in the second vee of the leading flight, on the starboard side. The second group of six Lancasters formed up half a mile behind.

With a signal from the leader, everyone turned on course and climbed to a thousand feet for the flight over England. They were going to drop down to only fifty feet over the Channel.

'No fighter escort either,' Wills said.

'They haven't got the fuel to reach where we'll need them,' Barrymore told him.

Branner said briskly, 'Keep the intercom free of unnecessary chatter.'

'Nose to Pilot, the coast is ahead, skipper,' Barrymore replied, as if it excused him.

'I see it, Geoff.'

The flight leader had signalled a drop down to low level at the same time.

The early morning sunshine was breaking through scattered clouds. The aircrews could see the huge areas of alternating shadow and sunlight move across the ocean. The sea was an inviting blue under the sun, but a cold near-grey colour beneath the clouds. A Royal Navy destroyer was steaming quickly south, her bow-wave visible as a curl of white. It was a raked, business-like looking warship. An Aldis light flashed a signal at them as the bombers passed overhead.

'Good luck, I think,' Sexton said to Branner.

'Looked like it,' Branner nodded. 'The Navy chaps are bloody quick on the signalling. Someone should tell them to slow down for blokes like us.' He added for the benefit of the others who couldn't see, 'We just overflew a Royal Navy frigate and she wished us luck.'

'Ask them to stick around skipper,' Flanders said. 'If we get into trouble on the way back, we can parachute straight down their chimney stack. Save us stuffing around with that bloody dinghy.'

'We won't be getting into any trouble. This mission has been well planned and thought out. If we carry out our orders, we'll be back safe and sound in time for a late supper.'

The silence that followed this was more damning than any comment.

When they crossed the Belgium coast and were over enemy-held territory it was different to the Frisian Island raid. The ground was close and threatening, as if the very soil had been instilled with a German menace.

'Landfall, skipper,' Barrymore called automatically. He had a momentary glimpse of a thin strip of beach before it became green pastures in orderly, hedge-rowed squares.

'We're in the thick of it now, lads,' Branner announced, again for the sake of Baxter and Flanders. 'Keep your eyes peeled—'

'Shit, skipper! There's a flak battery dead ahead.' Barrymore's panicked report made them all jump.

Branner searched the countryside in front and spotted the upright barrels of a dozen guns in their path. Everything happened quickly and his reactions were too slow. It was the same for the Germans, who Branner saw desperately running to their guns in an attempt to open fire. The Lancasters swept over the battery in a roar and were well past before the barrels could be swung down to a low trajectory. If any guns got off a shot at D-Delta's formation, no one on saw it.

'Too slow, you useless bastards,' Wills cried out gleefully as the Germans vanished behind. 'Bloody hell, I should have given them a spray.'

'Save your ammo,' Branner snapped. 'We're going to need it now. That bloody thing wasn't meant to be there. They'll tell every Luftwaffe fighter squadron on the continent about us. We were hoping for a bit more breathing space than this.'

Daniel called in, 'I think I can see muzzle flashes behind us, but no flak—hang on, wait. There it is, way too high. They must be having a go at the second flight without bothering to re-fuse their shells. It'd take a bloody lucky shot.'

'Unlucky, you mean,' Flanders reminded him. 'What'll happen if they shoot down Munk? Do you reckon he'll talk his way out of it?'

The anti-aircraft battery had been prepared for an attack using shells timed to explode at the same altitude as bombers flying much higher. The Lancaster's surprising low level rendered them almost ineffective except for the possibility of a direct hit as the rounds passed through the formations to detonate harmlessly above.

Flanders told them, 'Skipper, we're still on the first dog-leg and ten minutes away from the turn. At least they won't have a clue where we're going.' Their course included false headings to trick the Germans about their target.

'Apart from the next ten minutes,' Barrymore commented wryly.

Branner sounded strained. 'All right, everyone listen closely. Watch for fighters coming in low. At this height they won't even have their bloody wheels up before they can reach us. Gunners, don't waste your ammunition blazing away at long distance. Make sure you've got a decent chance of beating the buggers off. Remember your training. Keep the intercom clear unless you've got something damned important to say.'

The litany rang in Daniel's ears and jarred his nerves. He wished Branner would shut up. He wasn't telling them anything the whole crew wasn't acutely aware of. The Perspex of the turret suddenly seemed to leave him very exposed and with poor timing Daniel remembered the ground crew chief, Sergeant Granger, commenting on how the German fighter pilots liked to use the RAF fuselage roundels for a target.

They flew on in silence until Flanders asked Barrymore for a sighting of the next landmark, his question making everyone start nervously again.

'That looks like the river ahead,' Barrymore squinted at the distant countryside, unwilling to take his eyes off the horizon where he'd be most likely to see incoming fighters.

'The leader's signalling a turn,' Sexton called, seeing an Aldis flash. 'I'd say he's keen to get off this heading too.'

It was only a small comfort as they changed course. The enemy would be expecting tricks and casting their nets wide. As the sun climbed higher it felt like the Lancasters were being unfairly revealed. The aircraft weren't keeping to a strict height anymore but easing up and down with the contours of the land, hugging the ground as closely as they could. It gave the best chance for their mottled green and brown camouflage to blend with the country below and let them escape the attention of fighters searching for them from higher up. The formation had spread apart slightly, and the planes moved independently like boats on the open sea.

It was Daniel who announced their luck had run out.

'Mid-upper to pilot, aircraft on the starboard beam, skipper. Flying on the same course as us. Fighters, no doubt. I can't pick what type yet. I see six.'

'I see them, Danny. Pilot to crew, they'll be pulling ahead for a beam attack or maybe going around the front for a head-on out of the sun. Still can't recognise them, Danny?'

Daniel was cursing the moments during those lectures about aircraft recognition when his mind had drifted, lulled by the lack of urgency. The black silhouettes and cardboard cut-outs had seemed toy-like. Now he worried he'd missed some vital lesson that would cost them dearly today. He also remembered the WAAF and her clear frustration at making the men take her seriously, and he promised the gods to offer her an apology—if he got the chance.

Were they Focke Wulfs or Messerschmitts 109's? Did it even matter?

Yes, Daniel told himself. Because along with machine guns, the ME 109 had a twenty-millimetre cannon mounted in the wings that would make short work of their Lancaster with a single round...

Hang on. So did the damned Focke Wulfs.

Then there was that new ME 109 with a third cannon firing from the nose.

No, it doesn't matter after all, because they're all armed to the bloody teeth.

'They're Focke Wulfs,' Barrymore called as soon as they pulled into his line of sight. 'You can't mistake that fat engine cowling even from this distance.'

Wills asked with mock innocence, 'They're not Yank P-47's coming to help out?'

'Very funny. I wish they were.'

Branner was too absorbed in his flying to bother with yet another reprimand about chatter on the intercom. A village was directly ahead. Would the fighters attack if there was a risk of their firing also hitting the civilians below. Belgian civilians?

They probably wouldn't care.

The bombers thundered over the village, shaking tiles from roofs, terrifying animals and young children, and bringing the villagers out into the open to stare at the retreating aircraft. Some men shook their fists angrily, assuming the bombers to be German—and perhaps not concerned if they weren't.

'Here they come,' Sexton said, the rising excitement in his voice. 'A beam attack from the starboard side. They'll be all yours, Danny.'

'Not bloody yet,' Daniel grunted, his turret hard against the forward stops. He couldn't fire directly ahead or to thirty degrees either side of the nose to prevent him inadvertently shooting his own pilot's cockpit. There was also an interrupter gear to stop him hitting the tail rudders. He was waiting for the Focke Wulfs to draw closer. A beam attack like this suggested the Germans were either very skilled or quite the opposite— inexperienced. It was the hardest aerial shot to achieve with maximum deflection required. However, there was a benefit too. Of their group, only the two starboard-side Lancasters could provide defensive fire from their mid-upper turrets alone. The other RAF aircraft would risk hitting their own.

It was just the two guns out of the formation's combined eighteen.

The fighters came at them as six black streaks against the sky, moving incredibly fast at a closing speed of 450 miles per hour. Daniel opened fire in almost desperate hope, aiming well ahead of the Germans and intending that they fly into his tracers. The Browning machine guns filled his turret with a deafening clatter and the vibration blurred his vision to nearly useless. Empty cartridges spilled over his boots. He sprayed from side to side slightly, allowing for each of the Focke Wulfs as they took their turn strafing the formation before the Germans went howling with supercharged motors across the top of the Lancasters and away to the north. The fighters at close quarters were a momentary vision of streamlined grace and beauty—with deadly sparkling along their wings. Tracers lanced through the air and around the bombers, leaving contrails like paper streamers tossed at a departing ocean liner, an image only glimpsed before the bombers passed on and the white vapours were shredded by the slipstreams.

Torn apart, too, was the leading Lancaster on that starboard side. The Focke Wulfs had concentrated all their attack on the first aircraft and left D-Delta untouched.

It was their flight leader, A-Alpha, and she had shaken violently as the cannon shells tore into the fuselage. More telling were the myriad of holes on the port side flowering outwards as the rounds passed through. Pieces of the plane were spat out into the air. The mid-upper turret vanished in a shower of broken Perspex and a sickening mist of red. Even as the last fighter passed overhead a curl of flame and thick smoke grew from both motors on the bomber's starboard wing. A-Alpha's nose dipped and she headed for the ground.

'They haven't got a fucking chance,' Branner snarled as he instinctively pulled on the control column to clear the oily smoke. Black spots smeared his windscreen. The stricken bomber needed only seconds to drop and plough a fiery scar in the green fields. The plane exploded as it came close to stopping, then detonated hugely as the bomb load ignited. Only Wills saw this, the others feeling the rear of D-Delta shudder from the blast.

'Christ, are we hit?' Flanders called in fright.

'Shut up!' Branner told him. 'No, we're not hit. But that might change in a bloody hurry.'

In the distance, he could see the Focke Wulfs banking smoothly into a turn that would bring them back for another beam attack on the port side. It gave D-Delta some shelter and a brief reprieve, although not for long.

Then the voice of the pilot of B-Bravo, a man called Houghton who had automatically assumed duties as the flight leader, crackled calmly in Branner's headphones.

'This is Flight Leader. Break to port on my call. Don't acknowledge, out.'

It was the end of radio silence, but if everyone acknowledged the order that would give an alert German listener elsewhere an indication of how many aircraft were in the formation.

Houghton ordered the turn at the last nerve-wracking moment. The Lancasters swung raggedly to the left, the formation coming apart as the pilots concentrated on avoiding collisions rather than keeping their positions. The bombers came inside the turning circle of the Focke Wulfs, who tried to compensate. The last three still managed to get off head-on bursts at D-Delta. Rounds zipped around the Lancaster past the cockpit, over the wings and between the engines. Wills chased the Focke Wulfs with a hurried shot, giving up as they vanished behind within moments. He expected to hear Branner snarl at him for wasting bullets.

Instead Branner asked, 'Where are they? Can anyone see the bastards?'

Wills replied, puzzled and disbelieving, 'They kept going. I think they've gone.'

Daniel stared through his Perspex at a point in the sky where the fighters had disappeared. 'Charlie's right, skipper. They kept going west. I reckon they know about the second group and they're going to give them some hell.'

'Are you going to warn them, skipper?'

'That's not my decision to make,' Branner said grimly. 'Besides, we shouldn't assume the Jerries know for sure there's another six of us following. A message like that could give the game away.'

Houghton's voice came on the radio again. 'This is Flight Leader. Come back on course and try to close up. D-Delta come forward if you can.'

The Lancasters were scattered all over the sky and none had any height advantage for catching up. It took some time before they re-established a semblance of the double-V formation, still dodging hills and taller trees in the process. D-Delta took A-Alpha's place in the front row.

'Oh good,' Sexton said. 'Now everyone will think we're the flight leader. Will the skipper get extra pay? It can be his shout at the pub next.'

'That's including the German fighters, you realise?' Barrymore asked unhappily.

'Jesus Christ, that was funny, Barra,' Sexton explained with dry patience. 'It was supposed to make you laugh. By the way, Morgan. Are you still with us?'

Sexton saw Branner jerk with surprise. He hadn't done an intercom check that everybody was unharmed. The chatter had done that anyway—except Baxter was his usual, silent self.

'Radio to skipper, I'm fine. Scared shitless, but I'm fine.'

'Glad to hear it,' Branner said. 'So far, so good.'

***

Dianne was busy preparing for another raid, a part of the diversionary tactics. A group of Wellingtons from Waddington's second squadron were going to bomb a suspected U-boat pen on the French Coast. The Germans were getting clever about these installations and burying them deep beneath thick concrete. It made them harder to destroy. Bomber Command was always trying to attack them before all the defences were in place. It may have been a diversion, but it was still important.

Chalking up the crews to a dozen aircraft, Dianne had her mind busy. She kept an ear open for news of the Augsburg raid. Some of the staff in the Operations Room knew about the mission's destination now—those who wouldn't see the outside world until the bombs had been dropped on both raids.

A WAAF holding a piece of paper went over to Simmons. 'Message from A-Alpha, sir,' she announced, just loud enough so others in the room heard.

Simmons was sitting at his desk, a pile of forms spilling around him. He took her hint and said without looking up, 'All right, share it with all of us, Corporal Aveson.'

'They overflew a new Jerry flak battery as they crossed the French coast, sir. I'm afraid the game's up already.'

It was enough to make Simmons stop his work and look at her grimly. 'Damn, I was hoping they'd get a bit further than the bloody beach before the Germans knew they were coming. No mention of losses?'

'Nothing said here, sir.'

'Very well. We'd better all cross our fingers a bit harder.'

The mood of everyone darkened. It was a tough mission from the beginning and didn't need to get worse. Dianne bit her lip and stared at a blank part of the blackboard for a moment, forcing herself to stay calm.

Damn it, this was exactly why she shouldn't be getting involved with Daniel.

It was too late for that sort of regret now.

The moment passed and the Operations Room filled again with the restrained hubbub of people carrying out their tasks. Phones rang constantly. From beyond the walls, a single aircraft engine started up. It was loud enough to make the taped glass rattle in its pane and everybody had to raise their voice.

Different staff were entering and leaving the room all the time. Many were frequent visitors and didn't rate any attention. Dianne noticed a pair of unfamiliar officers come in and make a point of searching the room for Simmons before going briskly to his desk and bending close to whisper into Simmons' ear. She saw his face show surprise, then sadness, before he nodded agreement at the officers. They left just as quickly. Simmons waited until they had gone from the room, then he stood up and cleared his throat loudly.

'Everyone listen to me, please,' he called with an uncharacteristic insistence. Normally he would need to ask two or three times for their undivided attention. The room went quiet.

'You are all confined to base until further notice. Absolutely no exceptions, I'm afraid, so married personnel who are used to nipping off home for supper later on, don't bother trying. You'll be turned back at the gate. I repeat, until further notice. This has nothing to do with the operations we're running now. Don't assume when the lads come home safely that the restriction is lifted. Understand? Thank you—carry on.'

Simmons sat down again and went back to work, a set to his shoulders and an expression on his face discouraging any attempts to ask him what was happening. It didn't stop the rest of the staff exchanging puzzled comments. Beatrice feigned a need to inspect the blackboard and stand close to Dianne.

'What on earth's that all about, do you think?' she asked out of the side of her mouth.

Dianne shrugged. 'I thought it was just the normal lock-down during operations until he said that last bit.' She kept chalking as she spoke. 'Something's up, that's for sure. Probably another spy scare or perhaps it's just an exercise?'

'Surely not? We've got enough on our plate without messing us around with a bloody training drill. They're not that silly, are they?'

To answer, Dianne raised her eyebrows at Beatrice, who rolled her eyes as she walked away.

Dianne wasn't so calm in her own mind. Something about the intensity of those visiting officers, their whispered orders and the look on Simmons' face, all told Dianne something serious was wrong. This was no training exercise.

As Beatrice had said, as if they didn't have enough to worry about.

***

Barrymore stayed in the nose gunner's position and glumly watched the green fields below speed towards him at a dizzying rate. Over friendly territory it had been fun, even though the novelty had worn off a little. Here on the wrong side of the English Channel it felt more like asking for trouble.

A fanciful part of him imagined the Germans infesting the land as a horde of trolls from a fairy tale, like the savage Huns of old who attacked the civilised Roman Legions and defeated them with sheer, animal ferocity. Somewhere in fiery pits they would be relentlessly hammering out new weapons of war, while they raped and pillaged the terrified locals around them...

Shaking his head, chasing away the fantasy, Barrymore wondered if he should be on the lookout for targets to strafe as they passed, like that flak battery. Barrymore knew Branner would be angry about wasting ammunition on anything except a threatening fighter—but what if it was a legitimate target? A Panzer Tank? Hitler himself, taking a drive in the countryside?

It was hard to know. What about a German fighter on the ground? A Messerschmitt destroyed like that was one less they had to worry about. It would be a "kill" too—Barrymore was almost certain. At least, he thought it was in the RAF. Many of the German aces had amassed high, personal tallies by wiping out half the French air force while they were still parked on their runways. Some of the enemy became aces before they even had a dogfight.

Barrymore realised with a guilty start that the rushing, green fields below were mesmerising him into daydreaming. He keyed his intercom switch.

'Nose to Pilot. Skipper, this feels like the best way to wake up all of Germany and let them know we're coming.'

Flanders replied before Branner did.

'I've got some bad news for you, laddy. That flak battery will have called Hitler direct—not to mention Rommel, Goebbels and every bloody one else. They know we're coming.'

Sexton told him dryly, 'Suits me. Goebbels is little more than a glorified newspaper boy and Rommel's in the army. Not much to worry about there.'

'All right then, the fat bastard who runs the Luftwaffe,' Flanders tried.

'You mean Goering. He was an ace in the last war. He might try and shoot us down himself, except I don't think he could fit in a fighter anymore.'

'Skipper, how did we manage to get such an educated smart-arse for an engineer?'

Branner replied, 'The same way we got an idiot for a navigator. I don't mind a bit of chit-chat to keep you blokes on your toes, but perhaps you should change the subject? Something a little less taxing.'

Flanders said, 'Maybe Daniel could tell us again about his night staying at the pub with Dianne. The real story, not the hogwash he's been giving us.'

'Don't start that again,' Daniel groaned, not interested. After the fighter attack, he needed no incentive or idle gossip to stay alert and watch for more.

'I think I've got some bad news,' Wills called. The tone of his voice put them all back on edge. 'Skipper, I reckon M-Mother is dropping back. I think he's feathered their port outer. They must have taken some hits during that last scrap.'

'Danny, can you see?'

'Wait a second, skipper.' There was a pause and they felt the slight vibration of Daniel rotating his turret. 'Yes, definitely. That motor's gone and she isn't keeping up. We'll leave her behind quick smart if we don't back off.'

'I'm sure Houghton has seen it and we won't be slowing down. You fellows heard the orders about lame ducks.'

They had, during the briefing, and now the full meaning of it struck home. M-Mother was going to be left behind to fend for herself. Alone, her chances of survival were next to nothing. Especially if they still tried to reach the target.

So it was with relief that Wills reported that M-Mother was turning back, his dismay for her fate turning to a tinge of envy. He watched the bomber swing away in a wide arc to reverse course, an Aldis lamp flickering a brief signal.

'She's scrubbed herself, skipper, and going home. The lucky sods, they'll get to notch this one up as a sortie and—Christ. Those bloody fighters are back. Port beam on an opposite course!'

'I see four,' Daniel snapped. 'They're altering course. They've bloody seen us, that's for certain.'

'They won't be the same ones,' Branner told them, fighting an instinctive urge to turn away or corkscrew—do anything except maintain this heading. 'We should wish they were because the buggers would only have half their ammunition.'

Daniel watched the black shapes turn towards them. They were easily closing the gap, but then they veered away. Daniel saw what was happening and reported dismally, 'M-Mother's course has taken them smack into the Jerries. They mustn't have seen them before making the turn. They won't stand a chance on their own against four of the bastards.'

'Forget them and watch out for others,' Branner ordered. 'There's nothing we can do for M-Mother now.'

The distance between the remaining bombers and M-Mother increased quickly. The action, when it took place, was like seeing tiny insects whirling around something larger at the end of a garden.

'I see tracers,' Wills said, and added a moment later. 'And a smoke trail—there's a crash. Someone's gone down. Maybe the boys got a Focke Wulf?'

Daniel could see it too and he didn't share Wills' optimism. The thick scarf of smoke had been low and flat. He guessed it was the Lancaster on fire and struggling briefly to keep her scant altitude before crashing.

Branner didn't have any doubts either. 'Look sharp, lads. We'll be next on their menu and it won't take them long to catch up.'

Again Daniel felt a flash of resentment at Branner's constant warnings. With the loss of two from their flight, things were beginning to feel desperate, and nobody needed bloody reminding to stay alert.

It seemed luck was on D-Delta's side. The Focke Wulfs also saw the approaching second flight of Lancasters and turned their way. It was easier than tail-chasing the remaining four aircraft of the first group.

Daniel reported the thin, glittering lines of tracer coming to life again behind them. Wills offered a final comment.

'You know, I was worried about being in the first flight,' he admitted. 'With the Jerries having full fuel tanks and all their ammo to throw at us. I think I've changed my mind.'

***

No one saw the third attack coming. Flanders had just called to say they were only minutes from entering Germany and that had heightened their senses once more. Still, they were taken by surprise.

The first thing that Barrymore knew about it was seeing a row of eruptions bursting from the soil in front of D-Delta. It was as if the ground was trying to reach up to them. It puzzled him momentarily. Then he noticed the tracers spitting into the earth before the explosions. With a shock, he realised it was cannon shells fired down at them from above, the enemy fighter over-compensating for the bomber's speed.

Then Daniel almost screamed, 'Fighters directly above and behind. Coming out of the sun. Skipper, do something.' He wanted Branner to break to either side. Daniel caught a sinister silhouette crossing the glare of the sun and he fired wildly, squinting into the painfully bright flare that stopped him seeing either his own tracers or any enemy.

The four Lancasters had changed to a diamond pattern formation. The evasive action split them up again, scattering them wide across their own flight path.

'We've got one on our tail,' Wills told them breathlessly. Bursts from his machine guns could be heard over the intercom.

'Then that makes two that I know of,' Daniel called, searching frantically for the other German. He could see Wills' tracers curving out from the tail, hosing from side to side as the fighter weaved in their wake. The enemy was keeping low and Daniel couldn't depress his guns far enough to open fire as well. He only caught glimpses of the Focke Wulf as it appeared briefly on each quarter. Cannon shells from the German sprayed around the bomber in short bursts, coming at Daniel with deceptive, slow speed until they flicked past like lightning. Nothing hit them. Either the pilot was put off by Wills' firing or his own twisting and turning. Daniel had a moment to think the Lancaster was an impossibly large target to miss.

Sexton shouted, 'Danny, on the starboard beam.'

Daniel swung the turret around hard and saw the second fighter coming back. These were Messerschmitt 109s, their pointed noses and arched cowlings unmistakable. This one was attacking F-Freddy to starboard, punching tracers into her fuselage before hedge-hopping that Lancaster to continue on at D-Delta. It appeared to approach at a fantastic speed and Daniel allowed too much for deflection. He opened fire and saw his shots looping well in front. He tried to compensate and went too far, his tracers now trailing the German. A few went close. There was an instant of shooting at it head-on, so short he didn't know if any of his bullets hit, then the Messerschmitt roared over the top close enough that Daniel ducked his head instinctively. He knew better than to try and track the fighter or fire at a receding target. He swung his turret after it anyway in readiness for another attack.

In the heat of the moment, Daniel hadn't thought of anything else except to shoot at the fighter. Now he worried if they had been hit.

Glancing down into the fuselage he saw bars of sunlight like he'd seen in the crashed Wellington weeks before. Several rounds from the fighter had passed through D-Delta.

'Skipper, we took some hits. I'm all right. Gun seems fine.' He waggled the turret to make sure.

'Check in, everyone,' Branner said.

'I'm too fucking busy,' Wills snarled. They heard more firing.

'Charlie, if you can't hit the bastard, give up and save your ammo. We're going to need those bullets.'

Wills let go of the triggers and watched the Messerschmitt warily. The German had stopped firing too but continued to follow them at a teasing range.

The rest of the crew reported they were alive and unhurt. Flanders sounded shaken. A bullet had passed over the top of his navigation desk. He could almost stretch his arms wide and plug his fingers into the holes on each side of the fuselage.

'I think this bloody Jerry's run out of ammo,' Wills said carefully.

'Exactly. He just wants you to waste yours,' Branner replied with vindication.

The countryside was hilly and dotted with small forests. Branner was twisting D-Delta among them, still hugging the ground as much as he dared. At least the fighters couldn't get beneath them.

'I can't see where the other bugger's gone,' Daniel called, swinging his turret around. He had a crawling feeling on his back, expecting the fighter to jump them again.

Barrymore said hopefully, 'He probably had a go at all of us, one after the other, and he's run out of bullets too.' He was frustrated, despite his fear. Everything seemed to be happening to the rest of the plane and hearing it all on the intercom grated at his nerves. He longed to shoot at something—he was sure it would release the tension gripping his whole body. None of the enemy had come into his field of fire.

Then again, he figured that if he could aim at a Messerschmitt, the fighter could shoot back directly at him, and that wasn't so appealing.

D-Delta crested a rise and entered a large, shallow valley of farmland. Several miles to the south another Lancaster flew out of the hills. Then a third appeared on the opposite side.

Daniel told them, 'We've got a friendly to port and one to starboard. I can't see who they are yet.'

'Anybody see a fourth?' Branner asked. 'Charlie?'

'Hang on, that Jerry's just scarpering,' Wills answered, watching the ME109 bank away with an insolent disregard for any further attempts to shoot it down. 'No, skipper. I can't see anyone else.'

A minute later the ridge of hills was far behind and there was no sighting of the fourth Lancaster. There was a chance she had been pushed a long way off course and was continuing towards the target alone or had suffered enough damage to force them back.

There were no signs of the second flight either.

Flanders had recovered from his fright and told them laconically, 'If anyone's interested, according to my calculations during that little hoo-ha back there we crossed into Germany. Now the fun should really begin.'

'Confirm our course?' Branner asked.

'Should still be zero-eight-zero, skipper. A straight run to the target from here. If they want to guess where we're going, they'll get it right now.'

'Yes, it won't be much of a mystery anymore,' Branner nodded to himself as he spoke.

***

Simmons' phone rang and he picked it up absently, his mind on too many things. Dianne was watching him, and he caught her eye as he hung up. He gestured Dianne closer with a small wave that surprised her with its familiarity.

'Yes, sir?' She moved behind him to look at his paperwork.

He spoke quietly. 'I've been asked to send you to the Sergeant's Mess for a while. Sergeant DeCourt's there. She's been involved in a little unpleasantness and she's asked for you. I said we can do without you for a short while.'

Dianne was startled. 'What sort of unpleasantness—ah, sir?'

'Can't say, I'm afraid. You'll probably know more than me soon enough.'

'Okay, if you're fine with it, sir—' Dianne was nonplussed. It was so unusual. 'So, how long have I got?' She resented being dispensable from the Operations Room. Simmons put her mind at rest.

'Thirty minutes at the most. I'll need you here. Nothing is more important than what we're doing and anything else can wait, I'm sure. We have work to do.'

'All right, sir. I'll be as quick as I can. Ah... sorry about this.'

He gestured a dismissal. 'Not your fault, sergeant.'

Dianne hurried across the base towards the Sergeant's Mess, her mind running wild with possibilities. Alarmingly, a Military Policeman stood outside the Mess, guarding the occupant—which had to be Susan.

'I'm Sergeant Parker,' she told him, although he wasn't attempting to stop her. 'Can I go inside?'

He nodded quickly. 'She's expecting you, sergeant.'

The mess was empty except for Susan, who sat at a table with an overflowing ashtray in front of her. Another cigarette smouldered between her fingers.

'Hello,' she said in strange tone to Dianne. 'Sorry to drag you away from the Op's.'

'Susan, what on earth's going on?' Dianne sat next to her.

'It's a bit of a story,' Susan gave her a strained smile. 'You know that girl, Robyn, the Warrant Officer's daughter? She didn't turn up at the parachute shed this morning, so eventually I had to go looking for her. It was quite some time before I had a chance, what with the two missions going on and everything. Well, I certainly found her.' She emphasised this by mashing her cigarette into the ashtray.

'Is she in trouble?'

'You could say that. She's dead. I found her completely by accident, where they're building that new tractor shed behind our quarters. Something caught my eye and I went over and... there she was.'

For a long second Dianne could do nothing except stare at her friend. 'My God, what happened to her?'

'She's been killed—murdered, I mean, apparently murdered. That's what the MP's are saying. Strangled, in fact.'

Scrabbling for a smoke from Susan's packet on the table, Dianne used the time to recover from the shock. 'I don't believe it... this is horrible. God, you're very calm, I must say,' she said, lighting up with trembling fingers.

'Well, I've had a bit more time to think it over. Besides, we've all seen worse in the last year or so, haven't we? With the Blitz and things. I have, anyway.' Susan was avoiding her eyes.

Something dawned on Dianne. 'Bloody hell, do they suspect you?'

Susan looked confused for a second. 'Oh! You mean the thug outside? Goodness, no. He's supposed to protect me in case the killer tries to get me as well. Someone said they think he was hoping to bury poor Robyn in the foundations of the new shed. Covered by concrete forever, I suppose. I might have even disturbed him in the act.' Susan lowered her voice. 'You know, I didn't see anyone, but it's nice to worried over.'

'Susan, are you mad? Plainly, there are more urgent things to—'

'All right, all right. Just teasing.'

'How the hell can you tease at a time like this?'

'Well, what else can you do? Besides, you've heard the chaps in the pub joke all the time about losing mates. It goes on all the time.'

The news crowded in at her and Dianne was exasperated, unable to think of an argument. She took a deep breath and tried to adopt Susan's cool attitude. 'All right, then... look, ah—all right. I hate to sound a bit mean, but what's this got to do with me? What am I doing here?'

'Oh, you're just my shoulder to cry on. The men were convinced I couldn't endure such a traumatic experience without going to pieces. They sort of stood around and waited for me to start crying. When I didn't, they decided it was just stiff-upper-lip stuff and offered to run me home to my mother where I could sob in privacy. I think it might be standard RAF procedure for troublesome females—ship 'em back to dear old mum.'

'All the way to Wales?'

'No one bothered to ask me where she lived,' Susan said dryly. 'Anyway, I refused. Then, just to shut them up, I asked for you. I thought you might like a cup of tea and a fag.'

Dianne nodded jerkily, puffing hard on her cigarette, her mind still racing. 'I wish I could be as calm about it as you. I suppose this is why everyone's confined to base—no exceptions. Simmons was quite adamant about that and had us all puzzled.'

'Have they? Not surprising... still, it makes you really want to go to the pub and get sozzled, doesn't it?' Susan's eye drifted to the unattended bar behind them.

'Don't even dream of it,' Dianne said warningly.

'Of course not,' Susan said unconvincingly. 'How long have you got?'

'Time for another cuppa. That's about it. Simmons said half an hour.'

Susan stood up and went towards an urn in the corner. She said over her shoulder, 'On your way back, can you find Warrant Officer Giles for me? Ask Julie to come and rescue me? I need to get back to work, not sit around here twiddling my thumbs.'

'I'll try.'

Dianne watched her friend's back as she busied herself making the teas. Unseen by Susan, she shook her head in disbelief.

***

'Welcome to sunny Augsburg,' Branner told them, eyeing the city stretched out in front of the bombers. Wet streets below shone in the sunshine that had followed showers. With the town in sight they had changed to a long, line-astern formation with D-Delta second. Ahead and in the distance Houghton's B-Bravo weaved above the houses. As if speeding over the countryside at minimum height hadn't been dizzying enough, hurtling across the rooftops was terrifying. Branner was even climbing, then dropping again, to accommodate the taller chimney stacks.

Three bombers from their flight still survived. For them, the low-level flight plan had worked so far, the Lancaster's camouflage hiding them against the darker earth from fighters they regular spotted searching for them. It certainly helped with the anti-aircraft batteries. The few that had reacted fast and fired off shots had been wildly inaccurate and unprepared for the fleeting opportunity.

With every extra mile the raiders journeyed into Germany, it felt like they were pressing their luck impossibly.

Houghton came over the radio into Branner's headphones. They were so close to their destination that secrecy didn't matter now.

'Flight Leader here. I've spotted the river and I'm turning north. We seem to be on the right track. Good luck, everyone.'

The aircraft would identify and bomb the target separately. If everyone blindly attacked whatever Houghton bombed and he was wrong, the mission would be an utter failure. Each Lancaster was held responsible for hitting the diesel plant.

Branner acknowledged Houghton's call, then said, 'Bombardier, we're in your hands now. What do you see, Barra?'

'I've got the river too, skipper. Looking for an arched bridge—there it is, well to the north. We've done well, coming in on this side of the town. Follow the water and we should spot the stacks of the factory within a minute.'

'All right. I'm opening the bomb-bay doors now. Keep sharp, everyone.'

Daniel was straining to look in all directions at once, swinging his turret ceaselessly. They were so low that the smog of the city had cut down visibility, hiding them. It obscured approaching fighters too. Like Branner earlier, he wondered if the Luftwaffe fighters would shoot them down over the city, risking civilian casualties below.

'We did over London, you idiot,' he reminded himself. These few minutes over Augsburg wouldn't offer a reprieve from the Messerschmitts and Focke Wulfs.

As bomb-aimer, Barrymore was effectively steering the aircraft now, telling Branner where to go. While they easily traced the river through the congested city he had little to say, but coming on to the target would require precise manoeuvring. Nervousness ate at his stomach. He was lying down in the very nose of the Lancaster. He felt twice as vulnerable even though the forward turret where he'd been for most of the flight was only a foot or so above him.

'Don't stuff this up, Barra,' Flanders said quickly, risking a rebuke from Branner. 'I don't want to have to come back. The natives are definitely not very friendly.'

'Shut up, Bruce,' Branner said, predictably. 'Geoff, what's happening?'

'I think I see the stacks ahead, skipper. B-Bravo is dead in line. Hell, is that tracer? They must have ack-ack around the bloody factory itself.'

'I see it,' Branner said grimly. He was trying hard not to simply follow B-Bravo. Everyone had to be certain they bombed the right building. 'And there's B-Bravo's drop. Hopefully they've already done the job for us.' The explosions ahead were boiling clouds of black smoke after a flash of angry red.

D-Delta flew along the river, so low her slipstream frothed the water. A barge in front of them laden with timber turned toward the shore, afraid of the approaching bomber. An instant later it was gone, flashing behind them. Branner shook away a crazy idea to fly under the arched bridge— it was impossible. He lifted the aircraft over it with inches to spare. Everyone heard Barrymore swear in fear. When he spoke next, his voice was rough.

'Ah, skipper, that's got to be the target. Everything fits into place. I say come left about five degrees for a second, then we'll swing back to fly straight along the roof lines.'

Branner did as he was told without acknowledging. The intercom was to be kept perfectly clear for any instructions from Barrymore. The long days of training and now the hazardous trip to the city all hinged on the next thirty seconds. It seemed almost unfair, or somehow ridiculous, that the actual bombing of the target was just a brief moment amongst a much greater, drawn-out effort.

'Come left...' Barrymore said slowly, squinting through a bombsight. 'Left as much again... hold it there, please.'

The rising smoke from B-Bravo's bombs raced towards them. The cluster of larger, factory buildings was a comforting indication it was the diesel plant. Suddenly tracer curled lazily up at them from several gun emplacements, all of it flicking past the starboard wing and Branner only just stopped himself from swinging the bomber away. Then D-Delta lifted sharply, and he feared they'd been hit until Barrymore's excited call registered in his mind.

'Bombs away, skipper. Let's get the hell out of here.'

D-Delta banked sharply to port, the tracers chasing futilely after her. When the German gunners gave up, the range quickly beyond them, Branner came back to a wide starboard turn that was the agreed flight plan. He looked ahead for B-Bravo and couldn't see Houghton's plane. The whole crew was waiting on Wills' report.

It was unexpectedly subdued.

'Looks good, skipper,' Wills called, so calm that some of them wondered if he was describing the bomb strikes at all. 'I say we bracketed the main building, as we wanted. B-Bravo was close too.'

Wills was disappointed that the factory and everything around hadn't vanished in some cataclysmic eruption. It seemed only fitting after the tension and fear of the past hours. Instead, the bombs appeared to detonate on target, but even these were partially hidden by the smoke from B-Bravo's attack. It was anti-climactic.

'Are you sure?' Branner asked, suspicious that Wills wasn't his usual exuberant self.

'No doubt about it, skipper. We hit the largest shed.'

Flanders put in, 'Well, I'm glad to hear it.'

'I'd rather hear a course for home from you,' Branner replied. 'What about it?'

'Course is two hundred exactly, skipper. A straight bee-line for home and a pint of lager.'

The wide turn after the bomb run had brought them close to an opposite heading and they could watch the attack of the last Lancaster, F-Freddy. Sexton nudged Branner to get his attention, pointing across. He mouthed, "Good luck" without using the intercom.

F-Freddy bore in with what appeared stoic determination. The last minutes of a bomb run where the aircraft couldn't deviate from the flight path were by far the most dangerous. The tracer rose up to greet the Lancaster. From the viewpoint of D-Delta it seemed to surround the bomber and Branner, holding his breath, told himself it always looked worse than it was. Then F-Freddy jerked slightly, and a thin streamer of smoke appeared from one wing. She kept going and the black shapes of her bombs tumbled out to fall into the existing fires. The timed fuse delays did their job, the bombs exploding as F-Freddy pulled away. Her profile changed as she altered course to follow D-Delta. The burning in her wing lessened but didn't stop altogether.

'F-Freddy took a hit,' Wills reported glumly.

'We saw it, Charlie. Fingers crossed for her. It might not be too bad if they can get the damage under control. All right, everyone. The job's only half over. Now we have to get home.'

It was hard to believe. With the bombs dropped, it felt like the job was finished. Now they had the journey home to survive.

***

They didn't catch up with B-Bravo. Although they were all on the same course and heading for home, it didn't need much for the aircraft to lose contact permanently after taking evasive action. Staying at the tree-top heights made it more unlikely they would see each other.

In the meantime, the stricken F-Freddy fell slowly behind. Wills offered hopeful updates on her position, but soon the third bomber faded into the distance. There was still no sign of the second flight. Each of the Lancasters were on their own now.

'All right, let's do the rounds,' Branner said, sensing a dangerous lull in the silent intercom. 'Morgan, are you awake?'

'Wide awake, skipper. Nothing on the radio to worry us.'

'Bruce? Do we know where we are?'

'In deep shit, I'd say, skipper. Which means we're on course in the middle of Germany.'

For once, Branner didn't rebuke him. 'Gunners? How's your ammo? Nose to tail, you first, Barra.'

'I haven't fired a bloody shot,' Barrymore replied unhappily.

Flanders said, 'That's because the Luftwaffe waits in fear of when you do. Dead-eye Dick Barrymore, they call you.'

'As usual, shut the hell up, Bruce,' Branner said automatically. 'Daniel, what's your situation?'

'Plenty of ammo yet, skipper. I've got a numb arse from this bloody canvas seat though.'

'Charlie? You were blazing away for some time back there. What have you got left?'

Wills sounded offended. 'I nearly got him several times. I've still got a bit to shoot off.'

'Make sure it lasts. We've got a long way to go. Dave, how are you going?' Branner asked Sexton, although he was right beside him.

'I'm fine, skipper. The old girl is flying beautifully. We can do the trip twice, if you like.'

This brought a chorus of abuse.

Branner didn't talk about himself. If he had, he could have told them about his sore back from the uncomfortable seat and hardened parachute under his rump. He'd been clenching the control column too tightly and his wrists and fingers ached. A trembling anxiety wouldn't leave him, gnawing at his gut. All manner of problems, disasters and their possible solutions all chattered loudly inside his head at the same time, driving him crazy, when he was trying to concentrate on the hazardous low flying.

Nobody could take over the piloting and give him a break. No one else knew how to fly the plane, although both Sexton and Flanders had some flying experience before failing to make the grade as pilots. In an emergency, they might cope. There was no co-pilot seat in the Lancasters. Everyone had their task and Branner's was to pilot the plane. It was accepted that even on the furthest missions, he was stuck in the driver's seat for however long it took.

'A pair of fighters to port, skipper,' Barrymore called with dread. 'At about ten o'clock. Turning our way—they've seen us, the bastards.'

'Stand by, everyone,' Branner said. 'Charlie, remember what I said.'

There was a click as Wills turned on his microphone to reply, then apparently thought better of it.

The fighters were Focke Wulfs again. They came at D-Delta in a wide, banking turn with their wingtips almost touching, a perfect display of formation flying and an ominous sign these were no novice pilots. The Lancaster shook as the last of their strafing attack ran across the fuselage. In his turret, Daniel was hard against the stops, waiting for them to come into his field of fire. He tried to lift himself up as the aircraft underneath him filled with an awful noise, like a giant was running amok with a steel pipe and smashing it against the metalwork.

The Fock Wulfs howled over the top, uncaring of Barrymore's tracers spraying wide. By the time Daniel had recovered from his fright, the fighters were too far away for a shot.

'Come on, where the hell have they gone, somebody?' Branner shouted.

'Swinging to the west to come back again,' Daniel told him, watching the two specks streak against the background.

Branner banked D-Delta to port, putting more distance between them and the Focke Wulfs. When they eventually caught up it would bring two of the Lancaster's guns to bear.

Wills gave everyone a running commentary, his voice tight.

'They're swinging in behind us, skipper... staying higher. Danny, you take the one on the left. Jesus, these bastards are fast.'

He opened fire a second before Daniel, who wanted to be sure not to waste any ammunition. Two streams of tracer looped out of the Lancaster towards the Focke Wulfs. It was good shooting, not accurate enough to cause any damage, but it split the Germans apart and their co-ordinated attack didn't happen. Both shot at D-Delta from maximum range and didn't hit, although Wills was frightened enough to pull his feet up as a line of cannon shells fell away directly beneath him.

The fighters stopped firing and appeared to hover undecided behind D-Delta, biding their time. Abruptly they peeled away and vanished against the dark background of the country.

'We scared them off,' Wills declared triumphantly. 'I reckon I hit one of them. Did you see it, Danny?'

Daniel replied calmly, 'No, they ran out of ammo, Charlie. They've only pissed off to re-arm and refuel so they've got a chance to catch us again—or anyone following us.'

'Well, I saw a hit. You were watching the wrong one—'

'We got hit ourselves,' Branner broke in grimly. 'Dave's got trouble here. What can anyone else see? Report in, everyone.'

One by one they confirmed each man was alive and unharmed. Baxter reported, 'Navigation aids are gone, skipper. No damage here, so it must be somewhere else.'

Daniel went last. 'We took a lot of rounds below me, skipper. It's hard to see how bad from the turret. Want me to have a look?'

'No. Bruce, you go.'

There was the smallest hesitation before Flanders replied, 'On my way, skipper.'

He crawled out of his navigation space and into the main fuselage. The sight that met him made Flanders groan.

A dozen cannon shells had ripped through the body of the Lancaster. Some were almost neat punctures in the metal skin with corresponding exit holes on the other side. In several places the fuselage had been torn open like a sardine can, making holes big enough to put a man's fist through. Smashed, electrical wiring flapped crazily in the wind now howling through the plane and a long smear of oily liquid ran down one side, coming from shattered pipes. He saw the wooden seat for the rudimentary toilet in the middle of the aircraft had been blown off. It was a down pipe straight out of the bomber and was now adding to the rush of air stream whirling through.

There was nowhere to plug into the intercom. Flanders had no choice but to struggle back to his seat.

He reported breathlessly, 'Hard to say, skipper. They've made a right mess under Danny's feet. Some cabling is all fucked up and there's a lot of oil coming from somewhere.'

'Stay calm, everyone,' Branner said. 'We're still flying fine. Oil, you say? We must have lost some hydraulics, probably in the undercarriage. Danny and Charlie, your turrets are still okay?'

They both tried to move and experienced the same thing.

'Shit, things are getting a bit sluggish,' Daniel answered. 'That's our bloody hydraulic oil too, or part of it.'

Branner ordered, 'Bruce, go back and see if you can't crimp the broken ends closed. I don't know if it'll do any good, but it's worth a try.' Out of the corner of his eye he saw Sexton shake his head. He shrugged back and didn't change his mind. D-Delta was starting to fly lop-sided and he motioned about this with his hand at Sexton.

Sexton told him, 'I daren't trim any of the fuel between the tanks, skipper. What if they're holed? We could lose half of it before we realise and not get home.'

'Fair enough. I'm going to be bloody left-handed by the time we land.'

Back in the fuselage, Flanders found the leaking pipes and was trying to bend them over completely to crush them closed. He was getting his hands and face covered with the thin, strong-smelling oil. After a minute, Flanders didn't seem to mind. At least he was trying to do something to save the aircraft, rather than just sit at his navigator's table and wait for it all to end somehow. It didn't matter how filthy he got. In fact, he felt kind of heroic and thought it had to be good for a few pints out of the lads when they got back. The girls would be impressed too. It was a shame he didn't have a small wound to go with it. Something painless with a bit of blood for dramatic effect.

A tiny voice of reason reminded him the hydraulic fluid was made partly of ether. The fumes were making him silly. Christ, before long he would be singing bawdy songs over the intercom.

Flanders had the presence of mind to clamber back to his seat once more. In the process, the fuselage had stretched out impossibly before him for a second, then the hump of the wing spar was an almost insurmountable obstacle. He flicked on his microphone and mumbled that he was back.

'How did you go, Bruce?' Branner asked.

'I don't know, skipper.' Flanders' voice rang strangely inside his own head. 'I tried. Now I'm pissed as an owl from the bloody ether, I think.'

'Lucky sod,' Wills said.

'Try and stay awake,' Branner said. 'Use some oxygen.' He didn't really care. They were flying a straight course home and Flanders could take his time to recover.

Daniel thought it was best to use the turret's hydraulics as little as possible and conserve any movement for when it was absolutely needed. As a result, he scanned the sky by twisting and turning in his seat. It was difficult. His neck and back ached as he wrenched against complaining muscles.

He didn't like their chances if they were found by any more fighters. Otherwise D-Delta was still flying well. That was all that mattered.

***

'That port inner is getting damned hot, skipper. Any higher and I'll have to shut it down. It might catch fire.' Sexton didn't want to admit the gauges had been climbing slowly for the past hour. Branner had enough on his mind. 'Something's finally given up the ghost, I'd say.'

'Let's keep it as long as we can,' Branner said. 'Don't take your eyes off it.'

It was only a few minutes before Sexton said, 'I'm getting nervous as hell, skipper. We should stop it.'

They heard Branner's sigh. 'All right, close it down and feather it. We can get by on three.'

"Feathering" meant changing the pitch of the propellor blades until they presented the least resistance to the airflow, edge-on towards the front. If the engine was free, the propeller could still spin slightly with the slipstream, but this one was seizing up. It was a forlorn sight, looking out the window and seeing the blades unmoving. Branner climbed a few feet higher too, just in case. The bomber wasn't so responsive with less speed and power. A new vibration shuddered through D-Delta. Nothing obvious caused it and Branner mentally shrugged with a false bravado.

'Cheer up, lads,' Daniel tried to be sincere. 'We must be back over Belgium by now. The Channel can't be far away.'

'What do you say, Bruce?' Branner said.

Flanders' reply was thick, like he was ill. 'About forty minutes to the coast, I say. Shit, I feel crook. I'm never going to drink again.'

In the tail turret, Wills was talking to himself.

'Forty minutes... forty bloody minutes. Only thirty-nine, if I say it sixty times over...' He stopped himself. Like Daniel, he resisted the urge to use his turret's hydraulics to search around. They had spotted several aircraft too far away to identify and it had provided for some anxious moments. Nothing had come closer.

**

Dianne slipped back into the Operations Room, hoping in vain no one had noticed her absence. Curious gazes came her way from all over the room. Simmons gestured her to his desk.

'Everything all right, Sergeant Parker?' he asked quietly.

'It's a rotten mess, if you really want to know, Wingco,' she whispered back. 'Do you know what's happened?'

'Just the gist of it—no details.'

'I'm afraid I can't tell you much more,' she lied, because it felt the wiser thing to do. 'I was just a shoulder to cry on. It's a bad business.'

'Yes, well...' he looked disappointed. 'Best to keep it to yourself for the moment.'

'Yes, sir.'

'Go back to your post, please. Things are getting busy again.'

Dianne went to her desk and wasn't surprised to find Beatrice standing beside her within seconds. Dianne got in first.

'What's been happening, Beatrice?' Dianne asked.

'What? Oh—ah, it looks like the Augsburg lads are on their way home. They took a pasting, I'm afraid. Houghton's in command and on his own. He isn't saying if they got scattered or he's the only one left.' She shrugged at this. 'It pays to be careful.'

Dianne nodded calmly, although the news turned her stomach upside-down. It was true, too, that Houghton had no need to tell the world and possibly the Germans, even with encoded messages, how many Lancasters were still in the air. 'What about the rest?'

'You wouldn't believe it. Most of the diversionary raids have come back untouched. It's like the ones we wanted the Jerries to pay attention to got ignored, while the raid that was supposed to sneak past everyone got a bloody nose. It just goes to show, doesn't it?'

'I suppose so.'

'So, where did you run off to?' Beatrice dared.

Dianne looked grim. 'Can't say, I'm sorry. Simmons is watching like a hawk, making sure I don't.'

Beatrice raised her eyebrows. 'Sounds very interesting.'

'It's a bit more than that,' Dianne said, before she stopped herself. 'Enough chatter. When's Houghton due back? Have they amended it?'

'No, the flight plan hasn't been changed. What we don't know is how many Lancasters are using it,' Beatrice said wryly, gesturing at the blackboard. 'In about thirty minutes, the Observer Corps will spot them. They'll be almost over the Channel then.'

***

'There's the Channel,' Barrymore said. He was still in the forward turret and his fingers were nearly locked on the handles of the guns even though he hadn't had another chance to fire them. It had been hours since the last attack from the two Focke Wulfs that had done so much damage. Neither of the rear turrets could move, the hydraulic fluid gone. Daniel and Wills were still at their places on the lookout and in the slim hope that if more fighters came, the Germans would obligingly fly straight in front of their sights.

'Don't get lazy now,' Branner said. 'If the Jerries have ever figured out the one place to catch us napping, it's here.'

No one argued. Even Branner stared at the approaching strip of ocean glinting in the afternoon sun like it was a finishing line they only needed to cross. The trip over the Channel was as dangerous as the rest of the flight, but there was something symbolic about escaping the coast and enemy-held territory.

D-Delta roared across the beach at less than fifty feet, kicking up a spray of sand then a mist of white foam from the breaking waves close to the shore. A flock of seagulls erupted from the low dunes and miraculously avoided the speeding bomber, although a couple came so close that Barrymore cried out and threw up a hand at the fleeting shapes in front of him.

'All right, the last lap,' Branner said through a deep breath. 'Barra, we're going to need some landmarks quick-smart when we reach the other side. We haven't got the fuel to get lost over England.'

'Where are we going, skipper?' Flanders asked, sounding better.

Branner opened his mouth to answer "home", then changed his mind. Without hydraulics they probably didn't have an undercarriage to lower. That meant a belly-landing on a grass strip and although they could try that beside the main runway at Waddington, the emergency fields closer to the coast at Mablethorpe were a safer option.

'Let's find Mablethorpe,' Branner decided. 'Or whatever comes first. We'll work out where we are exactly, first. When we get there, we'll find out if we've got any legs to stand on.'

It reminded everyone that they were far from safe. A risky wheels-up landing might be needed yet.

'Oh shit, look,' Sexton said, his tone adding to their dismay. 'Dead ahead and high.'

Three menacing shapes were dropping down from the sun. They were in a perfect formation, very disciplined and no doubt would make short work of the crippled Lancaster.

'What the hell are they?' Branner lifted a hand to squint between his fingers. 'Shut up, whoever that is!'

Someone had been swearing monotonously, probably one of the rear gunners trying to get their seized turrets to move.

'Messerschmitts, if anything,' Sexton said. 'They're not Focke Wulfs. I reckon they're coming back from a sweep over Blighty. Hopefully they used all their ammo over there.'

'It doesn't bloody look like it,' Branner said.

'What are we going to do?'

'Not much. Jink a bit, but I want to keep heading for England as fast as we can. Maybe they'll make one pass and piss off home.'

'Fingers crossed about that.'

In the nose turret, Barrymore was lining up his twin Brownings and waiting to open fire. The glare was making his eyes water. He still had plenty of ammunition and they were close to England. He planned to fill the sky with as many bullets as he could and hope they had some effect.

The fighters were abruptly in range.

He pulled the triggers and saw his tracers cut between the attackers, so close he thought he'd scored some hits, and he stifled a savage cry. It only lasted a second. The fighters broke apart like frightened minnows and Barrymore's shooting was rendered useless as he couldn't decide which plane to track. Two went either side, while the third barrel-rolled straight over the cockpit.

Daniel yelled into the intercom, his voice cracking, 'Jesus Christ! They're fucking Spitfires. You bloody idiot, Barra, stop firing!'

Away from the sunlight and with the graceful roll above him, the distinctive shape of the Spitfire's wings shocked Daniel. He didn't need the blue and red roundels that were suddenly so obvious. His call was too late, and Barrymore had already lost sight of his targets anyway.

'What...? They're what?' Barrymore choked.

A cultured voice, clipped with anger, burst into Branner's headset from the VHF radio.

'Cease fire, you fools! Are you blind?'

Branner gave Sexton a stricken look. What was he supposed to do? Apologise, for God's sake? Then his expression went cold and he flicked on his own radio. He spoke in the same way.

'Sorry about that, but you should try damned-well identifying yourselves before you come out of the sun like that. We've had a bit of a rough trot today.'

There was a silence, then the fighter pilot replied, 'This is Blue Flight Leader, you should be clear for the rest of the trip. We'll keep an eye on you.'

'Thank you, Blue Leader. We appreciate that.' Branner turned the radio off, pulled his mask down and yelled at Sexton, 'Bloody upper-class twit.'

The rest of the flight was uneventful. In the tail gun, Charlie Wills almost relaxed watching the Spitfires flying higher and weaving to and fro behind them. There was nothing else he could do. Barrymore called out a quiet hurray as they crossed the English coast ten minutes later—his attempts to shoot down a friendly fighter already forgotten in his relief—and he spotted a lighthouse and small village that he recognised. He reported it to Flanders, who instructed Branner to follow the coastline south, telling him that the long emergency airstrip at Mablethorpe would soon be easy to see.

A few minutes later Mablethorpe was a wide and inviting green strip below that cut through several fields and fences.

'All right, Dave,' Branner said reluctantly, after radioing in their intention to land. 'Let's try the undercarriage.'

Sexton gave him a thumbs-up and a smile, then pulled the lever. The grin faded when nothing happened. Usually the increased drag of the lowering wheels was evident straight away. He tried the control twice more, then shook his head at Branner.

Branner called, 'Daniel, did anything happen back there?'

'That bloody oil squirted out everywhere for a second, skipper. Then it stopped.'

Branner swore. 'Okay—everyone listen. We're going to do a wheels-up landing on the grass. It might get pretty rough, but they happen every day and the crews usually get to have a pint afterwards. Everybody stay strapped in. Geoff, you'd better get back aft somewhere and get a good grip.'

'Right, skipper.' Barrymore wasn't happy. He might get bounced around the inside of the fuselage if the landing went badly. However, his chances securely strapped in his gunner's seat in the nose of the Lancaster were worse.

'No point in hanging around,' Branner said. 'Let's put her down.' He called to the airbase that they had no landing gear.

He brought D-Delta in by flying a long, shallow approach to the grass strip. It made the tension draw out unbearably. The approved method was to touch down at a speed as close to stalling as possible to lessen the impact. Poor judgment could see the aircraft fall out of the air and slam to the earth.

'You're doing great, skipper,' Sexton told him, staring at the flat grass rising to meet them.

'Kill everything the moment we hit,' Branner said through clenched teeth.

Sexton put his hand on the throttles in readiness.

For an eternity D-Delta seemed to hesitate above the runway, so long that Branner wondered if they had actually touched down and the whole thing was much easier than he'd thought. Then the propeller on the starboard inner engine hit the dirt and tripped the Lancaster to the ground. She landed almost straight, jarring everything inside. Glass smashed somewhere and one of the motors screamed briefly as the propeller broke away before Sexton hauled the throttles closed so hard he lost his grip when the levers struck the stops. Branner fought the controls although he had no influence now—but he couldn't simply let go. The noise was surprisingly innocuous, a juddering, grating sound like someone pushing a giant shovel through gravel, nothing like the howl of tortured metal that occurred when aircraft crash-landed on bitumen. D-Delta was sliding smoothly across the long grass as they'd hoped and expected.

The Lancaster finally came to a graceful halt angled across the runway. The following silence was stunning in its own odd way.

Branner broke it by ripping off his mask and yelling over his shoulder, 'Get the hell out, everyone. We could be on bloody fire for all we know.'

This galvanised everybody. Daniel dropped awkwardly out of his turret and was the first to reach the rear hatch which he yanked open too hard and it rebounded off its hinges, catching him a painful blow. At the last moment, he thought of Wills and stepped back from the inviting exit to crawl to the rear of Lancaster. He hammered ineffectually on the doors of the tail turret with his hands.

'Charlie? Are you alright?'

A cursing came from the other side, then a gap appeared of about an inch.

'The bloody thing's stuck, Danny. Don't go! Give us a hand, will you?' Wills sounded panicked.

'I'm not going anywhere. On my count, ready?' Daniel curled his fingers into the space and felt Wills' hands do the same. It was difficult to get any leverage. 'One... two...three... now.'

The doors separated another ten inches with a protesting screech. Daniel turned awkwardly on his rump, placing his back against the side of the fuselage, and put his boot on the inner edge of the door.

'Here we go...'

With three hard kicks the doors opened enough. Like an escaping animal, Wills came out so fast he started clambering over Daniel and caused a tangle of limbs.

'Bloody hell, Charlie. Let me get out of the fucking way, will you?'

They fought their way back to the hatchway and dropped out the opening. Spilling gratefully out on to the grass, Daniel felt his collar gripped by someone and he was hauled bodily over the ground before he had a chance to regain his feet. Beside him, Wills was getting the same treatment. The bells of emergency vehicles jangled all around.

Daniel was dropped in a heap, a group of flying-booted legs around him. More hands picked him up onto his own feet. Unsteady, he found himself surrounded by the rest of D-Delta's crew and several panting ground crew in fire suits.

Daniel growled, 'I could have done that on my own, you know.' He hopped on one foot a moment, easing a twisted ankle, and nearly fell over.

'Stop complaining. You're in one piece, aren't you?' Flanders said, his voice shaky with relief. 'It's more than we can say for the old girl.'

Daniel turned to look at D-Delta.

The bomber was a forlorn and strange sight. All four propellers were missing. The cannon and machine gun fire damage was sobering with lines of deadly holes stitched across the fuselage. Seeing them from outside, it seemed a miracle no one was hurt.

Wills said quietly, 'Bloody hell, they won't make us pay for that, will they?'

***

Unexpectedly, they were piled into a truck and driven the ninety miles back to Waddington. It was the last thing the crew needed. They were too taken by surprise to complain, and it wouldn't have had made any difference. It was close to dark when they started and the journey was long, the truck sometimes crawling through the night with its shuttered headlights. Most of the men fell asleep in impossible positions and were woken frequently from aching muscles and stiff bones.

They were deposited outside the briefing hut at Waddington—this was expected. No matter what happened, every mission was followed immediately by a debriefing. The hut was otherwise empty of aircrew and the Intelligence staff looked like they had been waiting a long time.

'Everyone else done?' Flanders asked with mock cheerfulness.

'There wasn't that many to do, from your flight at least,' an officer answered after a silence. 'So we're glad to see you've made it, at least.'

Flanders hid his discomfort by lighting a cigarette.

They endured the painstaking debriefing with their eyes blinking back tears of exhaustion and their bodies sagging into the chairs. Everyone stayed together and when the session was eventually declared over, Branner stared at the clock.

'The pub bloody closes in ten minutes. Do you think we can get there?' he asked with enthusiasm that rang false with his tiredness.

'Sorry, you're all restricted to base,' an Intelligence Officer called Whitely told them quickly. 'Everyone, that is.'

'What? Why?'

'Bad business, I'm afraid. One of the WAAF's has been found dead on the base. Strangled, they say. We're all locked in while they start the investigation.'

Flanders was the first to react. Stunned, he asked, 'Bloody hell. Who? Do you know?'

'The Warrant Officer's niece, the pretty one. Someone told me her name, but I can't remember.' Whitely frowned at his own lapse.

Daniel turned to Baxter, recalling that he'd been with Robyn the night before. The shocked expression on Baxter's face was enough to stop Daniel saying anything.

After a long, hopeless silence, Barrymore groaned, 'The damned Mess will be shut too. I can't just go to bed. I'm wound up like a bloody alarm clock.'

Squadron Leader Eagleton had been in the background, listening to their accounts of the raid. He stepped forward from the shadows and said in a low voice, glancing at the Intelligence staff, 'Alec, take the lads to the back door of your Mess and knock loudly. I've made arrangements. Tell them who you are.'

'Thank you, sir.' Branner threw him a relieved salute. 'Can you join us?'

'I might, later. Things to do...' Eagleton nodded at a table filled with papers.

Although they were deeply tired and it wouldn't have taken much to talk the crew of D-Delta into their bunks, now they felt obligated to take advantage of Eagleton's kindness. They found themselves alone in the mess, served by a silent corporal who knew better than to ask questions. Anyway, he needed only to listen as everyone drank several pints and talked about the raid. Baxter stayed very quiet. No one commented, since it wasn't unusual. Only Daniel seemed to have remembered that he had spent time with the murdered girl on the night she was killed. For the moment he kept it to himself and avoided Baxter as best he could. He just didn't know what to make of it and didn't know what to say.

By the time Daniel made it to his bunk, he was staggering with the alcohol and fatigue. He didn't know what time it was except that it was near midnight, nor did he care. If he could have seen Dianne, he would, but knew it was far too risky. Now, with the murder investigation, it would be very foolish to be creeping around the WAAF quarters.

He found an envelope on his pillow with a single sheet of paper inside.

The note read, '*I heard you made it safely back. Thank goodness. I'll see you tomorrow. Dianne XX.*'

Daniel stared at the two kisses at the end. They lifted his heart. He put his lips to the paper and let himself collapse onto the bunk, pulling the blankets over him without bothering to get undressed. He kept the note in his hand, pressing it close to his face, and convinced himself he could smell Dianne's scent on the paper.

Twelve

The next morning, the crew of D-Delta were taken off the duty roster for three days rest. Their aircraft was written off as a wreck and the station's medical officer grounded them as a precaution against undiscovered injuries. There was a worry that the seven men might be split up to fill vacancies in other crews, until Branner firmly told them it wouldn't happen—Eagleton had given him an assurance.

Everything was explained by Branner at a lunch he ordered everyone to attend at one o'clock. They managed to secure a table to themselves and scowled discouragingly at anyone who threatened to join them. When they all had a meal in front of them, Branner outlined what was happening, including telling them about their days off.

Flanders asked everyone, 'So does this mean the bloody Jerries technically shot us down, the sods?'

'Probably,' Wills frowned at his plate. 'That last bastard has probably painted us on the side of his cockpit already.'

'Hardly,' Branner was annoyed. He didn't like to think they'd come off second best either. 'He didn't see us go down—no one did, for that matter. We crash landed. Does that make you feel better?'

'Landed, yes. We still buggered the plane good and proper,' Flanders said.

'So, we get a new one.'

'Really? When?' Flanders wasn't serious. Branner surprised him.

'This afternoon, they tell me. Arrives at three, weather permitting—which it should. Brand, spanking new from the factory. It'll go to our usual dispersal for Granger and his lads to give it the once-over. I thought I'd go out there and have a look. Anyone else?' He asked offhandedly.

'Of course, we'll all be there,' Daniel answered, in case someone had missed the hint. 'What call-sign will she get? What's next in line?'

'No, they'll re-assign D-Delta to her,' Branner said. 'I was going to ask that anyway, and they've already done it.'

Flanders asked glumly, 'Wouldn't that be bad luck or something?'

'Don't be ridiculous. That kind of nonsense doesn't help, you know.'

'Good luck, more likely,' Wills offered hopefully. 'The last D-Delta got us home, right?'

'Only just.' Knowing that Branner wouldn't be pleased, Flanders covered his face with his mug of tea.

Barrymore changed the subject. 'What's the use in getting three days off if we can't leave the base? What an absolute pain, that poor girl getting bumped off—a real tragedy, I mean,' he added hastily. 'Who would have done a thing like that?'

Daniel eyed Baxter, who was quietly eating his meal without contributing anything to the chatter. He didn't appear to hear Barrymore.

'She was a lovely looking girl, too,' Sexton said. 'They'll never catch who did it, if you ask me.'

Daniel said, 'What makes you say that? She was the Warrant Officer's niece, remember? He'll turn this place upside down until he collars the bastard—then hang him by his balls. I almost feel sorry for the bugger.'

Sexton only shrugged. 'How do we know the murderer is still alive? It'd be a bit hard to find someone who's dead. It's not like you could bring them in for questioning or anything.'

'You're saying he could be one of the blokes on our raid? Someone who got knocked down? You're joking!'

'It's possible,' Sexton replied calmly. 'Even worse, it might have been someone who did her in because he was going on our raid. He might have been thinking, "Hell, I'm not going to come back from this one. I'm going to have a bit of fun before I go." That kind of thing.'

Half-laughing, Wills burst out, 'What a load of bullshit. You're a bit cracked in the head, I'd say. Did one of those Jerry cannon shells give you a whack on the scone?' He looked at Daniel for support. 'Come on, one of our fellows wouldn't do anything like that.'

Sexton could see they were taking it personally. He backed down with another shrug and said, 'I'm only saying that now's the perfect time to commit a crime—any crime, really. Who's to say the killer hasn't been clobbered himself? Or you could make it look like someone who is on the Missing list. You know a raid's going out and it's reasonable to assume they won't all come back. With a bit of planning…'

Branner said, 'You're forgetting that even we didn't know the mission was on until they woke us the next morning.'

'It's not hard to sense something's brewing though, is it?'

'All right,' Branner pushed his empty plate away and stood up. 'That's enough of this amateur Sherlock Holmes rubbish. Let's everyone meet at the dispersal at fourteen thirty, okay? Just in case someone else tries to nab the new plane in front of us.'

The rest of the crew got up and followed as if leaving the table had been an order. Trooping down the steps into weak sunshine, Flanders asked over his shoulder.

'Anyone for a game of darts in the Sergeant's Mess? The bar might be open, since the main gates are bloody shut.'

'That's worth a look,' Barrymore agreed instantly.

'Don't get sozzled,' Branner told them. 'Remember where you're going to be at three o'clock.'

'I thought we were on leave?' Flanders reminded him.

Branner pulled a face. 'Yes—well, aside from that… don't forget, that's all.'

It was normal, too, for Baxter to linger behind the others and keep to himself. Daniel made a point of staying with him, touching his elbow to stop Baxter and let the others draw even further ahead.

Daniel called to them, 'I've got a couple of packets of fags in my locker I owe Morgan. We'll get them and catch up in a few minutes.'

Flanders answered with a wave without looking back.

Baxter was watching Daniel with a resigned expression, knowing what was coming. Now Daniel grabbed his arm and led Baxter around the corner of a building. After making sure no one was close, he cornered the wireless operator against the wall.

'Well?'

'Well what?' Baxter said, a mixture of sullen and feigned ignorance.

'You know what the bloody hell I'm talking about. You were with that girl at the pub. I know for a fact you walked her home too.' Daniel was lying, but figured it was worth the bluff.

'I was starting to hope no one else remembered.'

'I can't believe they haven't all said something. Have you told the police?'

'Are you mad? They'd lock me up straight away.'

'Well, maybe you fucking well should be!'

Baxter dropped his head. 'I didn't do anything, Danny. Honest. I just walked her back to the barracks and left her where we always do, well in the distance so nobody gets into any strife. She chatted with me all the way, saying how everyone's saying cruel things about her that she doesn't deserve. I agreed, of course... so she'd like me, more than anything. It got me a kiss on the cheek and a half-promise of seeing her the next night.' Baxter smiled a moment at the memory. 'Then she headed off for the barracks.'

'Did you see her go inside?'

'Christ, you know what it's like in the blackout. Pitch bloody black. I didn't see a damned thing. I didn't even wait around to see. What's the point?'

'Did you see anyone else?'

'No, not for ages.'

Daniel was getting exasperated at Baxter's calm. 'How can you be sure nobody saw you?'

Baxter shrugged. 'Same thing. It's too bloody dark'

'Morgan, this is not a good idea. Someone might have been hiding and saw you—even known who you are. Maybe they killed her and they're going to slip your name to the police...' Daniel spread his hands to suggest everything falling apart. 'You have to tell the police you walked her home before someone tells them for you. It'll look bad if that happens.'

Baxter turned stubborn. 'Nobody's said anything yet. I've already made up my mind to wait a bit. Did you reckon I haven't been worrying about it? I can't think of anything else!'

Daniel shook his head and stared away into the distance, thinking hard. 'I don't know, Bax. It doesn't sound good to me.'

'Are you going to turn me in then?'

'No, but I will say something, if I think we'll get into trouble for covering for you.' Daniel wasn't so sure he meant this. It seemed the right thing to say. 'I'll give you another day, all right?'

'Then what?'

'How the hell should I know?'

Daniel abruptly turned on his heel and strode away angrily. He dimly heard Baxter softly say, 'Thanks, Danny.'

***

If Baxter had been convinced to confess to anyone, it wasn't apparent when the D-Delta crew gathered at the dispersal point to greet their new aircraft. The wireless operator was his normal self, quiet and withdrawn from the others—so nobody noticed anything different. Only Daniel sensed a reluctance in Baxter to be too close to anyone, especially him, no doubt in case another argument began.

'All right, where is it then?' Sexton asked the sky. It was filling with rain clouds and he pulled a face, tugging the collar of his jacket tight.

Sergeant Granger stepped out of his makeshift hut to stand behind them. 'Still twenty minutes away, sir. By my reckoning.' He had a mug of tea in his hand and suddenly looked concerned he might have to offer the same all around. He held it at waist level, as if it wasn't there at all.

Branner said cheerfully, 'Looking forward to getting your hands on a brand-new Lanc, sergeant?'

'The last one wasn't so old, sir,' Granger replied with a deadpan face. 'We'll have to start all over again, getting to know every nut and bolt, making sure she's come from the factory all right—'

'Yes, we had a bit of bad luck,' Branner cut him off. 'We'll try and look after this one a bit better.'

Granger nodded and retreated from the hard surface of the dispersal, where he could light his pipe.

'Cheeky sod,' Branner said to Sexton. 'Who the hell does he think he is?'

'The crew chief,' Sexton said. 'Closely related to God himself, in some circles. Actually, he was pulling your leg, skipper. He's got a funny sense of humour. You missed it.'

Branner sighed, his doubts about how the others regarded him whispering around inside his head again. Now they included the ground crew.

'Hello, this sounds likely,' Barrymore said loudly, eyeing the west where a rumbling was growing.

Flanders said, 'That's a single-engine job, you idiot. Can't you tell?'

'Rubbish, it's a multi of some kind. Are you deaf?' Barrymore saw that Flanders was teasing him. 'Bastard. It's a good thing you're not in one of our turrets with those bloody aircraft recognition skills. You'd shoot down your first Spitfire in no time—' He abruptly shut up, knowing he had set himself up.

'You can talk,' Flanders said with a smug grin. 'I seem to remember someone in the front turret—'

'I couldn't see those bastards at all. No one did.'

'Now, now children,' Sexton stopped them, pointing at a shape that appeared against the clouds. 'Enough bickering. I'd say this is our new girl.'

The lone Lancaster dropped down towards the runway, too fast to land.

'Not exactly going into a circuit pattern, right skipper?' Wills said for them all.

'No, the tower must have asked for a fly-by,' Branner agreed.

They watched with growing appreciation as the bomber over-flew the main strip at a steady height, the pilot's hand sure and confident. At the far end the plane climbed steeply and banked into a perfect "split-s" turn, swinging around hard to line up the runway for a landing. This was done with a single touch, the tail wheel dropping gently in time for the Lancaster to turn easily into a taxiway.

'Smart arse,' Branner decided. 'Why isn't he bombing Berlin instead of farting around the country ferrying new planes?'

'Probably too old. Some joker who flew in the last war,' Sexton said, matching Branner's grudging tone to please him.

'Maybe he's got no legs, like Douglas Bader?' Wills said. 'Hey, it's not so silly,' he added at their disgusted looks.

'You're bloody silly,' Flanders muttered.

The roar of the Lancaster silenced them. The aircraft taxied onto the dispersal, pressing the men backwards to join Granger on the grass. The ferry pilot blipped the port engines and spun the aircraft in a tight circle. One wingtip passed close to the hut and the cowering crew, the propeller wash blasting around them and causing much swearing and clutching at clothing. When the Lancaster's engines switched off and began winding down, the plane was positioned exactly in the centre of the dispersal.

'You'd have to say, very nicely done. Wouldn't you, gentlemen?' Granger called above the ringing in their ears.

'Well, if it's all you have to do all day,' Branner finished this with a shrug. 'Let's see him do it with the Luftwaffe trying to shoot his bollocks off.'

Members of Granger's ground staff were moving towards the aircraft, one of them carrying a ladder. D-Delta's crew followed and gathered at the rear hatchway. It swung open and the ladder was hooked on the bottom.

A petite and pretty young WAAF appeared in the door, her tousled blonde hair escaping her cap and framing a pair of bright, blue eyes. She was wearing overalls that were a snug fit, achieving things they were never designed to do.

'Hello!' Flanders was quickest. 'Look what Bomber Command has sent us. Jolly good, did you catch a lift? Have you been posted here?' He couldn't keep the hopeful tone from his voice.

'Something like that,' she replied coolly, tossing a small rucksack over his head to one of Granger's men.

Ignoring Flanders' outstretched hand, she stepped onto the ladder, coming down backwards with practiced ease. Most of the men took advantage of the view offered by the overalls. When she reached the ground and turned around, there was some hasty re-arranging of facial expressions. She looked for Granger and pushed through the others towards him.

'Hello, chief. Everything's ship-shape except the rudder feels a bit tight on the port side. You'd expect it to loosen up during the flight, but it didn't.'

'We'll give it a look, Bette,' Granger nodded. 'Thanks for that.'

'Is someone coming to get me?' She stared towards the main hangers.

'Soon, you'd think.'

'I can't be bothered waiting. Is there a pushbike I can borrow?'

'Take mine.' Granger pointed the stem of his pipe at a red-framed bicycle leaning against the hut. 'I should be glad of the walk later.' He patted his midriff.

This had cut off a chorus of similar offers rising from the D-Delta crew. They lapsed into disappointed silence.

'Thanks ever so,' she said, taking her rucksack back and slinging it over her shoulders. 'I'll leave it in front of your mess.'

She mounted the bike gracefully and pedalled away one-handed, waving with the other. The ground staff returned the gesture with familiar cheerfulness. Of the aircrew, everyone except Daniel tried to call an engaging farewell, none of which seemed to make an impression.

'Oh well,' Flanders sighed heavily. 'Maybe at the pub.'

Branner poked his head inside the hatchway. 'The pilot's taking his time coming out. I wonder if there's a problem?'

'I told you,' Wills said. 'He's got no legs. We'll have to carry him out.'

As Branner gave Wills an annoyed look, Granger said, 'Sir, why don't you jump in and find out?'

'All right, chief. I might as well get any bad news straight from the horse's mouth, so to speak.' Branner climbed the ladder and disappeared towards the cockpit.

No one else went in. There were no guns in the turrets, robbing most of the appeal for Daniel and Wills. The others took their cue and stayed on the ground. They lingered at the hatchway and waited for the ferry pilot to disembark.

Branner came back alone.

'I don't understand,' he called to Granger, who looked back blandly. 'Where'd he go? Out the front hatch—no, of course not.' That required a tall ladder and a lot of fussing about. It wouldn't have gone unnoticed. Branner's expression changed to disbelief.

'You've got to be bloody joking!'

'There's nothing funny about Bette's flying, sir,' Granger told him with ill-concealed delight. 'They say that in a Spitfire she could shoot down Goering himself, if they gave her a chance.'

In the silence and missing the point, Wills declared, 'Anybody could knock down that fat bastard.'

Flanders had caught on and he burst out, 'Don't be ridiculous.' He climbed the first steps of the ladder and leaned in past Branner's legs, searching the interior. His voice echoed out to them. 'You can't tell me that wisp of a girl was piloting the bloody plane. Girl's can hardly drive properly, for God's sake.'

'Steady on,' Sexton said quietly, glancing at the two women who were a part of Granger's crew. 'You'll start a riot these days, spouting stuff like that.'

'No, seriously, this is a prank, skipper. He's in there somewhere. They probably pull this one every time a new plane arrives.' He looked over shoulder. 'Look at 'em all grinning like Cheshire cats.'

The ground crew melted away to their allotted tasks. Someone called out that the armorers were coming, pointing out a truck grinding heavily over the grass their way.

'Believe me, there's no one else in here,' Branner said gruffly, pushing Flanders off the ladder and coming down. He said to nobody in particular,

'She did a smart job, that's for sure. But I'm not convinced it's a good idea having women ferrying these big brutes around. There'll be an accident one day.'

'Then I'd say it'll be a pretty spectacular accident, skipper,' Daniel said, gesturing at the far end of the runway where Bette had displayed her slick, split-s manoeuvre.

'Yes, that's exactly what I'm talking about,' Branner said, turning to Granger, who alone of the ground crew hadn't moved. 'I guess there's not much we can do here after all, chief. I mainly wanted to make sure nobody tried to poach her off us.'

'We'll get the call-sign on quick smart, sir.'

'That'll do the trick.'

Barrymore had wandered towards the front of the bomber and was staring up at the Perspex bomb-aimer's position. 'What about putting something on the nose, skipper?'

'What?'

'A lot of the Wellingtons have it. Their crews give the aircraft a nickname and paint something on the nose—something funny, or clever.'

'That counts us out,' Flanders said.

'Like what?' Branner waved at him to be quiet.

'I don't know. We'll have to come up with something together that we all agree on.' Barrymore shrugged at them from the distance.

Sexton said enthusiastically, 'I'm sure we could come up with something brilliant over a few pints. What about it, chief? Can it be done?'

Granger was scowling, unimpressed with the selection criteria. 'As long as it's something decent—sir,' he allowed unhappily.

***

The station curfew was lifted late that afternoon, in time to trigger a rush to the local pubs. Daniel managed to arrange meeting Dianne. His joy was soured a little when he found her sitting at a small table with a glum-looking Susan beside her. Something else was obviously wrong, apart from the pall of depression caused by the murder. They had grimly saved a third chair and were at least glad to see him and stop the endless requests for the empty seat. The girls hadn't explained the poor mood before the rest of D-Delta's crew had gathered close too, homing in on the familiar faces and claiming space on the table for their drinks. The pub was filled beyond capacity, spilling into the street. The crowd pressed in, jostling everyone.

'I've had an idea,' Wills announced, fighting to keep his space and not slosh his beer. 'For naming the Lanc', I mean.'

'All right, what is it?' Branner asked suspiciously.

'Well, the call-sign is D-Delta and I was just thinking we might be able to come up with something that was made from all the first letters of our girlfriend's names. Like, Danny can give us "D" for Dianne, see? I could maybe, well...' He looked hopefully at Susan, who didn't take the hint.

'Perhaps,' Branner shrugged, and added with a touch of defiance, 'So there's "C" for Cheryl, too.'

Flanders didn't let it pass. 'Ah, yes—the mystery girl at home, skipper. How could we forget? What about you, Charlie? You don't have a girlfriend, and let's face it, you're not very good-looking. I don't know if you'll ever have a girl. In fact, it's odd you came up with the concept, considering'

'You can talk,' Wills snarled. 'What about you? I can't see you fighting off swarms of girls either.'

'I'm saving myself for the beautiful Bette,' Flanders said dreamily. 'She can hold my joystick anytime.'

Amid the howl of derision, Sexton said, 'I might have to offer my mother.' This immediately silenced them, and they waited pointedly for him to explain. He looked uncomfortable. 'Her name's Alice. I don't have a steady sweetheart either and—well, it looks like we could do with the vowel.'

'I don't think this is going to work,' Dianne said wryly, adding to Flanders, 'And you are disgusting.' He looked pleased.

'What about something Biblical?' Barrymore said. 'About the wrath of God and all that nonsense?' This brought another groan of dismay, followed by outrageous suggestions along this theme to mock Barrymore. Daniel took the opportunity to lean close to Dianne and whisper in her ear.

'Susan's a bit glum. Is she all right?'

Dianne did the same, putting her lips so close he felt her warm breath on his neck. 'It's her fighter pilot boyfriend, the one stationed in Portsmouth. He's been posted as missing after a sweep over France.'

'Oh? I didn't even know she had a fellow.' Daniel glanced at Susan's sad face with a new understanding.

'Well, she didn't—she wasn't sure, at least. Now I don't suppose it matters.'

'No doubt about it?'

'From what we hear. No parachute, they said. The rest is just a formality. You should warn the other lads not to try their luck with her tonight. Especially Charlie. She's feeling a bit fragile.'

'I'll try and pass the word,' Daniel said, although he figured that since he'd have to yell this news over the crowd noise, he wouldn't have much chance of being discreet about it. Also, now he didn't fancy his chances of discussing his deal with Dianne. She was supposed to uphold her promise to commit herself to him—or at best, think about it, after surviving the Augsburg raid. This didn't feel like the right time or place to remind her. Dianne had taken on Susan's sombre mood in sympathy.

'I've still got two days of leave left,' he tried cheerfully. 'What about you?'

Dianne seemed reluctant to admit, 'No, I'm not on the roster tomorrow either.'

'Really? Why don't we go to London together?' The idea was out before he could stop it.

Dianne looked just as surprised. 'What? In your car? I don't think so—'

'No, the train, of course. I'd love to see it. We only passed through on the way here. You could show me around.' Daniel realized he was talking too loudly and was risking everyone else inviting themselves along. He lowered his voice. 'Go on. It'll be fun.'

She gave him a wan smile. 'I'm flat broke until pay day.'

'My treat. Please say you'll do it.'

They both knew what this was really about. Of course, Dianne hadn't forgotten her promise and was partly glad the crowd and Susan's grief was providing an excuse to avoid the issue. She knew she had made that deal with an unspoken, but clear understanding of what would happen between her and Daniel if he came back from the mission.

To be true to her word, she should now let go of her misgivings and take that next step.

On the other hand the loss of Susan's fighter pilot friend had brought back with a fresh insistence all the fears and uncertainties of having a sweetheart during wartime. It felt destined for a bad ending, no matter what. It wasn't like Daniel now had a safe posting away from the fighting. He had only flown two missions. It was just the beginning.

Suddenly she had an idea—both a decision and a way of avoiding things just a little longer. The car drive to the countryside pub had been a disaster, what with the crashed German bomber and everything. Instead, she could use this London trip to really get to know Daniel better and make up her mind if he was worth the risk. To figure out if she'd regret whatever time they spent together, however brief or long, were she only to lose him to the war.

'I'm worried about Susan—leaving her,' she said finally, thinking at the last instant that it might be good taking to London some insurance in case her decisions left Daniel upset. 'Do you think she could come, too? She needs cheering up.'

'Sure... of course,' Daniel said, about to give up she'd ever answer. With a straight face he furiously considered this development. 'Why not? Just her, though. No one else.' His eyes slid towards Wills.

Dianne put a finger to her lips and winked. Daniel returned this with a secretive smile, already trying to work out a way to convince—or even bribe—Susan to stay behind.

***

The three of them walked with linked arms back to the girl's barracks. With Daniel in the middle he tried to include Susan in the fun. She endured his attempts with soft laughter and a smile he couldn't see in the dark. Away from the presence of the others, she was more relaxed and herself, letting her sadness show, and she was grateful that Daniel had, on her behalf, also rejected all offers from the D-Delta crew to walk her home. Wills in particular had been almost encouraged by the news of the missing fighter pilot. Only memories of having similar thoughts about Dianne's lost Blenheim pilot had stopped Daniel from getting angry with him.

'Bloody hell, how are we supposed to find our way anywhere in these damn blackouts?' Susan said, tripping for the third time.

'Your language is shocking,' Diane told her mildly. 'It's the booze, you know.

'Of course, I know. I bloody drank it, remember? You don't sound so—erudite yourself.'

'Goodness, that's a word,' Daniel said.

'Yes, it is. You tell him, Dianne.'

'Tell him what?' Dianne was concentrating on keeping in step with Daniel, which seemed important.

'I don't know. Just tell him.'

'All right, consider yourself told, Daniel.'

'Fair enough.' He frowned, and decided it was too difficult to understand. He pulled them to a halt. 'This is as far as I dare go. There's your barracks. See them?'

'That black, round shape among all those other black, round shapes?'

'That's the one. I'd better not go any closer. The place will be surrounded by military police just dying to arrest some poor bastard.'

'Poor?' Susan asked quietly.

'He might be, if it's the wrong fellow. They can be a bit keen, you know.' Daniel imagined Baxter being dragged away in the night, protesting his innocence. 'It's certainly put a wet blanket on things. Will you two be all right?'

'Of course, we will,' Dianne said loudly, pushing Daniel aside so her arm could slip though Susan's. 'Together we're a match for anyone.'

'Ah, right,' Daniel sensed he'd just lost his opportunity for a goodnight kiss. 'So I'll see you both bright and early? In time for the eight o'clock train?'

'Not me,' Susan answered. 'I won't be coming.'

'What? Why not? We'll have great fun!' Daniel tried to sound disappointed. Dianne was protesting too.

'Give me credit for some brains, you two,' Susan said. 'You do not want me along.'

'I do,' Dianne said with a trace of desperation.

'So do I,' Daniel said lamely. Dianne gave him a look he fortunately didn't see.

'No, you don't.' Susan held up her free hand.

'Just a minute,' Dianne said, then made a point of speaking firmly at Daniel's dark shape. 'Good night, Daniel. It's time for you to leave. I need to have some private words with my dear friend here.'

'Honest, you're very welcome to come too, Susan,' he tried again, failing.

'Daniel,' Dianne warned him. 'Good night. I can assure you that Susan hasn't made up her mind completely. I'd say you'll be seeing her in the morning.'

Daniel lingered for a few more seconds, hoping for the kiss, then beat a retreat mumbling his farewells in the dark. Dianne didn't move until his crunching footsteps had faded into the night.

'What are you trying to do to me?' she demanded, pretending to be angry and tugging Susan's arm hard towards the barracks.

'I'm not doing anything. You don't want me to go either.'

'Quite the opposite, thank you. I want the moral support.'

'Hah! Since when do you need any help with a fellow?'

'I don't want help. Just a bit of company, if things get out of hand.'

Susan was incredulous. 'Like how? I'd say you've got the chap well under control.'

'It's not like that, this time—' Dianne stopped, hearing footsteps behind them. She spun around, taking Susan with her.

'Daniel? Is that you eavesdropping? How dare you.'

No one answered. Dianne would have sworn someone stood silently just a few yards away. 'Daniel?' she tried again. 'Come on, this isn't funny now.'

'Who's there?' Susan called, squinting into the dark. 'We can see you, you know.'

Still there was no reply. Dianne was suddenly torn between being afraid and making a fool of herself at an imaginary figure. The alcohol made her vision swim on its own.

'Look, who is that?' she snapped, her voice breaking treacherously. 'If you think this is some kind of a joke coming back from the pub…'

'Bugger the blackout,' Susan said, trembling and rattled too. 'Use your torch, Di. Let's see who this twit is.'

'I haven't got my torch. Where's yours?'

'Oh bugger—wait a second…' Susan rummaged blindly in her bag.

At that moment footsteps ran away into the darkness. From the distance a stumbling noise came, followed by a curse, then silence.

'Oh God,' Dianne breathed. 'There was someone there.'

Susan belatedly shone a hooded beam at where the figure had stood. There was nothing to see.

'Christ, who do you think it was?'

'Who do you think?'

'Then we'd better tell someone—quickly.'

'No—no, wait…' Dianne was unsure. 'Let's not jump to any conclusions.'

'What?'

'Seriously. Remember what Daniel just said? It might have been someone innocent that we just scared the pants off. They panicked, like we nearly did, and just ran.'

'From two women?'

'If it was the murderer, would he have run away?'

'Maybe he was waiting for us to split up, or he was—oh, let's get inside first. I've got the creeps standing out here.'

They turned and hurried towards the barracks, Susan shining the torch at the ground in front of them. If someone complained, she had a ready answer.

Where the hell were you two minutes ago?

A shiver of fear ran down Dianne's back as they finished the trip. They rushed through the doorway and blackout curtain, and both fell against the wall in weak relief. The barracks had a very dim light at floor level to help late comers find their bunks. It was enough for Dianne to see Susan's white, frightened face. Susan could have told her that she looked the same.

'Now what do we do?' Susan whispered, glancing at the sleeping figures in the nearest beds.

'I'm not sure. We're safe, aren't we? Perhaps we should wait until morning, if we do anything at all.'

'What about the others?'

'What others?'

'All the other girls still at the pub. Some of them might find themselves walking home alone.'

'Oh damn—of course,' Dianne bit her lip. 'Bloody hell, I can't think straight… all right, but let's do it quietly.'

There was a telephone for the entire barracks beside the door. Dianne used it to call the guardhouse, explaining in a hushed tone what had happened. Some of the bunks' occupants began to stir at the noise, raising their heads to blink owlishly their way. Susan tried to calm them with exaggerated arm-waving.

Within a few minutes, a Landrover filled with four military policemen roared to a halt in front of the barracks. Dianne and Susan were waiting outside, hugging themselves against the cold now, and they intercepted the MPs as they were about to storm inside. It took more furious whispering to repeat their story, which didn't seem to impress anyone as much as Dianne expected.

'Have you been drinking, ma'am?' the sergeant asked in an odd tone.

'Yes, we've been at the—' Dianne began.

'And you, ma'am?' He turned to Susan.

'Yes, as a matter of fact,' she growled at him. 'We're probably both a bit squiffy, but we know what we saw.'

'What you didn't see,' he said meaningfully.

'You know what I mean, sergeant.'

If the MP was supposed to feel outranked, he didn't show it. 'Why didn't you call for help? We have men patrolling everywhere tonight. Someone would have heard you.'

'Everyone's full of bright ideas afterwards, aren't they?' Susan said. 'At the time, we weren't sure what to do. We've called you now, haven't we?'

The sergeant sighed in the darkness and tapped his baton against his leg. 'You'll have to give a full report to the Warrant Officer in the morning. He wants to be told everything, no matter what. The smallest bit of information might help.'

Susan said quickly, 'Sergeant Parker here has to go to London tomorrow on official business. I can do it.'

The blackout hid Dianne's shocked expression.

'What sort of business, sergeant?' The MP stared at her in the dark. Susan answered for her.

'Official, I said. Don't breathe a word, Dianne. You know how important it is.'

The MP considered this a long time, making Dianne nervous. 'Then I suppose you'll have to do it on your own,' he agreed reluctantly. 'Make it at 0800 hours. I'll meet you there.'

'All right. Good night, sergeant. Thanks to you and your men for coming so quickly.' Susan gave him a thin smile he couldn't see.

The MP didn't like being dismissed. 'Good night, sergeants. We'll be having a look around for a while. You may hear us. Don't be alarmed.'

'Oh, no. We'll feel much safer now.'

He couldn't decide if she was mocking him. He moved away, issuing orders at the others to search the area.

Back inside, Dianne turned on Susan. 'Thanks for that, but it was a silly risk. We could both end up in the brig for telling whoppers like that. Official business indeed!'

'No harm done,' Susan said lightly. 'You still go to London, that's the main thing.'

'But you don't.'

'I didn't want to, remember? It's all worked out well, really.'

Dianne was tempted to say she would cancel her trip too. She knew it would start an argument she probably wouldn't win. Giving up, she gave Susan's hand a squeeze as they headed wearily for their bunks.

***

The next morning, Daniel tried to look crestfallen when he saw Dianne alone, standing in the sun near her barracks.

'You couldn't change her mind then?' He made to hook his arm through hers. She dodged gently aside.

'Don't. We have to look serious, at least until we get out the gate—and don't pretend you're disappointed about Susan.'

'Serious? What do you mean?'

'There's an MP about who thinks I'm going to London on official business. If I could have gotten a message to you to meet me outside, I would have.'

The mention of an MP was enough to make Daniel behave. He said quietly, 'Hell, this all sounds very cloak and dagger stuff. What on earth did you do?'

'Not me—well anyway, I'll explain when we're out of here.'

They walked through the crisp morning air, almost marching to compound the ruse they were going somewhere important. Daniel copied Dianne's concerned frown.

The guards at the base entrance left their gatehouse only to offer a cheerful good morning to Dianne, grudgingly including Daniel at the last moment. Worried that the MP sergeant from last night was lurking inside, Dianne returned their greetings with a touch of formality. One of the guards wasn't to be so easily discouraged.

'Off to Lincoln, ma'am?'

'No, to London. Not for any fun, I'm afraid.' She gave him a wan smile.

The guard glanced at Daniel as if this were his fault. 'Surely it doesn't have to be all work and no play, Sergeant Parker? Not in London.'

'Well, perhaps not.' She brightened her expression a little. 'Tell you what. I'll do my best to have a drink for you.'

'Only wish I could join you, ma'am.' He threw her a jaunty salute. His grin turned sour as Daniel tried to contribute to the deception as he followed Dianne out.

'Yes, you never know, sergeant. But there is war on, isn't there?' he said.

'We had noticed, sergeant,' the guard replied, pointedly keeping his hands at his side, stilling Daniel's beginnings of a casual salute of his own. 'Have a good day, all the same.'

The two of them continued marching away from the base until they had rounded a bend in the road that hid them from the gate and out of earshot. Then Daniel grabbed Dianne's arm and stopped her.

'All right. Now what in Heaven's name is this all about?' he demanded gently.

'Calm down and I'll tell you.'

'I am calm.'

'You could have fooled me.'

Daniel guiltily let go of her elbow and they started off again, this time slowly. Dianne took a deep breath and told him of their fright the night before that turned into an encounter with the MPs. Every time Daniel tried to interrupt, his alarm growing, she silenced him by holding up a finger.

'That's it,' she allowed him finally. 'This morning we both felt a bit silly. We might have made a mistake and frightened the dickens out of some poor fellow who was just staggering home like us. I hope Susan will sort it out for the best with the RAFP. Just in case, I had to make her little fib about the official business look good.'

'I don't care about that,' Daniel was annoyed at himself. 'From now on, I'm walking you up to the very door of your barracks. They can arrest me if they like.'

'I don't know what the right thing to do is,' Dianne said. 'They might arrest you and then what would happen? Especially if it's after I've gone inside and can't vouch for you.'

'It's bloody stupid,' Daniel grumbled.

Dianne didn't answer that. She quickened her pace again. 'Come on, let's make sure we get good seats on the train.'

All through the train journey to London, Dianne was quiet, keeping Daniel at a distance. He managed to hold her hand and move close enough to rub shoulders, but her mood discouraged him from doing more. Finally, a few minutes after they pulled away from the last stop before Victoria Station, he got desperate.

'Dianne, are you going to be like this all day?'

'Like what?'

'You know what I mean. It's going to be rotten if you keep this up.'

She bit her lip. 'Look, I know I agreed to all that stuff about you and I after that last mission and everything, but I still don't know if it's a good idea. What about poor Susan's bloke? The fighter pilot? Look how upsetting things can be, if it all goes wrong. It's been preying on my mind since she told me, that's all.'

The train began to brake again, throwing the carriages together with a clatter of couplings. Victoria Station and a disastrous day were approaching fast. Daniel was tempted to be petulant, saying she had promised and was going back on her word. He guessed it wouldn't help. Instead, he took a moment to silently curse the missing fighter pilot and his poor timing in getting himself killed.

'All right, just one day then? Today, together in London having a nice time, then let's see how we both feel. Forget about everything else we've said before, okay?'

Dianne shook her head. 'I'm sorry, I'm being selfish. You don't have to do that, Danny. I'm just upset and still a bit spooked from last night.'

'I don't want to force you into anything you don't want to do, either.' Daniel felt a renewed confidence he had things back under control, although he wasn't sure how. The train was slowing so much now that they had to brace themselves. Time was running out to make sure. He smiled encouragingly at her.

She returned it with a weak one of her own and a small, apologetic shrug. 'No, you're right. Let's just worry about having a lovely day.'

'That's the spirit.' He gave her shoulders a hug.

Dianne had turned to watch the platform sliding by, her face reflected in the glass.

'You're bloody tricky creatures,' he muttered, disguising it under the noise of the train halting.

They stepped from the train into clouds of filthy steam drifting back from the locomotive. Everyone else around seemed to be in a hurry, pushing past Daniel and Dianne as they moved into clearer air.

'Okay, what's first?' Daniel said, waving his hand in front of his face.

'Some late morning tea, I think.' Dianne looked around and saw the cafes at the other side of the station. 'Perhaps not here. Let's find something nice out on the sidewalk.'

Emerging from the station, Dianne was struck by how so many people were wearing a uniform of some kind. She mentioned this to Daniel adding, 'Is anyone still at home?'

'Someone's answering my letters, so there must be.'

'More to the point, I suppose they're all hoping to go back home some time, like you.'

'Yes, there is that.' Daniel feared this could lead to another awkward subject and quickly changed it. 'We're not too far away from lunch. Do you just want tea or something else with it?'

Dianne laughed. 'Lesson number one in London, Daniel. With all the rationing, you never know what you'll find in the restaurants or shops. So if you see something nice, grab it and eat it before someone else does.'

They found a tearoom with tables outside under a tree that somehow grew in a tiny alcove between the buildings. The shade from the leaves and walls was enough to make it a chilly spot. Daniel was fascinated by the constant stream of people going past. He stayed there while Dianne went to scrutinize the cakes and sandwiches inside. She came back looking disappointed.

'Just a cuppa here, I'd say. Nothing in there makes my mouth water. While we have tea, let's work out what we can do. We don't have a lot of time, really.'

He ignored what that might mean and nodded at a Sikh sergeant passing by wearing a turban. 'There's all sorts here,' he said. 'It's like a circus.'

'Hmm, you're definitely a country lad.'

An ageing waiter arrived and emptied a tray of tea, cups and some tiny, complimentary biscuits onto the table. Dianne thanked him, before telling Daniel, 'You should go to the city more and get that hayseed out of your hair. Come to think of it, you haven't told me about your farm much. What sort is it again? Didn't you say sheep?'

'That's right,' he said absently, now watching a Scots Guardsman in a kilt stride by.

Dianne said, 'I have a cousin who owned a sheep farm, I'm told. Out in the Cotswolds somewhere. Quite big, I believe. How big is yours?'

'Hmm? Oh—well, we're a fair way into the country.'

'Ah, out in the famous "outback" Australians are always talking about,' she said wryly, 'Like it's something from Alice in Wonderland. I suppose you've got those bungyip things in the rivers too.'

'Bunyips,' he corrected her with a smile. 'Close, but no, I've never seen one on our property.' He narrowed his eyes to scare her. 'That doesn't mean we don't have any. They're quite mystical creatures, you know. Not to mention the occasional swagman's ghost at the billabongs. Besides, there's plenty of little nooks and crannies I've never been to they might be hiding in.'

She frowned, puzzled. 'What do you mean?'

He was suddenly embarrassed. 'You see, we've got over thirty thousand acres. I reckon there'd still be rocks and logs even my old man hasn't looked under, if you know what I mean. Sometimes you don't get off your horse for a while.'

One of the biscuits had crumbled in Dianne's fingers. Her eyebrows had shot up comically. 'Thirty thousand acres? That's bigger than Ireland, isn't it?'

'No, not quite.' He buried his face in the cup of tea and stayed quiet while she thought this over.

She asked after a moment, 'So, how many sheep do you have then?'

'It depends on the season. If it looks like there'll be plenty of feed, Dad might run two or even three to an acre. If the rains didn't come as much as we'd want and things are a bit bare, he'll keep it down to one.'

'No wonder you can afford to buy cars and go to London at the drop of a hat. You're like landed gentry with buckets of money—' Dianne stopped self-consciously. 'Something like that.'

He shrugged awkwardly. 'Yes, something like that, as you say. It's still all Dad's, of course. It can depend on how good the market is each year. Things go up and down. We've had our lean years. I must admit, I struggle to spend the allowance they send me and it mounts up a bit. That reminds me, I need to pop into a bank for a minute some time. Do you mind?'

'Goodness, I'm sure they'll roll out the red carpet for you,' she said, recovering. 'Tell them about the sheep. I don't think there's that many in England.'

'Don't you believe it. There are hundreds of thousands of the bloody things everywhere. You should see them from the Lanc', when we're flying low-level.'

Dianne leaned towards him. 'You know, I would like to see that. Do you think I might be able to cadge a ride in your bomber one day?'

'You're joking, aren't you?' It took only a second for Daniel to realise she wasn't. 'Why on earth would you want to do that?'

She looked annoyed. 'Just because I'm a girl doesn't mean I don't find that sort of thing exciting. God, why do men insist on believing women are only interested in dolls and damned knitting?'

'All right, I'm sorry.' He held his hands up in surrender.

'I'll tell you something, Daniel Young.' She tapped the table angrily with her fingertip. 'I know plenty of WAAFs who would be keen to go on a bombing mission, even if it meant stowing away.'

'Well, you'd have to,' he said quickly. 'The skipper would have a fit if he thought we had to take a WAAF with us over the Channel.'

Dianne made a scornful noise. 'What about Bette, that ferry pilot? She could fly rings around Alec—no offence, but she could. We might be safer over Germany with her in the cockpit.'

'Maybe, but that's never going to happen, is it?' Daniel mentally apologised to Branner for not putting up a better fight on his behalf.

'What about a training flight? I only want to have a ride, not steer the rotten thing.'

'Can't you make it official somehow? Ask your Wingco to slap up some paperwork?' He was stalling, hoping it would sound too difficult.

'No, it's easier if one of the crew just slips you in a back door. They usually don't mind and think it's quite fun,' she accused him with a glance. 'It happens all the time, but not many have snuck into a Lancaster yet.'

'Surely not?' Daniel was shocked. 'Don't tell me you've done it.'

'No, I'm not going to say a word now,' Dianne turned sly. 'You look like the type to go telling tales, if you ask me.' She began gathering her bag and cigarettes. 'Come on, we'd better get a move on with our sight-seeing.' She stood up.

He was taken by surprise, but glad to escape the topic. 'Oh... right ho, then... where are we going?' Daniel hurriedly slurped down his tea and dug into a tunic pocket for change.

'The usual, I suppose.' Dianne pointed along the street. 'We'll pop onto the Tube and go into the middle of the city. Then it's Trafalgar Square and St Paul's cathedral-—all the normal stuff. We'll just keep walking until we're tired or hungry. Don't forget to stay on the lookout for a nice lunch.'

As they left the café, Daniel stole a look over his shoulder and saw the waiter furtively retrieving the uneaten biscuits, no doubt to be put back into their stocks. It struck him as both funny and sad, and it didn't surprise him so much. He made a decision not to be so surprised by anything anymore.

Certainly not, when it came to Dianne Parker.

**

The sunshine was smothered when the weather turned to scattered showers, the thicker grey clouds looming over the skyline when they were least expected and catching people in the open. Daniel didn't care. He couldn't have been happier than walking, mostly arm-in-arm, around the old city and wondering at the marvels he'd only ever seen in books and scratchy film reels. Dianne took on her role as a tour guide enthusiastically, reciting everything she knew of the monuments and famous buildings. They pointedly ignored the tremendous amount of bomb damage, as did everyone else in the streets.

At one point, Daniel saw a bank and they went inside. Dianne sat in a comfortable chair and watched from a distance as a teller's attitude towards Daniel changed from barely disguised tolerance to near fawning at his every word. She couldn't help noticing the wad of notes he stuffed in his wallet was rather thick.

They had a good lunch of a meat pie, potatoes and drinks in a smoky pub claiming to be over a hundred years old. The meat tasted so nice that

Daniel didn't spoil things by asking what it was—since the menu avoided the issue too. Refreshed, but weighed down by the meal, and in Daniel's case two pints of bitter, they again found a nearby Tube station and rode to Marble Arch, before setting off to walk around Hyde Park.

Directly opposite the gates of the park, they saw a nondescript building which might have been offices or flats—it was hard to tell—that had been hit hard. One middle section of the place, nearly a third, was a crumbled mess of broken brickwork, blackened walls and exposed beams. The rest of the building stood precariously like a cracked shell around the impact point. This time Daniel couldn't help stopping, pulling Dianne to a halt and staring across.

She said quietly, 'It's incredible they haven't hit anything important—I mean, historical or precious. Everything's important, of course.'

'I suppose we're trying to do exactly the same thing to them, aren't we?' Daniel answered grimly.

'Are we? I was asking myself the very same thing, last time I came to London—' Dianne didn't remind him of the bombing of the fish and chip shop, which he knew about. 'Are we bombing civilians and city centres too? As well as strategic targets? We never see the target maps.'

'I'll have to get a few more trips up my sleeve before I can honestly answer that, but I like to think not.' Daniel shrugged. 'It's better not to worry about it. We've just got to beat the bastards any way we can. The Japs, too.'

Dianne guided him through the gate, turning away from the bombing. 'What about that? Do you worry that you should be back home fighting the Japanese instead of being here and putting up with our problems?'

Daniel laughed softly. 'I reckon if the Japs do invade Australia, they might be in for a bit of a shock. North Queensland's not much like this,' he gestured at the impeccable gardens around them. 'Unless you've got crocodiles hiding in the rose bushes.'

'And deadly bunyips,' she reminded him, pleased to get it right.

'Those, too. They're not to be taken lightly, you know,' he told her seriously, then added in a lighter tone. 'Besides, the situation seems to have gotten better in New Guinea, and with the Yanks around, things are looking up. I'm sure someone will come and get us, if we're needed. If you believe some of the letters the chaps are getting, it's more like we're being invaded by Americans, not the Japanese.'

As they walked further through the flowerbeds, Dianne told him the story of the young shop assistant who was so pleased the Americans had come. Now it sounded funny and didn't reveal the sad side. Daniel found it amusing, at least.

They took their time, sometimes dodging under trees to huddle together against a fresh shower of rain. Daniel enjoyed the closeness and Dianne didn't seem to mind either. Deeper in the park they found some anti-aircraft batteries, the guns placed there because of the clear fields of fire they had in the open space. The crews looked almost bored. The tense expectations they'd suffered in the days of the Battle of Britain and the Blitz were gone. At one gun, some street urchins dared to go close, watched carefully by a scowling sergeant.

Just as Daniel believed he'd seen enough roses to last him a lifetime, Dianne took him out a different entrance and back onto the streets, explaining they were heading for no less than Buckingham Palace itself. His interest was tempered by signs pointing towards Victoria Station and he wondered if Dianne was thinking of making this a last attraction before heading home.

The palace had the normal numbers of touring servicemen peering between the bars of the wrought iron fence, imagining they might actually catch a glimpse of the king. Many had cameras and took hopeful shots as well, avoiding the glaring guards who suspected one and all as German spies. Dianne, having seen it many times, waited patiently for Daniel to be satisfied. He lingered longer than he wanted, feeling obligated to appear awed in the presence of the very throne of England.

Finally he took the risk and asked, 'Well, what next?'

'What do you want?'

'I wouldn't mind finding somewhere warm and cosy to sit down for a while. It feels like I've been walking for a week.'

'A pub, in other words?'

'Well, since you insist.'

217

Dianne rolled her eyes and wearily grabbed his hand. 'This way, you incurable drunkard. Lucky for you, I do happen to know of a few in this area.'

The lounge bar was like many others, with a low beamed ceiling and lead-lighted windows, the furniture wooden and stained, the whole place reeking of a long history. It was late enough in the afternoon for the first after-work drinkers to be there. Daniel and Dianne found an empty table close to a fire. The burning wood looked suspiciously like pieces of a building frame, probably scavenged from a bomb site. Questions about this—and like about that meat in his luncheon pie—Daniel guessed, should never be asked.

The two of them chatted comfortably. Dianne was drinking a gin and tonic, while Daniel was acquiring a taste for Guinness. Both of them happily wreathed themselves in cigarette smoke. The only thing spoiling the moment for him was the awareness it was getting dark outside, heralding the time they must leave.

With a sigh he said, 'When are you back on duty? First thing in the morning?'

'No,' she answered casually. 'I've got a shift in the afternoon starting at 1500. Don't know why. Probably a training run for some new girls.'

'You don't have to go back tonight?' Daniel sat up straighter, blinking at the smoke.

'I didn't say that.'

'Oh—no, I suppose you didn't.'

She watched him carefully for a second. 'What else do you think we could do?'

He cautiously weighed his reply. 'Well, we could certainly have a nice dinner at a restaurant and maybe see a show, if you found one you liked. Perhaps we could go to the pictures? Of course, we'd have to stay the night in a hotel…'

'I'm glad you said that last, as if it's the least important of all.'

'Would you like to stay at your parents? Will they let me sleep on the floor?'

Dianne laughed so abruptly and loud that several patrons turned to look. She clamped a hand over her mouth and said, between her fingers, 'No, ah… I—I don't think that would be a good idea. Definitely not. It'd have to be a hotel.'

'All right,' Daniel kept calm, though his stomach was churning. 'Which hotel? Any one you like, it's your choice.'

She felt a flush of guilt, because for a moment Dianne was tempted to use his money to indulge herself. She said, 'No, I've changed my mind. Perhaps we'd better go back.'

'No, you don't—I'm sorry.' He shook his head theatrically. 'It's too late already. You can't change your mind now. I've had visions of a real bed, instead of those worn-out door mats the air force calls a mattress.'

'You don't have to go back. I can catch a train by myself, you know.'

'If you go back, I'm coming with you.'

'That's not fair. You'll make me feel bad.'

Daniel ticked things off with his fingers. 'Look, we'll have a nice dinner, go to a show of some sort and stay in a nice hotel, then catch the first train back in the morning. You can have your own room, by the way.'

'I can't afford a room anywhere.'

'It's my treat, remember? I told you last night.'

'Daniel, you don't know how hard it is for me to agree with that. It doesn't feel right.'

'I'll telegram the old man to flog off a few extra sheep. He won't miss them.'

It made her smile. 'You know that's not the point.'

'It is, you know. If I don't start spending some of this money he keeps sending, he'll stop. I need to splash out a bit.'

She didn't know what to say and couldn't deny that a large part of her would love to stay in a nice hotel. Perhaps she could have a real bath? The idea was so tempting, but what would it really cost her? For that matter, would she mind paying?

Daniel said gently, 'Come on, Dianne. Do it for me? Let's have a great night in London, while we can.'

She took a deep breath. 'Can I lock my door?'

'You can even throw away the key.'

'Promise you won't get drunk?'

'No.'

'Fair enough,' she shrugged.

***

Dianne hugged herself with delight—when Daniel wasn't watching—when the clerk at the Dorchester Hotel readily offered them adjoining rooms. The half crown that Daniel slipped into his hand went into a pocket with deft practice.

Heaven forbid, they could run her a hot bath immediately.

They decided to give each other an hour and a half to freshen up before going out again to look for a dinner restaurant, although this was purely for Dianne to have her bath really. Neither had a change of clothes.

Dianne was overjoyed at walking into her room and seeing the large, comfortable bed, soft furnishings and expensive decorations. She touched everything happily, listening to the maid running a bath for her in the small ensuite, and wished she had a clean uniform to put on. It came to her that wearing something civilian didn't appeal, making her smile. Civilian clothes and her civilian life weren't a part of this, she knew. She was determined not to feel guilty about Daniel paying for it all. He had insisted. Sometimes, you had to have faith that things would work out the way they should.

Next door, Daniel was doing the same for different reasons. He fingered all the linen and furniture just to occupy himself, immediately bored, and decided to have a quick bath too and spend the rest of the ninety minutes in a quiet bar somewhere close, slowly having a few drinks. He couldn't suffer sitting around for an hour or so waiting for Dianne to finish whatever it was girls did for half the night in a tepid bath. Besides, his hopes for what might happen later, despite his assurances to her, could torture his imagination in this empty, alcohol-free room.

Inspired, he knocked on the interconnecting door and heard a near-startled reply.

'Yes? Who is it?'

'It's me, Dianne. I'm going to nip out a bit later and buy tickets for a show, if I can. Save us queuing up. Is there anything you fancy?'

She sounded relieved and called back without opening the door. 'No, anything good you can get into, I don't mind.'

'I'll scout around for a good restaurant too and be back in time to pick you up.'

'Whatever is best. Don't panic.'

Dianne was relieved. She felt better about relaxing in the bath and enjoying herself without worrying that Daniel might be impatiently pacing the floor in the next room. She had no doubts he would end up in a pub somewhere, and she trusted him to behave.

Daniel went into his own ensuite and ran a bath for himself, although he could have called a maid. As he hurriedly soaped himself it occurred to him it was a pleasure rarely experienced these days, but he'd promised Dianne tickets to a play or maybe a musical and he couldn't afford to linger. He towelled himself dry and dressed again, feeling a little shabby since he was clean and his uniform wasn't. Checking he had his watch, wallet and the key to the room, he set off closing the door quietly so not to disturb Dianne.

By then she was luxuriating in a deep, hot bath and oblivious to anything beyond the walls. Most baths in London had a "plimsol" line on them, like a ship's maximum draught, to help with the rationing of the valuable coal that heated the water. The maid had smiled that Dianne was in the air force and forgot to turn the water off in time.

***

Daniel discovered the streets of London weren't so easily navigated, especially after dark and without Dianne to push and pull him in the right direction. Outside the hotel, he tried to guess which way to go, gave up instantly and turned to a doorman lurking in the shadows.

'Excuse me. I'm supposed to find a show and a decent restaurant for a meal. I wouldn't have a clue which way to go.' Daniel spread his arms helplessly.

The doorman looked him up and down knowingly. 'You'd be wanting Soho, I'm guessing, sir.'

'Soho? Isn't that where…?'

'Yes, sir. And all the theatres and dance halls. You only need to know exactly where to go.' The doorman regarded him as if this were a charade he went through frequently. 'Can I call you a cabbie?'

'No thanks, I'd better walk. I need to waste some time.'

'Yes sir, I suppose it is a bit early for that sort of thing. Here, let me show you.'

He led Daniel to the middle of the footpath and gave him precise instructions, pointing with his flattened hand and mimicking each turn with a wave. Daniel didn't have the heart to admit most of it meant little to him and tried his best to remember what he figured were the most important bits. After giving the doorman a generous tip, he set off in the first direction he'd been given.

Ten minutes later he took an abrupt change of course into a blackout curtain that promised a bar behind and ordered a pint of Guinness. It went down very quickly, and mindful he still had a lot of time to pass, bought another to drink more sedately.

Near the end of this pint he asked the barman, 'Apparently, I should go to Soho and see a show. What's the best way there?'

The barman opened his mouth to begin explaining, then stopped. 'Call a taxi,' he decided.

'Good idea,' Daniel nodded, tipped him and walked a little unsteadily out the door to stand on the curb. He hailed a cab within a minute.

'To Soho, please,' he said, collapsing gratefully into the back seat.

'Where else?' the taxi driver replied good-humouredly, engaging the gears. 'You're an Australian, right?'

'Sheep farmer,' Daniel nodded, since it had apparently impressed Dianne that day.

'Is that right? What do they expect you to do, shear Hitler to death?'

'Ah, no. Bomber Command. Mid-upper gunner in a Lancaster.'

'Those big, new buggers? Good on you, son. Give 'em hell for me.'

Daniel was relieved to be let out of the taxi at Piccadilly Circus because it was somewhere he recognised from their day's sight-seeing.

'Soho's that way,' the driver told him. 'Stay out of the small side-streets on your own, all right? They're no place for sheep farmers.'

Daniel thanked him and waved away the change due on the fare. He set off down the nearest street towards Soho, as he'd been told. It was much colder and the showers were persisting, chilling a breeze and making the pavements dangerously slick. It helped to shake some of the Guinness fog from his mind and Daniel realised the second pint had been a bad idea. He needed to sober up a little before he went back.

Soho was a place that came into its best after the sun went down, which wasn't helpful with a wartime blackout in force. The result was doorways with hooded, red lights and shadowy figures calling out, advertising their wares. The more respectable taverns and bars had the standard signs, barely lit, but Daniel wasn't after another drink. The trouble was, he couldn't quite figure out what he was looking for. The streets were surprisingly crowded by what he assumed were servicemen moving from one door to next. Everyone else seemed to know where they were going.

A voice hissed out at him from the gloom.

'Looking for some fun, son?'

Daniel went over and peered at a small, older man standing in a darkened doorway. 'I'm trying to find some kind of decent show. Where the hell are you supposed to go?'

'We've got the best show right 'ere. Downstairs. Two quid to get in and you get a free pint.'

'Two quid? Really?'

'You get a free pint,' the man whined. 'And you see the show for as long as you like. Unless something else takes your fancy.'

'What do you mean?'

A group of men loomed behind Daniel and waited for him to get out the way.

The doorman was suddenly impatient. 'Come on, son. Make up your mind. Everyone wants to see our show and you won't all fit in.'

'What sort of show is it?'

'Christ, does it matter? They're all the same, you know. Ours is better, that's all.'

Daniel was confused and more than a little suspicious he was in the wrong place, but he needed to get inside somewhere. His bladder was starting to require urgent attention and the idea of finding a toilet, some decent light and someone to ask proper directions all added up to two quid's worth of good value.

'All right, bugger it,' he said, pulling out two pound notes from his pocket. His wallet was buried inside his jacket—strong advice against pickpockets from Dianne earlier in the day. The doorman gave him a grimy playing card as a receipt.

'For your drink,' he said, turning to the group. 'Step up, lads! Best show in town!'

Steep stairs on the other side of the door took Daniel unawares and he nearly fell. At the bottom he turned a corner and found himself in a dim, sour-smelling room with a bar at one end and lounge chairs scattered throughout, all of them roughly facing a makeshift stage at the opposite wall. From somewhere a gramophone played a scratched record too loud, distorting the music. Daniel was annoyed there was hardly any more light than out in the street. Only a dozen people were there with just two standing at the bar. It was already looking like a bad choice except for the "Gents" sign beside the stage. He was unbuttoning his fly even as he walked across the bar.

The urinal bore no resemblance to his ensuite at the Dorchester. It brought Daniel such sweet relief he felt in much better shape to cope with whatever the place could offer. In fact, he figured he might as well drink his free pint and get his money's worth.

The girl behind the bar was so scantily clad that Daniel could hardly believe it. The other two customers had melted away.

'Here you go, love,' she said with a smile that revealed lipstick-smeared teeth.

'How long before the show starts?' Daniel asked, sipping the beer. It was watery and too warm, making him pull a face.

'Have a seat. It won't be long.' She winked to encourage him.

By now, Daniel knew he was definitely in the wrong place—at least, not the kind of establishment he could bring Dianne. He would have left, only he had a stubborn insistence to drink at least some of the lukewarm pint. To be really honest with himself, he hoped to get a peek at the show, if there was time.

Time! He fumbled at his watch, which had a leather cover over the face, and tried to see the dial. The luminous hands swam in and out of focus for a second, then he worked out he had less than twenty-five minutes before Dianne would be expecting a knock on the door.

'Damn, I've hardly got time to get back,' he groaned to himself, sinking down onto a vacant double lounge chair. He nearly went through it, the springs and cushions useless. A good portion of the beer spilt on his trousers. Swearing, he wiped at it with his sleeve.

'Oh dear, you're not having a very good night, are you?'

Daniel looked up in time to see a girl dressed in a high skirt and black stockings sitting next to him.

'No, wait a second…'

Too late, she sat and fell against him, the ruined sofa throwing them together. She giggled and put a hand familiarly on his thigh to push herself upright.

'Sorry about that,' she said breathlessly, putting her face close to his. 'Hello, my name's Josephine. What's yours?'

Daniel guessed she wasn't more than twenty. She was plump in the face and thighs—the dress had ridden up so he could see most of them—and her make-up was heavy. Dark and curly hair dropped to her shoulders and smelled of something above her cheap perfume. Bright eyes flashed at him in the gloom.

'Hello, I'm Daniel. I was just about to go…'

'But you haven't finished your drink.'

Daniel tried to make some space between them. The sofa wouldn't allow it. 'I don't like it. I only came down here to see what sort of show it is, but I've run out of time.'

Josephine put on such an expression of tragic disappointment Daniel feared she would burst into tears. 'I can get one of the other girls for you, if you like,' she said quietly.

It took a moment for him to understand. 'No! No, it's not anything to do with you. I really shouldn't have come down here. I was looking for something else.'

'That's what everyone says.'

'No, honest! I was looking for a show to take my—ah, my sweetheart. I got kind of lost. The bloke at the door talked me into coming down here.'

'You have a sweetheart?' Josephine examined him with a critical eye. 'It doesn't sound like you're so sure about it.'

'Well, I think I have. She's waiting for me back at the hotel.' Daniel was getting desperate to escape, but he had the presence of mind not to mention the Dorchester. This girl would instantly equate that with a fat wallet.

'Goodness, aren't you a bad boy?' Josephine wagged a finger at him. 'Coming to a place like this when your lady's waiting back in the room? You're Australian, aren't you? You Aussies are all the same. Very naughty.'

Lesson learned, Daniel didn't mention sheep. 'Yes, I am—Australian, I mean. I've really got to go. I'm sorry, don't take it personally.' He tried to get up and was foiled by her hand on his arm.

'So, where are you going to take her, Daniel?'

He started getting annoyed at her persistence. 'I don't know, and I haven't got any damned time left to find anywhere—'

'Buy me a drink and I'll tell you where to go.' She pouted at him.

'Really, I'd like to sit a while, only I've already told you—'

'You don't have to stay and drink with me. Just buy me one and I'll tell you all the good places to go, all right?'

Daniel gave in. 'Fair enough, but you'd better be quick.'

Josephine signalled at someone and within seconds the barmaid appeared with a docket book on a tray.

'The usual, Jo?' she asked, looking at Daniel.

'Gin on the rocks, love,' Josephine said.

'That'll be a pound, soldier.'

'What? Is it the whole fucking bottle?'

Josephine shushed him with a finger to her lips, her eyes wide. 'Keep it down. You don't want the lads chucking you out the back door.'

'For God's sake...' Disgusted, Daniel threw a pound note on the tray. Unfazed, the barmaid walked away. 'How long will she take?' he nearly snapped.

'Oh, I'll be having it later. Can't drink while I'm working.' She winked and Daniel fumed. Winking seemed to excuse anything in this country.

'That's it, I've had enough.'

This time he managed to rise, but Josephine grabbed his wrist and stopped him leaving. He thought about getting very angry. With her free hand, she beckoned Daniel to bend down and share a secret. Reluctantly, he did so and she put her lips close to his ear, giving him an uncomfortable reminder of Dianne waiting for him at the hotel.

Josephine whispered, 'Go back to Piccadilly Circus and look for Bert near the kid's roundabout ride. He scalps tickets to nearly every show around here. Wait until the last minute and he'll do any deal to get rid of them.' Without warning, she placed a wet kiss on Daniel's cheek and fell back with a laugh.

'Thanks, I think,' Daniel said, wiping at his cheek. 'Enjoy that bloody expensive drink.'

He left without waiting for an answer, moving towards the steps and discovering a small crowd in his way. Someone called out to him that the show was about to start. Daniel ignored this and pushed through to the stairs.

Outside he welcomed the fresh air with relieved, deep breaths. Combined with the unpleasantness of the last ten minutes, he felt almost sober. His vision still shifted a bit, but his thinking was clear.

'Be damned to this, I'm going home,' he decided. He'd failed miserably in finding a show or a good restaurant, and he figured that being too late back to the hotel would only make things worse.

Someone gave him directions back to Piccadilly Circus and Daniel found it easily. He went straight to the curb for a cab and while he waited saw a likely-looking fellow that could be Bert next to the closed roundabout, standing beside a small cart selling something. Daniel was tempted to change his plan again, then a taxi pulled up in front of him and he climbed gratefully in the back.

'The Dorchester, thanks,' he said, glad to be certain of where to go for once.

'The Dorchester? Are you sure, lad?' The cabbie stared at him over his shoulder. In the darkness, the whites of his eyes were large.

'Yes, I'm staying there.' Daniel guessed what the problem could be. 'I spilled a damned drink all over me, that's all.'

'You look a mess, if you don't mind me warning you, sir,' the cabbie grunted, pulling away from the curb. 'Nice perfume, too.'

The doorman at the Dorchester greeted him with a grin. 'Didn't like the show, sir?'

'Something along those lines,' Daniel grumbled without stopping. He didn't notice the odd stares he got as he crossed the foyer.

Dianne was dressed only in a thick, white bathrobe when she answered the door. The sight took Daniel's breath away. She looked radiant until her expression changed to mild shock.

'What on earth happened to you?'

Daniel worried she was just a moment away from slamming the door in his face. 'Can I come in?' he asked and pushed through anyway. 'I've just had a terrible time.'

'I can smell how terrible it was,' she said, putting a hand over her nose. She kicked the door closed.

'Someone tipped nearly a pint of beer in my lap,' he explained weakly. He sat down quickly in the nearest chair, figuring Dianne might not kick him out so readily if he wasn't standing.

'Really?' She didn't come closer. 'Did they shower a whole bottle of cheap perfume over your jacket too?'

'Oh? Look, believe me, everything just went really wrong. I ended up in the most God-awful place.'

'It must have been shocking,' Dianne said flatly. 'Because that lipstick doesn't suit you at all.'

'Oh shit—you're kidding?' Daniel turned to face a mirror and saw the bright red smudge on his cheek. His hair was everywhere and a white coating on his shoulder could only be make-up from Josephine after she'd fallen against him.

'Oh no,' he flopped his head onto his hands. 'Can I use your bathroom for a minute?'

Dianne still hadn't moved. 'No, you can't. I think you can stay right there and tell me exactly what you've been doing before you do another thing.'

Daniel decided that honesty was the best policy, took a deep breath and poured out the story of his last hour or so. When he finished, he looked up to see her reaction. The scowl on Dianne's face was fierce.

'I didn't mean any of it,' he pleaded. 'I went out to buy tickets and maybe have a quite beer, and ended up in this… this—'

'Prostitute's arms,' Dianne finished for him grimly.

'No, that's not true,' He held up a finger. 'I didn't let her put her arms around me.'

'She wasn't interested in anything above your waist, Daniel.'

'No, only my wallet, more like it. God, a whole pound for a gin on the rocks! How can they?' He dropped his head back down again in despair.

Dianne burst out laughing and couldn't stop. She stumbled over to the bed and sat down, tears in her eyes and her shoulders shaking. Whenever her mirth began to subside, she needed only to glance at Daniel's forlorn figure and it would set her off again.

He didn't know what to do, so he sat there and took it. Finally, when a spate of hiccups attacked her more violently than the laughing and she might hear him, he said, 'All right, I admit I did a very poor job of the whole thing. It's not that funny. I wasted a lot of money.'

Dianne managed to blurt out, 'Yes, you poor, innocent thing. Taken advantage of like that.' That started her giggling uncontrollably again.

Daniel stood up. 'I think I'm going to give you a great, big hug for being so understanding.'

Her laughing turned instantly to a scream. 'No. No, you don't! You can sit right back down again.'

'What am I going to do? I stink!'

'Exactly. Just sit down.'

Daniel did as he was told and Dianne edged closer, dropping to her knees and keeping her face averted. Reaching as far forward as she could, she undid the laces on his boots and pulled them off.

'What are you doing?' he asked.

'We're going to give your uniform to a maid and ask if she can sponge it down.'

'How long will that take?'

'As long as it has to. We can't go out with you smelling like this.'

Now Dianne was closer and undoing the buttons on his jacket. Daniel could smell the bath salts and shampoo in her hair, and the bathrobe gaped teasingly. He was mesmerised.

'No, you'll have to do it yourself,' she said, falling back with a gasp. 'God, you smell awful. I'll get you a robe and call room service while you get undressed. Don't forget to empty your pockets.'

She found another robe in the cupboard and draped it over the back of the chair, then pointedly turned her back on Daniel as she spoke on the telephone to room service, explaining what was needed. When she hung up, she asked without turning, 'Have you finished?'

'I suppose so.'

Daniel stood in the robe, his stockinged feet looking a little incongruous. His trousers, shirt and jacket were in a heap on the floor.

Using her fingertips, Dianne put them in a laundry basket. At that moment there was a knock on the door. Dianne went over and let in a young maid, who blushed at the sight of them both.

'What do you think? Can you help him?' Dianne asked the young girl, after showing her the clothes and ignoring her embarrassment.

'I don't know if I can get it all out without a proper wash, ma'am,' the girl said in a low voice, her head down as she examined the stains. 'It does pong a bit, doesn't it?'

'Yes, it does,' Dianne agreed, with a look at Daniel. 'Can you have it back in an hour?'

'I'll do my best, ma'am.'

'Thank you. Daniel? Have you got something for this poor girl's extra trouble?'

'What? Oh, right.' He took some change from a table and gave it to the maid, who was so thrilled at how much it was that Daniel wondered himself.

When the maid had gone, Dianne turned off the main light, leaving a bedside lamp on, and went to stand directly in front of Daniel, close enough to touch him. She said softly, 'What do you think we should do for the next hour?'

He had to clear his throat. 'Ah, I'm not sure. Have you got any ideas?'

Dianne put one hand inside the fold of his robe and ran it down his chest slowly, dragging her fingertips. Then she did the same with the other hand, pushing aside the lapels of the robe to make room. Daniel didn't move and hardly dared to breathe in case it stopped her. Dianne encircled his waist and pulled herself hard against him, raising her face for a kiss. It became a passionate embrace, their lips together hungrily, until Daniel tugged Dianne's robe from her shoulders to kiss her neck. The gown dropped to floor revealing Dianne naked underneath. After a moment she stepped back, taking his hand, then tugged Daniel towards the bed.

'Come on, we've only got an hour,' she whispered.

He followed obediently, using his free hand to rip impatiently at his own gown.

Thirteen.

It wasn't until the Second World War that opposing forces had the ability to strike at the industrial capability of their enemy. Before this, the soldiers fought each other equipped with weapons, food and provisions as best their homelands could provide. In the Great War of 1914-1918 the Germans carried out a U-boat campaign against convoys from the United States, hoping to starve Great Britain of supplies, but apart from some rare exceptions using Zeppelin air raids that were more shocking for the populace than destructive, they never directly attacked the British or American factories or farms, or the people who worked them. Similarly, the First World War Allies couldn't reach the manufacturing plants of Germany.

In 1941, after the Dunkirk evacuation and Hitler's headlong rush through Europe had halted at the English Channel, fighting the war over vast distances began in earnest. For the Germans it again turned into ferocious assaults on the Atlantic convoys from America, since it was from there the real source of the Allies' strength came, shipped in vast amounts. In turn, the British and, soon afterwards, the Americans used long-range bombers to attack the industrial heartland of Germany's Ruhr valley and other important centres, trying to destroy the German's ability to manufacture anything in the first place. It was a high priority. The basic theory was that every German soldier, airman and sailor should be ill-equipped and lacking supplies before any battle was even fought. Especially during any counter-invasion of France.

The United States Army Air Force and the Royal Air Force Bomber Command approached the problem of bombing Germany in entirely different ways, primarily because each believed their method was best and regarded the other as flawed. The Americans, after building up their strength on the British mainland, flew in large formations in daylight, releasing their payloads en masse from high altitude (controlled by a master bomber-aimer) but nonetheless suffering intense anti-aircraft gunnery and fierce opposition from Luftwaffe fighter squadrons.

The RAF attacked at night, which required much lower altitudes, and using a unique "streaming" formation. It was like a close, single file of bombers, akin to a line of ants crawling across the ground except obviously airborne, sometimes numbering up to a thousand with each aircraft strictly maintaining a different, pre-determined height to avoid collisions. Viewed from the side, that single line was stepped or staggered. Every bomber was responsible for aiming and releasing their munitions on the target when they arrived. If, as often happened, the bomb-aimer didn't get a good look at the target and didn't release, the aircraft would circle around for a second or even third pass.

The greatest danger apart from that posed by the defenders was a risk of being hit by "friendly" bombs from above. Keeping a correct altitude was simple for an undamaged bomber, but a precise speed was something different. The vagaries of the winds at alternate heights or aircraft that had mechanical problems slowing down resulted in planes arriving at the target together, unseen in the night. The amount of bombers severely damaged or bludgeoned out of the sky from bombs released above them was much higher than the odds of such a thing occurring might suggest. Incendiary bombs, relatively small but dropped in clusters, could set an aircraft below alight in seconds. The Germans even used bombing an enemy formation from above as an effective defence.

The main advantage was that the stream presented a formidable defence against fighters from the sheer number of guns the bombers brought to bear on any attacker. Bombers that maintained their position in the stream were significantly safer from fighter attack. However, unlucky, single aircraft that strayed might be detected by radar and quickly picked off by a German night-fighter guided in by radio.

The Germans countered the stream tactic by surrounding their cities with massive anti-aircraft batteries to deal with the lower-flying RAF bombers, and by concentrating the night-fighter's efforts within a nearby radius where stumbling across a bomber was likely in the vicinity of the target. It helped, too, that the burning factories both lit the large aircraft from below, or silhouetted them from above.

It was 1430 and the crew of D-Delta was wasting time on the perimeter of the dispersal, grabbing the opportunity for a cigarette and watching the ground crew do much the same, fiddling with last-minute checks they had performed several times already. A raid had been planned and briefed, but an unknown delay let the men stay out of the aircraft for the moment. The afternoon was fine, so all they knew was it couldn't be a weather problem. The target was to be ammunition dumps and German troop concentrations around the French Le Havre coast, just a short trip over the Channel. There was a rumour a storm front was moving across France and the waiting was to let it pass.

Flanders grumbled loudly, 'More likely the sky's full of bloody Me 109s and we're waiting for them to run out of bloody fuel.'

'Cheerful bastard,' Barrymore tossed the dregs from a mug of tea at him, making Flanders yell angrily and dodge to one side. 'I'll take that poor weather theory, before your damned fighters.'

Branner was ignoring them, staring steadfastly towards the Control Tower in the distance. A green flare was going to announce the raid would start. A red one meant a total cancellation. He couldn't decide which he wanted. Being so close to going, a part of him wanted to finish the job, get it over with and chalk an operation up against their name. Especially since it might be a quick trip. Avoiding the whole dangerous business was always attractive too.

Daniel had wandered over to Sergeant Granger, who was in his usual position near the hut, his pipe alight and a mug of tea in his hand.

'They know how to muck us around, right, Sarge?' Daniel said amiably. It could be a gamble how Granger might respond. Friendly and ready to chat, or tense and preoccupied with his work.

He answered slowly, nodding, 'I suppose they have their reasons. Greater minds than ours are planning these things.'

Feeling safe, Daniel said, 'Sergeant, do you mind if I ask you something? Have you ever heard of... well, ground staff and people like that stowing away in the bombers for a ride?'

Granger raised an eyebrow at him. 'Why on earth would they want to do that?'

'That's what I thought. Someone was telling me it's quite a popular idea. For a bit of a thrill, I suppose.'

'To go on a raid?'

'Perhaps, if they're game enough, or just a training run.'

'Like who?'

Daniel detected a gleam in Granger's eye that suggested the sergeant wasn't going to give him anything. 'Ah, perhaps I'd better not talk out of turn. Wouldn't want to get anybody into trouble for nothing.'

'There's trouble enough.' Granger said easily, punctuating it with a cloud of tobacco smoke.

'So… you've never been tempted? To hitch a ride?'

'I get plenty of flying time, usually with my arse hanging out the door and a brace of spanners between my teeth while I try and fix some bloody thing.'

Daniel laughed at the image. 'I suppose so. You don't want to see a raid?'

Granger gave him another sideways look. 'I've seen my share of Germans too. They over-ran our airfield during one of the big pushes in 1918. I was trying to burn the last of our buggered SE5a's, before running like hell to a waiting truck to skedaddle. Their infantry were walking across the landing strip, bold as brass, and spotted me. I tossed a match at the plane and sprinted for my life, so bloody terrified I don't know if the thing caught fire.'

'You were in the last war?' Daniel was awe-struck. Looking at Granger more closely, he realised the sergeant could be old enough.

'Just, in the last year only—and that was too long.' Granger fell silent and looked into the distance. Daniel figured he wasn't about to say more, but Granger added thoughtfully, 'I was barely old enough to join up and guessed I'd be safe as an aircraft fitter well behind the lines. It let my mum sleep at nights, anyway. When those Huns came like grey ghosts out of the mist, I nearly soiled my britches. We came close to losing the war that day.'

'Christ, you were almost captured? Imagine that.'

'I reckon I was almost shot,' Granger said dryly. 'They weren't taking too many prisoners that day.'

Daniel shook his head, letting out a long breath. 'Now you've got to do it all again?'

'No, you have to do it this time. You won't be finding me sneaking a trip on any bloody bombing mission.'

Daniel gave him a lop-sided grin. 'Come on, Sarge. I'll bet you know of someone who's gone for a jaunt, who shouldn't have.'

Granger pursed his lips. 'I've heard there're plenty of staff officers who feel obliged to have a peek or just take the risk once or twice. But…' He tapped the side of his nose. 'Like you said, let's not get anybody into any trouble.'

Branner broke in, calling, 'Here we go, lads! Green flare!'

A bright green light was arcing across the sky, fired from the Control Tower.

The crew scrambled urgently into the Lancaster, although they knew there was plenty of time. In their positions, the standard checks were redone again. Over the intercom, Branner confirmed the mission was on and began his routine for starting the engines. Daniel was in his turret and could see in the distance other bombers from their squadron scattered around the airfield at dispersals. All of them were coughing blue smoke from their exhausts, the giant propellers beginning to turn.

Next came the long taxi to the end of the runway. Daniel willed himself to relax, closing his eyes and taking deep breaths. Once they were airborne, it was a luxury he couldn't afford. He felt the Lancaster rumbling along and the slight sideways pressure as Branner guided it around bends. Then D-Delta stopped and Daniel guessed they were awaiting their turn at the end of the strip.

'Everyone wave cheerio,' Wills called.

Daniel opened his eyes to see a large group of people gathered to see them off, standing at the same spot Dianne and Susan had suffered the ageing deck chairs. The onlookers were enthusiastically sending off each bomber. Dianne, he knew, was inside the Operation Room and couldn't be there, so Daniel didn't look for her.

Wills reported for the sake of those who couldn't see, 'There's a big gaggle of girls wishing us luck. A few blokes too,' he added dismissively.

Flanders said, 'Danny, I suppose your new sweetheart is there, right at the front and waving her knickers?'

'No, she's on duty,' Daniel replied levelly. 'I'll tell her you said that. You'll be in big strife next time she sees you.'

'I'm surprised she can even stand, considering what you must have been up to all night in London.'

Daniel hadn't revealed anything to the others about his time away with Dianne, although it had been plain to see their relationship was closer. Flanders was fishing for details, as always.

'You don't give up, do you?' Daniel said.

'He gives up now,' Branner interrupted as the Lancaster started to shake and move forward with a roar. 'Cut the chatter while I concentrate on getting this girl off the ground.'

D-Delta was loaded with a clutch of incendiary bombs and a single 4000-pound cookie. The bomber gathered speed along the runway like an unstoppable beast. With plenty of room to spare they could feel the wings had enough lift and Branner pulled back on the controls. D-Delta left the runway gently, the undercarriage groaning as the burden eased. Moments later Sexton retracted it and they began the climb to their allotted altitude.

'Piece of cake,' Flanders said over the intercom. 'Do you think we'll be back in time for a pint?'

'You could bail out now and be in the pub in half an hour,' Barrymore answered him. 'We don't really need you. Even I could find our way to France. Come to think of it, what do you do in your little box back there?'

'He gives me a bloody course for the target,' Branner said. 'Come on, Bruce. Pull your finger out.'

'Skipper, steer one-two-on until we hit the coast, then turn into the stream on course oh-nine-five.'

'All right. Tell me again when we get there.'

D-Delta gained height for another ten minutes, then levelled out. Ahead of them, the English Channel shone in the afternoon sunshine as an inviting curve of blue on the horizon.

'Tail to pilot, test guns, skipper?'

'One at a time, all of you. Don't waste anything—and don't hit anybody.' All around them in the distance the sun glinted off the wings and glass of other bombers making their way towards the coast.

'Me first,' Wills said. He pulled the triggers of his four Brownings and grinned as the guns clattered deafeningly, vibrating the turret. The tracers vanished into the sky like a cloud of deadly fireflies.

'Mid-upper testing,' Daniel said crisply, letting off only half a dozen rounds from each of his two barrels, sending them high.

In the nose, Barrymore had been checking his bomb sight. With a curse he clambered up to his gun position, made sure nothing was directly in front, and fired the guns. The empty cases dropped around his feet. He said to himself, 'And that, I hope, is the only time I need to shoot at anything. The damned Luftwaffe can stay at home, thank you very much.'

As they drew closer to the coast an impressive sight was gathering around them. It was Daniel who broke the silence.

'Bloody hell, skipper. It looks like we're going to a fair old shindig.'

'It's a big raid, all right,' Branner replied.

The sky seemed filled with aircraft, mostly four-engine bombers, coming from all parts of the English mainland to converge into the stream and head for France. Everywhere Daniel looked in a broad sweep behind them planes were silhouetted against the heavens or the ground below. The sun sparkled off canopies and turrets in all directions. He guessed there were over two hundred within his limited vision alone. Wills, no doubt, would be able to see many more. Some were getting close as they came together at the stream's starting point.

In front of them, the bombers had formed into the gaggle structure, similar to a flight of geese that flew in a line, but at staggered heights. With the backdrop of a darkening, eastern horizon many of the bombers were lost to sight, but Branner could still pick out dozens above, below and near the same altitude as D-Delta. The closest was less than three hundred yards ahead and about four hundred below them.

Flanders reported, 'Navigator to pilot, I say we should be coming to that oh-nine-five course any minute now, skipper.'

'You can say that again, navigator. I'm turning now. Double-check our allocated height, please.' Branner added nervously. 'It's pretty bloody crowded up here.'

'We've got 15,250 feet all to ourselves,' Flanders said. 'Should be at 190 knots, skipper.'

'Looks about right,' Branner muttered, glancing at the throttles and resisting giving them a tweak.

Flying D-Delta in the stream was a demanding, exacting business. Each bomber was separated by only 300 feet of altitude and would have been almost nose to tail, if they'd been at the same height. Viewed from the side they were indeed like a flock of geese—a gaggle—or a giant set of stairs in the sky. There was little room for error. In daylight, aircraft that drifted out of position, by mistake or through damage, at least had a chance of being seen and avoided by the others. In the night raids every bomber relied on the skills of each pilot, flying blind with only instruments, to keep station in the stream. Near-collisions were common, saved by the glimpse of an exhaust flame or glint of moonlight off Perspex at the last instant. Too often the planes touched and wreaked fatal damage. Some aircraft limped home with frightening amounts of structural wreckage.

Flying like this, the bombers presented a strong defence with their amassed turrets and overlapping fields of fire. The German fighters rarely attacked the stream itself, instead waiting like scavenging wolves to finish off aeroplanes stricken by the anti-aircraft gunners.

D-Delta had another three Lancasters in front stepping upwards in height, before Branner could see the allocated altitudes reduced again. Beyond that, he couldn't tell. Behind them, he knew they went upwards again. D-Delta was the lowest plane in a vee section, which was just one part of an enormous rollercoaster structure of aircraft that now stretched for miles across the English Channel.

'Just like training,' Sexton said with a strained grin, seeing a bead of sweat form on Branner's brow.

Branner unclipped his mask briefly, so he could yell at Sexton without the others hearing on the intercom. 'Christ, imagine doing this at night. In the pitch bloody black.'

'I don't have to,' Sexton replied over the system. 'I'm sure we'll get a night op' soon enough.'

Branner nodded nervously, his eyes glued to the instrument panels except when they flicked at the nearest bomber in front.

Well over the Channel, everyone got serious about keeping an eye out for German fighters. Long banks of innocent-looking clouds above and to the north were ideal for an ME 109 or a twin-engine ME 110 to dart out and chance an attack. In his turret, the canvas sling already biting achingly into his rump, Daniel swung constantly from side to side, his eyes nearly watering from the effort of watching so hard. He kept returning his gaze back to those clouds.

'If I were a Jerry fighter, that's where I'd be,' he said to himself.

'Tail to skipper,' Wills sounded only half alarmed. 'The bloke behind us keeps creeping up something rotten. Their nose gunner was staring right at my crotch a minute ago.'

'Where is he now?' Branner twisted to look over his shoulder. It was too awkward, and he didn't like taking his sight off his own controls for more than a second. Sexton stood from where he crouched at some instruments and did the same. He couldn't see much more through the rear bubble of the canopy, but he immediately thought the head-on silhouette of the Lancaster following did look too close.

'He's dropping back again now, skip,' Wills reported. 'I don't know if he's correcting himself or just flying all over the bloody place.'

'Mid-upper to skipper,' Daniel cut in. 'I was thinking he's shaky too. Charlie beat me to it.'

Branner said, 'Maybe it's his first op' and he's a bit nervous. Perhaps he'll settle down after a while. There's not much else we can do. Keep a sharp eye on him when we get close to the drop zone, Charlie.'

'I'll shoot the bastard down if he looks like dropping his pills on my head, skipper.'

Branner didn't answer that. He checked their airspeed again and touched the throttles with his fingertips, fighting a fresh urge to add another notch and stay ahead of the rogue Lancaster.

It added a further tension to the next twenty minutes as they approached the target area. In the rear turret, Wills was on edge trying to gauge the right moment, if it arrived, when he should tell Branner the aircraft behind was too close again. It kept coming to the tip of his tongue, his fingers caressing the intercom button, then the bomber's shape would dwindle in size a fraction telling him it was drawing away.

'Useless bastard,' he told it, imagining putting a burst from his Brownings across the pilot's windscreen to make a point.

'I see flak well ahead,' Sexton reported, tapping Branner on the shoulder for good measure. He rarely sat on his fold-down canvas seat beside the pilot. Sexton was always on the move checking gauges, making tiny adjustments to knobs and valves, and visually inspecting any part of the bomber he could see. He also regularly popped his head up beside Branner, both to examine the dashboard dials and survey the skies around them. It was during one of these moments that he'd seen beyond the closest bombers the flowering, dirty brown smudges of anti-aircraft fire in the distance.

Branner raised his sight from the instruments. 'Okay, I see it. Coming up on the target, lads. Navigator, do you agree?'

Even though this was obvious with the aircraft all heading in the same direction and the flak beginning, Flanders was still supposed to confirm the target with his navigation.

'I say we're five minutes out, skipper,' Flanders said smoothly. 'Barra? We should have a forked river to the east with a largish village between the two. Quite a way off from the coast, really.'

'I can see it clearly, Flanno,' Barrymore confirmed.

Branner ordered, 'All right then, Geoff. Drop down to your bomb-aimer's position now. You'll be taking over in a few minutes.'

'Right-ho, skipper.'

It was Branner's last chance to set them up as best he could. He rechecked everything and allowed himself the tiniest adjustment of the throttles. After a final, deep breath he said, 'Geoff, whenever you're ready. I'm opening the bomb bay doors now.'

As if it were a signal for the flak to aim towards them, the airbursts started around D-Delta. They were widespread and plentiful, telling them the Germans had a lot to shoot and no shortage of ammunition. Nothing came close. Only a few explosions were near enough for the flat, cracking noise of the shell's detonation to be felt as well as heard. Otherwise, it was a procession of loud bangs adding to the overall clamour of the aircraft. Nobody took the flak lightly. They were aware of the old adage about a sniper's bullet—you never heard the one that kills you.

'I see the target, skipper,' Barrymore called excitedly. 'We're looking spot-on at the moment.' The rows of large sheds that were assigned to their load were ahead, although not within his bomb sights viewfinder yet.

In his turret, Daniel was trying hard not to flinch at the flak bursts around D-Delta. He had a fleeting recollection from his childhood, when he'd wanted to stop himself cringing at the lightning and shattering thunder from a close storm. He never managed it. Daniel pushed the memory away angrily. This was no time to be reminiscing.

It was a time for courageous Luftwaffe pilots to sneak close, risking their own anti-aircraft fire and claim an unwary enemy. Daniel stared upwards, thinking it was a smart thing to do since everyone else was probably looking down at the target and falling bombs. What he saw turned his blood cold.

He called urgently, 'Bloody hell, skipper! You'd better pull back. I'm looking straight into someone's bomb bay directly above and they haven't dropped yet. We'll cop the fucking lot!'

Branner jerked in his seat and glanced above them. Even in this emergency he wasn't willing to take his eyes off the instruments too long. He felt a wash of chilling fear, seeing what had happened. They had crept up on the Lancaster in front and were now flying almost under their hanging bomb load. It was his own fault, he knew. That ounce of extra speed to escape the bomber pressing them from behind had got them into twice as much trouble.

'Christ—easy does it,' he said through gritted teeth, edging the throttles back, although he felt like dragging them completely down to their stops. He needed to be careful and not shave off too much speed and the height they'd lose with it.

With agonising slowness, the Lancaster above pulled ahead.

Barrymore had his face pressed to the bomb sight. It had taken all of his willpower to stick to his job, shaken by the exchange in the intercom. He asked weakly, 'Skipper, are we still on? We need to come left a little. The target is close.'

Branner swung D-Delta a fraction.

'Left a little more skipper... a bit more... shit, can you split the difference back to the right? That's it. Steady... steady... bombs gone.'

They all felt the Lancaster lift as the weight of the bombs fell away. Branner struggled to keep the aircraft straight and level for a while longer until their bomb cameras had faithfully recorded the impacts. It was a long fifteen seconds until Barrymore called, 'Okay, let's get the hell out of here, skipper.'

Branner didn't need to ask what that meant—the photographs were taken. He banked D-Delta away onto the return course. It was at a lower altitude, giving the bomber stream a chance to dive and increase speed away from the flak. Everyone else was doing the same. D-Delta was now in a long line of tightly formated aircraft fleeing back towards England.

'Well done, Danny,' Branner breathed though a long sigh, once he was confident of their position. 'Bloody good thing someone was looking up.'

Daniel made light of it. 'I can't look anywhere else, skipper.'

'Okay, everyone. Let's get home in one piece and we can chalk this one up on the nose too. Keep an eye out for fighters.'

In the tail turret, Wills was mimicking Branner's last words, rolling his eyes. His electric suit was feeling heavier now that the worst of the mission was over and some of the adrenalin was ebbing from his bloodstream. Everything felt slower and longer. The Lancaster following them was now behaving perfectly.

'That'd be bloody right,' Wills told it. 'Now you haven't got any damn bombs to drop on us by mistake.'

For D-Delta it was an uneventful trip back to base, although they were to discover later that a dozen aircraft were lost during the course of the afternoon. It had been the normal, tragic cycle for the downed bombers. Flak had damaged them to an extent they couldn't stay in the stream. Drifting off like boats scattered in a stormy sea, German fighters called in by radar finished them off.

By the time D-Delta heaved to a halt at the dispersal, it was dark. Granger's ground crew hurried with a ladder to the rear hatch and met the airmen tumbling gratefully out. Immediately they walked to the edge of the concrete, tugging at the cigarettes in their pockets Cupped matches were shared around. No one commented on the trembling fingers or the first long, drawn-out lungful of smoke that came out a little shaky.

'Well, that was pretty easy,' Wills decided, looking squat and ungainly in his suit. 'Better than Augsburg.'

'Anything will be better than Augsburg, what do you think, skipper?' Flanders said sourly.

Branner was looking wide-eyed and vacant. Even though they had split away from the stream at the English coast to make their own way back, he still hadn't recovered from the long stint of intense piloting. He blinked at Flanders.

'Let's do one of these jobs at night, first. You might change your mind.'

'Look out, here comes our lift,' Sexton said cheerfully, before Branner's sombre reply could take hold. He pointed at a pair of covered headlights coming towards them, the labouring truck barely heard above the noise of another Lancaster landing.

Barrymore clapped his hands together. 'Not much to say at the debriefing. If we're quick, we might get an hour in the pub.'

'Why waste time going to the Arms? The mess is closer,' Sexton said.

'I'd rather go to the pub,' Daniel said, raising his voice above the approaching lorry.

'In other words, you think the girls are there,' Flanders said wryly.

'Not necessarily,' Daniel replied unconvincingly. 'We didn't make any arrangements in case we landed back here too late.'

'The girls?' Wills asked hopefully. 'Both of them? Do you think Susan will be there?'

Flanders said,' You really would flog a dead horse, wouldn't you? Can't you ever take a hint from that girl? You know, Susan and I would be getting on quite famously, if you didn't keep interrupting us all the time.'

'What bullshit. She's forever trying to escape your grubby little fingers, pinching her bum.'

The arguing went on while they piled into the truck, as well as more discussion between Daniel and Sexton about the merits of going to the pub or their mess. Already they were leaving the fear and strain of the mission behind on the tarmac of the dispersal, the more important subjects of girlfriends and drinking beer taking over. The debriefing would temporarily bring back the tension as they were asked to recall everything they could, especially anything that might explain the blank spaces on the blackboard for missing aircraft.

D-Delta had survived again, proving their belief that it would always be the "other bloke" who got shot down. It let them forget the tense, terrifying moments and gave them the courage to fly again. After all, the war had its advantages, like the excitement and steady wages.

Many men would say the bombing raids just got in the way of having a thoroughly good time.

Fourteen.

Barrymore couldn't understand why he felt so tired all of a sudden. This last minute of a bombing run was no time to be taking a nap. Besides, how could he sleep after there had been that loud bang and bright light? Much closer than all the other flak shells that exploded in the night sky all around them, while Bremerhaven burned like Dante's inferno below.

Something had slammed so hard into his chest that he felt numb—not pain. When Barrymore prodded curiously at himself, his fingers encountered warm wetness and the grit of broken Perspex. There was a strong wind inside the plane, which was odd. He wasn't sitting right either. Instruments and other things dug uncomfortably into his shoulders and lower back this way. Barrymore remembered he was in the middle of something important—something he was supposed to do or he'd get into serious trouble. His eyes focused on the bomb release on its stalk beside the bomb sight.

'Ah, that's it,' he sighed with relief. Barrymore went to reach over and press the button, but his right arm wouldn't move. Frowning at the inconvenience, he worked his left arm away from the bulkhead, stretched forward and placed an unsteady finger on the teat, working the switch.

D-Delta lifted sharply, causing Barrymore to curse good-naturedly as he was thrown back against side of the aircraft.

Voices in his head sounded insistent, but he didn't really care. It was funny, but he just didn't care.

Moments earlier, Branner had to fight the Lancaster back on course following the close burst of flak that punched them several degrees to port. The target zone was hot—very hot. The Germans must have brought in extra anti-aircraft batteries or perhaps they'd been cleverly hidden from the reconnaissance missions in the first place. Right now, speculating was pointless, although it meant Branner certainly didn't want to come around for a second run.

'Are we all right, Dave?' he asked Sexton urgently. The engineer was hastily scanning all his gauges.

'Everything looks okay, skipper. We took something, I'm sure of it—and look.' Sexton held up his hand. What he meant was to feel the chill breeze swirling inside the aircraft. 'We've got a hole somewhere. Is she flying right?'

'Seems fine.' Branner was aware the target could only be seconds away. 'Whatever's gone wrong, it'll have to wait. Geoff? Geoff! What the hell's going on? Are we still on target?'

Control of D-Delta had been handed over to Barrymore seconds prior to the flak burst. By now the bomb-aimer should have been calling the minute corrections to their heading. His silence was ominous.

'Maybe it's just his intercom?' Sexton said.

'I hope that's all it is—it still fucks up our bomb run,' Branner replied bitterly.

'Shall I go check on him?'

'Like hell, I want your eyes glued to that panel in case something lets go. Someone else can—shit!'

D-Delta had climbed sharply with the loss of her bombs, taking Branner by surprise. He forced the plane down again and counted slowly to twenty, resisting the urge to bank away too soon before any photographs were taken. Since no one had announced the bombs were dropped, he didn't expect to be told the pictures had triggered either.

'That's it, we're leaving,' Branner announced to everyone, swinging the bomber towards the next course in a shallow dive.

Now the cockpit windscreen filled with just as frightening a sight. Up ahead, the black sky flickered with a continuous, heavy anti-aircraft barrage. "Flaming Onion" rockets streaked upwards from the ground in large numbers.

Sexton tried to sound calm. 'Christ, skipper. Are you going to go through that?'

'That's our course and this close to the target I'm not going to leave the stream. There'll be Jerry night-fighters everywhere just hoping someone will try and go around that lot on their own. We'll chance the flak, rather than those bastards.' Branner wasn't convincing himself, let alone anyone else, but his logic made sense.

Sexton said, 'At least Barra pressed the tit. He must be all right.'

'Did he aim them or just dump the bloody things? That's what I want to know. Bruce? Can you hear me?'

'Right here, skipper.' Flanders sounded startled.

'Come forward and check on Geoff, will you? We haven't heard a peep from him since that near-miss. Someone's left a window open too.'

'Ah, on my way, skipper.'

Flanders wasn't happy about it. He'd been sitting hunched over in his tiny navigator's cubicle hearing the anti-aircraft shells burst all around, the concussion slapping against the fuselage. Half of him was glad he couldn't see what was going on—it would only make things worse. The other half wondered if witnessing the barrage might lessen the panic it caused him. After all, none of the gunners were complaining and they would have to feel dreadfully exposed in their Perspex turrets.

'Stupid bugger, Barra,' he said loudly, the roar of the Lancaster easily smothering it. 'Why don't you stick your head up and say you're all right? Save me the bloody trip.'

Flanders used a tiny lamp in his position to read his maps and it was enough to diminish his night-sight. The rest of the aircraft was an unfamiliar, dark obstacle course lit only by the flashes from the flak shells outside. The wind gusting through the plane made Flanders groan. It was a bad sign. Branner was weaving the plane as an added precaution to the enemy lining them up in their sights—be it a night fighter, anti-aircraft gun or a searchlight. The motion sent Flanders reeling from one side of the plane to the other and he swore with each change of movement. He had a flashlight in his pocket but preferred to leave his hands free to reach out to either side like a tightrope walker and cushion his falls against the walls.

As he got closer to the front of the bomber and Barrymore's position, he could see more of the flickering, lightning-like flashes of the flak barrage ahead coming through the Perspex of the front turret and the bomb aimer's position. The sight made his mouth go dry and he hesitated, unwilling to go past the perceived safety of the metal fuselage. Then he saw the silhouette of Barrymore slumped against the side of the aircraft and it hurried Flanders on into the nose. It was such a cramped space that Flanders had to straddle the other man's legs to get close enough. Barrymore didn't appear to register his presence. Until that instant Flanders had convinced himself it would be a simple problem, like a broken intercom line. Even now, he figured that at the worst, Barrymore might have banged his head and knocked himself out. As he was about the yell into Barrymore's pale face, the scene beyond the Perspex filled Flanders with horror.

Below and to starboard another Lancaster lit itself up with a long feather of flame from one motor. White fire streamed backwards in a long tail. Like moths drawn to a light the anti-aircraft batteries turned their aim to the target they could plainly see. A concentration of explosions followed the bomber through the sky, and seconds later, a searchlight brilliantly exposed it further.

'Corkscrew… dive—do bloody something,' Flanders told it, dreading what he knew would happen next. The bomber was having enough trouble trying to stay in the air. Evasive action was probably the last thing on the crew's minds. He hoped, instead, they were frantically bailing out while the pilot held the plane steady.

The end came seconds later, turning Flanders' sickened stomach. A fuel tank ignited in the Lancaster's wing, and it abruptly turned into a ball of flame plunging towards the ground. He watched it drop, desperate for a glimpse of parachutes, and saw none.

Flanders couldn't shake the terrible images of what must have happened to the crew inside—until he realised the Perspex he was staring through had two holes, one small and the other larger. Even though the second was still only the size of his fist, the speed of D-Delta's passage was pushing the freezing, cold wind into the bomber.

Flanders snapped back to the task he had, supporting either side of Barrymore's face with his fingers. 'Jesus, Geoff? Come on, stop fucking around. Are you all right?'

Barrymore groaned, inaudibly with the noise of the aircraft, but Flanders saw it. Now he fumbled his flashlight out and shone it on Barrymore. His eyes remained closed and the deathly pallor of his cheeks and forehead frightened Flanders further. He ran the torch downwards and gasped at the blood-soaked jacket.

'Oh shit—oh shit, what the hell got you?'

Flanders' hands hovered over Barrymore, searching for something to do. He suddenly pulled away and climbed up to the cockpit. The closest thing was Sexton's leg and Flanders yanked on that, startling the engineer who had been staring anxiously at his panels of gauges. It took Sexton a moment to see that Flanders had no intercom connection, so he bent his head down.

'Barra's been wounded,' Flanders shouted. 'Pretty bad, from the looks of it. A piece of flak, maybe two.'

Sexton nodded and Flanders saw him relaying the information to Branner through the intercom. Then he leaned over again.

'Morgan's coming to give you a hand. Pull Geoff back into the fuselage and see what first aid you can give him.'

Flanders reached up and slapped Sexton's shoulder to show he understood and dropped back down to the lower section. He got back to Barrymore and waited helplessly until Baxter arrived a minute later. The wireless operator knew from the intercom that Barrymore was badly hurt. Even so he too was momentarily mesmerised by the flak explosions now surrounding the plane. They were flying over the last line of batteries and the Germans were putting up a wall of bursting rounds.

'Jesus Christ,' Baxter mouthed, his eyes wide. Flanders read his lips.

'My sentiments en-bloody-tirely,' he yelled. 'Let's get him out of here.'

It wasn't easy dragging Barrymore, who was a silent deadweight, back to a section where there was enough room to lay him straight on the floor. Flanders twisted his ankle badly at one point, trying to get the purchase to lift Barrymore over the wing spar. His boot slipped and wrenched under the extra load. They finally heaved the injured man to a flat space and placed a parachute under his head. Flanders used his torch again to examine the wound, this time unbuttoning Barrymore's sodden clothing to reveal his chest.

A seeping, red puncture was at the top of Barrymore's stomach. It welled an alarming amount of blood as they watched.

Flanders and Baxter put their heads close to talk.

'What do you think?' Flanders asked, his own face pale.

'Put a pressure dressing on it, wrap him in a blanket and hope for the best,' Baxter replied with a blank expression. 'There's nothing else we can do.'

'Christ…' Flanders found his way to the first aid kit and brought it back. With Baxter holding the torch he inexpertly taped a large pad to the wound. The blood over Barrymore's torso made it hard for the tape to stick and Flanders cursed at the flapping ends. In desperation he made Baxter help him lift Barrymore several times and passed a bandage completely around his abdomen. When they'd finished, almost the whole medical kit was gone. By that time, D-Delta had flown beyond the anti-aircraft defences and settled into a straight and level course.

'What now?' Baxter asked, doubtfully.

'Get back to our stations. We've still got to get home ourselves, let alone for his sake.' Flanders jabbed a thumb at Barrymore. 'I'll stick my head out as often as I can and keep an eye on him.'

Back at his Navigators desk, Flanders plugged into the intercom to hear Branner asking for him repeatedly, anxiously awaiting news. Before he answered, Flanders noticed his hands were covered in blood. They were also trembling. Grimacing, he looked around to find something to clean them, saw nothing and he wiped them on his trousers.

'Navigator to skipper, I'm back,' he said, cutting off Branner's latest demand. 'Barra's in poor shape. A shrapnel wound from the looks of it. A couple came through the Perspex and at least one hit him. In the chest.'

'Is he conscious?' Branner asked.

'No, skipper. He's out to it.'

'Are you sure he's—' Branner stopped himself. 'Is he comfortable? Is there anything else we can do?'

'Just get him back home quick-smart. I'll watch him closely in the meantime.'

D-Delta flew on through the night. Everyone concentrated hard on their jobs, but it was difficult not to keep thinking about Barrymore laying hurt. High cloud made the sky utterly black once they left the glare of the target zone with its burning buildings on the ground, anti-aircraft fire and sweeping searchlights. Wills watched it disappear behind them with a mixture of anger and relief.

During the flight, Flanders regularly checked on Barrymore. He found it was impossible to decide what condition he was in. The noise and vibration of the bomber swamped everything and his attempts to confirm a pulse or even breathing were hopeless. He could only report to Branner that Barrymore was still, at best, unconscious.

When they came to the course change that took them out of the returning stream and heading for base, Branner said crisply, 'All right, everyone. Let's not stuff this up now. Bruce, double check everything. Tonight of all nights, we don't want to get lost on the last leg. Morgan, radio in that we have a badly wounded man.'

Within seconds Baxter told him, 'There'll be an ambulance at the end of the runway, skipper. They'll be whipping him off in a hurry, so we can get off the strip.'

'All right. Everyone keep out of their way. They know what they're doing, and they'll have a stretcher.'

Twenty minutes later the flare path came to life below them. Branner lost height fast and put D-Delta down hard, making sure the aircraft stuck. Normally he would take the first taxiway off the strip, but this was three-quarters of the way along its length and he didn't see any ambulance. At the very end of the runway a hooded torch swung in a low arc to attract his attention. He eased the Lancaster to a halt.

Daniel had left his turret and was already undoing the rear hatch. He hauled it open to see four waiting men wearing helmets and Red Cross armbands, blinking up at him, bracing themselves against the wash of the idling propellers. Two had a ladder, which they put in place. The other pair carried a stretcher and they swarmed up into the aircraft with practiced ease.

'Up there,' Daniel pointed. They had flashlights out and quickly found Barrymore for themselves.

It was hard to tell what happened in the dark. The medics appeared to have a brief discussion, before manoeuvring Barrymore onto the stretcher and carrying him awkwardly through the bomber to the hatchway. The men outside caught one end of the stretcher and held it high and level, while the two inside negotiated the ladder again.

'Is he going to be all right?' Daniel yelled as they reached the ground.

The closest man answered over his shoulder. 'He's already gone, son. Has been for a while.'

Daniel was stunned and stood in the open hatchway, watching as they loaded Barrymore's body into the ambulance. As they drove away, the Lancaster lurched forward, taking him by surprise and throwing him to the floor. Branner had seen the ambulance leave and knew the way was clear to get off the runway.

This last taxiway was a longer trip back to their dispersal. Daniel sat in the open hatch, propping it with his boot, but he didn't see the dark, open field sliding past. He was avoiding the intercom, where he'd have to say something. Probably, Branner was getting angry by now that Daniel hadn't plugged himself back in.

Daniel had decided it was better to tell the others about Barrymore at the dispersal, to their faces.

Fifteen

The next day, D-Delta would have gone on another raid with a replacement bomb aimer taking Barrymore's place. Instead Granger managed to pull the aircraft off the roster so he could replace the entire Perspex bubble rather than just patch the holes. Plus a lot of blood had pooled or run into difficult places, threatening to short-circuit some electrics and it was a hard job to clean it. A reserve plane was assigned to the mission.

Branner gave his crew the day off to do as they wished, although they all agreed to meet at the Saracen's Arms at six o'clock to give Barrymore a proper send off. The debriefing the night before had been tiring and drawn-out because of the damage to D-Delta and Barrymore's death, as well as Flanders having to explain at length what he'd seen of the downed Lancaster in front of them. It became too late to get to the pub, and the few beers they had in the mess were token and drunk in near-silence.

In the morning, Daniel took the opportunity to tinker with his Morris, cleaning the spark plugs and checking every nut, bolt and screw he could find. It was a way of wasting time and keeping his mind off what happened. Dianne was on duty until the raid returned. She expected to get to the pub.

As Daniel was trying to decide if he wanted any lunch, a rain squall made up his mind for him, driving him away from the car and into the mess. Getting a sandwich and a mug of tea, he found a table on his own. Within a minute somebody flopped down beside him. It was Flanders.

'It's nice to have a holiday, but I'm going mad twiddling my bloody thumbs all day. What about you?' he asked, inspecting the contents between his own slices of bread.

'About the same,' Daniel admitted.

'Shall we go to the pub after this? The dartboard should be free at this time of day.'

'Better not. I'll be pissed as a monkey by the time everyone else gets there. That's not a good idea.'

'We could take it easy.'

Daniel let out a humourless laugh. 'Who are you kidding?'

They ate in silence for a minute, then Flanders said quietly, 'Well, I know one thing for sure.'

'Really? What's that?'

'From now on, when we're on an op', I'll be staying in my little hidey-hole all the way there and all the way back.' Flanders demonstrated this with a wave of his hand.

'I should hope so. You're the navigator.'

'No, I mean I don't need to see what I saw last night—not Barra, the poor bastard. I'm talking about all that flak trying to blow us to pieces and those flaming onions all over the place.' Flanders shook his head at the memory. 'It scared the pants off me. I'd rather not know what's going on, thanks very much.'

Daniel looked at him closely, trying to figure out how serious Flanders was and saw the navigator's hand shaking slightly as he picked up his mug of tea.

'It's not as bad as it looks, you know. Well, I know it looks like you can't possibly fly through some of that shit and come out in one piece, but most of us do. All of us, sometimes. A lot of it comes down to luck, I suppose.'

Flanders snorted. 'Like that Lanc' bursting into flames right in front of us? Was that bad luck or the Jerries shooting a week's worth of ammunition at us in five minutes?'

'It's not worth thinking about it too hard,' Daniel said, getting annoyed. 'I feel lucky and that's good enough for me. Besides, there's no point in dragging your feet around and believing you haven't got a decent chance.'

'No, I suppose not,' Flanders relented, blowing out his cheeks. There was a hint of embarrassment in his eyes, and he changed the subject. 'The skipper's already got a replacement for Geoff, did you know?'

'No, where did he come from?'

G.M.Hague

'The pool, I guess. Skipper's bringing him to the pub tonight to meet everyone.'

Daniel frowned about that. He turned it into a shrug. 'As good a time as any, really.'

'He'll probably look like a bloody movie star and completely cut Charlie out of Susan's sights.' Flanders tried to cheer himself up and grinned at the thought. Something in his eyes didn't match his expression.

'I don't think he's in Susan's sights,' Daniel said dryly. 'Only Charlie believes that.'

'Yes, and just enough to get in my way all the time, the rotten bugger.'

Daniel stayed silent about his opinion on Flanders' chances with Susan too.

Flanders finished his sandwich and swilled the last of his tea. Standing up, he said, 'I'm going for a walk around the place and see if I can't find a game of cards or something. Want to come along?'

Daniel shook his head. 'I'm going to catch up with forty winks. We don't often get the opportunity. I'll see you later.'

Flanders left the mess, whistling under his breath, his melancholy mood vanished as quickly as it came.

Daniel only managed to doze fitfully for an hour or so, frequently disturbed by other aircrew coming into the Nissan hut. Then the first rumbling of a returning bomber began to vibrate the walls and he gave up trying to sleep altogether, figuring he might as well watch the squadron land. Outside, he discovered the rain had settled in, so he turned back, retrieved his great coat and went dodging from one patch of shelter to the next until he reached a hanger overlooking the main strip. Here he huddled against the edge of the giant door out of anybody's way. Daniel lit a cigarette and kept it dry under the palm of his hand.

Another Lancaster was landing at that moment, throwing long plumes of mist behind the propellers from the tarmac as it struggled to pull up in time to swing into a taxiway.

Daniel didn't know how many aircraft had gone on the raid, so he couldn't tell if anyone was missing. Several bombers looked damaged and one in particular was running on only two engines. A thick smear of black along the cowling of a dead motor suggested they had put out a serious fire. It must have been some heart-stopping minutes for the crew.

'See, Flanno?' Daniel said aloud. 'I'm not the only bloke with a bit of luck on his side.'

He watched for a long time. Whenever he was tempted to leave, another far-off growl of an approaching bomber would make Daniel stay a little longer and make sure the aircraft landed safely. Finally it began to darken. The cold and damp seeped under his clothing and thoughts of the warm pub and Dianne beside him won over the remaining, returning bombers. He guessed there couldn't be too many more to come anyway. Wishing good luck towards the sky, he walked away from the hangers and headed for his quarters until Daniel realised within a few yards that he had no reason to return to the Nissan hut at all. He had everything he needed, so he changed direction and aimed for the main gate.

There he was allowed to leave without so much as a glance from the guards. He was puzzled to see they were closely questioning an airman returning to the station. His curiosity didn't last long. It was too cold and wet to do anything but hunch his shoulders and keep a fast pace to warm himself.

With many of the base personnel, both ground and aircrew, still involved with the returning bombers, the bar wasn't as crowded as it might be for this time of night. Daniel spotted Flanders, Wills and Sexton at a dartboard, saw they all had full pints, and bought himself a drink before joining them.

'Where's everyone else?' he asked, raising his glass in a greeting.

Flanders looked like he'd been drinking a while. 'Baxter's still AWOL and the skipper's bringing the new chap any minute now.' He squinted unsteadily at his watch. 'He's helping to move his kit into more permanent quarters.'

'And the girls?'

'No sign of them yet,' Wills said, disappointed.

Sexton came close to Daniel and lowered his voice. 'Have you heard the news?'

'News? No, what news?' Daniel expected something about the war.

'There's been another girl attacked. A farm girl this time, a few miles up the road. Same as last time, apparently, except he got frightened off before he finished the job, they say.'

'Jesus, hang on. You mean she's alive?'

'In pretty bad shape, but she'll certainly live.'

'So they know who it is?'

'Nope,' Sexton was enjoying telling the story. 'Covered her head with sack from behind and gave her a rough time. Trouble is, she's saying he got pissed off at her biting and kicking him. Says he swore like a trooper. Like a digger,' Sexton made the point with his eyebrows. 'She reckons he was an Australian, the way he talked.'

'Oh shit,' Daniel looked around the bar. 'Wait a minute,' he frowned at Sexton. 'How do you know all this?'

'The local coppers have been in here giving us all grief,' he said over the top of his pint. 'Gave Flanders some curry because he's been here half the day. The barmaids vouched for him though. It's different see, because that other girl—what was her name?'

'Robyn,' Flanders answered promptly, listening to them as he aimed a dart.

Both Sexton and Daniel gave him an odd look before Sexton went on. 'Robyn, right? That was on the base, so the police haven't had much of a look-in. Especially since she was the Warrant Officer's niece and he wants to lynch the bastard before anyone else gets their hands on him. But this is outside in the civvy world. Different thing altogether. You watch,' Sexton raised an eyebrow. 'This will be a Scotland Yard job and everything.'

'Just what we need,' Daniel said. He was more concerned they would be confined to the base indefinitely. Now he understood why the MPs at the guardhouse were questioning the airman returning. Anybody who was outside the base during the afternoon would be a suspect.

His thoughts were interrupted by Dianne and Susan walking through the door. They were accompanied by a muscular, handsome airman with Canadian flashes on his shoulders. Daniel could tell that Dianne was thanking him with an invitation to join them. The Canadian, after a glance towards the D-Delta crew, turned down the offer with a wide and friendly smile that made Susan almost glow.

'You're in trouble already,' Flanders baited Wills, who was also watching.

'I could deck the bastard,' Wills said.

'I can tell you without a shadow of doubt that man eats bears,' Flanders told him. 'Most Canadians do. He could eat you without even farting afterwards.'

'Shut up, Flanno.'

The two girls came over. Dianne gave Daniel a kiss on the cheek.

'Hello,' she said.

'Hello. Who was that?'

'A knight in shining, white armour,' she smiled demurely. 'He escorted us from the base, which is more than somebody did.'

'I didn't know it might be needed until two minutes ago.'

'It shouldn't be needed before you think of it.'

'I thought we weren't sure when you'd finish?'

'Early, as it turned out. Everyone came home and they're claiming some good strikes.'

'All right, I should have waited. I'm sorry.'

She touched his arm. 'It's not your fault, I'm only teasing. I could have been there all night, as you well know. God, this latest attack on the girl is absolutely horrid. What's the country coming to? You know, I didn't think the MPs were going to let us out the gate, they were so concerned about our safety.'

'I'm sure that's all they had on their minds,' Daniel nodded.

'Then Keith came along.'

'Keith?'

'The Canadian chap.'

'Oh, of course.

'Keith, the Canadian bear hunter,' Wills muttered. 'Bloody wonderful.'

'What?' asked Susan, since he had edged close to her.

'Nothing. Want a drink?'

'Thank you, Charlie. What about Dianne?'

Wills looked at Daniel, expecting him to do something.

'There's a good chap, Charlie,' Daniel said. 'A gin and tonic, right Dianne?'

'Yes, please.' Dianne beamed at Wills, who grumbled something under his breath and went to the bar. She pulled herself closer to Daniel. 'You could probably buy the whole damn hotel. Do the others know that?'

'We're not that well off,' he whispered back. 'And no, they don't know.'

Branner appeared among them followed by a small and wiry man with a sharp face and darting, intelligent eyes. His skin appeared dirty because he had been suntanned all his life until he encountered the mild, English climate. He looked at least thirty years old, which made him considerably older than the rest of the crew—in their estimation.

'Heads up, chaps—ah, and ladies…' Branner said. 'Meet our new bombardier, Billy Cook.'

'Cookie, like the bomb,' Cook said straight away, offering his hand to all of them as Branner introduced each person and their role in the aircraft.

'Cookie, it has to be,' Sexton said warmly. 'Where are you from?'

'601 Squadron until a few weeks ago.' Cook accepted the gestured offer of a drink from Branner.

'They kicked you out?' Flanders asked, already back at the dartboard and peering uncertainly at his target.

Cook's expression lost some of its humour. 'Not quite. We belly-landed after a bad night and only three of us walked away. Hardly a full crew, so we got split up.'

Flanders was trying to think of an answer when Dianne said gently, 'You'll have to excuse Bruce. He's an idiot.'

'Just what you need for a navigator,' Cook said, thanking her with a look. 'What happened to my predecessor? Finished his tour, I hope?'

'In a way,' Flanders grabbed the chance to get even. 'He took a piece of flak and now he's going to be pushing up daisies somewhere behind the hangers, I suppose. Poor old Geoffrey finished his tour a bit earlier than he expected. By the way, when's the funeral? Does anybody know?'

'They'll tell the skipper, no doubt,' Sexton said, trying to ease some of the tension. 'In the meantime, we should raise a glass in Barra's honour, right?'

Branner had returned and heard this. 'Wait a second,' he said, handing a glass to Cook.

'And me! Hold your horses,' Wills called, pushing between them with the girls' drinks and a fresh pint for himself.

With everyone supplied they returned Sexton's toast, murmuring Barrymore's name doubtfully as they touched glasses. No one was sure what should be said, and they changed to drinking instead.

'Damn,' Branner said, with foam on his upper lip. 'Where's Bax? I just realised he's missing. He's so bloody quiet you don't notice it when he's not here.'

Nobody had seen Baxter all day and as they were debating what might have happened, the wireless operator sidled among them with an apologetic smile.

'Sorry, I got caught up,' he said softly. 'Have I missed anything?'

'Just the main event, lad,' Flanders scolded him. 'Where have you been?'

'Did I? Can't we do it again?'

'Not really,' Branner looked annoyed too. 'It's a bit meaningless the second time.'

'Never mind, I'll do it myself.' Baxter lifted his pint alone. 'Here's to a nice bloke and a damn good bombardier. I wish he was still with us.'

The others responded automatically, some with wry expressions that Baxter had said something appropriate, compared to their own lame attempt. There was an awkward silence, then Cook changed the mood by introducing himself to Baxter. The gathering soon turned into a normal drinking session with Barrymore's death not mentioned again. Only

Dianne and Susan exchanged a look and a tiny shrug. This was a new event for the crew of D-Delta. The two WAAFs had been a part of many bar room funerals since the beginning of the war. Nothing surprised them anymore.

Daniel was bothered by Baxter's absence all day and what it meant, since it coincided with the attack on the farm girl. He felt helpless and annoyed he'd let his twenty-four-hour ultimatum to Baxter pass without action. It was too late to just confront Baxter and demand to know where he'd been this time, because if there had been any foul play no doubt Baxter was well beyond simply admitting it. Daniel wanted to hang onto a hope his suspicions were wrong. Revealing them to either the MPs or the police could start something very unpleasant that Baxter didn't deserve. There were plenty of things the wireless operator might be involved in that he didn't care for others to know about—things that had nothing to do with killing Robyn or assaulting the farm girl. God forbid, he could be having an affair with an officer's wife, or dealing in the black market. Nothing to be proud of, but no business of Daniel's to expose by voicing any unfounded accusations.

Over the next hour, the pub filled with aircrew and ground personnel who were finishing their duties after the raid. The noise of shouted conversations grew louder. Flanders was doing a miraculous job of keeping the dartboard, defeating all challengers even though he was swaying from too many pints and peering through bloodshot eyes smarting from the permanent cigarette in his lips.

Wills gestured some of them close and said, raising his voice, 'We still haven't named the plane, have we?'

'What?' Daniel asked for everyone as they exchanged puzzled looks.

'Remember? We were going to name the Lanc' after the first letter of everybody's girlfriend.'

'I thought that idea was chucked out?' Daniel said, smiling as Dianne quickly breathed in his ear that he could use "D".

'I said you could have my mother's name,' Sexton reminded them.

'I'm afraid I'll have to withdraw C for Cheryl,' Branner admitted reluctantly. 'I got a letter on Friday. She's taken up with some Yank and reckons it's not fair to keep it a secret any longer.'

'Shit, that was sudden,' Sexton tried to be sympathetic.

'I told you,' Flanders said mournfully, thumping another dart into the board.

Ignoring him, Branner told them defensively, 'Well, the mail takes a while, and I might have missed a letter. I expect he's a very nice chap and I am on the other side of the world…' He looked sorry he'd told them. 'I can't really blame her.'

Dianne touched his arm. 'Yes, you can, Alec. It's not right she's done this when you've come over here to fight the war. You're not having a holiday or something, right?'

'No—no, we're not here for the fun.' Branner dropped his eyes and tried to appear like he wasn't standing in the middle of a crowded bar, drinking beer.

Sexton asked, 'What about you, Cookie? Have you got a girl back home who's name we can use? If I remember, we're a bit short on vowels. How about an Anne, or Enid?'

'Ursula would be good,' Wills said, frowning with concentration.

'Afraid not,' Cook shrugged. 'All I can give you is M for Mary.'

'Better than nothing, which is all I've got,' Sexton said. 'Except for the old girl. So, are you married?'

'Hardly. She's my horse.'

'A horse? You ride horses?'

'Lots of them. I was a jockey.'

Susan said, 'I love horses.'

It made Wills scowl.

'Do you ride?' Cook asked her. 'Maybe we could hire a couple of nags one day and go for a trot?'

'Not 'round here,' Wills said. 'Too dangerous.'

No one took any notice.

'You'd have to remind me how it's done,' Susan gushed, excited.

'It's easy. You'll pick it up in no time.'

'Did you ever win anything?' Flanders asked, still from the dartboard.

'Quite a lot in the country, and a few in the city—in the lower classes,' Cook called back.

Flanders snorted, 'Nothing decent, like the Melbourne Cup or anything?'

Dianne was annoyed again. 'For goodness' sake, Bruce. Are you so clever?'

Cook said smoothly, 'Actually, I did race in the Melbourne Cup once. The highlight of my career, probably.'

'God, you're famous,' Susan said. 'Where did you come?'

'Fifteenth out of twenty-four,' Cook spread his arms. 'Not very good, I'm afraid.'

Wills said suspiciously, 'Aren't you a bit tall to be a jockey?'

'They only let me ride very short horses.'

'See, Bruce?' Dianne deliberately waited until he was aiming his next dart. 'What's your claim to fame?'

'Getting a double nine with my first dart,' Flanders replied, making his throw. It hit the wire and bounced spectacularly back into the crowd, bringing a chorus of cursing. 'All right, my second dart…'

Daniel had been watching Branner carefully. His skipper seemed in two minds, a part of him relieved that his admission about the letter from Cheryl had passed relatively unchallenged. He also looked disappointed to have missed the chance to talk about it. Daniel turned Dianne aside so they could talk privately.

'Dianne, let's go away again together. The next leave we get, to somewhere different.'

'In London?' She was confused. 'I thought the Dorchester was very nice—'

'No, I mean a different place. Somewhere beside the sea.'

'Oh, where we can gaze out at the anti-tank mines on the beach and the barbed wire?'

'I'm serious.'

Dianne stared at him for a minute. 'All right, Danny. I was only joking. That would be nice.'

'Just the two of us, nice and romantic. Don't say a word to the others.'

'My! How can I refuse an offer like that? I won't breathe a word.'

.

Sixteen.

'Skegness, here it is,' Dianne said, showing it to Daniel on a map. It flapped in the breeze, and she fought to keep it under control as they sat on a bench under the shade of a tree. It was in one of the few parts of the base that had grass and somewhere pleasant to be and wasn't allotted to only officers. In the past it had been a play area for children living on the station.

'Skegness? It sounds bloody awful. Familiar, for some reason.' Daniel studied the map.

'It's a lovely seaside place, I'm told. With nice beaches and a big pier out into the ocean like they have at Brighton. Not quite so grand, of course.'

'Ah, right. Flanno uses that pier as a landmark. He's always asking about it. You can see it for miles.'

'There you go. It's about sixty miles from here. We could do it in your car, if it will last the journey.'

'Hey! The old Morry would get us to London and back twice over without a hiccup, if you don't mind. I'd need to scrounge a few petrol coupons, that's all, but not many.' Daniel warmed to the idea. Anything that put them alone and together got his vote.

'How long have you got?'

'Three days. What about you?'

'I could probably wangle the same with a bit of swapping about.'

D-Delta had flown as many missions in those three days. Two night raids across the Channel to St Nazaire and Cologne, and the last another daylight gardening trip for mine-laying. They had come back unscathed each time; the entire squadron lost only a single plane. That was during the second evening. It wasn't that the Germans weren't fiercely defending the targets. The anti-aircraft barrage over France had been the usual, ferocious assault. The crews were feeling the strain of flying three successive missions.

Dianne had suffered with them, spending long hours in the Operations Room organising raids that had stretched their resources to the limits. After which came the endless waiting for the bombers to return, staring at the chalked names as if it somehow helped to bring the aircraft back safely.

Both of them were looking forward to the trip away.

'Look, we could leave first thing in the morning and be there in a few hours,' Daniel said, tracing a route on the map that allowed him to run off the paper and up her arm. 'Get a spot of lunch, find somewhere to stay, and then go and dabble our toes in the ocean.'

'It's a bit cold for anything else. It looks like I'll have to navigate this time—all the way.'

'Excuse me, there was nothing wrong with my map-reading last time.'

'We got lost, found a pair of dead Germans, and by sheer luck stumbled on that pub. It's not bloody likely I'll let you be in charge again.'

'Where's your sense of adventure?'

'I generally lose it along with my sense of humour when you get things wrong.'

'That's very unkind. Don't forget, we're not going to tell the others.'

Dianne hesitated. 'I don't want to sneak away, but you're right. We'd risk everyone inviting themselves along.'

'Not even Susan.'

'All right, not even Susan. Even though I trust her,' Dianne said pointedly.

'So do I. Still, at the pub tonight remember let's just keep it to ourselves.'

'As if you can keep a secret,' Dianne said wryly.

***

'Are you three comfortable back there?' Daniel asked, sounding as if he didn't care at all. The Morris was grinding down the road, the tail-end almost dragging with the weight of Susan in the back seat sandwiched by Wills and Flanders.

'It's a very small car to travel so far in,' Susan groaned. She added waspishly, 'Whoever has their hand under my bum, take it out or I'll break all your damned fingers.' She stared steadfastly forward, giving the culprit the chance to withdraw anonymously.

'I warned you,' Daniel said.

'I just wanted to see the seaside,' Susan replied, indignant. 'I was quite happy to leave you two alone to do your own business. You wouldn't even know I was there.'

'I'm the same,' Wills said immediately. 'Once we get there, I'll be right out of your hair. I'll think of something to do on my own…' he risked a sideways glance at Susan, who ignored him.

When Flanders didn't contribute his own excuse Dianne prompted him, 'Come on, Bruce. Exactly how did you invite yourself along?'

'Don't be like that, Dianne,' he said cheerfully. 'At least I'll be honest about it, not like some. It's the petrol coupons, dear girl. You can't expect me to just hand over my rations without something back in return, and anything that gets me away from Waddington and the Saracen's Arms for a change is well worth the company of a beautiful young lady and the discomfort of a smelly tail gunner.'

'How long have you been rehearsing that in your head?' Wills growled. 'Susan is not in your company by the way.'

'I'm not in anyone's company,' Susan said quickly.

'No?' Flanders raised his eyebrow. 'Then I won't have to worry about sharing my supplies, will I?' He produced a silver hip flask and waggled it in front of them.

'Goodness, it's only ten o'clock in the morning,' Susan said, her eyes lighting up.

'Yes, but it won't be ten o'clock for long, will it?' Flanders said with a wicked smile. 'Want a smoke?'

Susan accepted archly, 'All right, since you insist.'

Wills snatched one as well and while the three of them bickered about that, with Susan refereeing, Daniel was able to sigh at Dianne. She struggled not to laugh.

The previous night, in the Saracen's Arms, Daniel's plan to be discreet about their trip fell apart when he asked, innocently enough he thought, if anyone had any petrol coupons stashed away he could borrow. The others instantly sniffed a trip in the offing and started bartering between themselves over the places in the back seat. Neither Daniel nor Dianne found they had much say in the matter, except to eventually insist Susan was included to balance out the gender representation. Flanders had an impressive horde of petrol coupons—making Daniel suspicious —that out-bidded everybody. Wills managed to squeeze himself into the expedition by virtue of his size and a rash promise to be responsible for Flanders not spoiling everyone else's time away.

It was a transparent ploy to stay close to Susan that she accepted reluctantly.

'I'll be looking after myself, by myself,' she'd told him pointedly.

For once, Wills had the wits to stay quiet and accept his good fortune.

An hour away from Waddington, they were still driving through flat and open country. With the sunlight, everything was colourful. The green meadows glowed and spring flowers were out in large numbers. Whenever they passed paddocks with sheep the herds always had plenty of white, unsteady lambs among them. The two girls were delighted at the sight. The men discussed the best way to cook them. Overhead were aircraft of every type, flying high and low, trying to remind them the war couldn't be escaped altogether.

Soon there were at least four happy people in Daniel's protesting Morris, courtesy of Flanders' hip flask.

'I need to pee,' Flanders announced after they passed a sign.

'We'll keep a look-out for a big tree,' Daniel said.

'There's a pub up ahead.'

'You just want to get more booze.'

'No, honestly. I want to spend a penny. Quite desperately as a matter of fact.'

'Then we can stop right now. This hedgerow's good enough.'

Susan said, 'I need to visit the lady's room too. I don't want to be squatting behind some bush with these two trying to get a peek.'

'Yes, and I could probably do with a stop,' Dianne touched his leg.

'All right.' Daniel held up his hands in defeat and caused them all to cry out as the Morris drifted towards the verge.

The hotel was on its own surrounded by gardens and picnic tables. A village was a further mile up the road. Flanders dived out of the car before it had even stopped and ran to the door, disappearing inside. The rest followed at a leisurely pace and should have guessed Flanders had another agenda. By the time they all met at the bar to be on their way, he had a round of drinks ready. Only a few locals were at the far end, watching the visitors. The landlord appeared pleased with the early business.

'We weren't going to have a drink,' Daniel complained. 'We've still got a fair way to go.'

'You can hardly make use of a fellow's facilities and not buy something,' Flanders said, shocked. He began passing out the drinks. 'Just the one. Let's go and sit by the window—here's yours.' He pressed a glass into Daniel's hand and led the way to a table.

'What the hell's this?' Daniel asked, not moving and looking down at the drink in horror.

'Lemonade, of course. You're driving,' Flanders called from the window seat.

'What?'

'You're driving.'

'Like hell!'

Daniel lingered at the bar and eventually joined them carrying a pale beer. 'It's a shandy,' he explained grumpily.

They sat and talked loudly, teasing Daniel for his attempts to hurry them up. When his pint was finished, Flanders winked and told them he was only going to buy some smokes. When he returned, he was frowning.

'The publican won't sell me any more drinks,' he told them, outraged. 'He said you instructed him not to.' Flanders pointed dramatically at Daniel.

'That's right. He was very understanding,' Daniel said mildly. It had cost him a small bribe that he figured was well worth it. 'We have to get going.'

'You tricky sod,' Flanders said. 'I'll never trust you ever again. At least wait a minute while I see if he'll top this up.' He brandished his flask at them.

Further down the road, the flask drained once more, they were all singing and trying to dance inside the car, making the Morris sway alarmingly. Daniel didn't protest because he soon saw the first glint of a teary eye and stifled yawns among the mayhem. Fifteen minutes later he was driving in blessed silence apart from Flanders' soft snoring. The three in the back were sharing shoulders—much to Wills' enjoyment with Susan sleeping huddled into him. Dianne promised to stay awake, then promptly balled a jacket against the door for a pillow and nodded off.

Daniel wasn't complaining. The longer his passengers stayed comatose, the closer he would get to their destination.

Everyone stirred as they came into the outskirts of Skegness after Daniel changed gears and turned several corners, breaking the rhythm of their journey. Susan jerked guiltily seeing herself snuggled against Wills' shoulder.

'Good morning, everyone,' Daniel called loudly.

'Very funny,' Susan groaned, flexing her neck. 'What time is it?'

'It must be lunch time because I'm bloody starving,' Flanders said, yawning.

'That's about right, just after one o'clock.' Daniel nodded out the window. 'Welcome to Skegness. The French Riviera of east Lincolnshire.'

It was a holiday town that was hugely popular before the war because it boasted the railhead of a line that travelled through the midlands and the heart of Britain. Every year, thousands of people descended on the town for their taste of the seaside and Skegness catered for them with an impressive pier, clean beaches, theatres, dance halls and fairgrounds. With the war, it was no longer a destination for families on vacation, but the surrounding airfields and army training grounds provided a host of servicemen and women all with their pockets filled with wages.

This became obvious as Daniel slowly drove into the centre of town to the esplanade along the beach. Everywhere they looked the streets were filled with uniformed people, strolling casually and out to enjoy themselves.

'I thought the idea was to get away from the air force?' Susan said.

Dianne warned Daniel with a glance not to answer. She could tell he had a glib reply about who, exactly, had invited themselves along and could hardly complain.

She agreed, 'I must admit, I was sort of hoping for some untouched, charming beachside village. There's even a fair amount of bomb damage—look over there.' A row of destroyed buildings were the unmistakable victims of a stick of bombs.

'I can't wait to get my trunks on and go for a paddle,' Flanders said. 'Just as soon as the Jerries drop by and clear that lot out the way for me.'

He pointed at the beaches beyond the seawall that lined one side of the esplanade. The inviting sand was covered by long festoons of tangled and rusting barbed wire. It stretched for as far as they could see. Closer to the seawall, above the high tide line, deep concrete pits for tank-traps had been dug in overlapping patterns.

As they took in the forlorn sight Flanders said, 'Why would the Germans want to invade here? The fish and chips can't be that good.'

'Let's see if we can find out,' Daniel said with a forced cheerfulness for Dianne's sake. 'Come on, we shouldn't whinge too much. Really, what else should we have expected?'

They parked the Morris and climbed out, the back seat passengers making much of their aches and pains. It wasn't long before the fresh, ocean air and the carnival atmosphere of the place flushed away any disappointment. Walking together along the footpath, they were lured by the smells of frying batter, salt and vinegar to a café. Everyone contributed to buy a large serving of fish and chips and then continued on until they found a vacant picnic table on the foreshore. They unwrapped the newspaper between them, weighting the edges against the breeze with piles of chips, and instantly attracted a crowd of seagulls that wheeled around squawking raucous demands for scraps. Regardless, it was relaxing and they happily ate, squinting in the sunshine, and discussing what to do next.

'I'll need a drink after this lot,' Flanders waved a chip at them.

'No surprises there,' Susan said mildly. 'We probably need to find somewhere to stay before getting too stonkered in some pub.'

'Hmm, that might not be as easy as we thought,' Flanders gestured at the people passing in a constant stream. 'This place will be pretty chockers, if you ask me. At least, the cheap hotels.'

Daniel had set some rules the night before about who was going to stay where or, more to the point, that he wasn't going to be caught up trying to find a place to stay for all of them. Now he explained, 'I've managed to sneak a few quid up my sleeve and I'm going to treat myself and the girls to somewhere nice—' He stopped himself elaborating on how that arrangement might work. 'I don't know about you blokes. You might have better things to spend your money on.'

Wills was biting his lip with fierce concentration, no doubt wondering if it was worth spending a lot of money to stay in the same hotel, just in case Susan came knocking on his door in the small hours.

Flanders said casually, 'Oh, we'll find somewhere unless I get a better offer...' He twinkled his eyes at Susan. She rolled hers back at him.

'Okay, and our first course change is?' Daniel stood up and waited for Flanders, who did the same and sniffed the air like a hunting dog.

'There's a pub over there,' he declared, leading the way with long strides.

***

While they were having a few drinks in the hotel, Daniel quietly chatted with the owner about staying somewhere with a luxury suite. The landlord happily obliged him by calling a friend. A deal was struck and Daniel returned to the table pleased.

'I've found us a place,' he whispered to Dianne under the noise of Flanders trying to convince Susan he could catch crabs with his bare hands. 'It's just around the corner. I might grab the car, go and book us in, and I'll be back before anyone knows it.'

'What about Susan?'

'I got her a room on her own. I'll pay for it and she can make it up to me whenever she can,' Daniel added, seeing the question coming.

'Have you asked her? She might not want it.'

'Where else would she stay?'

'You know...' Dianne tilted her head a fraction towards Wills and Flanders.

'My God, you're joking. Which one?'

Dianne looked wry. 'Yes, you're right. That was silly of me. Don't tell them, though. They'll stop competing and it's rather fun to watch. I'll have a word in Susan's ear, if they give me a chance.'

It took twenty minutes for Daniel to organise everything and it was long enough for things back at the bar to have gotten very merry. Thinking that they had a night ahead of them yet, he talked Dianne into a walk out on the pier. They left the others behind and strolled at a leisurely pace, bypassing the kiosks and stalls at the beach end and going straight out along the long finger of the timber jetty. The sea was almost flat, lapping at the pilings. With the sun low in the west, many of the families had retreated, leaving the pier to arm-in-arm couples like Daniel and Dianne. They went to the very end, chatting about nothing as they did, and stopped to look out across the calm English Channel. The sky was clear and empty. Daniel guessed it wouldn't be long before the first of any night raids on France or Germany would be growling across the coast. A solitary fishing boat was a speck in the distance.

'It looks so wonderfully peaceful,' he said, pulling Dianne close. 'It's hard to believe there's poor blokes out there getting bombed and torpedoed, swimming for their lives. And the chaps who have to ditch on the way home.'

'Daniel, I was trying not to think of such things for once.'

'Sorry.'

'Besides, I know it does happen, having to ditch and everything. You should be glad you're not in the North Atlantic on those dreadful convoys, which is nothing like this. Out there it's freezing cold and stormy. God knows how they can do it.' She shuddered at the thought.

'Yes, I suppose if we end up in the drink, at least it'll be out there somewhere and not too far from home. With a bit of luck, the weather's like this,' he added ruefully.

'I hope you don't have to go swimming at all! Can we change the subject?'

'Yes, all right.' He took out his cigarettes, lit two and handed one of them to Dianne. Avoiding her eyes by blowing a plume of smoke out to sea, he said, 'Oh, I haven't told you yet. I booked us in the hotel as Mr and Mrs Young. I hope you don't mind.'

'What? Why did you do that?' Diane was more surprised than upset.

'The lady behind the counter looked a bit fierce and old-fashioned, and I didn't want to take the risk.'

'I'm sure she's seen plenty of couples who aren't married.'

'Well, I got nervous about it.' Daniel shrugged helplessly, making Dianne laugh at him.

'What about Susan?'

'I said she was a friend.'

Dianne lifted her hand and examined her bare fingers. 'I haven't got a ring, silly. What are we going to do about that?'

Without meaning to, it became an entirely different question and there was an awkward silence.

'Perhaps I can keep my hands in my pockets whenever she's around,' Dianne said at last. 'We'd better head back. I'm getting cold anyway. What about you?'

Daniel shivered to demonstrate and put his arm around her, pulling her against him as they turned to walk back. They had only gone a hundred yards before he asked hesitantly, 'Dianne, if I was shot down, would you wait for me?'

She considered avoiding the question, remind him they were on leave and shouldn't be so serious. She was afraid he might take that the wrong way. 'Oh Daniel, it depends on a lot.'

'Like what?'

'Well, how would I know if you're even alive? People just vanish all the time and no one knows what went wrong. How long would you expect me to wait before we accept something terrible has happened?'

'All right,' he accepted this with a nod. 'If I'm a POW and you know I'm alive, would you wait for me?'

'You really shouldn't ask things like this. It gets too difficult and upsetting.'

He didn't answer, his silence waiting for an answer. Dianne thought carefully before she replied.

'Okay, I'll make a deal with you.' They both smiled at the now-familiar arrangement. 'If we don't get any news, I'm not going to hope against hope like some of these poor women, expecting a miracle. I think we've all used up our quota of miracles in the last year or so. If I hear from the Red Cross that you're a prisoner of war, I'll try very hard to wait for you as long as I can. For how long, I have no idea. This war could go on forever, couldn't it? I can't promise to behave myself either. I would get too... lonely.'

'Then I don't like my chances of winning a deal like that,' Daniel said glumly. 'Someone will sweep you off your feet quick-smart.'

'You might be surprised. Women are a lot better at that sort of thing than men. If things were the other way around, you would be chatting up the next tart in the Saracen's Arms in no time.'

'What rot! I'd be heart-broken for the rest of my life.'

Dianne felt her face flush and hoped he didn't see it in the gloom. 'Well, that's the deal. It's not like we're married or anything. That would be different. We have to be practical and realistic in these times. I told you before.'

'All right. It doesn't make much difference anyway, because I'm not going to get shot down. I told you.'

Having seen so many erased pilot rosters and empty seats at debriefings, Dianne wished she could be so confident and was about to say something, then figured there was no reason to be openly pessimistic about Daniel's chances of surviving the war. It would only spoil the mood for the evening.

'So you keep saying, Danny. Churchill might want to know your secret.'

'Having a pretty girl to come back to, that's the secret.'

'That'll do.'

It was almost dark by the time they completed the return journey down the long pier. Back at the hotel, things were looking tired. Wills and Flanders were slumped around a table with half full glasses that had been there for a while. Susan was at the bar talking to a Scots Guard who, Daniel could tell, was using his rich brogue to its full potential, since every rolled "R" he uttered seemed to make Susan lean closer. It explained the morose expression on Wills' face.

'What's happening, lads?' Daniel asked brightly.

'We've got rooms here, upstairs,' Flanders replied, patting a yawn to extinction. 'I'm thinking about a short nap, before something to eat and then a foray into the night life of jolly Skegness. There's a dance club called the Kings Hall with a very good band on tonight, so I'm told. I suppose I'll have to take misery-guts here with me.' He jerked a thumb at Wills.

'Don't worry about me,' Wills said mournfully. 'I can look after myself.'

'Oh dear.' Flanders mimed playing a violin and hummed a tragic melody.

'What about Susan?' Dianne sneaked a look and thought the Scotsman was rather good-looking.

Flanders said, 'I think she's planning to have haggis on the menu this evening.'

At that moment they saw Susan kiss her companion on the cheek, give him a small wave, then she came over to them.

'Hello, you two. Did you have a nice walk?'

'Nice and peaceful with all that sea air,' Dianne said, watching the soldier leave. 'What have you been up to?'

'Not much. I'm going to check out the hotel—thank you, Daniel—and hopefully have a nice, long bath. I can't wait for that. Then I've got a dinner engagement.' Susan batted her eyelids.

'No prizes for guessing with whom,' Dianne said, seeing from the corner of her eye Wills sink lower in his seat. 'We're going to do something along those lines, right, Daniel?'

He nodded. 'A nice, romantic dinner for two somewhere, then later we might try this dance Flanno's talking about. Perhaps we could all meet up there for a bit of fun?'

Flanders said, 'You might have trouble finding me. I'll be surrounded by adoring women who know a nice chap when they see one.' He pulled a face at Susan.

'What about you, Charlie?' Daniel said.

'I can't dance,' Wills admitted pathetically.

Susan said cheerfully, 'Oh, don't worry about that. I'll take you for a spin and teach you a few steps in no time.'

'Would you? I'd be very grateful.' Wills looked like a drowning man who had been thrown a lifeline. Perhaps the Scots Guard wasn't going to provide more than a free feed, or maybe they weren't allowed to dance without their kilts? For some reason there was hope, that's all that mattered.

They split up, agreeing to find each other at the dance hall later in the evening without putting a definite time on that. Susan went with Dianne and Daniel back to their hotel and disappeared into her own room with a whoop of joy, followed by shouted declarations of love for Daniel through the walls.

Daniel led Dianne into an adjoining room which had a huge, four-poster bed and a bathroom with a deep tub. A bottle of champagne he bought earlier was nicely chilled on ice.

They both kicked off their shoes and jackets, then ran the bath, which they used together while they drank the champagne. Afterwards they made love and ended up snuggling in each others arms, fighting off sleep and trying to motivate themselves to get back up and dressed for a meal. Two growling stomachs finally had their way and they took to the streets in search of a good restaurant.

In an intimate café, they had expensive plates of grilled fish with vegetables. It tasted nice and Daniel wasn't about to complain, although it made him smile suspecting there wasn't much of a difference between the tastefully arranged fillet in front of him and the newspaper-wrapped lump of cod at lunch time. He was determined nothing was going to worry him for the next forty-eight hours, when they were due back at the station. Right now he was alone with Dianne at a candle-lit table, a bottle of red wine carrying on where the champagne had left off, and a night of more romance waiting ahead of them.

'Do you really want to go dancing?' he asked Dianne. 'I'm not that crash-hot at it myself, you know.'

She tilted her head. 'We should, while we have the chance.'

'There's always tomorrow night. Tonight, we could get some more champagne and a bucket of ice—'

'We can go to the dance for a while and still do that,' she cut him off gently. 'Besides, I'd feel a bit guilty, if we didn't show up after saying we would. Susan might worry.'

'You're just hoping she can tell you what they wear under their kilts.'

'Daniel!' She tried to look offended. The frown wouldn't stay and she changed it to an arch smile instead. 'You shouldn't assume I don't already know.'

'I can tell you don't.' Daniel leaned close and whispered. 'It's women's knickers. A reliable source told me.'

'What rubbish.'

'It's true.'

'Well, if Susan's friend is at the dance tonight, I'll tell him that you've told me this and you can sort it out, if he gets upset.'

'Of course, he'll get upset. The Scots don't like anyone knowing.'

Dianne stared at him for a moment. 'You are an idiot,' she told him mildly.

***

There was a bright half-moon that lit the streets better than the shaded blackout lamps would ever achieve. It glinted off the sea in silvery flashes and made a sharp outline of the pier and its buildings. Skegness had been regularly bombed during the Blitz and still suffered an occasional, dashing visit from the Luftwaffe as if the Germans were intent on preventing their enemies from having a holiday. The residents also maintained a healthy respect for any U-boats that might try and shell the town from offshore. Blackout curtains were kept tightly closed and humourless Air Wardens strutted about everywhere. It didn't prevent scores of people from strolling the main street looking for somewhere to drink, eat or dance. On warm nights the pier was popular late into the evening, as was the fine sand of the beach below it. Anyone walking the timber planks could hear the giggling couples underneath.

Kings Hall was an old Edwardian building with a swimming pool and public baths open during the day. Many visitors to the town chose cheap lodgings without a bathroom, knowing they could patronise the public baths. The water was half-saline, but special soap that lathered in salt water was available.

More than anything else it was a theatre. The hall section had a stage for performing plays and pantomimes, unless like tonight the seating was rearranged to create a large dance area in the middle of the floor. A makeshift bar was at either end of the room.

When Daniel and Dianne arrived there were plenty of people in the room but gathered around the edge while only the confident couples whirled about the dance floor. Those that needed a little alcohol and dim lights to improve their technique still waited. The air was thick with cigarette smoke and the smell of spilled liquor. The band was loud and echoed in the large space. As usual, almost all the men wore a uniform, while the civilian women provided the only splash of colour.

'Well, this looks exciting,' Daniel said with a tight smile, raising his voice above the noise. Watching the adept dancers suddenly had Daniel doubting his mother's despairing lessons from so long ago. This was no shearing shed bush-party.

Dianne's eyes were shining. 'It's fantastic! I haven't been to a place like this for ages.'

Daniel was disappointed to learn she had been to one at all. It only deepened his dancing paranoia. He grabbed her hand and led Dianne around the side of the room, threading a way between the crowd.

'How will we find anybody?' Dianne asked.

'Don't be silly,' Daniel said over his shoulder.

'Oh, of course.'

They easily discovered Flanders and Wills at the furthest bar, standing to one side and each nursing a beer. Daniel was glad to see they were both relatively sober. They must both have had a feed and a sleep. Wills, however, didn't seem to have improved his mood. His brief joy at the prospect of a dancing lesson from Susan had evaporated.

'Hello chaps,' Daniel said. 'Anything exciting to report?'

'Not yet, I'm working on it,' Flanders said. He and Wills looked at Daniel with the ill-disguised envy of men who knew he had been eating, drinking and sleeping with an attractive woman for the last few hours.

'Where's Susan? Have you seen her yet?' Dianne asked.

Flanders told her dryly, nodding at the dance floor, 'Keep looking in that direction and she'll be around soon—in fact, here she comes now.'

Susan appeared dancing with the Scots Guard. They made a striking couple, moving gracefully and without effort. Susan's new friend was obviously an accomplished dancer. It explained Will's relapse into melancholy and didn't help Daniel's confidence either.

'My, he's very good,' Dianne said admiringly.

Daniel pulled a face. 'Yes, I suppose so. Good thing he's not wearing a kilt after all, chucking himself around like that. He'd be scaring the seagulls.'

Dianne poked him in the ribs. 'I think you should meet the fellow before you decide to make awful comments about him all night.'

Daniel avoided answering that by offering her a drink. He disappeared, pushing his way towards the bar.

His timing was good. The band stopped for a break as Daniel paid for his drinks and so he missed the ensuing rush. When he got back to the others, he found Susan had joined them with her friend. His name was Michael Connors, and much to Wills' disgust he was a very likeable man. Connors was well built and looked physically strong with wide shoulders and large hands. He had red hair nearly as bright as Susan's and a big smile that took up all of his face.

Dianne and Susan went to the toilets, with Susan insisting she'd get Connors a drink on her way back. He waggled a finger at her. 'You'll not be getting me drunk and taking advantage of me, hear?'

'Wouldn't dream of it,' Susan said over her shoulder as they left.

Wills glowered at her. She didn't see it.

There was a moment of silent drinking and lighting of cigarettes, then Wills told Connors, 'We're bloody glad to get a break. We've been doing a bit of flying lately dropping millions of bombs it seems like. What about you, Mick? Have you've seen much action? I suppose you've got some sort of a desk job, since you're not over there with the invasion?'

Connors shook his head. 'I'm a front line man through and through. I had to come back for a bit of business. I can't wait to go back and kick their black, German arses.'

'Oh…' Wills faltered. 'Must have been important to bring you back.'

'Aye.'

Daniel said, 'You reckon we'll finish it before Christmas? The Jerries might just surrender to us, afraid they'll get thrashed by the Russians.'

'Not a hope,' Connors took a hard drag on his cigarette. 'They won't quit in a hurry. The Jerry top brass won't admit defeat in case bloody Hitler shoots them instead. I reckon you might be right about the Ruskies making the Huns a mite nervous. I want to be there when the bastards shake out the white hankies. Anyway, so what do you blokes do?' He fixed his eye on Wills. 'What about you?'

Wills was taken aback a second. 'I'm a tail gunner—in a Lanc'… our Lancaster bomber.'

Connors was delighted. 'Tail gunner? Just the place to be for shooting down Krauts. How many have you got?' With his thick accent Krauts sounded like Connors was clearing his throat.

Wills answered unhappily, 'None yet, but it shouldn't be long now.'

'Good for you. When you get your first Hun, put a couple of extra rounds in the fucker for me, all right?'

'That's—ah… not a problem, Mick. Be glad to.'

Connors turned on Daniel. 'And you?'

'I'm the mid-upper gunner. I haven't come close to hitting a bloody thing yet. I'm sure Charlie hasn't either. He's full of bullshit.' Daniel was trying not to laugh.

'Never mind, never mind. You will. What about you, Bruce? You must be the pilot, then?'

'No, I'm the navigator,' Flanders told him, deadpan.

Connors raised his eyebrows and scratched the back of his neck thoughtfully. 'Aye, well… someone's got to do those sorts of jobs, don't they?'

Flanders said, 'It's actually pretty damned important, otherwise we'd be dropping our bombs on bloody Edinburgh by mistake and you wouldn't like that, would you?'

The Scotsman grinned at him. 'Ah, I'm just pulling your leg. Susan told me what you all do while we were dancing, so I thought I'd have some fun. Talking of which…' He lowered his voice and gestured them close. 'None of you fellows mind if I try my luck with that lovely girl? We seem to be getting on very well, if you know what I mean, but I don't like to be thought of as a poacher or someone who—'

'Hell no, go for your life,' Flanders cut him off. 'She won't have a bar of us. I mean, we're all just jolly good friends. There's no funny business.'

'We appreciate you asking,' Daniel added, warning Wills with a look. Wills was a picture of simmering outrage. For once, Daniel agreed with

Flanders. He wasn't going to ruin Susan's night just to cater to Wills' hopeless ambitions.

'Fine, then. That's fine,' Connors relaxed. 'I owe you lads a drink for making me welcome.'

The room was getting full as they chatted more about the grim side of the war before the girls returned. Wills sullenly didn't take part. If Connors noticed or guessed why, he didn't say anything. As Dianne and Susan came back, everyone had nearly finished their drinks and the band began playing again, starting with a waltz.

Daniel hesitated and said to Dianne, 'I think I might be able to have a go at this one.'

'Are you asking me to dance?'

'Yes, I suppose so. Can we go in the middle, where it's all a bit slower?'

'You're leading, remember? Take me wherever you want to go.'

They walked into the centre of the dance floor where the participants were more swaying and fondling. As they held each other close and slowly turned, Daniel noticed Flanders and Wills having a heated conversation. Dianne saw it too as they came into her view.

'What's wrong with those two?'

'Michael fancies his chances with Susan and he asked us if it was all right. We told him it was fine, before Charlie said anything stupid. You can imagine he's a bit pissed off at us and now Flanno's copping it.'

'Well done. I'll make an officer of you yet. Susan would be rather miffed if you chased her handsome, dancing Scot away.'

'Do you want to dance with him?'

Dianne leaned back and looked into Daniel's face. 'What do you mean?'

He shrugged in their embrace. 'I'm serious. I know I'm not very good at this sort of thing, and I'm sure you'd like to do a couple of tunes with someone who can. I wouldn't get jealous, if you did.'

'I'd say Susan might, though… maybe. I won't ask, just in case.'

'Then I'll ask for you. Tell him about my sheep farmer upbringing and beg him to give you a real run for your money. Susan won't mind that.'

Dianne smiled at him and kissed him on the lips. 'Thank you. That's very thoughtful.'

Half an hour later, the hall was packed by a roaring mob having a tremendous time. The band was exhausting themselves trying to match the volume. The bars were doing a very brisk trade.

Flanders announced he was drunk enough to "give romance a shot" and he wandered off in search of a girl he could ask to dance. This left Daniel feeling guilty about leaving Wills alone while he was crippling Dianne with his dancing prowess. Dianne was being very patient during their adventures on the dance floor, but at times her smile was strained. Daniel grabbed at a chance to solve his problems when they were waltzing past Susan and Connors. He reached out and stopped them.

'Say Michael, I couldn't ask you to give Dianne a few whips around the floor, could I? I think I've broken both her feet and she won't be talking to me much longer.'

Connors looked a question at Susan, who laughed and broke away. She took Daniel's hand, pulling him towards the bar. 'Then I'm certainly not going to dance with you,' she said. 'You can buy me a drink instead.'

Daniel and Susan discovered a luckless Flanders back with Wills.

'I'll do another recce in a few minutes,' he said, trying to look unconcerned. 'You know, some girls just don't realize when their chance has come.'

'Exactly,' Wills muttered.

'Oh Charlie,' Susan scolded him cheerfully. 'Buck up and smile. We'll have a dance when I've had my drink, all right? I haven't forgotten you, I promise.'

Wills looked at his feet and feigned indifference. 'I don't know if I want to now.'

'Well you said you would, so you're not getting out of it.' Susan managed to sneak a look at Daniel. He pretended to wipe his brow with relief.

Susan lowered her voice. 'Say, did Michael tell you he met the King— the King himself! When he got his medal?'

'Ah, that kind of business...' Daniel murmured.

'That fucking figures,' Wills grated.

Daniel left to go to the bar and bought drinks. When he got back, there was only Flanders trying to appear as if he hadn't been abandoned by his friends.

'Good oh,' he said, taking a drink from Daniel. 'I was getting a bit parched.'

'Where is everyone?'

Flanders gestured at the packed dance floor. 'Making fools of themselves. I don't know what they're doing. Susan said it's very easy and dragged Charlie out there before he could complain.'

'He is being a bit miserable.'

'Unrequited love, the poor bastard. It can give you piles, I'm told. Not that I would know, of course.'

'Either would I.' Daniel couldn't help a smug smile.

'Yes, all right, you lucky sod. Don't gloat too much. I'm thinking of pushing you out of the bloody aeroplane the next time we're over Germany.'

'Now now, no need to be like that. It's not my fault if things are going well.'

***

For the rest of the evening, the airmen obliged the girls and occasionally danced awkwardly, drank beer with a lot more expertise and gratefully plied Connors with pints to fuel his efforts on the dance floor where he happily made up for their shortcomings.

At the end of the night with the lights being dimmed to hint it was time to go, no one was sure what would happen with Connors. Daniel and Flanders began to say goodnight with smiles and handshakes. Susan wrapped her arms around his neck and gave Connors a long kiss on the lips. She looked puzzled and stepped back, staring at his chest.

'What are you doing now?' Dianne asked, taking her turn to kiss him. 'Hey, what's this?'

Connors discreetly opened his jacket to reveal several bottles stuffed underneath. 'I took a detour past the bar and bought a bit of old stock.' He grinned at them.

'What are you going to do with it?' Flanders asked, suddenly rejuvenated.

'Go down to the beach and tell Hitler he can fuck off. Want to join me?' They understood better when he added, 'I was at Dunkirk. The bastards won't kick me off a beach again.'

'We can't, can we?' Susan said, delighted with the thought. 'It wouldn't be allowed.'

'What else can you do?' Connors said. 'Go home and go to bed?'

They looked at each other in the dark and Susan said, 'Well, not yet…'

Daniel whispered in Dianne's ear, asking what she wanted, and she nodded.

'Why not, Danny? God knows, it could be a long time before we do anything like this again.'

Daniel was enjoying visions of their bed with Dianne in it, waiting for him. He didn't say so. Besides, he figured she was right. Some moments had to be seized because the chance may never come again.

They all trooped down to the pier, jumped the sea wall and found a place on the dry sand above the high tide mark. Sitting in a circle, Connors passed the bottles around and they silently drank, toasting their health and silently being thankful the war had spared them so far.

Connors told them, 'You know, there was a time I promised myself never to set foot on a beach again, after what I saw over there. Then I changed my mind and vowed the next time, it would be when we went back, not before.' He raised a bottle to his lips. 'We practically walked ashore at Normandy, so that doesn't make up for Dunkirk. Remembering that place makes me very bloody angry. When I go back again, I know it helps to feel that way. It's no place for pity… ah, damn it! Excuse me, ladies. I'm being maudlin and rude. It's this god-awful shit they call scotch.'

Dianne and Susanne laughed quietly. Daniel said, 'I hear you've done all right so far. You got yourself a decent gong.'

Connors dismissed it with a snort. 'Ah, I was at the right place at the right time, that's all. Anyone would have done it. In fact, it happens every day, but no one sees.'

Flanders said wryly, 'I don't know how you managed to be noticed among a couple of million bloody Yanks telling you how good they are.'

It made them laugh again and eased the mood. A while later, Connors took Susan to the water's edge and they tried to dance slowly to the rhythm of waves lapping at the sand. Wills slipped quietly away. Flanders stayed and drunkenly lectured on the virtues of anything that occurred to him while he buried himself in the sand.

Daniel and Dianne held each other and listened to the cadence of Flanders' voice. The alcohol had them all lulled and sleepy by now, but no one wanted to move back to the hotel yet.

When Flanders fell silent Dianne asked, her voice slow and quiet, 'This is such a nice place. Why on earth did the Germans want to bomb it? They did, you know. Quite a lot. What's the point?'

Daniel whispered back, 'The pier. It would be hard to resist. It looks important.'

'They bombed the town.'

'Probably the pier says it's a big town. Maybe industrial—who knows what they think? If you miss your target, I suppose you look for anything likely instead.'

She shook her head. 'Can you imagine what it must be like to have a full squadron of Lancasters dropping their whole load on you?'

'They did it to us, don't forget. To you, at least—in London.'

'I know and it must have been terrible. I'm so glad I wasn't there.' Dianne sipped at the bottle of wine they were sharing.

'I know what would be worse,' he said, kissing her. 'Losing you. I don't know what I would do if that happened.'

'Me? How on earth can you worry about me? You're the one with a whole tour to finish.' For once the truth of what they were facing, the unspoken reality that no one was allowed to mention, was threatening to come out.

He quickly put a finger on her lips. 'I'll be fine, you'll see.'

'For God's sake, I'll worry, Daniel. Every time you fly I'll always worry.'

'Didn't you hear me? I'll be fine, I promise.'

Dianne hugged him close. She knew it was a promise very likely to be broken.

***

A red glow on the horizon came as a shock.

'What the hell's that?' Flanders mumbled, stirring and surprising a dozing Daniel.

Daniel squinted at the light. 'Shit, I think it's the sun.'

'Oh, is that all? Anything left in that bottle?'

'Is that all? Like hell! Come on, we'd better make a move.'

Daniel couldn't decide if he was drunk, sick or just hung over. Doing anything was hard work. They found Susan and Connors sleeping together in a sand hole. It took a minute to rouse them and get everyone stumbling through the pre-dawn darkness back along the streets of Skegness. Only a few air raid wardens called yawning, bored greetings as if couples emerged from the beach at this time of the morning every day.

They stayed together until Flanders turned towards his own lodgings. Everyone accepted now that Connors was going to join Susan in her room

'I suppose we'd better head back some time today?' Flanders asked tiredly.

'Not on your life,' Daniel replied. 'I can hardly make it back to our room, let alone drive to Waddington. Besides, I've paid for the place for another night. I'd like to try and sleep in the bloody thing.'

Flanders scratched at himself. 'Why not? So I'll see you at the pub?'

'It's your shout, if I remember.'

'Like hell. Good night, all. Good night, good night, good night...' Flanders continued to waver over his shoulder as he disappeared up the road.

Everyone else made it to the hotel and silently let themselves in, dreading the landlady would catch them. Susan and Connors hissed their good nights in the corridor.

In their own room, Dianne insisted they undress in the bath to collect the sand cascading out of their clothing, then she used a warm sponge to wipe themselves down. Finally collapsing together in bed, they fell asleep instantly.

Daniel dreamed of dancing in a huge, dark room with no roof, a starless night above him. Overhead the silhouettes of bombers swept in waves, the noise of their engines thunderous. He kept trying to dance well, but he couldn't take his eyes off the sky, waiting to see if they would release their payloads.

What was more frightening, his partner was a faceless, unknown shape in his arms.

Seventeen

The less experienced aircrews always assumed that Berlin would be the hardest target. Germany's capital, filled with symbols of the Third Reich and the centre of Hitler's power, would have to be the most heavily defended of all.

They were wrong. Key manufacturing cities such as Essen and Dusseldorf were worse. It was from these places the Nazi war machine fed its insatiable hunger for munitions, weapons and supplies. Factories were ringed by wide and concentrated batteries of anti-aircraft guns. The night fighters were the best squadrons the Luftwaffe had to offer. No price was too high to pay for the protection of Germany's industrial heartland.

Similarly, the Allies were willing to risk much in an effort to destroy it.

The Briefing Room was filled with a groan as the target maps were revealed. It was Essen. Someone called, 'Get her to chuck the bloody thing again.' It was a popular story that the commander of RAF Bomber Command, Vice Commodore Arthur Harris, chose his daily targets by inviting his daughter to throw a dart at a map of Germany. Where the dart landed, the bombers were sent.

'All right, this is going to be a late one, as you should have guessed,' Eagleton told them, tapping the map to get their silence before waving at the unseen night beyond the blackout curtains. Aircrews had been ordered to get plenty of rest in the last twenty-four hours. 'The idea is to be over the target well after midnight in the hope the Jerry defenders will be thinking they've got a night off. If it works, it should be a help for the first aircraft arriving, if nothing else. From that time on you'd expect the Krauts to have woken up quick-smart. Maybe they won't be able to shoot straight in their pyjamas.'

It got a laugh, but not much. There wasn't a lot to find funny about bombing Essen.

At the back of the room, sitting at a table with Branner, Cook and Baxter, Flanders nudged his skipper's arm and whispered, 'A bit of engine trouble on the way could come in handy, skipper. Like, all bloody four somewhere near our coast and we can drop into Mablethorpe for a cup of tea.'

'You want to watch what you say,' Branner replied out of the corner of his mouth. 'You'll get yourself shipped off as LMF, if you're not careful.'

'Lacking Moral Fibre,' Flanders muttered the euphemism for cowardice. 'They should call it HCS—Having Common bloody Sense.'

'Aren't you supposed to be paying attention to this part?'

Eagleton was tracking with his pointer the course home. He was saying, 'Most of you should be clearing the Belgium coast at around daybreak and landing here in bright sunshine in time for a proper breakfast. Don't be late or the Jerry fighter squadrons will make a morning meal out of you instead.'

Flanders sighed shakily and began making his notes.

***

The other three crew of D-Delta were already at the bomber when the men who attended the briefing arrived. There was time for the ritualistic, last cigarette on the edge of the dispersal before they got aboard.

'Why so late, skipper?' Sexton asked as they traded lit matches and lighters. In the night, the tiny flames illuminated their faces eerily, like they were ghosts.

'The top brass have a theory that the Jerries will be all tucked up in bed when we get there.'

'What? They won't wake up when the first blokes drop a swag of incendiaries down the chimney?'

'That's where the theory gets a little thin.'

Sexton laughed ruefully. 'That's putting it mildly. The boffins and their crazy ideas never cease to amaze me.'

'When we get where?' Daniel asked.

'Essen.'

'Oh shit. Next time, don't answer.'

'Look at it this way, chaps. If we do a really good job, we won't have to go back.'

'That's what they said in 1918,' Flanders grunted.

Branner dropped his cigarette and ground it out with his boot. 'Okay, that will do. Let's get in and double-check everything. We don't want anything going wrong on this trip.'

They were airborne thirty minutes later. Normally, even if they took off at dusk for a night mission, they would get enough sunlight to safely get to their allotted altitude in a circuit above the base before setting off. Tonight, with the risk of aircraft colliding in the black sky as they gained height at differing rates, Branner immediately put them on a course for the beginning of the stream, aiming to be at the right altitude by the time they got there.

High cloud and just a low, quarter moon robbed them even of starlight. Starting a mission at night like this gave each man in D-Delta a greater sense of isolation, strapped into their turrets or huddled at their instruments with only the loud, vibrating darkness around them. Beyond the Lancaster, landmarks for checking their position were going to be difficult to see. It made Flanders' navigation absolutely crucial, while Branner was flying almost blind and hating every second of it. He wasn't tolerating any idle chatter on the intercom.

It was nerve-wracking as Flanders gave them a course that put them inside the stream heading for Essen. Branner could sense, more than see, the other aircraft close around them. Several that were much lower gave a fleeting silhouette against the sea, which was a dull pewter with the scant moonlight. Above and in front of him he saw only black shapes against a darker background. His peripheral vision worked best. If he stared straight at them, the aircraft vanished in the night.

The stream's course dog-legged several times to confuse German observers on the ground and radar stations. Late in the night, when they finally came onto a course heading directly for Essen, it was still another twenty minutes until they would reach the target.

Only five minutes afterwards something far in the distance began to flicker and glow.

'So much for the gunners being asleep,' Sexton said.

'Oh, it doesn't look too bad,' Branner said lightly.

'You think so, skipper? We're still fifteen minutes away and we can see the flak?'

They were both right. The anti-aircraft batteries around Essen hadn't all begun firing yet, and the first bombers over the city enjoyed a small element of surprise. It didn't last long.

By the time D-Delta moved close enough, the defences had come alive with an enormous, dreadful beauty. The sky they flew into was filled with the eruptions of time-delayed shells, reflecting off the cloud base and making it appear like they were entering a massive storm. Flaming onion rockets streaked upwards in such numbers that it seemed impossible they might avoid being hit. Lines of tracer weaved through the sky. No one could tell if it was from night fighters or the turrets of other Lancasters shooting at shadows. Not the least of their worries was the feared searchlights. Dozens fingered the sky in slow sweeps. The power of the beams was impressive for all the wrong reasons.

D-Delta was being buffeted by the air turbulence caused from so much flak.

'How are you going, Cookie?' Branner asked, fighting to keep the plane steady.

Cook replied casually, 'We must be in the right party with all these champagne corks popping off, skipper. I'm buggered if I can see anything that gives a target reference, unless you just want to drop 'em where everyone else is. You can open the bomb bay doors in case I see something in a hurry.'

Branner did this and the Lancaster slewed through the air in a different way as the open doors hit the slipstream.

'Hang on, there's the river,' Cook called with relief. 'We're on the right track and it looks like everyone else is too.'

'Then you take over, Cookie.'

'Right you are, skipper. Come right for me… about the same again. Keep her steady there.'

There was a particularly bright fire ahead and Branner used it as a navigation point, keeping it in exactly the same place on his windscreen until it slid beneath the nose of the bomber.

'Still steady, skipper. Just a few seconds more… bombs gone.'

D-Delta didn't lift as the aircraft normally did with the bomb release. Sexton and Branner instantly exchanged a puzzled look.

'Are you sure, Cookie?' Branner snapped.

The tone in Cook's voice said he also suspected something was wrong. 'I pressed the tit, skipper. I felt something, but not much, right?'

'Dave, go back and have a look. I have a feeling we didn't lay all our eggs.'

As Sexton left the cockpit, making his way aft towards the bomb bay, Flanders asked anxiously, 'Skipper, do you want a course? We should need one by now.'

Branner replied as he put the Lancaster into a wide banking turn. 'No, Flanno. We're going round again. We've haven't come all this way just to drop half our bombs on a paddock somewhere.'

Branner didn't need to ask his crew how they felt about exposing themselves to the flak all over again.

Baxter passed on a message.

'Skipper, Dave says the incendiaries went, but the cookie's bloody hooked up. He thinks he can drop it with the manual release though.'

The main 4000-pound bomb, called a "cookie", hadn't fallen free.

'Then tell him to wait until we're over the target. Cookie, did you hear that? Your namesake is stuck in the damned bomb bay. We'll go around again and you give Bax a shout when to let it go.'

'Worth a try, skipper,' Cook answered doubtfully.

'Anywhere over the target area will do.'

'You can say that again.'

Branner felt oddly alone without Sexton close by as usual. He stared to his left and down, seeing the maelstrom of exploding bombs and firing flak batteries as it passed before they would turn into the steam again. It seemed a miracle they had survived it the first time and taking a second chance was madness. He briefly wondered what other pilots would do and if he was being foolish. The fires below were now so bright Branner could see other aircraft around them. It was like a late evening. At least the risk of a collision was reduced.

'All right, everyone. Here we go again.'

D-Delta came back to a course directly for the target zone. The bright flashes and streaking tracer filled Branner's windscreen like before. In their turrets, Daniel and Wills searched the sky around them for that first, tell-tale glimpse of a night-fighter. Cook had his eyes glued to the bomb sight once more, while Baxter anxiously awaited the moment to signal Sexton to manually release the bomb. Sexton was bracing himself against the blast of the open bomb bay doors and resisting a strange impulse to step through the opening. Only Flanders had nothing to do except wait and only imagine the ferocious anti-aircraft fire that slapped against the Lancaster's thin skin, threatening to claw them out of the air. He endlessly twirled a pencil through his fingers until his tendons ached.

Cook's bomb sight was so bright with the blazing destruction below he couldn't see a definite target. 'That'll do, Bax. Get rid of the bloody thing.'

Baxter gestured madly at Sexton, who needed no further urging. He could plainly see the target zone below and had the fleeting thought that the reflected light was enough to read by. He tripped the switches on the bomb panel and glanced over his shoulder at the hulking bomb, expecting it to drop into the void.

It didn't—and again everyone knew it had failed by the lack of sudden lift.

Baxter reported anxiously, 'The bastard's still stuck, skipper. Dave's having a fit.'

'He's not the only one! Can he see what's wrong? We sure as hell don't want to be landing back home with a cookie hanging out of our arse.' The slightest jolt, like touching down, might jar the bomb loose and kill them all instantly.

'Give us a moment.'

Sexton was clambering around the edge of the open bomb bay trying to see what was holding the cookie in place. He desperately wanted to solve the problem before D-Delta moved beyond the target zone. With every second the bomber farther, and making things harder, the glow inside the aircraft dimmed until he angrily pulled a flashlight from his pocket. More by luck its shaking beam fell on a likely fault.

'He's fixed something, skipper,' Baxter told them, seeing a thumbs-up from Sexton. 'Let her go?'

'No, we'll go around again,' Branner said calmly, which belied the shout of panic inside his head. The shocked silence from the crew was just as damning. At his navigator's table, Flanders allowed himself to put his head in his hands and rest it gently on the desk in front of him.

Branner turned D-Delta back towards the target and bypassed it to starboard in the same way. The section of city they were bombing was a roaring inferno and it seemed unlikely their cookie was going to contribute more. Branner grimly reminded himself it was the job they were meant to do. Besides, heavy machinery had been proven to survive fires before. The destructive power of the cookie was needed too.

Cook didn't bother using the bomb sight. There was nothing he could pin-point. It was a matter of dropping the cookie somewhere in the middle of the existing destruction and for that he could judge without the sight. He waited until the fires were passing through the bubble of his bomb aimer's Perspex.

'Any time now, Bax. Tell Dave to kick the bloody thing out if he has to.'

The bomb bay was vividly lit again and Baxter only had to nod and wave enthusiastically at Sexton, who shouted a prayer as he worked the manual release. This time the cookie vanished and D-Delta surged upwards. Whoops of delight filled the intercom and Sexton grinned fiercely at Cook as he hurried past back to the cockpit.

'Thank Christ for that, skipper,' Sexton said, after plugging back into the intercom.

'Well done, Dave. Let's not hang about any longer than we have to. What's our course, Navigator?'

Flanders replied in a cracking voice, 'Now you want to leave in a hurry?' He hastily added the course before Branner could reprimand him.

Branner put the aircraft into a slight dive to increase speed quickly. Their three passes over the target might have left them alone and straggling at the rear of the stream—easy pickings for a fighter. He wanted to catch up.

It was a long and uneventful journey back. In his rear turret, Wills watched a slow sunrise behind them as D-Delta approached the Belgium coast and the English Channel. There were no Lancasters close to the rear, telling him the stream had been spread wide during the night. Glinting Perspex in the distance showed him they weren't the last aircraft in line.

Similarly, Branner was breathing easier as the morning revealed the nearest aircraft in front. With daylight the chance of attack from German fighters increased rapidly, but it looked like the stream's flight plan would work and the Lancasters were going to reach the coast just as the sun broached the horizon. A white strip of beach passed beneath and of the crew began cautiously opening their sandwiches. The tea or coffee had already been drunk before it got too cold.

The ocean was an inviting blue under a clear day by the time D-Delta completed the Channel crossing and turned out of the stream for Waddington. By now the crew was carefully chatting, not wanting to irritate Branner who was fatigued by the lengthy spell at the controls. Someone even joked they should have overflown the target a fourth time, just for a sight-seeing trip. The others heartily abused the culprit.

They landed without incident and endured the taxi-ing to their dispersal, the final and painful minutes of sore backs and muscles, numb rumps and stinging eyes. As usual, the crew piled out as soon as the Lancaster stopped, accepting the congratulations of Granger's ground crew as they hurried to the edge of the bitumen for a much-needed cigarette. Here they loudly exchanged their thoughts on the raid, the tension rushing out of them in shouted jibes at each other and nervous laughter.

'A lorry's coming,' Sexton announced, fingering his ear as if he could dig out the deafness that still lingered. He nodded at an approaching truck.

Daniel winced at the thought of the hard, wooden seats in the back and wished the ride was a bit further away so he could get some circulation back into his rear end first.

'Look out, there's a lame duck coming in.' Cook pointed at an approaching Lancaster.

It was going to fly low over the base so that ground staff could confirm what the aircrew couldn't actually see—that the undercarriage hadn't dropped at all. The bomber passed overhead as the lorry pulled to a halt. Branner gestured for the driver to wait a while.

The Lancaster presented a sorry sight. It was blackened in several places from flak near-misses and one engine was stopped. They could even see holes and rents in the wings and fuselage. The aircraft had suffered a hard night, but some would say it was lucky too—it had made it home.

'This will be a belly-landing for sure,' Sexton yelled above the noise.

'Let's see her down,' Branner said. Everyone agreed and the driver of the truck guessed what was happening and took the opportunity to light a cigarette.

Dwindling to a toy-like size at the far end of the runway, the troubled Lancaster swept around to approach for a landing. Branner could see it was off to the left, towards D-Delta's dispersal, to use the grass beside the main strip.

'That's a smart fellow,' he said approvingly.

Daniel heard him and turned to agree. Beyond Branner he saw Granger frowning and chewing unhappily at his pipe. As if he felt Daniel's eyes on him Granger looked back and growled, almost unheard, 'Wrong bloody side of the landing strip—the fool.'

'What?' Branner asked, catching the end of this. Granger only nodded at the Lancaster to encourage Branner to watch for himself.

The noise of the aircraft's engines grew again in odd surges, the pilot nursing the throttles to lose most of his height quickly and give the bomber plenty of time to ease the rest of the way onto the ground. The Lancaster dipped alarmingly several times, almost brushing the earth too early, until it steadied to skim above the grass perfectly. D-Delta's crew collectively held their breaths willing the cripple safely down the last few feet.

The Lancaster obliged them by dropping abruptly, shearing off the propellers to send the blades wheeling spectacularly through the air, then the underside of the aircraft thudded onto the grass with a sound of crumpling metal. It kept going in a straight line beside the tarmac.

Nearly everyone at the dispersal burst into cheers even though the aircraft was still sliding fast and would take some time to halt. More than anything, the bomber hadn't tripped or cart-wheeled as it hit the ground. The hardest part of a wheels-up landing had been done. Still only Granger wasn't satisfied, puzzling Daniel, who had joined in the celebration.

Their joy was very short-lived. The Lancaster skated across one of the many taxiways and for a brief moment the metal underbelly met with the bitumen. There was an instant of brilliant sparks showering everywhere and in that same moment the bomber burst into flames, becoming a ball of flame as it continued its slide and now spin around slowly. Fuel spilling from ruptured tanks had been ignited.

The watchers were shocked into silence. The tragedy wasn't finished yet.

The Lancaster must still have had its 4000-pound cookie on board, exactly what Branner had gone to great lengths to avoid over Essen. Still moving fast, the stricken bomber blew to pieces with such a ferocity the explosion slapped at the D-Delta crew and caused a huge geyser of debris and earth. Then something incredible happened.

The rear turret was spat out of the bomber like a ball from a cannon. It rolled across the earth towards the amazed witnesses for several hundred yards until it finally came to rest on its side, still in one piece.

The lorry driver was leaning out his door. 'What the hell are you all waiting for?' he yelled.

He gunned the motor and only gave enough time for Daniel, Flanders and a half-dozen of the ground crew to scramble over the tail gate before the truck lurched into motion to race towards the turret. Again the driver shouted out of his window. It was incomprehensible to Daniel. One of the ground crew relayed the instructions.

'He reckons three of us hop out here, the rest go on to the wreck. You two get ready to jump.'

Daniel and Flanders didn't argue and edged back to the rear of the truck, hanging on grimly as it bounced over rough ground. It came to such a sudden halt they were nearly thrown off their feet. They managed to keep hold and get out. Another body thumped down with them.

The lorry roared off with a cloud of blue smoke, drawing aside like a piece of stage scenery to reveal the blown-out tail turret. From this close it didn't look so undamaged, but it was still remarkably complete. The three men didn't expect the same for its occupant, if the gunner was even in there. They hesitated for a moment, holding on to the slim hope the man had chosen to try surviving the belly landing inside the fuselage. The instant oblivion with his crew mates would have been better than the torture of the rolling, smashing turret, bludgeoning the gunner to death.

It was then they heard the monotonous, angry swearing coming from inside the turret. Daniel was stunned to recognise the pale blob of a face behind the smeared Perspex.

'Jesus Christ, he's alive,' Flanders choked.

They hurried to the rear of the turret and saw the doors were missing. The gunner's back was towards them. Daniel thrust his upper body inside to see his face. Inside, it stank of cordite and burning. Hundreds of brass cartridges lay everywhere. He could smell the man's sweat.

'Are you all right? Can you hear me?' Daniel couldn't believe the man was alive.

'Get me out of here,' the gunner whispered hoarsely. 'I—I can't bloody breathe.'

'Get out the way,' the ground crew man told Daniel, tapping his shoulder.

As Daniel stepped aside the crewman produced a large pocketknife and sliced through the seat harness. They managed to pull the gunner out and lay him gently on the grass. He didn't move, staring unseeing at nothing, but he looked unhurt. Daniel took off his own jacket and bundled it into a pillow under the man's head.

Flanders was saying loudly, 'God, that was absolutely fucking unbelievable. Who would ever have imagined it?' He sounded slightly hysterical.

'It's bloody amazing,' Daniel said, exhaustion setting in. 'We'd better try and wave down one of those ambulances. They won't expect us to have anybody alive either.'

'Did you see that thing bouncing over the ground like a bloody tennis ball?' Flanders asked and smiled with wide eyes down at the gunner. 'I say, you don't fancy a game of snooker when we get back? I'll bet you're a damned expert at it now.'

The gunner didn't reply. Flanders' grin slowly faded as he realised the man's gaze was locked on the pyre of smoke coming from the destroyed Lancaster.

'Sorry,' Flanders said quietly and embarrassed with his outburst. 'Don't worry, old chap. Some medical blokes will be here to take care of you soon.'

Again the man didn't answer. Flanders shrugged an uneasy apology to the other two instead.

Eighteen.

In late afternoon sunshine Daniel, Flanders and Cook were beside an improvised playing field watching a scratch game of rugby. Plenty of eager players lined the boundaries, rushing on to take the place of men who were tired or winded by a rough tackle, tagging someone as they staggered from the game. On the field there was a lot of friendly confusion about who was on which side and some men treacherously changed their minds when it suited them, but it was all in fun. Daniel wasn't interested and was only killing time before walking Dianne to the pub. Besides, he didn't particularly like the game. Cook and Flanders were keeping him company and wouldn't need much encouragement to join him in the trip to the village. Flanders was eyeing the game doubtfully.

'The idea is to get the ball from one end of the field to the other and over that line, right?' he asked.

'Right,' Daniel answered the obvious.

'But you're only allowed the throw the ball backwards?'

'You can run forwards and kick the ball that way,' Cook offered, knowing what answer was coming.

'Running only gets you clobbered by the other blokes, and kicking it is a waste of time from the looks of it. Passing it is best, but only if you can only do it bloody backwards. How silly is that?'

'It's only a game, Flanno,' Daniel said.

'Typical of the Poms though. To make it stupidly hard for themselves. How do they expect to win the war with that kind of planning?'

Cook said wryly, 'We don't have to now, remember? The Yanks are coming to do it for us.'

'Exactly,' Flanders pointed a finger at him. 'In their game of rugby you're allowed to throw the football forwards. In fact, it's positively encouraged. The Americans aren't shy to make things easy for themselves.'

'Yes, that's true,' Daniel nodded. 'Just ask the skipper. Has he heard any more from his girl?'

Flanders snorted, 'God no, what do you expect? Not as far as I've heard anyway—not that he'd tell us. She's a goner for sure. Buried under a mountain of stockings, chocolate and goodness knows what else. The Yanks don't know the meaning of the word "rationing", I'd say. Mind you, I suppose the skipper can always hope the bloke goes for a burton himself. Maybe she'll come back then.'

No one was even slightly shocked at the callous suggestion. Daniel was only curious. 'You seem to know a lot about it. You haven't been getting any Dear John letters from home yourself, have you? I didn't know you had anyone back there.'

'I don't. Only my sister, who writes quite regularly with all this kind of gossip.'

'Ah, I forgot about her.' Daniel added to Cook, 'Apparently Charlie's seen Flanno's sister naked. He reckons she'd do quite well out there.' He rolled his eyes at the game and made the shape of a large woman with his hands.

'I can't see Charlie coping with that sort of girl,' Cook murmured, wincing at a hard tackle right in front of them. From under the mound of tacklers the victim held a pleading hand towards them, begging to be tagged out of the game. They all looked back at him with feigned misunderstanding.

'That fibbing little bastard,' Flanders growled. 'We never even knew each other before the crew was put together, so he certainly hasn't met my sister—naked or otherwise.'

Daniel said, 'What about after the war? Surely, we'll all be keeping in touch? They might meet then, and you never know—stranger things have happened. You might end up as best man at Charlie's wedding to your sister.'

'I hope you're not serious.' Flanders gave him an evil look. 'Besides, you won't be there. You'll still be here, battling to feed Dianne and a brood of six little monsters in some East End flat, living off your war pension.'

'Hardly. I'm sure she'll come home with me.' Daniel felt a squirm of pleasure just thinking about this.

'Have you asked her? What do you think, Cookie?'

Cook had gone pensive during the discussion and looked unwilling to offer his opinion. Then he saw an easier way out. 'All I can say is you'd better make up your mind fast. Here she comes.'

Dianne and Susan were walking towards them from the direction of their barracks. They joined up with the men and Dianne gave Daniel a quick kiss on the cheek.

'Hello, are you all having a go?' she asked cheerfully.

Flanders answered for them mournfully, 'At this idiocy? What do you take us for?'

Susan said, 'I see. Well, it's not the kind of spirit that will see the Germans off. I suppose a few pints at the pub will get your courage up?'

'Now here's a girl after my own heart,' Flanders said warmly, turning to leave and holding out his arm to put around her shoulders.

'No, I'm not,' Susan said, dodging away from him. She surprised Cook by hooking her arm through his. 'Bruce, you're getting as bad as Charlie.'

Flanders frowned at Cook. 'At least I'm much more attractive than him.'

'He makes me look tall,' Susan explained, bringing a crestfallen expression to Cook's face. She let him suffer for a moment. 'Not really, Cookie. I think you're very sweet.'

'Sweet?' Flanders made it sound like a disease. 'What about your haggis-munching friend? The ballroom dancer?'

'Michael's not here, is he?'

'All right, you two. That will do.' Dianne held up her hands like a line referee, which was appreciated by some nearby players. They called to her jokingly to join the game. 'Are we going to the pub or not?'

They all walked together through the base and towards the main gate. As they approached it, seeing the guards on duty in the distance, everyone began to slow. Dianne voiced her thoughts for all of them.

'It's starting to be some kind of sign, waiting to find out if the MPs are questioning people coming back like they did when that poor girl was murdered.'

'Things look fairly calm from here,' Daniel said.

'Yes, I think so too. God, I hope they catch him soon.'

Flanders said, from in front of them, 'I reckon he's already got the chop or been posted away. That's why they haven't found him yet. Serves the bastard right if he's gone down.'

'What about the blokes who went down with him?' Susan asked.

Flanders shrugged. 'All right, let's hope he's been shot to pieces by the Jerries and he was a fighter pilot.'

'Not around here, he wasn't.'

Dianne interrupted, 'I'd prefer he's still in one piece and they catch him. That way we know for sure and we can all go back to the way things were. Nice and normal, and girls can go wherever we please at night and not have to worry about being escorted home.'

No one answered that because they had come close to the gate and were filing silently past the watchful eyes of the MPs. Outside and further down the road, Daniel made Dianne slow down a little and put a little space between them and the others.

'Dianne, after the war would you come and live in Australia with me?'

'Goodness, is this another proposal, Daniel?'

He answered seriously, 'Actually, it's more a question of being practical. Whether I'd have to stay here with you, or you'd come back to Australia with me…'

Dianne mimicked his tone. 'Dianne, would you like a drink? Dianne, do you want a fag? Dianne, will you come and live in Australia? God, Daniel! You do ask the most incredible questions without any warning. How should I know? Let's wait until we've won the war first, shall we?'

'I was only wondering,' Daniel said casually. 'By the way, I like escorting you home. I don't care if they don't catch the murderer for a while—as long as he doesn't hurt anyone else, of course.'

Daniel hadn't told anyone of his fears that Baxter might be involved, and that he wanted to prove somehow to himself he was wrong before an arrest did that for him. Apologising to Baxter after having someone else caught first wouldn't feel quite like the same thing.

***

The hotel was already busy with thick crowds around the bar. The only clear space was a thin corridor for the dart players to have their game. Being on the edge of this was a dangerous place to be, especially if a dart rebounded off the wire frame. Several bystanders had been impaled. The evening was closing in, but it was mild enough for people to stand in the beer garden, so many had migrated out there. In a back room, a billiards table that was constantly ruined by boisterous horseplay had been patched back into life. Half the challenge was to negotiate the balls over the many glued or taped repairs to the felt.

They discovered the rest of D-Delta's crew crushed into a corner. Even Baxter was there, silently nursing a beer and listening to Branner and Sexton argue about how well the bomber stream tactic had worked. This was after a discussion on performing a "corkscrew" manoeuvre, twisting the Lancaster through the sky in such a way that any night fighters on their tail would be shaken off. Wills had stubbornly insisted it would be better to keep straight and level so he could shoot the offending German down instead. Faced with his slightly drunk doggedness, the skipper and engineer changed the subject to the streaming debate, saving them from being forced to admit they had little faith Wills could shoot down anything.

Once they'd all exchanged greetings, Daniel asked loudly, 'What's the occasion? It's a bit crowded, even for this place.'

'We're celebrating dreadful weather on the other side of the ditch,' Sexton said with a happy smile. 'Most of Europe's well socked in, they say. At least, the bits we want to bomb. Not much chance of an early morning call, see?'

'Good, another day off.'

'Perhaps. At worst, we might have to do some training or cop a few lectures.'

Flanders said, 'That's all right. You can always catch up on forty winks during those.' He avoided Branner's disapproving eye.

It began a night of dedicated drinking with everybody assuming the same—that there would be no battle orders posted the following day. It seemed like the entire base had come into the village and was at the pub. The South African pilot, Munk, pushed his way through the crowd to them. No one from D-Delta had seen him since the preparation days for the Augsburg raid. Munk's aircraft had been a survivor among the second flight of six. They greeted him as one who had shared a dangerous time.

'Hello, chaps—and good evening, ladies,' he shouted back. 'Has anyone seen my navigator? He owes me a few quid and I'm broke.'

'He's probably lost,' Flanders said.

'You are funny. Has anybody got a sensible answer?'

Branner said, 'I don't think I'd know the bloke, if I did see him. Anyone know him?' They all shook their heads or shrugged.

'Never mind. I don't suppose you'd like to buy me a drink?' he asked Susan, turning to her.

'You've got to be joking. We don't get half the pay you pilots get.' Susan's laugh was strained, and she edged away from him slightly, pressing against Cook.

'No, I suppose not,' Munk replied. 'You're quite right. It's more appropriate that I buy one for you when I get some money.'

'Then you'll have to shout everybody a drink,' Wills said, taking them all in with a sweep of his hand. 'It's the way we do things in our little mob.'

'Mob,' Munk tasted the word. 'That's what we call sheep back home. Anyway, I doubt I'll be able to afford that.' He used this to appeal for sympathy at Dianne, who looked blandly back.

'Where's your spy pay from Hitler?' Flanders asked. 'You should ask him for more money. Some kind of hazard wages for having to drink in a place like this.'

'For some reason the bank won't honour his cheques,' Munk said. He sensed the girls weren't going to give him any attention and stood on his tip-toes, looking around for someone else. 'Are you sure you haven't seen him? A little fellow with big feet.'

Again, they all gestured no. Waving his farewells, Munk slipped back into the crowd.

'That chap really fancies himself,' Susan said as soon as he was gone. 'It annoys me.'

'Very cock-sure,' Dianne agreed, frowning. Her expression stayed a moment because she was beginning to feel a little ill. It might have been anything—the drinking and too many cigarettes, plus the dubious snacks that came from the bar. She didn't want to say anything to Daniel just yet in case she spoiled his fun. The feeling might go away just as quickly as it came.

Later in the night, the crowd began to thin. It was Flanders who noticed that many of the revellers leaving were WAAFs, dragging their male companions with them.

'I say, is it going to be a dirty ditty session or something?' he asked, squinting around. Sometimes the men would start singing some of their more bawdy songs, too offensive for the girls' delicate ears.

Susan gave it some thought and her face lit up with a memory. 'Oh, that's right. Attila the Hun's got half the girls doing a damned cross-country run in the morning. Honestly, that woman's a terror. God knows why we're expected to be fit for this job. What's the point?' She shrugged. 'Anyway, I've wiggled out of it. What about you, Dianne?'

'I haven't heard a thing about it and that's how I'm going to keep things. Don't say another word. Besides, I would call in sick,' Dianne said with a sincerity no one noticed. Her upset stomach wasn't getting better.

'That might be a sight worth seeing,' Flanders mused, imagining hundreds of WAAFs jogging past in their gym gear.

'I can't see you getting up that early,' Susan told him.

'We should all make the effort. Cheer the girls on, so to speak. What do you think, lads?' When Flanders got resounding silence from the others he said, 'What about Bax? Where is he?'

'He's going home to bed,' Wills said, pointing at Baxter, who was sneaking out the hotel door. 'He never says goodbye in case we tease him into staying longer. I don't think he holds his booze very well.'

'What, and you're a paragon of sobriety?' Flanders raised his eyebrows.

'A what? What did you call me, you bastard?'

As Flanders tried to explain, Daniel used the opportunity to talk quickly to Dianne.

'Damn, there's something I had to chat with Bax about too. Look—it won't take long. Do you mind staying here while I try and catch up with him? I'll be as quick as I can.'

Dianne was on the verge of asking to go back too and had been worried how Daniel would react, since he was enjoying himself. She saw a chance to make a trade. 'No, it's all right. But can we leave, when you come back?'

'If you like.' He added with a lopsided smile. 'I'll fall over soon, if I don't.'

With a squeeze of her hand he hurried to the door, dimly hearing Dianne explain his departure to the others.

Daniel was glad to find the night was well lit by a half moon and it wasn't long before his eyesight adjusted. He was only after one thing—an assurance that Baxter was only going back to the station. Confronting him was going to be another awkward moment and the alcohol buzzing in Daniel's blood threatened that it might be a bad idea. However, he was also thinking that even just asking Baxter might make him think twice if he had other plans. Daniel couldn't help the thought that several WAAFs could be on their way home without escorts. A clever killer might find an opportunity even with so many others making the same trip.

The road leading towards the base stretched clearly for some distance and he could see the shadowy forms of friends and couples making their way back. None of the moonlit figures struck him as Baxter, although it was hard to tell. Something made Daniel search to his left and he was in time to spot somebody moving deeper into the village. Without knowing how, he recognised Baxter. A cold feeling filled Daniel's stomach.

'Shit, where the hell are you going?' he asked aloud, momentarily torn by the idea of quickly getting Branner or Sexton to help him. That would be long enough for Baxter to get too far ahead.

Cursing, he set off in pursuit. Once Daniel was close enough to stay in touch, he slowed down again, figuring it might be best to follow Baxter for a while and find out exactly what he was doing. Stopping him now wouldn't answer any questions.

Moving silently through the darkened village wasn't easy. Some of the streets were cobblestoned, while others had potholes and broken paving to trip the unwary. Daniel was glad of the moonlight just to give him half a chance of not breaking an ankle. He spent most of his time watching the ground in front of him and the rest keeping his eye on Baxter, who seemed to be traveling a lot more easily like he knew where he was going. That worried Daniel too. Did Baxter have some pre-determined place he might prey on unsuspecting women? Some of the doorways sheltered the pinpricks of lit cigarettes and murmured conversations, the local village girls snatching final minutes with their sweethearts before going inside. These fell silent as Daniel passed and sometimes he could feel accusing looks on him, questioning what he was doing creeping through their streets alone.

The further they went, the more Daniel worried about leaving Dianne behind. He'd promised not to be long and he didn't want to worry or anger her. At least he had a good reason and decided to tell her everything when this was finished, regardless of how things turned out. Baxter would just have to put up with it.

It was almost grimly amusing for Daniel to realise that, while he had come into the town and its pub with nearly every chance offered, he'd had no reason to investigate the village further and was now in unfamiliar territory. So he was surprised to find himself close to the main centre with its wider streets and shop fronts.

Then, in distance, Baxter disappeared behind a large door. There was a gleam of orange light as he opened and closed it.

Daniel trotted across the road to the same entrance and pulled up with shock when the truth hit him.

'This is the last thing I would have thought of,' he groaned quietly. He took a step back again and stared upwards at the church spire silhouetted against the stars above. Quietly he pushed open the door and slid inside.

Several candles were lit on the altar with a few more down each side of the room, not enough to betray the village to German bombers through the colourful lead-light windows. Two rows of pews with an aisle between stretched empty to the small stage, except for the form of Baxter sitting bowed about halfway along. He didn't turn as Daniel entered but spoke as he eased the door closed behind him.

'Don't tell the others where I go, Danny,' he said very softly. 'Especially Bruce. I'll never hear the end of it.'

'It's no one else's business,' Daniel said, moving closer. 'I won't say a word.'

'Are you satisfied now? Now that you know where I go? Is that why you followed me?'

'I… thought you were going somewhere else. I was worried.' A part of Daniel didn't want to be convinced. Perhaps Baxter had seen him following and detoured into the church to mislead him?

'You thought I was going somewhere else,' Baxter echoed with a knowing smile.

'Is this where you go all the time?'

'Just about. Sometimes I go to a park on the other side of the village. It can be nice and peaceful there too. The Father always leaves the door open, and the candles lit for blokes like us. Particularly on nights we come back from a raid.'

Daniel glanced around expecting to see a priest emerge from the shadows. It seemed they were alone. 'I understand, Morgan. You don't have to explain anything.'

'I'm not especially religious, you know.' Baxter still hadn't raised his head or looked at Daniel.

'No? I don't suppose that matters, does it?'

'Not now, anyway. As a kid we went to church all the time and these days I get… guilty. More so, after a few too many beers. Odd, isn't it? Some blokes want to fight when they're drunk, others cry like babies. I get ashamed and come here to pray.'

'There's nothing wrong with that.' Now Daniel was feeling completely out of his depth and hoped he sounded sincere.

Baxter let out a quiet laugh. 'Except that I'm only interested in praying for myself. I ask God to let me see next week. I'm bloody terrified in that aircraft, Daniel. Every second we're airborne and heading for a target, I'm scared out of my wits.'

'We all are, Morgan. Don't kid yourself that you're the only one who's frightened.'

Baxter thought about this for a long time, so much that Daniel was feeling a need to break the silence when Baxter said, 'You thought I was going to try and find some girl to attack, didn't you? That's why you followed me.'

'I didn't know what to think, that's why I came after you. It would have helped if you'd told me about all this last time we spoke.'

'I brought her here, you know. Robyn, I mean. That night she was killed.'

Daniel tried to keep the sudden tension out of his voice. 'And what happened?'

'She laughed at me. Thought this was a funny thing to do. After she spent half the night telling me how proper she was and how she didn't like a lot of the attention her looks got her, I guessed she might like visiting a church. I was wrong and she thought it was funny.'

'So, what did you do?'

'Nothing. I took her back to the base. On the way, she began apologising for not taking me seriously and I think she really meant it. I already felt bad enough and it was too late. I couldn't get away from her too soon.' Baxter's head dropped into his hands. 'I could have walked her much closer to the WAAF's barracks—seen her to the door safely, despite how I felt. But I left her as soon as it was half-decent and Robyn

313

didn't complain. I think she wanted to be rid of me just as much as I did her.'

'Then you're a bloody fool, Morgan, if that's all that went on. Why don't you tell the police all this? You were the last one to see her alive.'

'That's right, and they'll lock me up forever until someone else owns up to it—if they ever have to. They've hung people by mistake in this country before, you know. Given the circumstances, would you take the risk?'

Daniel was disturbed to find he wasn't sure. It was fine to offer such calm advice from his side of the argument. 'Where were you when that other girl was attacked?'

'Here, alone.'

'Still, she won't recognise you. That's a good thing.'

'Only if the police and the MPs are convinced the same bloke did both.'

Baxter had plainly been giving the problem a lot of thought. Daniel had no answer for that one. He shuffled his foot uneasily on the stone floor. 'We can talk about that later. Things can only get worse, keeping secrets like this.' He paused, still uncomfortable. 'Look, I'd better be getting back. I told Dianne I would take her home. She'll be getting worried.'

'You promised you wouldn't say anything. Don't tell them I come here.'

'I said I wouldn't.'

'Can you stay just a few minutes more? The company helps me get things straight in my head. Then I might come back with you.'

Daniel suppressed a sigh. 'All right, but not long. I'll have to get back even if you're not ready.'

He saw Baxter nod and slowly lower his head to rest tiredly on the back of the pew in front of him. Daniel wasn't sure if Baxter was praying, so he didn't say anything more. He carefully sat down and gazed around at his surroundings. He couldn't remember the last time he was inside a church, and it was all very alien to him in the flickering candlelight, bringing back childhood ghost stories. Daniel knew he wasn't going to last long waiting for Baxter, but he had promised at least a few minutes.

They began to pass with a painful slowness.

***

'Now where's Danny gone?' Branner asked with the added authority of too many pints. He was left with Dianne after the others had spread around the bar.

'He went to chat with Morgan and hasn't come back for some time,' Dianne explained weakly. All she cared about now was the growing nausea in her tummy. The same drink was tepid and unwanted in her hand. 'I was rather hoping he would take me home soon.'

Branner noticed her pale face. 'Are you all right?'

'Not really. I seem to have picked up a bit of a wog.' She gave him a quivering smile.

He peered at her. 'No, I must say you don't look your usual brilliant self.'

Dianne came to a decision. 'Alec, I don't suppose you'd care to walk me back to the base? I'd go on my own, only it's a bit late and—'

'No, of course I don't mind,' Branner cut her off, but he had an edge of disappointment and added, 'Besides, I can always double back—that's not important. You need taking care of, that's all that matters. Just give me a second to tell the others.'

'On second thoughts, I'll be all right…'

'Nonsense! You don't look well at all. We can be off in a jiffy. With a bit of luck we'll cadge a lift.'

'Then don't tell Susan. It'll spoil her fun.'

'You call that fun? If you like.' Susan had been fighting off Wills, Flanders and several new suitors all night. Finding a safe harbour in Cook had helped and pleased the bomb aimer greatly, except it was never long before she drunkenly ventured away again.

'I might go out the front for some fresh air, while I wait,' Dianne told Branner, already moving for the door.

'Good idea. I'll be with you in a minute.'

Branner struggled through the fog of cigarette smoke to find Wills and Flanders at the dart board. 'Chaps, I just offered to take Dianne back to the base. Danny's done a disappearing trick and she's feeling a bit poorly, so I said I'd take her.'

'I'll do it, if you want, skipper,' Wills offered.

'Really? Have you had enough for the night?'

'Well, I suppose Susan will be going back with her?'

'They are like two peas in a pod,' Branner shrugged. 'My game's finally come up on the billiard table and I was feeling a bit browned off I'd have to miss out.'

'Let me check that Susan's going back too.'

From the dartboard line, Flanders said, 'You just don't give up, do you?'

Branner said, 'Thanks for that, Charlie. I'll owe you a pint.'

As Branner walked unsteadily back to the billiards table to see the status of things, Wills went in search of Susan, who he knew was in the backyard beer garden with Cook. He discovered them pressed close together by a crowd of airmen. Neither seemed to be complaining.

'There you are,' he said, startling them. 'Susan, are you going back to the station with Dianne?'

'No, it's the first I've heard of it,' she said, hurriedly dropping her arm off Cook's shoulder. 'Why? Is she going back?'

'Apparently. Danny's still off somewhere with Bax, so the skipper offered to walk her home. I said I'd do it, since I figured you'd be going, too…' Wills' voice tailed off as suspicions began to surface in his mind.

'I don't want to go back just yet. I'm having a wonderful time. Have you got a fag, by the way? Cookie's run out.'

Wills gave them both a cigarette as he frowned at the implications of this. 'Then I might stay too,' he decided. 'Since you are.'

Susan swapped a meaningful look with Cook. 'Charlie, I think you and I need to have a little chat in private. Do you mind? We can have a drink just outside of the garden here. Cookie, be a darling and go to the bar for us?'

'My pleasure,' Cook said carefully.

Wills was delighted and looked around to see if anyone else was witnessing his good fortune. In that moment, Susan leaned close to Cook and whispered, 'If I'm not back in ten minutes, for God's sake come and rescue me with those drinks.'

'Synchronising watches now, skipper,' Cook answered in a hushed tone. 'Gin and tonic and a pint in ten minutes.'

He slipped away inside. Susan took Wills' hand and led him through a small gate to the rear of the hotel where they wouldn't be disturbed. It was a lane way, part of the back boundary of the hotel with a high masonry wall topped by wrought iron spikes. Susan leaned her shoulder on the stone and Wills did the same, facing her.

She started heavily, 'Charlie, I wish you wouldn't follow me around so much like some lost puppy. It's very nice that you buy me drinks all the time, but it doesn't mean anything if I take them, right? I don't want to feel... obligated every time you do something like that.'

Wills' hopes were rapidly crashing. 'I don't understand. I only do it because I like you—a lot.'

'And I like you. You're a very good friend. But honestly, I don't think we'd ever really be anything more, if you know what I mean.'

'No, I don't. Not if you say we're very good friends.'

Susan took a deep breath and resigned herself that it was going to take all of those ten minutes to steer him through the emotional crisis of rejection and, she had no doubt, back to being a friend, before Cook returned. Susan wasn't worried, she had broken hearts before and young men like Charlie Wills were all the same. She knew what to say and do.

Inside, Branner had time to buy another drink. The last game on the billiard table was dragging out before his turn. He got himself a pint and noticed Cook leaning on the bar alone further around the room.

'Hello, Cookie. Have you been cut adrift too?'

'Something like that, skipper. Susan's taken off with Charlie.'

'Good-oh. He said he'd do that. Leaves me to take my chance at sporting glory. I must get back—the bastards will scrub you off the blackboard if you don't hang around.'

'Good luck then, skipper.'

Cook watched him go, puzzled by a misgiving that he'd missed something during the exchange. It wouldn't be long before he could clear things up. Four and a half minutes, to be exact. Just enough time to buy those drinks.

***

In front of the hotel, Dianne was huddled beside a porch support and waiting miserably for Branner to come out. The fresh air had helped, but now it made going back into the bar to find out what was taking so long impossible. The smells of stale cigarettes and spilt drink on the carpet would give her stomach that last, dreadful turn. It was getting cold too. Her jacket wasn't keeping out the chill. Dianne was certain now she was properly ill, not just drunk, and all she could think about was her warm bunk and help close to hand if she needed it.

The road leading back to the base was clear and inviting in the moonlight. She had done the trip so many times before, if not alone, then only with Susan and often feeling the worse for wear—and she'd never come to any harm. Sure, things were different at the moment, but what were the odds of getting into trouble on such a well-used track? Besides, she could probably be back at the station in the same time it would take to go back inside, find Branner and coax him into finishing his drink, say endless goodbyes and then get a move on. In fact, Daniel wouldn't be much better, even if he returned right now.

'Oh, bugger it. They can catch me up if they really care,' Dianne decided and set off across the road on the journey home.

It took her a few minutes to walk the straight section that was visible from the village. Dianne kept her head down, fighting off the nausea by concentrating on her footsteps. Nobody else was on the road with her, but while the front of the hotel was still in sight behind her—albeit in the distance—it felt safe. The first corner loomed as a more daunting prospect. Beyond it was another long, unbending piece of road, then after that several more curves bringing her close to the guard house. This next part of the trip was going to be the worst and Dianne hated the fact that just thinking about it made her even more nervous. There was no going back though.

Past the corner she tried to walk faster. It jolted a headache building behind her eyes. Perhaps she was getting a migraine? Dianne suffered from these about once a year and they made her ill too. It was a small comfort that maybe it wasn't some kind of food poisoning from the pub.

'Hello, Dianne. What are you doing walking back alone?'

Dianne let out a small squeal and whirled to face the man who almost magically appeared strolling beside her. She recognised the voice and could see his face in the moonlight. It was Munk. Dianne immediately started walking again. He kept pace beside her.

'God! You scared the hell out of me.'

'I'm sorry, I didn't mean to. Not very thoughtful of me, I suppose.'

'Where did you come from?'

He sounded embarrassed. 'I was behind the bushes there… a call of nature, you know? One pint too many.'

'I didn't see you before, on the road in front of me.'

He cleared his throat. 'Actually, I found it quite peaceful back there. It's a little clearing at the edge of the paddock. I had a smoke and looked at the stars for a while—I'm sorry, would you like one?' He deftly dug a cigarette case out of his pocket and flipped the lid open.

'No, thanks. I've been smoking like a chimney all night.' Dianne didn't want to admit she was ill.

'Then do you mind if I accompany you back to the station? It seems silly to walk apart.'

'No, of course not, thank you. I'm rather keen to get back.'

'I can tell,' he laughed gently. 'You're setting a cracking pace.'

He tried to make small talk and they continued on. Dianne could only answer in monosyllables, partly because she didn't like his company and also with her efforts to cope with the headache and nausea. She hoped he didn't take offence and get unpleasant, but she couldn't make a bigger effort.

Well before the next turning on the road Munk asked, 'Dianne, are you all right? You seem a bit... upset.' After a pause, he added softly, 'I suspect you don't like me very much.'

Dianne was alarmed. Something in his voice was lifting the hairs on the back of her neck and she felt an instinct to calm him. 'No, it's not that—really. I'm not feeling very well, that's all.'

'Oh? Why didn't you say something?'

She offered a wan smile. 'I just need to get back, that's all.'

'I'm surprised Daniel isn't here looking after you.'

In turn, Dianne was taken aback that Munk used Daniel's name with such familiarity. How did he know they were having a close relationship?

Dianne thought it was like he'd been watching them.

Calm down, you idiot. You're imagining things.

'Daniel got caught up in some other trouble. I'm sure he's searching the pub for me right now. I should have waited.'

'You look like you need to sit down for a minute and rest.'

Munk put an arm across her back, resting his hand easily on Dianne's opposite shoulder. She managed not to flinch at the unexpected touch.

She said, 'There's hardly anywhere to sit down. The main gate's not too far ahead. Maybe I'll stay there for a minute? The boys in the guard hut always look after me.'

'There's a small bench under this tree just ahead. Do you want to stop for a minute and catch your breath?'

'There is? I've never seen it.' Dianne didn't believe him. She searched the moonlight shadows ahead.

'Just there, next to the crooked fence post.'

She wasn't going to sit down. Still, Munk to pull her closer to the edge of the road.

Suddenly his hand went from her shoulder to clamp over Dianne's mouth and Munk threw himself sideways, dragging Dianne with him.

They fell through a gap in the hedge, the branches scratching at Dianne's hands and hair as she flailed for something to stop herself falling. They landed on soft grass, punching the wind out of her lungs. Munk rolled heavily on top of her and pinned her arms with his knees. Before she could catch her breath, he moved his hand back to press even harder on her lips, crushing them against her teeth. With his other hand he began tearing at the top buttons of Dianne's blouse and coat together, trying to thrust it underneath her clothing to the bare flesh beneath.

Dianne tried to beg him to stop and Munk understood what she was saying. He went abruptly still, bent forward and put his face close to hers.

'I don't care,' he hissed angrily, spitting. 'I'll be dead in a few days, or a fucking week. We all will be. Shot down or taken prisoner by the Germans. Until then I'm going to do exactly as I please with snotty bitches like you. I did it before at home and they never caught me then. Here, that farmer's whore didn't even see me. I'll be long dead and gone before anybody knows anything.'

He jerked upright and with a fast move delivered a stinging blow to the side of Dianne's head, stunning her momentarily.

'Be still and it won't hurt,' he growled through his teeth. They gleamed terribly at her in the moonlight. Munk's clutching hand now went behind him, pulling up her dress and scratching with his nails between Dianne's thighs, ripping her stockings.

Dianne was aware in her pain that she was sinking into the damp ground under her. There was a chance to wiggle her arms free, but Munk would feel it too. He was just too strong and Dianne couldn't see a way to fight him off. She knew he would soon get frustrated with her struggling and concentrate both hands at her neck, like he did the other girls.

Then he could do whatever he wanted.

***

Daniel had given up on Baxter and left him in the church. Baxter had begun to talk about his family and past, the words laced with self-pity, and Daniel had quickly figured he wasn't going to hear anything that was more important than getting back to Dianne. Making excuses, he hurried out of the door and into the street.

Daniel tried to retrace his steps back to the hotel. It wasn't so easy and he kept encountering dark lane ways that looked blocked and dead-end paths. Finally he got to the edge of the village and made his way around. The distant sounds of singing and laughter led him to the bar.

He went inside with a smile ready and rehearsing his first words to Dianne. That plan fell to pieces when he saw none of his friends or either of the girls. Then he spotted Branner far across the room under the light of the billiards table. He went straight over and had to wait anxiously for Branner to finish his stroke. The game had just begun and he took several shots before missing a pocket.

'Skipper, have you seen Dianne?'

'Hello, Daniel. You're back. Any luck?' Branner's expression changed as he realised he had no idea what Daniel might have needed luck for. 'Dianne? Yes, she went back to the base with Charlie and Susan.'

At that moment, Wills moved into the glow of the billiards table. He said unhappily, 'How's the game, skipper? Hi, Daniel. You were gone for a while.'

Daniel said, 'I thought you were walking Dianne and Susan back? The skipper just said.'

'No, Susan's out the back with Cook. She doesn't want to go home yet.' Calling Cookie "Cook" gave Daniel a hint what was happening, but he didn't care.

Branner said, frowning, 'Cookie said you were walking them both back to base?'

'No, only if Susan was going too. You said you were going to take Dianne back.'

Now Branner looked genuinely appalled, knowing he let something go wrong. 'Then she must be still waiting out the front. Bloody hell, she'll be ropeable.'

'No, she's not,' Daniel said, getting very alarmed. 'Damn it, she must have started back on her own. How long ago did all this happen?'

Branner stared at the billiards table full of balls. 'It can't be that long. You'll catch her up, if you hurry,' he said uncertainly.

Daniel turned his back on them and headed for the door.

'She'll be all right, won't she?' Wills called after him. Daniel didn't answer.

He burst back out onto the street and spent just a second looking around for Dianne sheltering in the shadows, but he was alone. The road back to the base was empty too. He set off at a trot, convincing himself Dianne must be heading back and had given up waiting for him.

She's angry and walking fast.

There was a chance she had found someone to walk with, but that was no comfort until he knew. Daniel broke into a run a couple of times, but the night's drinking took its toll and only gave him bursts before he ran out of breath. He got to the first bend, panting and holding a stitch in his side. He prayed that rounding the corner would reveal Dianne alone and close. All he saw was a moonlit couple in the distance, the man with his arm over the woman's shoulder.

'Bloody hell,' Daniel groaned, stopping to put his hands on his knees and get some breath back. He stared at the two people ahead, jealous they were three hundred yards further towards the station and therefore that much closer to Dianne. Maybe he could catch them and ask if they'd seen Dianne in front?

To his utter amazement the pair abruptly disappeared from the road. It took Daniel a shocked second to realise what had happened. The man had grabbed the girl and dragged her into the hedgerow. Suddenly, it wasn't in fun or lovers fooling around.

'Jesus—hey… Hey!' Daniel gave up calling out straight away, saving his breath to sprint down the road, ignoring the fresh pains that didn't care for his urgency.

***

Dianne forced her jaw open and felt the heel of Munk's palm between her teeth. She bit hard and tasted salty blood. Munk yelled and pulled his hand away, leaving something behind. Dianne spat it out and frantically sucked in air to scream. She saw Munk raising his arm high to smash her with a roundhouse blow and silence her. She could only turn her head aside and close her eyes in dreadful anticipation, her cry stifled by the fear of impending pain.

It didn't come. There was the sound of a grunt and heavy collision, and Munk's bulk was hauled off in a single movement.

Now two men were grappling on the ground beside her. They fought inexpertly, wrestling and landing ineffectual blows, swearing incoherently. Munk, she could see, had set his mind on escaping and kept trying to drag himself away. She heard a sickening noise of a fist landing on flesh, a punch to the face, and Munk jumped to his feet. His assailant grasped his ankle and was quickly kicked away. Munk scrambled off into the darkness as the other man tried to get up and follow.

Dianne choked, 'No! Please don't leave me! I know who he is.'

For the first time, she saw her rescuer's face and recognised Daniel. He crawled on his knees to her side, wrapped her in his arms and cradled her hard against his chest.

'Oh shit, it's you,' he said despairingly. Until that moment Daniel had prayed it wasn't Dianne he was running to help. Now in Daniel's stunned mind the worst had happened. Everything had gone wrong, he had let Dianne down, and she'd been brutally attacked. How could he ever say sorry enough? Why should she ever forgive him?

For Dianne, Daniel was the most welcome sight she would ever see in her entire life. That it was Daniel only added to the pure, intense knowledge she was going to live.

Nineteen

Daniel arrived at a late breakfast to ironic cheers from most of D-Delta's crew. All of them were present except Branner, who was checking the Battle Orders listings. Other men in the mess looked on curiously at the jeering and guessed what it was about—it wasn't hard with the evidence on Daniel's face. He waved them to silence and sat down with his plate of toast, baked beans and a mug of tea. This morning it was normal fare, not the ritual bacon and eggs they got before or after an operation.

Predictably, it was Flanders who got in first.

'How are you going to shoot down Jerries with only one eye?'

'It works all right. Just a bit black around the edges.' Daniel concentrated on scooping beans onto his toast and stopped himself touching his bruised cheek and eye.

'A bit black? He got you a beauty. What did you do, sit up like a bleeding rabbit and say "hit me hard, please?"'

'I didn't see it coming. It was more of a wrestling match.'

Sexton said, 'I wonder if they've got him yet?'

Cook told him, 'I heard the coppers were out scouring the land with tracker dogs. Fancy being chased down by a pack of hounds, hey?'

'Some people deserve it,' Wills said into his mug of tea.

'Yes, but do you know what pisses me off?' Sexton asked without waiting for an answer. 'That farm girl mistook his accent for a bloody Australian. How the hell do you get an Aussie accent and a South African one mixed up? He sounds German! We sound like… well, I don't know, but not German.'

'I think the amount of bad language might have had something to do with it,' Daniel said mildly.

'Ridiculous, we're no different from anyone else.'

Flanders now had Baxter in his sights. 'What happened to you, by the way? No one's told us what you and Danny were up to sneaking off like

325

that. Our hero here might not have arrived in the nick of time, thanks to you.'

'But he did, so what does it matter?' Baxter said, which amounted to almost a speech from him.

'Oh no, you don't. You'll have to do better than that.'

Daniel pretended to confess, 'Listen, I knew Bax was chasing one of the village girls who's a bit off-limits. I caught up with him and managed to talk him out of it. That's all.'

'Oh? Which one?' Flanders was delighted.

'Not on your life. That's all you get to know.'

'Morgan, you sly old dog. You can tell us…'

Baxter looked at Flanders through a cloud of cigarette smoke and didn't reply.

Flanders gave a snort of disgust. 'I'll get it out of you sooner or later. No one can keep secrets from me too long.'

'How's Dianne, then?' Cook asked Daniel.

'She's fine, if a bit shaken up. No serious injuries. Surrounded by bloody MPs like it's Buckingham Palace.'

'What? They think old Monkey will try to finish the job?'

'Hardly. It gives them something decent to do at last, I suppose.'

Wills asked meaningfully, 'Do the MPs need more people to arrest and beat up? Maybe we can volunteer someone?'

No one answered this. Cook asked Daniel, 'Can we get her some flowers?'

Daniel shrugged. 'We can ask. If you really want to do something, get her some fags. She'd appreciate them more, I think—oh dear, here comes the skipper. He looks serious.'

Branner walked up briskly balancing a plate and mug of tea. 'Battle Orders are posted chaps and we're on them. For a trip this evening, so don't make any plans.' He sat down and started eating straight away.

Everybody groaned with Flanders adding, 'I thought the weather over Hunland was rubbish?'

'It is now. Not by tonight.' As he was about to bite into his toast Branner did a double-take at Daniel. 'Bloody hell, can you see out of that thing? We'd better take you off the roster.'

'No, it's fine, skipper,' Daniel insisted quickly, louder than he meant. 'It looks a lot worse than it is.'

'What if a Jerry fighter comes in on your blind side?'

'I haven't got a blind side, honest, skipper. I'd tell you, if I did. I wouldn't put the rest of you blokes at risk.'

Branner regarded him thoughtfully and nodded. 'All right, if you're sure.'

***

Later that afternoon it was Flanders, not Daniel, who begged off flying the mission. As the crews approached the briefing hut, Flanders tugged on Branner's sleeve.

His face screwed up, he said, 'Skipper, I hate to say this. I'm having a bit of trouble staying out of the blasted crapper. My guts are aching like a bastard too. I can handle that. It's just having to drop my strides every five minutes.'

'Damn it,' Branner pulled to a halt and watched the others pass as he thought. 'Is there nothing you can take? Have you seen the doctor?'

'The nurse gave me some awful stuff and I've been drinking it like water all day. It doesn't seem to be working.' Flanders hoped from one leg to the other and grimaced. 'Not far off another episode to tell you the truth, skipper.'

'Christ, I don't want to miss a mission just because of one sick crewman.'

'Do you have any idea where we're going? Is it a quick trip?' Flanders looked hopeful.

'Not a clue. Could be Berlin for all I know.'

'Skipper, I'm not pulling your leg. I'd go if it was a shortish flight. But to Berlin and back…' Flanders turned pale at the thought.

Branner came to a decision. 'Okay, I'll chat to Eagleton right now and see if we can pull a replacement out of the pool or the reserve crew. You're absolutely sure? You realise what it means?'

'Well, obviously I can't do the op', that's all.'

'When we all finish our tour of thirty, you'll still have one to go. They'll probably stick you in the pool and make you wait until someone needs a fill-in, like us now.'

Flanders hadn't thought of this. He hesitated and said uncertainly, 'Maybe I can sneak in a run with someone else in the meantime. Make up the difference.'

Branner's mind had turned to the problem of replacing Flanders in time to do the mission. 'Don't worry about it now. Piss off before someone decides to look up your arse for evidence. Get a chit from that nurse to say you're too crook to fly.'

'Thanks, skipper. Tell the chaps what's happened and wish them luck, won't you?'

Waving, Flanders trotted off in the direction of the hangers where he hoped the nearest vacant toilet should be.

Sexton had been chatting to a friend from another aircraft and wandered back to Branner as Flanders left.

'Where's he going in such a hurry, skipper? Did the idiot forget something?'

'No, he's got a bad case of the runs, he says.'

'What's the greedy sod been scoffing that we haven't?'

'I didn't think to ask. It must be some stomach bug.' Branner let his annoyance show. 'I've just given him the night off. We have to find ourselves another navigator quick-smart or we'll all be scrubbed and they'll send the reserve plane.'

'Perhaps we should see where we're going first?' Sexton joked weakly.

'I'd rather get the op' on the board against our name.'

'I bet it'll be bloody Essen again,' Sexton muttered.

That night, D-Delta went to Nuremburg to an aircraft engine manufacturing plant. It was a hot target with plenty of flak, but they came back undamaged. Flanders' place was filled by a Canadian called Sweetman who did his job with such quiet efficiency that Branner had thoughts of trading the Canadian permanently. Sweetman didn't seem to doubt Branner's authority for a moment.

Two days later, D-Delta was being sent on a gardening trip to the Friesian Islands again. Flanders was fully fit by then and was sitting next to Branner in the briefing when their destination was revealed. As the sigh of relief went through the room at this relatively soft target, Flanders made a small, satisfied noise, as if he'd guessed correctly.

Branner asked him quietly, 'Have you got a crystal ball under your pillow or something? It sounds like you knew already.'

'I was just feeling lucky this morning, skipper. In the scheme of things, that's lucky.' He nodded at the map.

'Well, you certainly know which op's to miss and which ones to fly.'

Flanders took some teasing from the rest of the crew during the mission about his absence from the hazardous mission to Nuremburg and timely return for a gardening operation to the islands. He accepted it all good-naturedly and didn't put up much of a fight.

Listening in, Daniel figured that it was because Flanders was feeling guilty over dropping out of a raid, despite the perfectly good reason. If you were genuinely sick, of course you didn't go—nobody would. Daniel guessed, as Branner had told them, that Flanders would probably try and sneak into another crew for an operation and get his mission tally back on par with the others.

A week later after another two missions, both to French coastal targets, Flanders again had to drop out of a raid that proved to be nightmarish for those who went. It was an attack on the railway marshalling yards at Brunswick less than one hundred and sixty kilometres short of Berlin.

This time the circumstances were more serious for Flanders.

The crew of D-Delta were gathered together near the briefing rooms about to split up with Branner, Cook and Baxter, who expected to attend one meeting, while the gunners and Sexton went to a separate room to be shown the latest intelligence on night fighters in the area.

Flanders was missing and Branner was getting very irritated at the delay, watching the other crews filing into the briefings.

'Where the hell is he?' he asked for the fourth time.

Sexton said the same thing he'd already told him before. 'He ducked back into the mess for a second, that's all. I thought he was right behind us.'

'Want me to go and look, skipper?' Daniel offered half-heartedly.

'No, we'll only end up waiting for you instead—'

'Flying Officer Branner?' someone called. 'Which of you chaps is Branner?' A mess sergeant was moving towards the Briefing Hut as he asked aloud. Branner got his attention with a gesture that brought him over.

The sergeant saluted casually and said with a rush, 'I'm afraid your navigator's had a bit of an accident, sir.'

'For God's sake,' Branner growled. 'Will he be much longer?'

'They've carted him off to sickbay. I can't see him making your op', sir.'

Branner needed a moment to understand. 'Oh? I didn't realise... is it bad? What's he done?'

'He was grabbing a last cup of tea and poured boiling water all over his arm and hand. Nasty scalding, but it's not too serious, sir. He'll live.'

Branner's frown returned. 'Not when I get hold of him. The useless bastard.' While the rest of D-Delta's crew groaned at the news, Branner dismissed the sergeant and went in search of Eagleton, rueing that he had to make excuses and cause trouble for the Squadron Leader for a second time.

'Can we get hold of that fellow Sweetman again, sir?' he asked, hoping to make things easier.

'Sweetman?' Eagleton frowned and remembered. 'No, I'm afraid not. He didn't come back from Essen last night in F-Freddy with the 470 lads. They lost four aircraft all up. Not a good result at the end of the day. Listen, would you rather I pull your Lanc' off the raid altogether?'

Again, if Branner took the offer, they might miss out on an easy trip that comfortably added to the crew's mission score—or they may avoid the kind of operation that destroyed four bombers and killed good men like Sweetman.

'The job's still got to be done, sir. I'd rather we go if you can find us a navigator in time.'

'All right, that's the spirit, Alec. I'll get someone on to it straight away.'

On this occasion, Flanders' stand-in was a youth called Coward who found himself dragged into his first operation. He had been dropped out of his original assignment after contracting bronchitis and his replacement kept his place. It was no way to begin a navigator's career in Bomber Command with an unfamiliar crew already unsettled by Flanders' abrupt withdrawal and the report of Sweetman being missing. It was going to be a dangerous flight too—something the rest of D-Delta's crew didn't hesitate to grumble about to relieve their own tension.

Any thoughts of making jokes about Coward's unfortunate surname were quickly forgotten as the newcomer's nervousness grated on everyone the whole trip, an anxiety that somehow bled through the intercom even when the navigator wasn't speaking. It was hard for Branner not to snap at him to calm down. He told himself they must all have sounded just like him on their first raid.

They returned safely and were surprised to find Flanders waiting for them at the debriefing, even though it was very late. He looked sheepish and showed them his bandaged arm apologetically. The extent of his burns weren't much at all and Flanders should have been well worth some mockery. The returning crew were too exhausted from an event-filled mission to bother. Flanders was left flat by their lack of attention.

***

The following evening, D-Delta wasn't flying and Daniel grabbed the chance to slip away with Dianne in the Morris without telling anyone. They drove to the same hotel where they'd stayed on the night of finding the downed German bomber. The landlord recognised them—or Dianne, at least—and made them feel very welcome. After dinner, sitting relaxed in a corner of the bar, Dianne surprised Daniel when he mentioned Flanders' luck at having to miss the more dangerous missions.

'Well, it's not hard to do, if want to,' she said easily, lighting a cigarette. She seemed fully recovered from the ordeal of Munk's attack.

'What do you mean, "if you want to"?' Daniel asked curiously, holding his hand out for the smokes. 'We don't have a clue where we're going. In fact, you girls know before we do. Even the skipper isn't told anything until the cover comes off the target maps.'

'That's right, I probably do know before you, as do a lot of other people. The armorers, for instance. They might be loading mines onto the bombing trains when you're still tucked into your bunk with your teddy bear. So it's got to be a gardening trip, right? And the refuelers? They only pump in what you need, not much more. If it's just a few gallons, then you're headed for northern France or somewhere on the Belgium coast. It doesn't take a genius to work these things out. Get chummy with a few Erks and you'll know a lot well before any proper briefings, or you can have a good guess anyway.' Dianne gave a small shrug at Daniel's ignorance and added, 'It's not encouraged, of course, but quite common.'

It made sense too easily, disturbing Daniel. He didn't answer and scowled at his pint.

Dianne asked, alarmed, 'Good God, you're not thinking Bruce is deliberately pulling out of the rough missions? No one asks about for that kind of reason. It's more just to... I don't know. Have a bit of warning, I suppose.'

'No, of course not. But as you say, it wouldn't be hard. He told me once how scared he was when we're flying. It was after Geoff was killed and Flanno had spent some time in the nose over the target, seeing all the flak. It shook him up pretty badly, although I didn't notice that at the time.' Daniel sounded guilty.

There was a silence between them, then Dianne said, 'I think you're making a big thing out of nothing. Would somebody tip boiling water on themselves to miss a raid? I doubt it.' She shuddered.

'That's a point,' Daniel agreed with relief. 'I can't imagine it either.'

'I'd say Bruce is well annoyed he's fallen behind you fellows to the tune of two missions now. He'll want to catch up, you'll see.'

'Yes, I'm sure you're right.' Daniel changed the mood with a bright smile. 'Come on, drink up. I've finished mine. I reckon you should take a turn to go to the bar. That landlord's besotted with you. He might give them to you for nothing.'

Dianne smiled sweetly. 'You know, he might throw in a separate bedroom for free if I ask nicely. I could do with a good night's sleep.'

Daniel got to his feet immediately and reached for her empty glass.

***

Their next mission was a daylight raid put together at short notice and the first that the crew of D-Delta knew of it was an unwelcome shake out of their bunks in the predawn dark. They all stumbled from their respective barracks to the mess and met at a table for breakfast. They had half an hour before being due at briefings then at the equipment sheds to draw their parachutes and other gear.

No one was feeling very enthusiastic, thanks to the usual forays to the pub or the sergeant's mess the previous night. The nervous boiling in their stomachs added to the unease of the hangovers.

'Has anybody got any idea where we're going?' Flanders asked glumly. He had declared himself fit for active duty although his bandages were still on. It was wrapped in such a way that his fingers were free. He still struggled that morning with his knife and fork.

Daniel listened carefully.

'How the hell would we know?' Wills grumbled back. He took any opportunity to be morose at the moment since his private chat with Susan.

'You can guess, you know. Maybe someone's heard a bit of gossip,' Flanders said.

'I hope you use a bit more science than that when you're navigating.'

'Well, well, somebody got out of the wrong side of their bunk this morning—again.'

Sexton said sincerely, 'You know, I can't decide which I like better, daylight raids or night time jobs. Like, it's not good they can see us and everything, but there's a certain comfort in being able to see them at the same time.'

'Hey, perhaps we'll get fighter support?' Daniel said hopefully.

It brought a chorus of ribald laughs with Flanders adding, 'Our fighter chappies don't get out of bed before dinner time anymore. They don't like to get their silk scarves damp in the dew.'

Branner subdued them saying, 'It must be something important to be put on in a rush like this, so I wouldn't be hoping for any easy trip.'

'Augsburg again?' Sexton asked.

'God, I hope not. Surely even the RAF top brass can't be that silly?' Branner didn't sound convincing. 'What's the point in worrying? We'll find out soon enough.'

Forty-five minutes later they knew. It was a raid on some new submarine pens at Brest in southern France. Despite being unfinished, the Germans were already using the facilities to arm and provision U-boats that were attacking the Atlantic convoys. Some reconnaissance photographs the evening before had revealed a chance to damage the construction works and maybe destroy several submarines in port as well.

The usual anti-aircraft batteries surrounded the target, but flying across France in broad daylight was also going to tempt fate in the shape of Luftwaffe fighter squadrons. Support would come from Spitfire and Hurricane squadrons based in Portsmouth and Plymouth, but they could only go part of the way and pick the bombers back up on the return journey. It was small comfort that since D-Day the Germans had a much-reduced fighter force in France, or more to the point, didn't have the aviation fuel to fly them.

***

As always, at the dispersal the crew shared last cigarettes before boarding D-Delta. Bright morning sunshine was burning away a frost on the grass and warmed them unduly through their thick jackets. Daniel noticed that since the briefing Flanders had gone unusually quiet. Now the navigator looked almost furtive, fidgeting with his flying gear and glancing at the others as if he were too conscious somebody was watching him.

'All right, let's go,' Branner announced, tossing aside his butt and leading the way towards the ladder.

Everyone followed in silence, lost in their own thoughts about the hazards of this raid. Daniel saw Flanders lingering behind and stayed with him.

'Are you all right, Flanno?'

Flanders' eyes were darting left and right as he replied. 'Feeling a bit dodgy this morning, Danny, to be honest. Not a hundred percent, that's for sure. I hope I'm doing the right thing by keeping myself on the roster.'

'It's just nerves, Flanno. Butterflies in the guts. We've all got 'em. I feel like I'm going to throw up half the time.'

'Really? Well, I don't know about that. This might be something worse, I reckon. I don't know what it is… I'm not sure.' Flanders hadn't moved off the grass onto the dispersal, the final steps toward getting aboard the Lancaster. He rubbed at his stomach and fingered the bandages underneath his tunic sleeve as if he were searching for the source of his illness.

Or, Daniel thought treacherously, deciding which might make a better excuse to pull out of the crew again.

'Flanno, you'll be okay once we get going. You know how it is by now. Waiting around is the worst. Keep yourself busy and the op's over before you know it.'

Flanders glared at him. 'I really think I'm ill for God's sake. I'm not a damned coward, you know. Is that what you're thinking?'

Daniel didn't want to back down and said harshly, 'No, but somebody else might. If you think you're too crook to do this raid as well and pull out, people will start to ask questions. You'll start to look a bit flaky, Bruce. Is that what you want?'

Flanders' face collapsed for a moment before he collected himself. He said in a hoarse, despairing tone, 'You blokes tick off these missions like they bring you one step closer to finishing the tour and that's all. I envy you. I see them as one less before we go out on the one that kills us. God knows, I was all right until I saw the shit we fly through above the targets. Who the hell is going to survive thirty op's? I don't think we have a fucking chance of doing a whole tour,' he ended in a whisper.

'Well, I think we do,' Daniel said firmly. 'I have a really strong feeling I'm going to see this thing through, and we're all in the same plane, right? If I'm going to make it, we'll all make it. That's the way I see things.'

'It didn't do much for poor bloody Barra, did it?'

'Okay, that was just damned bad luck. One piece of stray shrapnel hits the Lanc' and Geoff cops it too. Maybe then we've had our share of bad luck?'

Flanders laughed without any humour. 'Shit, I wish I had your outlook on life. How can you be so naïve?'

They were interrupted by Branner yelling at them from the hatchway.

'Come on, what the hell are you two doing?'

'Coming right now, skipper,' Daniel called back. He stared at Flanders.

'Oh, fuck it—of course I'm coming,' Flanders said, grinding out a cigarette savagely with his boot.

Once they had taken off and settled into a holding pattern, awaiting the rest of the squadron, Branner took the chance to ask what had happened.

'What were you two doing back at the dispersal?' he demanded over the intercom. 'I told you to get aboard, not sneak another quick fag.'

Daniel answered hurriedly before Flanders could. 'Just a quick check of Flanno's bandages, skipper. While we could. One of them was coming loose.'

There was a silence, then Branner replied grudgingly, 'All right, but you could have told somebody. I was getting livid in here wondering what was bloody going on.'

'Sorry, skipper. It was a last-second thing.'

***

It was a large group of bombers and a daunting prospect for any German fighters even after the Spitfires had dropped back. A few Messerschmitt 109s snapped at the edges of the formation before diving away from the massed turrets they would encounter above the Lancasters. Most likely, they were low on fuel too. The bombing campaign was having an effect.

D-Delta enjoyed a trouble-free trip near the centre of their squadron's pattern. Wills complained several times he was being robbed of his chance to shoot down a German, until Branner told him to shut up in no uncertain terms.

As they neared Brest, the flak began in earnest. Hundreds of dirty, black explosions appeared among the bombers. A half-dozen came frighteningly close to D-Delta, slapping at the fuselage, and each time Branner told everyone to report in that they were all right. A minute out from the bomb run another flak shell rattled the Lancaster from the port side. This time Flanders didn't respond to Branner's call-up.

Branner didn't wait a second longer. 'Danny? Check on Bruce and get back to your guns quick-smart.'

Daniel was the logical choice. This was a rare formation attack and Baxter was needed at his radios to confirm the command to drop bombs, called from the lead aircraft, even though Branner would hear the order in his own headphones too. Cook was at his bomb-aimer's position, ready with the release, while Sexton was best kept at his engineer's station during such a critical time in their flying. With so much flak bursting around them, it was unlikely a German fighter would attack. It was a reasonable risk for Daniel to leave his guns for a short moment.

Daniel was glad to be given the task because he had a suspicion what he might find—and he was right.

Bracing himself again the swaying of the aircraft, his legs both numb and stinging from the turret's canvas sling and the now-returning blood circulation, he moved forwards and pushed past the blanket that covered the entrance to the tiny navigator's cubicle. In daylight, Flanders didn't need it, but had left it in place anyway.

Flanders was sitting absolutely still at his desk, a pencil poised frozen above a map. His eyes stared straight ahead at nothing. What struck Daniel the most was his deathly pale face.

Without his mask Daniel shouted against the noise. 'Flanno? Flanno! Are you all right? Have you been hit? You're not answering the skipper's calls.'

Slowly Flanders registered Daniel's presence and turned his head towards him. His expression was one of incomprehension.

'For Christ's sake, Bruce! Pull yourself together. Are you okay?' Daniel couldn't see any blood. That didn't rule out a wound on Flanders' hidden side, against the fuselage.

Finally, Flanders nodded and held up a shaking hand. Then he pressed his intercom switch and Daniel saw him mouthing a reply to Branner. This done, he gestured again at Daniel that he was unhurt and waved him out of the cubicle. Daniel hesitated, but there was nothing else he could do. He went back to his gun.

As he strapped himself back in, he heard the remains of a conversation between Branner and Flanders. The navigator was saying the close flak burst had jarred his intercom connection loose.

Branner was simply relieved he hadn't lost another crew member.

Two Lancasters were shot down by flak over the target as the bombs were released, then the aircraft turned together for the return trip. Not long after leaving Brest, Hurricanes arrived to escort them home. By then it felt a comparatively safe flight and there would be no more losses. The mood was confident for the rest of the trip back. Things had turned out much better than everyone had feared.

At the dispersal after they landed, D-Delta's crew were loud and boisterous with relief. Even Wills smiled around at everyone, although it faltered in Cook's direction.

Flanders was his normal self, making jokes at everyone's expense and rugby-tackling Baxter as they reached the grass. Only Daniel saw something different—that Flanders was avoiding his eyes. It wasn't worth the trouble it might cause mentioning it or asking why Flanders wouldn't look at him, since he already knew the answer.

Twenty

It was a fine, clear day and Daniel had invited Dianne, Susan and Cook on a drive out into the countryside. With the boot filled by a blanket and a makeshift hamper of sandwiches, fruit and a bottle of wine, they set off to find a hill. The girls had declared they wanted a view, not an easy thing to do in the flat expanse of Lincolnshire that was ideal for long runways and airfields.

So they travelled some distance and finally happened on a shallow valley surrounded by an escarpment that hardly qualified for the description, but it enough to let everyone lay on the grass and look out at the country below. They had to vault a rickety fence and brave the curiosity of some sheep, and Dianne and Susan were satisfied.

After lunch and most of the wine, Susan and Cook went for a walk, disappearing over the skyline with several of the sheep in pursuit. Dianne stretched out luxuriously on the extra blanket space and closed her eyes, gratefully feeling the sun's heat on her face. She heard Daniel light a cigarette and exhale a long plume of smoke. He sounded contented, but it was always hard to tell. Dianne had learned he was good at concealing his problems, although they talked about everything.

'How many trips have you done now?' she asked lazily.

'Nine.'

'Is that all?' It soured her mood a little and Dianne wished she hadn't asked. If she had guessed, her number would have been much higher. It just felt that way. She decided to persevere with a positive outlook. 'Still, that's almost a third of the way there.'

'Yes, not too many more before we're on the downhill stretch.' He gave her a small shove as if to send Dianne rolling down the hill.

'Don't or I'll make you carry me all the way back up again. What are you going to do when you've finished your tour?'

Daniel took a while to reply. 'What do the other chaps do?'

It was Dianne's turn to pause. 'I've never met anyone who's completed a tour—plenty do, of course,' she added hastily, if not completely sincere. 'I know there's several fellows not far off. I suppose it must be nerve-wracking, getting so close.'

'I don't think they promote you or anything—nothing much, anyway. I'll still be a sergeant and an air gunner, good for only one thing really.' He said this lightly. Dianne opened her eyes and turned her head to look at him.

'You'd sign up for a second tour?'

'I honestly don't know what I'll do. Perhaps we'll have won the war by then?' He smiled gently.

'By when? At the rate you're going, you'll finish your thirty trips in another two or three months at the most. I don't think even Monty would say we'll be reaching Berlin in that time. A second tour wouldn't take much more.' Dianne frowned at the realities. 'This war is just going to last too long.'

'It's hardly worth worrying about. Things never turn out the way we expect. Let's just see what comes along? I still believe I'm going to make it through in one piece. It's just a feeling I get, that's all.'

She sighed and reached up, asking for a drag on his smoke. Daniel obliged and plucked it back out of her fingers. When she handed it back, Dianne said, 'Do you think you'll all do a second tour?'

'Yes, I'd say we'll stick together.'

'Including Bruce?' Daniel had quietly told Dianne what happened.

He replied reluctantly, 'No, maybe not Flanno. He still doesn't seem to be coping very well at all.'

'I wouldn't be surprised if he doesn't make it through the next week.'

'Why on earth do you say that?'

'I've heard stories. They say that once the… the fear gets under your skin, it takes hold fast. Like a bad fever.'

'We're all scared. I don't mind admitting it.'

'Which means you can deal with it. It sounds like Flanno can't.'

Daniel suspected Dianne was right. During the last few days, even though they hadn't flown anything except training missions, Flanders had the look of a man on the brink of unravelling. On the ground inside the station he was waiting for the next, posted Battle Orders for D-Delta like someone expecting their own death penalty. It was a stark contrast to the jovial, skylarking Flanders who stalked the pub in search of a girl or free drink. Beyond the airfield gates, he was fine. On duty, and especially inside the Lancaster, the demons of imagination preyed too much on his mind. No one else had commented and perhaps Daniel saw too much in things, knowing what he thought he knew—that Flanders had deliberately avoided two missions.

Daniel asked Dianne, 'What happens if he goes to pieces and says he won't fly? Do you know?'

'He's declared LMF—Lack of Moral Fibre, and they quietly take him away, never to be seen again.'

'Bloody hell, to prison?'

'Not quite. They're demoted to the lowest rank and sent to be gardeners or kitchen hands at the POW camps. Something like that. They can't get a discharge and they're never promoted, stuck in the most menial jobs until the end of the war.' Dianne made it sound like a life sentence.

'And probably made to feel guilty as hell.'

'I don't think they'd need much help in doing that.'

Thudding footsteps and laughter announced Cook and Susan returning.

Cook called, 'Hey Danny? There's a farmhouse just over the way. I thought about popping across and asking if they might sell us another bottle of booze. Lazy-bones here doesn't want to climb the hill again. Want to come along?'

'Why don't you?' Dianne said to Daniel quietly. 'It'll give us girls a chance to talk.'

'Gossip, you mean.'

'Talk.'

'As if you need any more time to chatter. All right, but we'll be talking about you too.' Daniel got heavily to his feet.

'Say what you like, I don't mind.' Dianne poked her tongue at him.

Susan squeezed onto the blanket. As soon as the two men had gone beyond hearing, Dianne went cheerfully on the offensive.

'For someone who told me it was a bad idea, you're getting very friendly with Cookie.'

'Oh, I can't believe it myself. He's too short and much too old—and Australian. What will my mother think?'

'How old is he?'

'Ancient! Twenty-seven, I think. Five years older than me. That's almost cradle-snatching.'

'Dreadful,' Dianne murmured. 'What about your Scottish friend? Michael?'

'Didn't I tell you? I got a letter from him last week. He's joined some elite brigade that goes around with boot polish on their faces and a bayonet between their teeth, hunting Hitler or something. All a bit perilous, if you ask me. He sounded quite chirpy about the whole thing and sort of hinted it might be hard for us to see each other again for a while.'

'So Cookie goes to the top of ladder by default?'

'Don't be like that, Dianne. He's a lovely bloke.'

'Yes, he is—unless you ask Charlie.'

'Bloody Charlie! If I'd known he was going to take it so bad, I wouldn't have said anything. I was better off with him following me around buying lots of drinks. Anyway, what did you and Daniel talk about while we were gone? You were both looking very serious when we got back.'

Dianne pulled a face. 'Daniel's convinced he'll do two tours and survive without so much as a scratch.'

'That's something else that makes Cookie attractive, apart from his movie star looks. The fact he's in D-Delta with indestructible Daniel,'

Susan said, nudging Dianne to make her smile. 'If Danny's so sure, Cookie will get through too. As long as they're always in the same plane.'

'I believe Danny had a chat with Flanno along those lines,' Dianne said wryly. 'Have we forgotten so quickly?'

They exchanged a long look that for a heart-breaking moment revealed the truth behind their false bravado.

Susan said sadly, 'We've gotten use to forgetting them quickly. What else do we do, when the worst happens?'

Dianne asked, softly too, 'Are we just a pair of stupidly optimistic fools? What hope do we really have?'

A tear came into Susan's eye and she instantly dashed it away and smiled determinedly. 'Hardly any at all. Don't let the lads catch on what we know.'

***

They got back to Waddington late in the afternoon and made the effort to go to the pub. It was a good night, despite Wills' continuing surliness anywhere near Cook. Finally, Daniel walked Dianne as close to her barracks as he dared—which was closer these days—kissed her good night and made his way unsteadily towards his own Nissan Hut. He was surprised by Flanders coming out of the shadows as he approached the door.

'Flanno, what are you doing? Wouldn't you have more luck lurking around the WAAF's quarters?' Daniel regretted the poor-taste joke. Flanders didn't notice it anyway.

'Have you heard, Danny?'

'Heard what?'

'There's going to be a huge raid on tomorrow night. The armorers are piling incendiaries and cookies up to the sky and there's three extra fuel tankers called in. Big loads for the entire squadron. That means somewhere deep inside Germany.'

Daniel tried to push aside the dulling alcohol and think clearly. 'So you have been checking around? Did you know those two raids you missed were going to be risky?'

Flanders was a dark shape in the night. 'I—I got some word from a friend.'

'Jesus, tell me you didn't pour boiling water on yourself.'

'I didn't mean to—it was like pulling a damned tooth. I did it without thinking. It hurt like hell and I regretted it, but for a moment it was a good idea and I just…' Flanders fell silent and then with a quivering breath said, 'Fuck Danny, I don't think I can go. I don't know whether I'll be able to get inside the plane.'

Daniel was sober by now and deeply disturbed. He felt out of his depth. 'Then you have to talk with the skipper. Perhaps we should find him now.'

'God, no. That's about the one thing that keeps me going. The thought of the way everyone will look at me, when they know. I couldn't stand it. Especially the skipper.'

Frustrated, Daniel said, 'Then what the hell do you expect me to do?'

'If I'm not here tomorrow, don't let them run around searching for me. Tell them I've gone. I don't want to cause any more trouble than I have to.'

'That's ridiculous. You'd better make up your mind sooner than that. If you're going to let people down, give us some time to do something decent about it.'

'I don't want to let anyone down. I want to be there and do my job. I'm just hedging my bets, Danny. If I'm not there, you know what's happened.'

'For Christ's sake, we're all fucking scared, Bruce. Why the hell should you get to run away and hide?'

'My sentiments exactly. So I'll see you tomorrow, I hope.'

Before Daniel knew it, Flanders had melted into the darkness.

He felt angry and confused. Should he find someone and report this conversation to them? It was impossible to think straight and Daniel's mood got worse as he tried.

'Damn you, you'd better be here,' he said eventually, kicking at the ground. He felt sorry for Flanders, but this was no way to deal with these things. It might get everyone else into trouble they didn't deserve.

***

The next morning Daniel was shaken awake by a nervous-looking recruit. It was early, but a grey daylight was creeping past the nearest blackout curtain.

'Sergeant Young? Your crew's on Battle Orders today, put in at the last minute. Flying Officer Branner sent me to give you fair warning.'

'Thank you,' Daniel groaned, rubbing at his eyes. 'What the hell is that, rain?'

'A steady drizzle, sergeant. Not enough to keep you on the ground, they're saying.'

'I thought summer was just around the bloody corner?'

'Yes, sergeant. It rains in summer in Blighty too. A lot, really. I—I have to keep going…'

'Yes, thank you.' Daniel groggily swung his feet onto the floor. It was an unwritten rule that people who were supposed to be roused from their bunks were deemed awake if they did this. The recruit would be blameless should Daniel fall back asleep afterwards.

Dressing and donning a great coat against the rain, which seemed ridiculous after the sunshine of the previous day, Daniel made his way to the mess. Everyone was there including a subdued Flanders. They all looked damp and unhappy, mostly from hangovers. Daniel was glad to see Flanders, more because it took away any need to confront Branner with what he knew, rather than any assurance that the navigator would fly. There was still plenty of time for Flanders to vanish.

For once, no one spoke about the upcoming mission. Usually they would guess loudly or make bets on where the target might be. This morning a shared, odd reluctance to talk about it kept them all to just idle chatter about nothing. Daniel understood it as he sat down, without knowing how. Only Branner mentioned the raid as he stood to leave.

'Briefings start at 1500 for a long trip tonight, that's all I can tell you,' he said. 'You blokes know the drill.' He walked away with a wave.

Cook murmured, 'Yes, a thoroughly boring day when I won't catch a wink of sleep.'

The rain persisted enough to keep them indoors. Daniel went to the sergeant's mess to write a letter to his family. It was easier on the tables there instead of balancing a pad on his knees lying on a bunk. When he had finished it, he was taken by a strange impulse to write something to Dianne too. It was hard to avoid the clichéd beginnings like, "If you're reading this, I haven't come back this time," or any of the other painful and inadequate opening lines that came to him, but he realised in his heart it was the kind of letter he needed and wanted to write. Despite his confidence about surviving the war—which he truly felt—today, Daniel wanted to tie up loose ends. Perhaps it was the mood at the breakfast table, or Flanders' conviction that they wouldn't finish their tour. Nothing was definite in his mind except the idea, All right, just in case.

He told Dianne how beautiful she was, and what she meant to him. It wasn't perfect prose and Daniel was tempted to tear the letter up several times in frustration. Finally he wrote that he loved her—and that made Daniel pause a long time, his pen poised over the page.

'Damn,' he told the overflowing ashtray in front of him. He hadn't actually said this to Dianne directly, to her face, and suddenly it was important.

There was no chance he could find her or the right moment to say anything about love if he did. The momentum of the day was building towards the evening's raid and that all began much earlier for Dianne. She would be hellishly busy, Daniel knew. Too busy even to be told he loved her.

Torn by indecision as to whether he should try and snatch a few minutes with Dianne, he finished the letter and carefully addressed it. Daniel took it back to his barracks and made sure it was plainly a part of his personal belongings. Someone would find it, if it became their job to sort such things out.

***

'The rain isn't your concern,' Eagleton announced loudly as he stepped onto the stage, silencing the gathered crews. 'The met' boys will tell you more, but basically it's not raining where you're going.'

'Brighton Beach?' someone called, getting a chorus of laughs.

'Tonight's target isn't on the ocean. This particular place is about as far from Brighton as you can get.'

The laughter turned to groans, which swelled again when Eagleton revealed the target map.

Outside the door, Daniel had lingered before heading off late for his own briefing to make sure Flanders entered with Branner and stayed there. He heard the dismay of the pilots with their navigators and wireless operators. It was all he needed to hear—the specifics of the target didn't really matter. He wondered how Flanders was dealing with knowing his worst fears had been confirmed.

At least Daniel felt certain Flanders was going to do the mission. Surely, if he intended to somehow stay back, he would have made his move by now? Pulling out of the raid after the briefings, whether he managed to convince Branner it was for a real reason or not, would result in the entire crew being scrubbed from the operation this time. What if the reserve aircraft was shot down? Daniel guessed that Flanders would never want that on his conscience.

The briefings took quite a while, and the day was greying to a wet night as they gathered at the dispersal. Daniel, Wills and Sexton had been there for half an hour already when a truck pulled up and the remaining crew tumbled over the tailgate. Flanders came last, giving Daniel a tense moment as he began to think he wouldn't get out, but the navigator seemed his normal self as he cursed a plume of exhaust smoke that enveloped him when the truck splashed away.

'Last fags, lads,' Branner called, leading them to huddle against the side of Granger's hut. It was poor shelter from the rain.

'So, where to, skipper?' Daniel asked, shaking out a match. For security reasons, the one thing the gunners hadn't been told at their briefing was the target. It was a bad sign.

'Essen, again.'

'Christ, what did we miss last time?'

'Nothing. I think the idea is to bomb the place out of existence. Don't give the Jerries time to rebuild.'

Wills said, 'Jesus, back to bloody Essen. I reckon we wouldn't want to bail out if we get hit. The locals will be well pissed off with us by now. They've been getting a hammering for weeks.'

Daniel nodded. 'That's probably why the intelligence chaps think there's an extra night fighter squadron they talked to us about. They're getting a bit sick of being clobbered.'

'Look, it's not our problem,' Branner said firmly, holding up his hands. 'Nobody is going to be bailing out. Not from D-Delta at least. We'll drop our pills down their bloody throats and be back in time for breakfast.'

'Maybe there'll be a birthday cake waiting for me?' Wills said.

'Birthday? Whose—yours?' Branner raised his eyebrows. Everyone looked surprised.

'Twenty-one and never been kissed,' Wills said with a wry smile.

'Bloody hell, Charlie! Why didn't you say? We could have gotten you something. It's a bit special, your twenty-first.'

'Buy me a pint tomorrow night, skipper.'

'We'll all buy you a pint.'

'I'll kiss you,' Sexton added.

'Thanks, Dave. Just my luck, when none of the bloody girls will.'

Daniel noticed that for a moment, Cook was in two minds whether to be sympathetic or annoyed. Sometimes Wills was taking this business about Susan too far.

Thoughtlessly, Branner said with a wink, 'Don't worry, Charlie. I'm sure both Dianne and Susan will oblige a birthday boy.'

'Let's stick with the pints, skipper. I don't want to be stealing Dianne away from Danny. We know he's not shy of a fight, and I don't want to blacken his other eye.'

They laughed and chided Wills about his nerve.

Branner became business-like. 'All right, chaps. Let's get on board and check everything. Sergeant Granger? Is the old girl ship-shape?'

'In tip-top condition, sir,' Granger appeared from the growing gloom. He looked thoroughly wet, hunching his shoulders.

'We'll bring her back exactly the same way.'

Branner moved towards the ladder, taking everyone with him. Daniel half-expected Flanders to balk again, so he was ready for it when Flanders drifted behind and stopped.

Branner sensed it as well and turned around.

'What's up, Flanno?'

Something in Branner's voice told Daniel that their skipper wasn't so unaware after all. There was a challenging edge to his tone, as if he had been prepared for this and wouldn't take any nonsense.

Absorbed in their own tasks, chatting among themselves, the rest of the crew kept moving toward the ladder. Only Daniel stayed back.

'Your bandages need checking again?' he asked, offering Flanders an excuse.

Flanders' expression abruptly changed as his face fell and he whispered, 'Fellows, I'm dreadfully sorry—I don't think I can go.'

'What?' Branner snapped, loud enough to stop the men climbing into D-Delta. He turned and told them coldly, 'Get to your stations, lads. We won't be a moment.'

Daniel said quickly, 'Damn it, skipper. Some of this is my fault. I knew this was coming and I should have said something—got Flanno to take some leave… we were talking the other night—'

Branner cut him off harshly, 'This isn't anything to do with you, Danny. No matter what's been said. What the hell are you saying, Bruce?'

Flanders looked a different man from the brash and confident one they knew. He wilted in front of Branner. 'The truth is I'm fucking terrified, skipper. Of where we're going and what's waiting for us. So bloody scared, I don't think I can do my job.'

'Are you mad? They'll have you shot.'

Risking Branner's anger, Daniel said, 'Skipper, that's not true. He'll just be... taken away. It wouldn't be the first time.'

Branner glared at him, but his next words were calmer. 'Bruce, do you realise what you're saying? Do you understand what will happen if you keep this up now?'

In the background, some of the nearer Lancasters were starting their engines, masking the conversation and saving Flanders from being overheard by the rest of D-Delta's crew.

He said pleading, 'Believe me, I don't want to do this, skipper. Only it's getting like I can't even think when that flak starts bursting around us. I freeze up and can't breathe.'

'For Christ's sake, we're all like that. What about you, Danny?'

Daniel was taken aback. He managed to say, 'Scared bloody shitless the whole trip, skipper. Every time.'

See, Bruce? You're no different from anyone. I need you to get in that plane and do your damned job like everybody else.'

Curious faces were framed in the Lancaster's door, defying Branner's order. It wouldn't be long before they guessed what was happening.

After a tense silence Flanders hung his head and said, 'Yes, of course you're right. Count me in, skipper. I suppose one more trip won't kill me.' He grunted a humourless laugh.

'It won't kill any of us,' Branner said relieved, but his manner still hard. 'Good man. Get a move on and climb aboard. I need a quick word with Danny here to sort out what we'll say to the others. Their ears are bloody burning. I'll tell you what—tomorrow I'll see about getting you a spot of leave. You just need a decent rest, most likely, that's all.'

'You're probably right, skipper. Things are getting on top of me, I reckon, Thanks.' Flanders nodded and trudged to the ladder.

When he was beyond earshot, Branner told Daniel brusquely, 'Don't say a word to anyone. First thing tomorrow I'll have a word with

Eagleton. Like you said, they'll shuffle Bruce off somewhere and we'll never see him again. There's no need to upset the lads with it tonight. We've got enough to worry about.'

'Whatever you say, skipper,' Daniel said tiredly. He wasn't surprised. There was nothing else Branner could do and clearly Flanders was close to breaking down.

Over the intercom as they taxied towards the runway, Sexton inadvertently provided an excuse for the delay back at the dispersal.

'Were you three cooking up a nice birthday surprise for Charlie, skipper? I'd be wetting my pants, if I were you, Charlie. Or maybe we'll all just put in and buy you a willing girl?'

'I'm not saying a word,' Branner replied with a hint of conspiracy. 'We'll be chatting about it later.'

'Steady on, chaps. Be nice. It's my birthday,' Wills complained. 'Come on, skipper. Look after your crew.'

'Don't worry. Nothing nasty for a twenty-first, I promise you… look sharp, lads. Here we go.'

The bombers were taking off in quick succession and Branner swung D-Delta onto the runway as they were given the green light to go. Ahead of them in the last of the twilight the aircraft ahead was kicking back a plume of mist from the wet tarmac. The plane lifted away into the darkness as Sexton pressed forward D-Delta's throttles and they roared forward. The bomber lumbered at first with the weight, then as the lift built under the wings D-Delta began the transformation into a thing of power and grace. The undercarriage left the ground in a single, smooth movement and the Lancaster swept upwards.

Branner asked five minutes later, 'Navigator, what's our course?' They had been steadily climbing and circling the station until they broke through the weather into clear sky. It was lighter at this altitude, the dusk renewed and the setting sun given them a wide strip of orange from below the clouds. Around them other Lancasters glinted in the last rays.

Flanders' reply was bright and confident. 'Course is southeast on one-three-five degrees, skipper. No mucking around tonight with any tricks, boys. We're taking the express route to Essen.'

Cook said dryly, 'The top brass probably think that even the Germans won't believe we're hitting Essen again. A real course is just as likely to fool them.'

'There's merit in that,' Branner said. 'All right, let's all keep our eyes peeled. There's a lot of chaps flying with us tonight. We don't want to bump into anyone.'

In his turret, Daniel was marvelling at Flanders' tone. It was as if the confrontation on the dispersal had never happened.

***

Night fell completely as D-Delta crossed the English Channel. The stream tightened together above Belgium and Branner's mood soured as he concentrated on his flying. No one could tell now if the cloud cover was still in place below. It wouldn't hide them from the Germans' radar or any night fighters in the air with them, but the bomber crews always felt safer and preferred to be out of sight from any angry eyes below. That is, until they reached their destination, where seeing the target was paramount to getting the job done quickly and sending them home without delay.

Above the Lancaster, a million stars were bright in a moonless sky. They kept dragging at Daniel's attention with their beauty and he wished Dianne could see them with him. Occasionally he spotted the silhouette of another aircraft sliding across the constellations. The sight made his heart skip a beat. With so many bombers in the air it wasn't unexpected, and Daniel was careful not to over-react. He needed to identify any enemy fighters and call a warning, but false alarms would get dangerously on everybody's nerves.

It was a three-hour journey to Essen. Sixty minutes out from the target an eruption of anti-aircraft sprayed into the night far away to starboard. Daniel reported it, although he knew Branner must have seen.

'I see it, Danny,' Branner replied. 'Looks like a diversionary raid of some kind, although no one told us about it.'

'Maybe somebody's wandered way off course and blundered over a flak battery,' Cook said, adding, 'Unless we're the jokers off the track and that's the Jerries having a go at the stream. Any chance of that, Flanno?'

Flanders answered immediately, 'I make us bang on course, Cookie. You just make sure you drop those bloody pills first time, so we can go home. I want a hot breakfast.'

Among the distant, bursting shells something flared briefly and curved towards the earth in a fiery comet. Wills said sombrely, 'Looks like somebody bought it over there, the poor bastards.'

Daniel tried, 'Perhaps it was a Hun night fighter? You never know, someone might have got in a lucky burst.'

No one answered him.

***

'Target ahead, skipper,' Cook called as bombers far in front attracted the first barrage from Essen's defences. More guns quickly joined in and within a minute the sky ahead of them was filling with streaks of tracer and bursting flak shells.

'I make us about ten minutes out still,' Branner told him. 'The place looks hot, chaps. Be prepared for a rough ride.'

D-Delta bore on through the night with only a gentle weaving by Branner to throw off any night fighters sneaking behind.

Baxter surprised them by saying, 'Just the once this time, all right, skipper? If that cookie hangs again, I'll throw the bloody thing out myself before you have a chance to go around.'

Sexton told them all, 'I checked that blasted thing a dozen times and so did Granger. If it gets stuck, you can chuck me out the bomb bay instead.'

'Speaking of which, you can open them now,' Branner ordered. The target zone was close and already brightly lit by hundreds of fires. The reflection was enough to see clearly inside the Lancaster and it also revealed other bombers close by. Branner grimaced at the thought that D-Delta, too, must be plainly in sight. It was a small miracle none of the searchlights had found them yet. 'How are you going, Cookie?'

'I'll take her now, skipper. Keep her on this line. We're looking good.'

As if prompted by Cook's taking over, flak shells started to explode close around D-Delta. A couple were near enough to punch the aircraft aside and slightly off course. Branner quickly brought the heading back before Cook asked for it. Something rattled against the fuselage and a weak voice on the intercom cursed strangely. Branner didn't ask—they were coming onto the release point. Nothing else mattered for the next minute or so.

'Come right a bit, skipper…' Cook said calmly. 'A bit more… half that again. Good, hold her steady there.'

In his bomb aimer's position, the glare lit Cook's face ghoulishly through the site's eyepiece. He forced himself not to flinch at the flak and stared resolutely downwards. It took all his will power to ignore another startled cry on the intercom.

Sexton had been staring at Branner, willing the bombs to be dropped so his skipper could turn them away from the anti-aircraft barrage. Beyond Branner and outside the cockpit, close enough to catch the pilot's eye too, a large cylindrical shape drifted down past the port side windows. Sexton believed he could have reached out and touched it, if he was fast enough.

'Fucking hell, what was that?' he jerked out, although he knew the answer.

'It was somebody else's cookie,' Branner said shakily. 'Have we got some bastard on top of us? Danny? Can you see anything?'

Branner fought every instinct to bank away. Their own bombs would be released at any moment. Where there was a 4000-pound cookie falling on them from above, a brace of eight incendiary bombs should be too.

Daniel was twisting frantically in his turret, swinging the gun about and pushing himself against the harness. 'I can't see a bloody thing, skipper. No one on top, at least. He must be well upstairs.'

Cook brought them back to the job at hand, announcing firmly as D-Delta lifted sharply, 'Bombs gone, skipper. Hold her for just a few seconds more.'

Now Branner struggled to compensate for the sudden weight loss, shoving D-Delta's nose back down. He told himself the threat from overhead was gone. All bombs, big or small, fell at the same rate and the incendiaries must have passed unseen. Still, a crawling feeling ran down his spine.

'The camera has gone off, skipper. Let's go home.'

Branner put D-Delta into a sharp turn to port. 'Right-ho, Cookie. You don't have to tell me twice. Get back up to your gun. The trip out doesn't look too healthy either.'

The German flak guns were getting plenty of opportunity to farewell the attackers with a storm of fire.

'Confirm our course, Bruce. We don't want to lose the stream tonight.' Branner was shouting against a succession of air bursts. When Flanders didn't reply, he snapped, 'Bruce, what's our course? Are you all right?'

'Course should be two-nine-zero, skipper,' Flanders answered in a drained tone. 'Sorry, I—I'm going bloody deaf back here.'

'We'll be out of this lot in a minute.' Branner didn't bother to weave the aircraft now. It was a case of flying beyond the reach of the gun batteries as quickly as they could.

There was a long minute of silence over the intercom as D-Delta fought through the shell bursts. Finally, nothing was exploding in front or around them. Only Wills and Daniel could still see the anti-aircraft barrage as it dropped behind them.

Wills said fiercely, 'Bloody good riddance too.'

In that instant D-Delta was shaken violently by a tremendous blast and the aircraft was sent plummeting downwards. The change was so abrupt nobody had time to do anything except yell out in fear at the numbing realisation they were being hit hard. The Lancaster didn't spin but had a terrifying swaying movement that alternatively pinned the crew in their places, then threw them in the opposite direction. It was all Daniel could do to hang onto the grips of his Brownings for support. A lancing pain stabbed under his ribs.

Now the intercom was filled with Branner and Sexton shouting at each other as they struggled to co-ordinate their efforts to bring the aircraft under control. The sickening plunge continued. Just as Daniel was going to take his chances and release himself from the turret, expecting to bail out, D-Delta skidded into a near-level flight. There was a list of several degrees to starboard and the plane felt like it was tearing through the air with all manner of things wrong. At least they were maintaining an altitude.

Branner called desperately, 'Everyone report in. Does anybody know what the hell happened?'

Only Cook, Sexton and Daniel confirmed they were all right. The intercom was scratchy with waves of interference. Daniel could feel a rush of swirling air. A slick dampness under his clothing told him he'd been hurt and was bleeding, but the pain was manageable. The plane, he worried, was in worse shape.

The fuselage had been punctured many times, he was sure. Looking downwards, he saw in the light from the burning target behind them a line of jagged holes along the floor. The entire length of the aircraft that he could see was shattered by gunfire.

'Skipper, it must have been a night fighter,' he called, his eyes flicking at the night sky around them. 'It looks like we got strafed from end to end.'

'Then we must have lost him as we fell, thank Christ,' Branner decided. 'Danny, I can't spare Dave and I want to keep Cookie close— did you hear that, Cookie? Stay at your gun in case I call for more help. The old girl's flying about as well as a crate of Guinness. Danny, you'll have to try and see how much trouble we're in and check on the other blokes.'

'Skipper, you want me to leave the gun?'

'There's no one else, Danny. Just be quick about it.'

Daniel released his harness and let himself carefully onto the floor of the Lancaster, keeping his helmet and intercom connected. Something burned in his side. He realised the pain was serious—he was definitely wounded—but nothing he couldn't deal with, and he had no choice anyway. They had bigger problems. He was facing to the rear and in that moment, Daniel discovered why he could see so clearly inside the fuselage.

The rear turret was gone. A gaping hole was all that remained of the entire mechanism and the man, Charlie Wills, who had sat inside it. The tail of D-Delta had been sheared off like a man clipping the tip of a cigar. In the distance behind them Essen's fires were framed in the ragged edges of the opening.

'Christ, skipper. You're not going to believe this—Charlie's gone.'

'He's dead? Are you sure?'

'No, I mean he's bloody gone! The whole fucking turret's been blown away.'

There was a silence and he heard Branner curse in stunned disbelief. 'All right... Jesus. Then find out what's going on with the others.'

In the cockpit, it made dreadful sense of the way D-Delta was flying. Without the weight of the tail turret and its gunner, the aircraft was decidedly nose-heavy. Branner had the control column almost pulled all the way back, fighting to climb against the Lancaster's desire to dive. Sexton was huddled on the floor beside him. It was the best way to get an extra grip on the controls and add his strength to the non-stop tug-of-war.

At his gun in the forward turret, Cook was battling to stay at his post. It seemed pointless when there must be more urgent things to do. He kept looking over his shoulder, but the bulk of D-Delta's internal equipment didn't let him see far.

Daniel had disconnected his intercom and was turning himself carefully, holding on to something at all times and feeling he might be sucked out the end of the fuselage although the air whipping through wasn't that strong. He dreaded what waited for him behind the flapping curtains of the wireless operator's position and then Flanders' navigator's desk.

He checked on Morgan Baxter first.

Baxter was dead, his lower body torn apart by a cannon shell. There was no doubt he had been killed instantly. All the radios and the aircraft wall were coated in his blood. In contrast, Baxter looked peacefully asleep in the dim light, his body slumped with his forehead resting on the shattered dials in front of him.

Feeling sick, Daniel pulled himself to the next opening.

Flanders was covered in blood too. He sat with his knees pulled up and hunched against his table. His pale face and blinking, frightened eyes told Daniel he was alive.

'Flanno, are you badly hurt?' Daniel asked, squeezing in close. Flanders didn't reply, although his gaze followed Daniel like he wasn't completely in shock. Daniel fumbled at Flanders' clothing without knowing if it was the right thing to do or how he might deal with whatever he found.

The navigator had several deep wounds on his left side that were bleeding profusely. Daniel guessed they must be shrapnel from the cannon shells that struck Baxter in the next compartment. It might be the same thing that had his own uniform soaking in blood.

'I'll be right back with some bandages,' he shouted into Flanders' face. Flanders gave him the smallest nod in reply.

Despite the urgency of stopping Flanders' bleeding, Daniel took some precious seconds to jam his intercom back in.

'Morgan's dead too, skipper. Flanno's badly hurt and I'm going to give him some first aid.'

Branner sounded exhausted. 'Do what you can, Danny. We can bail him out, if you think he's got a better chance on the ground.'

Daniel was shocked by having such a decision put in his hands. He imagined Flanders being found by German civilians. Why would they bother trying to save him?

'What's the point, skipper? Let's try to get him home.'

'See if you can get a parachute on him anyway and keep yours close. We might all be bloody jumping in a minute. Are you certain about Bax?'

'No doubt about it. He's... never mind, skipper. I'm sure.'

Daniel found the first aid kit and took it back to Flanders. He also found a torch, since the light from Essen had faded. The lamp had a weak battery and no matter where Daniel balanced it, the flashlight fell over a few seconds later. In the gloom, he ripped the first aid kit open and spilled most of the contents everywhere. Finally he located some bandages and thick pads and attempted to put pressure on Flanders' injuries. The amount of blood welling out of the ripped flesh was troubling and Daniel tried not to let his dismay show. He doubted Flanders would survive. Apart from the severity of his wounds, Flanders' silence had an ominous quality about it.

Next, he struggled to put Flanders' parachute on him. It was impossible to do this the normal way, so Daniel got the two leg straps in place and left the rest in readiness for someone to help. He tried not to think about what he should do if the aircraft suddenly began to fall again. How long should he risk himself, trying to help Flanders, before bailing out and leaving the wounded man to perish in the crash?

'Just keep us in the fucking air, skipper,' Daniel said to himself. 'That way I don't have to worry about it.'

He went back to Baxter's position and pulled the wireless operator's bloodied parachute from beside his body, returning with it to Flanders, where he used it for a pillow. Flanders' eyes rolled questioningly towards it, and Daniel yelled with a grim look, 'Bax doesn't need it anymore.'

He gave Flanders a sip of water from a bottle and left it cradled it in the navigator's arms. He told him, 'I'm going back to my gun. Don't worry, we'll come and get you if we have to bail.'

Again Flanders only nodded before closing his eyes. For a moment, Daniel feared he had died until he saw his chest lift laboriously.

Daniel discovered his turret was useless with no hydraulics again, like the last time they were hit. He reported in, 'I'm back in the mid-upper, skipper, for what it's worth. My hydraulics are buggered.'

Branner answered, 'What's the news on Bruce?'

'Not good, skipper. But I'm no medic. I've done all I can, and I'll check on him every few minutes. Are we going to make it back?'

'We've lost one motor. Three's more than enough to get us home. Flying forwards is not the problem. Going in the direction we want is the hardest part.'

'That sounds pretty good to me, skipper. If anyone can get us there, you can.'

Branner didn't reply. Daniel's faith touched him in a way that seemed a little ridiculous, given the trouble they were in. This was no place or occasion for such emotions. At the same time, Branner's determination to fly them back to England reaffirmed itself and gave his aching arms a fresh injection of stamina.

Daniel had gathered up some fallen bandages, but he didn't want to take off his clothing and risk losing his own body heat. Instead he stuffed them inside his shirt, wincing when he came close to the wound, hoping he might be somehow staunching the bleeding.

The next two hours were a grind of tension and a physically exhausting time for Branner, who couldn't release his grip from the controls for a moment without losing some height. Sexton took turns with Cook to help keep the pressure on the column, even devising a lever between Branner's legs to force against the bottom of the shaft. Then with the Channel only ninety minutes away a second motor sputtered to extinction. Luckily, Cook was helping Branner, and Sexton was able to make hasty adjustments on his engineering panel. It was a good time to call for help and Branner tried without expecting any result. He was right because all the radios were destroyed.

The real problem now was D-Delta very slowly losing height regardless of their efforts.

When the realisation sunk in, Sexton asked for everyone, 'So we're going to crash-land after all, skipper?'

'No, I still think we'll make it. We've got enough altitude to come close to Blighty, at least.' Branner hesitated. 'We'll be too low for any bailing out long before that. If anyone would rather jump, you'd better make up your mind soon.'

'You're not going to jump, skipper?'

'No, I'm trying to get Flanno back to one of our hospitals, and the plane back too.'

'Then I'm not going to bail either.'

'Nor me,' Daniel said. He was back in his turret. Flanders was unconscious and beyond any more help Daniel might try. Daniel's abdomen was numb and sticky, and for once the canvas sling seat was the most comfortable.

'Or me,' Cook echoed from his front gun.

Branner admitted with a wryness they heard over the headphones, 'Actually chaps, I'm no hero. I'd just would rather get home than be a fucking prisoner of war.'

'You've got my vote on that, skipper,' Cook said. 'All of us, I'd say.'

***

Closer to home, the weather had cleared and Daniel saw the incongruous sight of a late moon rising through the wreckage of the Lancaster's ruined tail. They had just crossed the coast and the sea below began to shimmer silver with the light. It reminded them it was uncomfortably close too.

By now, Branner's face was white with the prolonged exertion and his arm muscles trembled uncontrollably. Sexton was trying to keep him distracted from the pain by constant reports on the motors' conditions and anything else he could think up.

'Hell, skipper. I just realised that if we have to ditch, at least we got the practice right. Remember they made us treat Flanno as a casualty?'

'He volunteered to stay behind, if I recall,' Branner said, his voice husky and quivering.

'We won't take him up on that. We'd better chuck him in the dinghy with us or he'll swim ashore and give us hell for the rest of our lives.'

'I don't think the old girl will float long enough to bugger about with any dinghies. Not with the arse blown off her. Do you?'

'Ah, that's a point.'

'You'd better start worrying about the undercarriage instead.'

'Where are we going to land?'

'I haven't got a bloody clue. The first paddock, at a guess. In which case, we'll belly-land... again.'

It was no great feat of navigation that Branner had steered them back to the Channel and England. But without Flanders' pinpoint skills and his estimations about crosswinds or how much losing any engines affected their flying, they could be crossing the coast anywhere. Branner was hoping for Lincoln, but it was wishful thinking. At least they would have some idea of their landfall from the amount of time it took them to cross the sea—by how wide the Channel was at that point.

'Skipper I can see the coast. You've done bloody well,' Cook called from the nose turret.

Ahead of them, the ocean turned into a darker mass of land. There was no white beach, but that didn't tell them much. Branner again found some reserves of strength, seeing they would make it over the land.

Then D-Delta's run of bad luck changed for the better.

'Shit! Is that a flare path to the north? Can anyone else see it?' Cook was almost babbling with excitement. A line of lights had come on in the distance.

'I see it,' Branner said. 'Someone's turned on the welcome mat for somebody. Let's hope they leave the damned things on when they hear us coming.'

D-Delta crabbed through a shallow bank to starboard. It was the first serious course alteration since they had been hit and the aircraft felt like it might suddenly topple earthwards. They lost more height than Branner had bargained for. Still at Branner's feet and adding his weight to the controls, Sexton exchanged a look with the pilot.

'I know,' Branner said. 'We're not going to get a second chance at this. There'll be no coming around for another run.'

He kept the thin glow of the flare path in the middle of his windscreen and prayed D-Delta would make it all the way. Then the flare path vanished.

'Oh no, you bloody fools! Can't you hear us coming?' Branner snarled.

'Now what, skipper?' Cook asked anxiously.

Branner recovered and shook his head. He said, 'See that dent in the coastline? I put them at around ten degrees to starboard of that. That's where we're headed and hopefully the idiots will figure out what's happening.'

'Maybe they think we're a German bomber?'

'Do we sound like a German bloody bomber?'

'We've only got two engines running, skipper.'

'Damn it, then turn on our navigation lights, if they're still bloody working. Show 'em how big we are.'

Awkwardly Sexton reached up and flicked a switch.

'They're on, skipper,' Daniel said unhappily from his turret. It was inviting an easy attack from any German night fighters lurking nearby. He wasn't sure it was a good idea—and it was getting harder to think straight.

D-Delta kept falling through the dark, heading for an imaginary point on the ground that might turn into an airfield. A dark line of sand with breakers flashing white sped underneath.

'No need for the dinghy,' Cook reported.

'Get up here, Cookie,' Branner told him. 'There's no telling when we'll hit the dirt.'

'On the way, skipper.'

The moonlight showed them the ground rising to meet them. Banner was becoming mesmerised by the racing earth in front of him.

'Come on, come on,' he breathed, uncaring that anyone heard him.

The flare path abruptly came to life again, bright with its nearness. Branner let out a yell of triumph, then swore at how much they needed to swing left to come even close to the strip. He turned D-Delta and his stomach flipped at the way the aircraft wobbled and skated in the air, but he didn't back off and the flare path edged into the middle of his windscreen. They were going to land at an angle across the strip, not actually along it. That was better than nothing and Branner was satisfied not to risk more turns.

'Hang on, everyone. This is going to happen sooner than you think.'

Sexton asked worriedly, 'Skipper? You want the undercarriage down or not?'

'Too late for that, Dave. It won't do us any good anyway. When I say go, kill the throttles.'

'Ready when you are.' Sexton didn't mention he wasn't strapped in and he bit his lip at the thought of what the impact might do to him.

'Nearly… nearly there… now.'

Sexton raised himself to his knees and grabbed the throttle levers, hauling them backwards with all his strength.

D-Delta slammed to the ground short of the flares and careened through them, shattering several in a shower of sparks. Then the aircraft was sliding across grass and turning as she went. Branner could do nothing except watch the dark world spin by. He felt Sexton gripping his leg for support. The Lancaster rocked and bucked beneath them, the belly being torn apart as the plane hit rougher ground beside the airstrip. It brought them to a halt sooner with a final heart-stopping lurch that was like one last attempt to destroy itself, before everything became a black, deafening silence.

***

The four survivors stood back from the wreckage and watched ambulance men carry Flanders gently out. He was still alive, but in a bad way. No one wanted to guess if he would live. With an urgent jangle of bells, the ambulance pulled away.

The empty tail where Wills' turret had been seemed to accuse them, or taunt them. Nobody could put into words the strangeness of it. That Wills was gone without a cry for help, a final curse or even a single bloodstain. It felt somehow impossible and vaguely unfair.

Hunched over, Daniel asked softly, 'What happens now, skipper?'

Branner replied with an utter tiredness. 'A debriefing for us, then it's back to Waddington where I'd say they'll split us up.'

'You think so?' Sexton found the energy to sound outraged.

'We're hardly a full crew anymore just looking for a replacement. We'll be snatched out of the pool one by one, as we come back from leave. To replace others in the same boat.'

All of them were smoking. Branner could hardly lift his hand to his mouth, the tendons in his arms and shoulders locking with fatigue. For Daniel, everything was starting to spin and he realised how silly it'd had been to say nothing of his injury in the interest of getting Flanders seen first. A ground staff corporal came over from a truck and scrutinised the crew until he saw Branner's rank.

'Sir, they've told me to drive you back. Are you ready?'

Branner nodded at the plane. 'We'll wait a moment. There's still someone to come out.'

'Is there?' the corporal asked, puzzled. Then he understood. 'Oh, right.'

Respectfully he drew back a few steps and watched with them as they brought out Baxter's body. Nothing was said as the blanket-covered stretcher was loaded into a second ambulance. Branner turned on his heel as the doors were closed.

'All right,' was all he said. The others followed. Daniel began to stumble. Branner stared at him. 'What's wrong?'

'I might have copped a small bit flak, skipper. Nothing serious. I didn't want to worry anyone until Flanno was looked after...' Daniel's knees began to buckle and the others caught him.

'You bloody fool, Danny,' Branner snarled. 'For God's sake.'

Another nearby ambulance was called over and Daniel sat in the back while a medic probed at his clothing. 'A lot of jam in here, lad,' he said. 'You're going to need a lie down for a while.' They pressed Daniel backwards to stretch out in the van. He gave in with a groan.

Branner waved the ambulance away, both annoyed and grateful Daniel's wounds weren't serious. 'Bloody idiot,' he said. 'Anyone else got a problem you're being heroic about?'

No one replied and they set off for the transport lorry again.

The corporal walked beside them, gesturing towards the anti-aircraft guns. 'We nearly shot you blokes down, you know. Coming in with no radio contact and all that.'

It seemed like nobody was going to answer, then Branner jerked a thumb over his shoulder.

'I think the Germans did it for you.'

Twenty-One

Branner was wrong about being split up, except for Daniel, whose wounds put him in hospital for three weeks with an even longer convalescent period following. The long deep slash in his side had to be stitched after a piece of shrapnel was removed from near his hipbone. None of it was too serious and the doctors pronounced early that Daniel would eventually be fit for active duty again. However, the surviving three men of D-Delta's crew wouldn't be waiting for his return. They were flying seven days later with permanent replacements for the dead Wills and Baxter, and Flanders who was still seriously ill from his wounds.

A mid-upper gunner joined them too, a pleasant young man who might have stood aside for Daniel when he was well enough, but everyone knew it wouldn't be asked. By the time Daniel was fit, all kinds of new bonds and friendships would be forged between the crew. In the hyper-compressed environment of the bombing raids it would soon all be different. Branner's next aircraft didn't even have the D-Delta identification letters.

Everything quickly changed. Daniel would have thought this impossible only weeks before. The original crew had believed they'd embarked on the grand adventure of the war together and were inseparable, to see it through or suffer the worst as one. Now he knew better.

The idea of an armistice in time for Christmas became just a dream too. The war bogged down in the mud and snow of Belgium, then in mid-December the German army mounted a counter-offensive in the Ardennes forest that wreaked havoc on the Allies before it was stalled by heavy winter blizzards and a lack of real strength. It became known as the Battle of the Bulge and showed there would be no dramatic collapse of the Third Reich's forces any time soon. The fight would be taken all the way to the centre of Berlin.

The raids didn't slacken. More aircraft were used dropping record amounts of bombs. Sophisticated methods for aiming the drops brought better results. However, as the Germans were pushed back and squeezed against the Russians coming from the east, so their anti-aircraft defences were concentrated. They had perfected synthesising fuel oil as well, which kept both daytime and night fighter squadrons in the air in dangerous numbers.

Daniel missed it all until the beginning of the new year, 1945. He'd spent a week following his hospital release doing nothing except rebuilding his strength, a period of inactivity which nearly drove him mad and thinned Dianne's patience. For all of December he was allowed to drive one of the support trucks taking crews to and from the aircraft at all hours of the day and night. He saw them leave full of life and nervous excitement, then return exhausted and with wide, staring eyes. On some nights the dispersals remained tragically empty, the aircraft lost.

Throughout these weeks he met with Branner, Cook and Sexton for drinks, just like old times. It wasn't the same and everyone felt it. Cook stayed closest to Daniel because of his relationship with Susan. The two couples spent a lot of evenings together.

Daniel insisted on spending Christmas Day with Dianne at her home in London. It was going to be the first time he'd met her parents and she relented only after he agreed to strict instructions on what he could say and do. She wasn't relishing the prospect of celebrating with her family anyway, since much more fun was on offer at Waddington among the aircrews with no relatives in England, and things could only be worse with Daniel put under intense scrutiny by her mother. But there was no denying him.

'Don't tell them about your own home,' she said, sitting with him in the pub several days before Christmas. Fresh problems kept occurring to Dianne at any time. There was so much she needed to allow for.

'They're bound to ask me,' he replied, scratching at the bandages underneath his tunic.

'Stop scratching. All right, tell them you come from a small farm.'

'I do.' The itch persisted and Daniel blinked at the effort to ignore it.

'By your standards, perhaps. My mother will think you're richer than the King if she knew the details. Don't tell her about the sheep either, how many you've got.'

'I probably am. This war must be costing him a fortune. All right, I'll say we've got a dozen rather small ewes. Nothing to speak of.'

Dianne pulled a face. 'Nobody English would find that very funny. We're still paying for the last one.'

'What? Oh—the King… sorry.' It had taken him a moment to understand which part had offended her. The British love for their monarchy baffled him. He nodded at white flakes icing up a window ledge. Snow delighted him. 'Do you think it'll be a white Christmas? It looks like it. My parents will be green with envy when I tell them. At home it will probably be a hundred degrees and without a breath of wind.'

'Just because it's trying to snow here doesn't mean a thing in London. Besides, there it would be a grey Christmas. It turns into filthy stuff, full of soot and smoke and God knows what else. It soaks everything and chills you to the bone.'

'My, you're just full of the festive spirit. It still sounds better than having a heat wave. Have you ever tried cooking a roast turkey when the front veranda is hotter than the oven? Hey, there's a thought. At least I can buy the turkey. We'll say it was won in a raffle.'

Dianne stared at him. 'Are you mad? We'll be lucky to have any meat at all. Where would we find one? My best hope is for a tough bit of mutton.'

'They're having turkey here,' he frowned.

'That's the privileges of being in the services, silly. The civilians are still utterly rationed. Turkeys you can buy in the butchers will be as rare as—well, hen's teeth.'

'Then we'd better get one here and take it with us.' Daniel leaned back, pleased with himself. His blithe solutions to everything sometimes exasperated her.

'Well, you'd better hurry up, hadn't you?' she said. 'I'm warning you, by the time my mother's finished with it, it'll still taste like mutton.'

Daniel wasn't sure she was serious. Before he could ask, they were interrupted by Beatrice appearing from the press of bodies. She snapped at a young airman as she pushed past.

'Get out of the way, you cheeky sod. Keep your bloody hands to yourself or I'll tell your mother.'

Beatrice dropped a folded newspaper on the table in front of Dianne. It scattered ash from the ashtray. 'There's an early Christmas present for you, Di. Have you seen it?'

'Seen what?' Dianne scanned the page and Daniel tried to read it upside down. Beatrice didn't wait.

'They're going to hang your mate Munk on next Tuesday. For Rosalyn's murder. They're giving the rotten bastard one last Christmas, then wringing his neck like a turkey. Not a day too soon, if you ask me.'

Dianne was subdued as she read the first few paragraphs. 'I heard they found him guilty, but there was no mention of the death sentence. It's to be expected, I suppose.'

'It's what he deserves. I would have been at the trial cheering the judge on. I can't believe you didn't go.'

'They didn't need me unless the murder charge wasn't going to stick,' Diane murmured. 'There was the farm girl before me, don't forget. God, what a mess.'

'It's not surprising. He was practically German, when you think of it.' Beatrice was eyeing their near-empty glasses. 'Are you going to bar, Daniel?'

He took the hint. 'I guess so. Can I get you something?' He stood up and offered Beatrice his chair. 'I say, I don't suppose you'd know where I can get hold of a real turkey?'

'You must be joking—' Beatrice stopped and went suddenly sly. 'As a matter of fact, I might have heard some rumours. I can't quite remember. By the way, Bill and I are hoping to slip away together for a quiet Christmas Day, just the two of us, but we've got no transport. You wouldn't know someone who's got a small car we can borrow? Like a Morris or something?'

'What a strange coincidence,' Daniel gave her a wide smile. 'What was your drink again?'

A small part of Dianne resented their chat. It was more important procuring a Christmas turkey, or borrowing a car, than acknowledging a man was going to be hung. Wasn't there enough death? The sounds of the bar roared in her ears as she stared unseeing at the newspaper, remembering Munk's hands tearing at her clothes and clamping around her throat. The printing shifted as someone took the newspaper away and Dianne looked up to see Beatrice watching her with a gentle expression.

She said softly, 'Dianne, he won't be doing it again to you or anyone else, that's what matters. It's not for us to judge if he should get the noose, but I'm glad he is. I'll sleep easier at nights knowing he can't possibly come back.'

'It seems odd, hanging someone like this when so many chaps are getting killed by the fighting... oh, I'm not making sense, I know.'

'Maybe God will make a trade? Let someone like your Daniel off the hook, because we send him bastards like Munk?'

'There's a thought,' Dianne managed a smile that got better. 'Yes, maybe he will. Damn it, I do hope Munk rots in hell forever. We should make it a toast, if Daniel ever gets back with our drinks.'

***

Normally the public transport and centre of London would be sparsely populated on a Christmas day. With the war and tens of thousands of service personnel all trying to make it to their homes, the trains and buses were crowded, while the streets themselves were packed with people all hurrying to the next Tube station or bus stop. Many of the shops were open to give passers-by a chance to buy that last, forgotten present. Everything looked busy and everybody appeared anxious. Peace and goodwill to all men seemed a scarce commodity. Hopefully the Germans were having similar problems and didn't have the time to launch any of their long-distance rockets. No one had time for any enemy attacks.

Daniel had endured the train journey from Waddington with the treasured turkey in his lap, wrapped in wet cheesecloth and kept in a leather bag. He'd expected the freezing weather to prevent the bird from spoiling and he hadn't counted on the heat from the packed bodies in the train. He worried his piece de resistance to Dianne's mother might be tainted—along with her first impression of him—by the time they arrived. Dianne watched him all the way, amused and refusing to offer any help.

Daniel was also prepared in other ways. Packed in his carry-bag were two bottles of sherry and one of whiskey. He figured that if all else failed, he could resort to drinking and dulling any awkward moments.

He was tired of lugging the weight around by the time they reached Clapham just after lunch. Dianne couldn't help much, burdened with a large satchel herself with their personal belongings. It was trying to snow as they walked up the street towards Dianne's home and the result was exactly as she had told Daniel. A thin grey slush lay on the footpath or half-melted in the gutters. It was hardly the fairy tale Christmas that Daniel wished for.

'Here we are,' Dianne announced with a deep breath as she paused at the gate. 'Home, sweet home.'

'Very nice,' Daniel said, staring up at the tenement house that looked exactly like every other home in the street.

'Let's not start off on the wrong foot, shall we?' Dianne said tightly.

As always, the curtain was twitching, and the front door swung open before Dianne got halfway down the short path. Her mother appeared in the frame, wearing her best dress, a long pleated skirt and matching blouse that were more suited to a warmer season and she looked out of place in the freezing weather, complete with fine drifting snow settling on her breast.

'There you are! Merry Christmas, love,' she called loudly. 'You did bring your friend.'

'Merry Christmas, Mum. I told you Daniel was coming. God, what are you trying to do, get pneumonia? Get back inside before you catch your death.'

Dianne gave her a hug. Gesturing her daughter past, Beryl trapped Daniel on the step and embraced him. His hands full, he couldn't ward her off and self-consciously pecked her cheek to return the sentiment. He smelled sherry and was glad. Getting a drink in early wasn't going to be a problem, apparently.

She bustled him through to the kitchen. Daniel was nonplussed at the size of the house. It was tiny, compared to what he was used to.

George Parker rose from his customary seat at the kitchen table, kissed Dianne on the forehead with a greeting and reached for Daniel's hand.

'Welcome to our house, lad. And Merry Christmas.'

'Thanks, Mr Parker. Merry Christmas to you.'

'You can call me George.' He turned to Diane. 'Do you want to put your things upstairs, love? Stop them cluttering up the kitchen?'

'I'll give you a hand,' Daniel said immediately, not wanting to be left alone with the Parkers in the first minute.

'I'll be fine,' Dianne told him. 'Where are we putting Daniel, Dad?'

'I've cleared a spot in the lounge and he'll just fit on the sofa. He's a strapping young feller,' George beamed at Daniel.

'Have you? Good-oh,' Daniel smiled back weakly. This was news to him. It hadn't occurred to Daniel he might be sleeping anywhere except in Dianne's bed. 'I hope I'm not putting you to any trouble.'

'Not at all, not at all...'

'Oh, good... then. First things, first. I've—ah, brought you this,' Daniel told Beryl, hurriedly pulling the cheesecloth from his bag as if it might somehow improve the night-time arrangements. 'Did Dianne tell you I got us a turkey? Won it, I mean.'

'She certainly did. How lucky for us!' Beryl's enthusiasm sounded a bit forced. Daniel gave her the benefit of the doubt. She took the bird from him and weighed the bag in her hand. 'Ooh, and it's a big 'un. Isn't it, George?'

'A beauty,' George agreed quickly.

'Well, it'll do,' Daniel murmured. He thought it was disappointingly small. He even worried it wasn't a turkey at all, but a large chicken or maybe a duck. 'I hope it survived the trip. It was quite warm in the train.'

'I'm sure it'll be fine,' Beryl assured him, heading for the stove.

They organised Daniel's overnight bag in the lounge, giving him a preview of his bed for the night—a lumpy two-seater sofa with rock-hard armrests. He instantly gave up hope of getting any sleep unless he was comatose from the whiskey. There was a tricky few minutes alone with the Parkers while Dianne was upstairs, then finally everybody took places around the kitchen table except for Beryl, who fussed at the stove. Daniel had a sense that the preliminaries were finished with and the excitement was over.

Dianne's mother asked over her shoulder, 'So, what have you both been up to, since we last saw you, Dianne?'

Dianne tilted her face at Daniel. 'Tell Mum what we've been up to, Daniel. She's tired of always hearing my news.'

He looked like a cornered animal. 'Ah, all right. But does anyone want a drink first?'

**

The day wore on with no excuse for the visitors to escape the kitchen. The pubs weren't open and the weather wasn't encouraging for a stroll outside. Clapham Common was just down the road. Its charms weren't enough to entice anyone into the freezing cold. Dianne would have disappeared upstairs for a nap, but that meant leaving Daniel in the clutches of her mother and while that might be worth a laugh, it was just too cruel.

At least the sherry and whiskey kept them all in a good mood and when the evening meal, the traditional roast turkey, appeared on the table, it was greeted with a chorus of approval. Everyone pulled crackers and donned paper hats, blew the roll-up whistles in each other's faces and wished one and all a merry Christmas once more.

The dinner was another testimony of Beryl Parker's culinary skills. The turkey was overcooked, dry and tasteless, the vegetables boiled to death. Afterwards, there was an indescribable pudding, Beryl's contribution to the menu, which Daniel didn't dare ask what it was supposed to be. He manfully ate a bowlful and flapped his hands regretfully at her offers of a second helping.

Dianne was finally beginning to believe they might get through the day relatively unscathed. There was only a bit of cleaning up to do, perhaps a last drink together and everyone should succumb to the stifled yawns and sleepy looks that were beginning to show.

'Well then, young Daniel,' George began, lighting his pipe. The two women were noisily washing dishes at the sink and his tone made the hairs on Dianne's neck rise. 'This little farmlet you've got back in Australia. A family concern, is it?'

Daniel had drunk too much of the whiskey—the Parkers had preferred the sherry—and the alarm bells he should have heard didn't ring loud enough.

'It's been in my dad's name for over sixty years, George,' he replied, taking a cue and having a cigarette. Beryl had been discouraging about smoking in the house all day but relented due to the occasion.

'You'll be carrying on after your father?'

'Oh, we all just pitch in at the moment. That sort of thing doesn't matter yet.'

'Still, it's nice to know you'll have something to go back to after all the fighting's done.'

'I suppose so. Nobody thinks about that either. There's still a big job to do. The Jerries aren't giving in easily.'

George puffed a cloud of smoke out, obscuring his face. 'Ah, but it won't be for much longer, if you blokes keep up the good work.'

'Well, let's say I don't reckon they would have had too many Christmas dinners in Berlin today.' Daniel briefly allowed himself the credit for the entire war effort and rewarded himself with another sip of whiskey.

'So how serious are you about our Dianne then?'

At the sink, Dianne let out a tiny groan and her shoulders sagged. No one noticed.

'Oh, very serious, Mr Parker.' Daniel tried to sit up straighter. 'Under the circumstances, of course. I mean, with the war and everything. We're very fond of each other.' He didn't risk looking at Dianne's reaction to this.

George nodded sagely, encouraging Daniel's wisdom. 'And what happens when it's all over and done with? Do you expect Dianne to leave here and go back to Australia with you?' His manner had changed, his words flat, a father waiting to hear his daughter was going away. Beryl dropped a plate into the drying rack with a clatter and stared at Daniel.

Daniel faltered. 'It's a bit soon to know. I haven't—'

'Daniel's already asked me, Dad,' Dianne interrupted briskly. 'Like he says, it's all a bit soon to know. Nobody is making any decisions like that yet.'

'You'd go and live in Australia, Dianne?' Beryl asked in a trembling voice.

'What did I just say, Mum? Come on, you two. Don't spoil your day with something like this. Danny and I might have the biggest fight ever tomorrow and I never speak to him again.' She made it sound like a certainty. 'Plenty of things could happen before the end of the war. It's not worth worrying about.'

In the silence that followed, Dianne wiped her hands dry, gave her mother a comforting touch on the shoulder, then lit herself a cigarette and sat next to her father.

She said lightly, 'Besides, today it'll be a hundred-degree heat wave in Australia. Who would want to spend Christmas Day like that?'

'That's true, I might even stay here,' Daniel said cheerfully. 'I quite like it and I love the snow. Perhaps there's a little house around here somewhere I could buy?'

Someone kicked him in the shin hard and he managed to change his grunt of pain into a smoke-induced choking. He waved an apology, tears in his eyes.

When he could see clearly, Dianne's expression told him that all Daniel's good point-scoring for the day was wiped completely from the board.

***

When everyone was preparing to go to bed, they heard a distant, roaring explosion. Daniel was taken aback by the Parker's stoic acceptance of this. Beryl only paused as she shuffled towards the stairs, wishing all a good night.

'I'll have a look, love,' George told her, heading for the front door. Daniel followed and they both stood on the step, the cold night biting at their faces as they stared at a glow in the sky towards the east. No searchlights shone.

'A doodlebug,' George announced. 'Not big enough for a V2.'

'Should we go down to the basement?'

'It looks like just the one. A Christmas offering from bloody Hitler.'

They waited a few minutes, but nothing else happened and the chill drove them back inside. Dianne and her mother were already upstairs. George took Daniel to the lounge and gave him a torch as Daniel sat on the sofa, testing the cushions.

'Thanks for a great Christmas, George,' Daniel said quietly. 'My parents will probably write you a letter and thank you, too. They're like that.'

George Parker watched him silently for so long that Daniel thought he'd said something wrong. Then he said gruffly, 'Beryl will be dead to the world in a few minutes with so much sherry in her. A bomb won't shift her. Dianne's door is the one on the left. No funny business, mind. For God's sake, make sure you're back down here in the morning before mother wakes up.'

Daniel was astounded but blurted out exactly the right thing. 'I promise.'

'All hell will break loose, if you let me down, son. Good night.' George disappeared without another word, finding his way in the dark.

Daniel didn't lie down in case he dozed off. He counted out ten long minutes, just to be safe, then crept out of the room and began climbing the stairs. Each tread groaned treacherously, and he tried to stay near the edges, but it didn't help. He masked most of the torch's globe with his fingers. At the top, some impressive snoring from behind the door on the

G.M.Hague

right was comforting. Even if one of the Parkers was still awake, they wouldn't hear anything past all that racket.

Dianne's bedroom opened easily, and he saw her sit up in bed instantly, her white face blinking at the flashlight.

'Who is that? Is that you, Dad? What's wrong?' She was alarmed.

'Shush! It's me.'

'Daniel? Are you insane? Get back downstairs before someone catches you.'

'It's all right. Your dad said I could, as along as I got out before your mother wakes up.'

'Liar!'

'It's true. I promised no funny business, of course.'

'Of course,' she mimicked him, stunned. She collapsed back on her pillow and pulled the covers over her head, muffling her voice. 'I was having such a lovely sleep.'

'Oh, sorry.' Daniel tentatively sat on the edge of her bed. 'Small, isn't it?'

'Too small.'

'I could sleep on the floor next to you.'

She sighed. 'Oh, for God's sake, get in. Don't take all your clothes off, you idiot, You might have to bail out quick-smart.'

Dianne pressed herself against the wall and grumbled as Daniel undressed and squeezed in beside her.

'At least we'll be warm,' he said.

'I was already warm as toast. Shut up and go to sleep, and don't forget to wake up.'

'How can I sleep? I've got a lump on my shin like a cricket ball, thanks to you.'

'Now what are you talking about?'

'When you kicked me under the table, after I said I might buy a house here.'

'I didn't kick you.'

'Now you're lying. Say sorry and I'll forgive you.'
'I did not kick you.'
'Then who did?'
The only answer to that was so surprising, neither of them said it.

Twenty-Two

Daniel and Dianne returned to Waddington on Boxing Day to discover many of the aircraft had been sent on an operation. The weather over the Ardennes forest had finally cleared enough for Bomber Command to assist in the vicious fighting there and a raid had gone to bomb German troop positions at St Vith.

Dianne quickly changed her uniform and went to the Operations Room to see if she might help. Daniel found some extra clothing, then made his way to the motor pool and signed out a covered lorry. He drove it to the edge of the hangers where he could see the Lancasters land, and he settled down to wait. He had no idea when the first aircraft was due to return, but he had nothing else to do. Despite the cold, eventually he dozed off and was woken by a rumbling of Merlin engines. The sun was low and he must have been sleeping for over an hour. The Lancasters began to arrive in numbers and circuited to land from the west, silhouetted against the dusk.

The airfield came awake with Daniel, the air throbbing with the noise of the bombers. Vehicles streamed out towards the landing strip. He joined them, choosing a taxiway and heading for the furthest dispersals. He saw an unattended bomber pulling to a stop and turned towards it.

The crew was climbing from the rear hatch as Daniel braked to a halt. Knowing they would want to have a fag on the grass before getting in the back of the truck, Daniel got out and went to join them. He recognised the crew. The pilot was a Flying Officer called Oldfield.

'Hello, Oddy,' he called as he walked towards them. 'Back in one piece, I see.'

'Danny,' Oldfield eyed him carefully. 'Just my luck you'd come to get us.'

'Why? What have I done? Don't say you owe me a few quid and I've forgotten?'

The members of Oldfield's crew exchanged looks. Oldfield said, 'No, it means I might as well be the one to tell you that Alec Branner and his lads got jumped from behind by a Jerry fighter. They got knocked down. We saw five 'chutes for certain, maybe more.'

'One was late,' someone added. They waited to see what Daniel would do.

'Shit,' he said, feeling the energy drain out of him, his feet dragging to a halt. Nothing seemed the right thing to say. 'Oh, shit. That's not good news… the poor bastards. What side of the lines did they jump, do you know?'

'What lines?' Oldfield asked dryly. 'It was just trees and fucking snow for all we could see. It was after we dropped our pills and turned away, if that's any help.'

Daniel nodded slowly. 'Thanks, Oddy. At least it's better than no news at all. It will be something to tell the girls.'

The bomber crew's conversation changed to recounting the raid. Daniel stayed quiet. Someone patted him on the shoulder sympathetically and gave him a cigarette. A few minutes later they brushed the snow from their clothing and got into the lorry. Oldfield rode in the front with Daniel. As soon as the door was closed the pilot leaned his head against the window and appeared to fall asleep. He didn't stir during the short journey back to the hangers. Daniel couldn't think of anything to say anyway.

***

They went to the pub to have a proper drink in honour of the lost Lancaster. It was a tradition of sorts and Daniel had never complained before—any excuse for a few beers would do. Now he was closely involved with the missing men, it felt more like a mockery and disrespectful. Still, he put on a brave face for Susan, who was feeling the loss of Cook deeply.

The usual drunken formalities had been done leaving Daniel, Dianne and Susan sitting at a table and nursing their drinks.

'How many times has this got to happen before we bloody learn?' Susan said bitterly.

'We never get used to it,' Dianne agreed. 'You can't live like a monk in a monastery either.' She felt strongly for Susan and would miss Cookie too. As for Alec Branner and Dave Sexton, her friendship with them had faded since Daniel stopped flying with them. Yes, they had often still met at this pub, but something had been missing that even Daniel felt. That close kinship from shared danger, the crew mentality that he was excluded from had put Daniel, and therefore Dianne too, on the outside of the inner circle.

'You shouldn't be so despairing,' Daniel told Susan gently. 'Look on the brighter side. There was a lot of good news. Five 'chutes came out for certain, one was late and the Jerry fighter hit them from behind. Cookie would have been in the nose aiming the bombs, so he's got the best chance of being one of the survivors. The late 'chute must have been Alec jumping after making sure everyone else was out—everybody who could get out, of course.'

He left unspoken that the tail gunner had a high chance of being killed from a rear attack, leaving one other crew member as the unlucky, missing parachute. Unless Branner never left the controls to make sure everyone bailed.

'You think he'll be captured?' Susan asked.

'They might have landed on the American side of the lines and the cheeky sod's drinking bourbon and chewing gum right now. At worst, he'd be wise to lie doggo for a while and wait for the Yanks to roll over the top of the Jerries. They're expected to break out any time now with the good weather.'

'Good weather? The snow will be up to the poor little bugger's neck.'

'All the better for Cookie. He can just pop up out of his hidey-hole when the time is right.'

'Or he's been caught and on his way to a POW camp,' Susan said morosely.

'How bad is that?' Daniel spread his arms. 'That will only last three or four months, a year at the most.'

'And what am I supposed to be doing in the meantime?'

Daniel and Dianne glanced at each other. Dianne said, 'I didn't know it was that serious. Between you and Cookie, I mean.'

'Either did I until he was posted missing.'

Dianne reached across and took her hand. 'Chin up, Susan. Hope for the best. The chances are good, like Danny says.'

Susan said quietly, 'It's all right for you. Danny's not flying anymore.'

'I will be next month, I reckon,' he said before thinking about it. It got him an alarmed look from Dianne and he added to her, 'They've always said I'd be going back on the active duty roster. The last extension I got for my medical exclusion was until the new year. The doctor even told me to have a happy new year, like he was saying I'd be flying afterwards. I did tell you all this, remember?'

'Yes, I do now. I'd forgotten,' Dianne nodded unhappily. She hadn't given it much thought at the time because next month was a long way ahead in war. Now it was less than a week away.

***

They saw in the New Year with a huge party in the sergeant's mess. It wasn't just to bring in 1945. This was the first New Year's eve since the landings at D-Day, and things were going well on the continent—the American army were pushing the Germans out of the Ardennes—and bomber losses were less. Everybody could sense victory in the air and a real chance of surviving the war at last.

There had been no news about Branner, Cook or any of their crew mates, but that wasn't surprising. Sometimes it might take up to six weeks before the Red Cross brought information about prisoners of war. If the men were making their way back to England courtesy of the US army... well, these things could take their time too. No one believed the worst yet.

The mess was filled with new faces. Young men with bright eyes and hopeful expressions. For some, it was the opportunity to be a part of the war before it all ended. A taste of the excitement and danger while it lasted. Many of the raids sent out now suffered less than five percent casualties, perhaps three or four aircraft out of an average of two hundred that took to the air. These were good odds.

It was past midnight. Streamers and confetti littered the floor. Many of the revellers wore party hats. A gramophone squawking in the corner barely competed with the noise and couples danced in an awkward circle in the middle of the mess. This suited Daniel's style and he swept Dianne out for a few circuits. With her head on his shoulder, looking around at all the unfamiliar people as they turned in front of her, Dianne put her lips to Daniel's ear and asked, 'Are you still going back on the active roster? They probably won't miss you, if you don't.'

'That's not my decision,' he said lightly. 'You know that.'

'You've made yourself quite useful around the base. I'm sure if you kept low, they might not fuss. I mean, do you have to go looking for it?'

'No, but I don't want to avoid it either. I'm keeping an eye out, hoping I can slot into an experienced crew. I've put the word out. If I wait until someone notices I should be flying and they bundle me in with some new chaps, it could be a bit risky.'

Dianne's gaze drifted across to Susan who was standing near the wall and fending off the attentions of two men. She was smiling and laughing with them, which they found encouraging, but Dianne could tell her friend's heart wasn't really in the game.

'I suppose you know best,' she murmured. It was still the newer crews who got wiped from the blackboards more often than the old salts. Some things didn't change.

'Not when it comes to dancing,' Daniel said. 'Did I just break your toe again?'

'Don't worry, it was the same one. Just try to leave the others intact.'

A commotion stirred near the bar. Somebody took the needle from the record with a loud scratching sound that made everyone wince. The dancers stopped and waited. A hubbub of complaining started to grow as the music wasn't replaced, then Squadron Leader Eagleton popped up above the crowd standing on a chair. He motioned everybody to be quiet.

'Sorry to upset the festivities everyone, but Group's done a backflip on us and are posting a battle order on the board for this morning.' A collective groan went through the crowd. They had been promised a day without operations and many people were misbehaving accordingly, expecting twenty-four hours to sleep it off. Eagleton held up his hand. 'It's up to you whether getting any sleep will help at this late hour, but I expect you to take it easy with the booze from now on, if you're on op's.'

He stepped down, disappearing. There was a rush of bodies to get outside and see which crews were posted on the board. Daniel led Dianne back to Susan, who was suddenly alone.

'Aren't you glad you're still on the sick list?' Susan asked him with a crooked smile.

'I feel brilliant at the moment, but I imagine things would get a bit woolly by take off time,' Daniel agreed.

The celebrations got back some momentum from people who had seen they weren't flying that morning. Daniel danced with the two girls in turn, both them enduring his inexpert shuffling with good humour. Everyone in the room seemed determined to see the dawn on this New Years eve. It was going to be a special year. Besides, the mess was by far the warmest place to be. No one relished the idea of the freezing barracks and cold, uninviting bunks.

Daniel felt a tap on his shoulder and turned to see Tony Bishop, the pilot of S-Sugar in his squadron.

'I say, Danny. Are you still looking for a run with a decent crew?'

Daniel felt Dianne tense beside him. He said carefully, 'Yes, I haven't found a spot yet. I don't want to get bunged in with some kids still wet behind the ears. What's wrong with your chap?'

'I let him slip away to London for the evening and he won't know about the op'. We're on the battle orders. Do you want to fill his shoes? I don't want to get landed with a novice either, this late in the game. It could make all the difference and you'd get to chalk one up.'

Daniel could hardly say no unless he had a good excuse, which he didn't. 'All right, I can help you out. I don't suppose you've heard any rumours where we're going?'

'Not a thing. It can't be too bad at short notice, wouldn't you say? Especially a daylight job.'

That didn't make any sense at all, but Daniel agreed with a nod.

Dianne said with a forced smile, 'I can probably square up the paperwork.'

Daniel winked. 'There you go, Bish. All under control.'

'Well done, thanks, Dianne. Briefing's at 0600. Meet me there and I'll introduce you the rest of the blokes.'

Bishop melted away leaving Daniel and Dianne looking at each other.

'Just like that,' he said casually.

'Yes, just like that.'

***

It didn't seem like such a good idea three hours later, when Daniel hauled himself aboard S-Sugar and started to re-acquaint himself with a Lancaster's mid-upper turret. A hangover pounded at his head and every muscle ached. The rest of the crew were in the same shape, and someone passed around a portable oxygen bottle. A quick whiff of this did wonders. Daniel suspected he was more drunk again, rather than sobered up. It remained to be seen if the instant cure would last long.

At least the raid was going to be a milk run. A relatively safe operation to bomb the Dortmund-Ems Canal in Holland. A photo-reconnaissance flight had confirmed the Germans had repaired the canal from previous raids and the waterway was thick with laden barges, fresh troops and supplies heading for the front.

It was a six-hour trip and a successful one. The worst of it came as they closed the target. The defences were in better shape than expected and a wall of flak greeted the bombers as they began their bomb run. Daniel found himself flinching with every cracking explosion that slapped at the fuselage. He wondered if it was heavier and more accurate than he'd known before, or if he was just out of practice for ignoring it. No one made any comments over the intercom.

When they were well clear and heading home, somebody drawled, 'Maybe we should fly every op' half pissed, skipper? Things went smooth as a baby's bum.'

Bishop replied, 'We're not home yet. Stay awake and keep your eyes out for fighters.'

Someone started snoring and the navigator asked Bishop if he would come aft and tuck him into bed.

After they landed, the crew gathered around Daniel at the dispersal and took turns shaking his hand and thanking him.

'Any time, it's always a pleasure to fly with a top-notch crew,' he said, feeling it was a safe offer to make.

'We'll each shout you a pint at the pub tonight,' Bishop said.

'How can I say no to that?'

***

That evening, Daniel held them to their promise and met the S-Sugar crew at the Saracen's Arms for some drinks. Dianne was coming later. Bishop was the last to arrive and he had a strange expression on his face, but he didn't explain it until they began a formal toast to thank Daniel for his help.

'Just a second,' Bishop said as they raised their glasses. 'We can also welcome Danny to the crew permanently if he wants the job.'

Everybody was surprised and puzzled. Daniel was quick to say, 'Oh, I wouldn't want to cut your regular chap out of a job.' Their mid-upper gunner still hadn't returned from London. He was expected to walk through the door any moment. Daniel couldn't imagine how the man had been so unpopular to warrant replacing this easily and he thought Bishop was being a bit unfair.

'You won't be,' Bishop told them all. 'Smithy got himself run over by a car last night in Soho. He's not feeling too crash-hot.'

'Bloody hell,' Daniel said, the loudest among the chorus of shock. 'Is he all right?'

'A bit flatter than he used to be, but he'll live. He won't be flying again for quite a while, so you can take his spot, if you like.'

The others asked Bishop questions about Smith's condition and Daniel used the time to consider the offer. It was, in fact, exactly what he'd hoped for. A place with an experienced crew that might see him to the end of his tour—or the war, whichever came first. To get a milk run on his first trip with them was a good omen. They could be a lucky crew too.

'I'd be glad to join you, skipper,' Daniel announced, when he had a chance. It got him a cheer and they finished the toast.

'That's settled then,' Bishop said. 'I'll shuffle the paperwork.'

Twenty-Three

Throughout January they flew an assortment of raids, some dangerous and others comparatively safe, and Daniel never had to fire his twin Brownings. The Germans were still putting up a stiff fight, but it was the weather more than anything that kept the enemies separate. Many of the missions relied on radio-direction finding equipment in the bombers to bring them close to their objective and often they released their loads in hope over an obscured target. The flak batteries on the ground were likewise guided by radar and a barrage of anti-aircraft almost magically came up through the clouds to greet the Lancasters. Casualties stayed at an average of around five percent, although some of these were caused by the poor conditions. During one operation, eight Lancasters were lost due to mid-air collisions alone and on another, two crashed while taking off with ice-covered wings.

S-Sugar came back each time nearly untouched. Daniel didn't like to rely too much on superstition, but the feeling it was a lucky aircraft grew. He got some more good news in the third week. Billy Cook was in an American field hospital, suffering from exposure and frostbite. He had hidden under the snow for three days until he was certain the passing soldiers were US troops, then he had carefully surrendered to a patrol. He was expected to make a full recovery, minus a few toes. There were no reports about Alec Branner or Dave Sexton. It was assumed they had been captured and were in a POW camp. Susan was overjoyed when she heard and began to flirt with every man she could find as if she was on borrowed time.

At the start of February, the winter abated and Bomber Command took full advantage of the improved weather. It was during another daylight raid on the Dortmund-Ems Canal, this time on an aqueduct, when Daniel finally got to fire his guns in anger on S-Sugar's behalf.

The flak during the run in was heavy again and three Lancasters had already been hit, toppling them out of the stream leaving a trail of smoke and flame. It wasn't the kind of losses the crews expected anymore, and it was making everybody nervous. S-Sugar made her approach buffeted by near-misses and with shrapnel slicing through the fuselage in places. It was a miracle nobody was wounded.

'Christ, skipper. They'll use us to strain the peas in the kitchen when we get back,' someone called.

'Nearly there, lads,' Bishop answered almost absently, his focus totally on keeping the plan straight.

An instant later the Lancaster lifted as the bombs dropped away and Bishop gratefully turned hard to port, heading for home. They cleared the flak quickly and they found themselves in open skies.

'Okay everyone, time to go home—' Bishop began, but he was cut off by Daniel, whose heart had stopped at the sight of a menacing shape closing on them fast from behind.

'Skipper? We've got a fighter coming up on our tail quick-smart!'

'Tell me when to corkscrew, Danny,' Bishop ordered.

It was all in the timing. Twist the big bomber away too soon and the pursuing fighter easily compensated. Too late... was too late.

'Wait, skipper... wait,' Daniel hated making the call that might save them or doom them, but he was in the best position.

Something about the approaching fighter puzzled him. It was flying in such a straight line, not jockeying for the best position. At this rate it was going to pass their starboard side.

'What the hell's happening, Danny?' Bishop demanded.

'It doesn't look like he's interested, skipper...'

Carlton, the tail gunner, added, 'What the fuck is it?'

Only seconds were left to make a decision. The silhouette of the fighter, the shortened stubby wings and the single rear engine, suddenly became clear to Daniel. He shouted, 'Bloody hell, it's a doodlebug. It's going to fly right past us.'

It was a V1 rocket that by sheer coincidence was going to overtake S-Sugar. Daniel was already tracking the flying bomb with his turret and he opened fire, pouring a steam of tracer at the V1. Carlton did the same but only had a few moments before it pulled abreast of the Lancaster and his turret couldn't bear. Daniel kept firing and saw his bullets spraying around the sleek shape. Only later did he consider how dangerous this was. If the V1 had detonated, it might have severely damaged S-Sugar as well.

Instead, the rocket appeared to abruptly trip in the air, its delicate balance ruined by the striking bullets and it cart-wheeled downwards and out of sight.

'Hey! I shot the bloody thing down,' Daniel told them, absolutely amazed. 'They're never going to believe me, but I shot the bastard down.'

'I saw it falling,' Bishop confirmed, just as astonished. 'And you're right, they're never going to believe us.'

***

It was extra cause for celebrations that night. The Intelligence officers at the debriefing had to take Bishop's word for it, although no other aircraft had seen the shooting. It was assumed the V1 was aimed at Antwerp, which would explain why it was moving slowly for a doodlebug—it would have been close to its ballistic zenith and about to descend. One of the officers was very interested because shooting down V1s was still not a perfect science. He warned Daniel that he might be hearing more about the episode.

Daniel was just pleased to be a hero for one night, and a unique one at that. He had to retell the story of his "kill" to just about everyone in the pub. For the cost of a pint, of course.

'We're never going to hear the end of this,' Susan told Dianne, watching Daniel at the bar explaining his feat to a bored-looking barmaid.

'I'm just glad he can shoot straight,' Dianne replied quietly. 'Wingco told me today he thinks Group are going to really put the pressure on. Back-to-back op's until we knock Jerry out cold. Daniel reckons S-Sugar is a lucky plane and this little shenanigan only encourages him. I hope he's right, because I'd say the lads are going to need all the luck they can get.'

'It can't go on much longer, can it?' Susan asked.

'No, but you know what keeps me awake at night? Some poor bastard, maybe quite a lot of people, will be killed on the last day of this war without even knowing it. It's almost inevitable. How tragic would that be? For every bit of good luck, there must be some bad to balance things out. So it worries me, too much good luck.'

'You worry too much,' Susan gave her a poke in the ribs.

'I hope you're right.'

Twenty-Four.

'This is Kleve,' Eagleton announced, pulling aside the curtain on the target map. He let the assembled aircrews take this in for a moment. 'It's nothing much to speak of and not exactly a jewel in Hitler's crown, but the Jerries have decided it's where they're going to make their next, big stand as well as at a place called Goch just up the road. That's someone else's problem. This is ours,' he tapped the map with a pointer. 'Later today the 15th Scottish Division will attack Kleve in strength. They won't have too much trouble because you chaps will have blown the defences to bits. That's the job today.'

Tactical daylight raids in support of army operations were becoming common. Eagleton went on to explain the plan in detail. Anti-aircraft fire was expected to be heavy, since the Germans had made a point of retreating far enough to establish themselves well. After three days of snow the weather was cloudy, but there was nothing beneath five thousand feet and the bomber stream was going to fly under that. Despite the blanket of white below, because the town had been virtually untouched by the war so far, RAF Mosquito Pathfinders had plenty of recognisable landmarks for dropping their flares, identifying the targets for the following bombers.

A total of nearly three hundred Lancasters would be bombing Kleve that day.

In the Operations Room, Dianne was being stretched to the limit. Every available aircraft was going to be used and she had to do some juggling to have them all crewed. She had a moment to think that even if Daniel hadn't joined S-Sugar, today would be a day she couldn't have avoided putting him on the roster. In a way, it was good that the decision hadn't become hers. So far, it seemed Daniel had made the best choice.

The sky was clear over England and when the aircraft took off at midday there was a washed-out sun that offered little warmth. Inside his turret, Daniel held his gloved hands near the Perspex in line with the glare like it was a hearth fire. His fingers still tingled with cold.

Bishop didn't mind chatter on the intercom as long as everybody shut up when it mattered. During the four hours it took them to reach the target area, most of the talk was about what everyone might do after the war. It felt so close lately. The struggle was more about beating the Russians to Berlin than any doubts over defeating the Germans.

'Look sharp, everyone,' Bishop cut through. 'Target is ahead and it looks hot. They're throwing everything up at us.'

He was right. The sky in front was covered in the black blotches of flak explosions and streams of flaming onions climbed with a deadly grace all the way into the cloud base. The bombing was accurate, and the town was burning fiercely all over. Pyres were reaching high and wide into the sky. However, with the wind behind the approaching bombers, the smoke was obscuring the target-marker flares.

'What do you want me to do, skipper?' the bomb aimer, Walters asked.

Bishop replied, 'Give it your best shot, Phil. If you can't see any markers, go for the centre of the existing strikes. Let's hope the blokes in front hit the targets.'

'All right, then keep her steady on this line, skipper. You're doing fine.'

The flak started to explode around them, some of the rounds close enough to punch at the bomber's skin. It burst all about Daniel's turret in flowering, deadly smudges.

Walters was talking Bishop through the last thirty seconds of the bomb run. It was that vital time when Bishop couldn't deviate from their course.

'I can't see markers, skipper. I'm going for the middle of the strikes.'

'Whenever you're ready, Phil,' Bishop said tightly. 'This is getting bloody hairy.'

A flak shell erupted just under the port wing, throwing the Lancaster into a half-roll before Bishop, acting on reflexes, managed to claw it back to nearly level. Walters was badly wounded by some shrapnel, but he had the presence of mind to press his teat and release the bombs. The bomber climbed quickly and threatened to drop her tail too far. Bishop prevailed, bullying the nose back down.

It was bad. S-Sugar had been abruptly transformed from an aircraft flying perfectly to a wreck moving through the air—and not for much longer. Bishop knew it. None of the controls were responding right and now the plane was descending. Soon it would be a steeper, uncontrollable dive.

The intercom was dead. He turned to his engineer, called Frankston, and saw blood pouring from his scalp. He was conscious and staring at Bishop in shock, waiting for orders. Bishop pulled his mask down and shouted, 'We're goners! Go back and tell them to jump! Jump, jump, jump!'

Even if Frankston didn't hear him the words were unmistakable. He nodded, blinking blood from his eyes, and staggered back towards the main fuselage to pass the word.

Daniel had suffered a strange injury. Shrapnel had perforated the main body of the Lancaster in a hundred places and one piece in particular had neatly severed his canvas sling in the exact moment Daniel let go of his guns to flex his aching fingers. He dropped without warning to the floor of the fuselage, landing badly, wrenching his back and ramming his head against a stanchion. In the next twenty seconds of S-Sugar's lurching around the sky, Daniel was thrown everywhere, hurting him more. When he finally came to rest he was stunned and trying to understand what had happened. For a moment he numbly thought the bomb-release had gone terribly wrong, that was all. Then he saw the myriad tears in the outer skin, felt a freezing wind swirling through the bomber, and he knew everything was wrong. The engines sounded like they were labouring. They weren't flying on an even keel.

With a cold shock adding to his pain, Daniel realised that they were in serious trouble.

He twisted around to look towards the cockpit and saw the bloodied engineer fumbling his way towards the main spar. Frankston caught his eye and drew a hand across his throat twice, yelling, 'Jump, jump, jump!' Daniel waved that he understood, although it filled him with dread. Frankston was now heading for the radio cubicle and the navigator's table, smearing red handprints on everything he touched. Daniel groped for his parachute on the floor beside him, got to his knees and managed to shrug into it, then ignoring the pains that shot through his lower back he made for the doors of the tail turret. He noticed he had to clamber upwards. The plane was in a shallow dive which would no doubt get worse, and they were only at five thousand feet to begin with. There wasn't much time.

The doors to the rear turret weren't there. Steel covered the gap. Walters must have rotated his gun fully and bailed out the back. Either that, or he was too hurt to bring the turret back to fore-and-aft. There was nothing Daniel could do.

Moving back to the rear hatchway, Daniel nearly lost his footing and could have gone tumbling down the length of the fuselage, the nose of S-Sugar had dipped that much. Sitting on his rump and bracing his feet under the sill, he undogged the catches and hauled the door. The hinges were on the forward edge and it swung open quickly, nearly knocking Daniel aside. Then he was faced with the daunting sight of open air and the ground below—a lot closer than it should be.

Torn between jumping and helping the others, Daniel stared desperately back up the length of the Lancaster. Frankston was back at the main spar and saw him. He gave Daniel two vehement thumbs-down, his expression terrible under the mask of blood, and then he gestured towards the cockpit. Daniel figured that Frankston was going to jump from the forward escape hatch and hopefully take the bomb aimer and Bishop with him.

There was nothing else left to do. Without giving it another thought in case he balked, Daniel grasped the outer edges of the hatchway, pulled himself forwards and somersaulted out the door.

No training could ever have prepared him for the transition from a roaring, bellowing Lancaster diving to its death, to the freezing silence of falling through the open sky. The white earth and grey clouds tumbled crazily around him, while the air tore at his clothing. A sound like a hurricane wind filled his ears. Daniel was frantic to find his ripcord—he didn't know what height he had bailed out and didn't care to try and judge it. Forcing himself to think, he found the cord at his chest, wrapped the trailing end around his wrist and pulled with all his strength.

White silk and thin threads billowed and rushed around him, threatening to tangle Daniel like a net until he was jerked upright with a suddenness that jarred every bone in his body. He found himself suspended under the canopy of the parachute and floating downwards at a less alarming rate. The relief was immense and overcame all other thoughts for a moment.

'Fuck me, it works,' he croaked with a grateful look upwards towards the parachute.

He kicked and swung around, enough for him to see S-Sugar below him and now diving steeply. Two parachutes blossomed like mushrooms against the background and Daniel cried out in triumph, then had the sobering thought they were a long way in the distance, such was the speed of S-Sugar's final descent.

He was going to be on his own when he reached the ground.

For the first time, Daniel looked downwards to see what fate awaited him there and was alarmed to see he must be falling into the town itself, towards thick smoke laced with dozens of fierce fires. There was no doubt the wind was carrying him directly into the target zone. More explosions rippled across the ground. They were still bombing.

'Watch out for me, you bastards!' he yelled upwards. It made him feel better, if nothing else.

Daniel stretched his feet downwards as he dropped into the smoke, like a man feeling for the bottom of a murky pool of water. He fully expected to hit any number of things, like a roof or fence, or get hung up in a tree. There was a good chance he'd fall straight into the clutches of German soldiers. After escaping death in the stricken S-Sugar, Daniel prepared himself to meet it in the next few seconds.

It was a surprise and huge relief to fall into a thick drift of snow piled against a wall that couldn't have offered a softer landing. It buried him up to his chest in a damp, cold sludge and Daniel had a brief view of empty ruined streets, shattered houses and raging fires, before the canopy of the parachute folded down around him. He grappled with it frantically, afraid he wasn't going to see advancing soldiers running to kill him while he was trapped. His head escaped the shrouds in time to see a stick of bombs detonate through a line of houses only two hundred yards away. The noise was deafening, the concussion a succession of hot slaps on his face. Daniel threw up his arms to protect himself, yelling a stream of curses that were drowned in the roar of the bomb blasts. When the last of the debris had dropped back to the ground he ventured another look, his ears ringing.

No one was coming to capture him. Nobody sane would expose themselves to the bombardment. There was even a good chance his descent hadn't been seen. The layer of smoke would have helped too.

He hastily gathered the parachute and stuffed it down into the snow at his feet, which also gave some purchase to push himself up and out of the drift. Daniel rolled down the ice and onto the street, picked himself up and experienced a lesser twinge of pain in his back, then he ran at a crouch to the nearest open doorway and went inside.

It was a butcher's shop, evident mostly by the smell of raw meat and a well-used chopping block behind a counter. There was no produce left and plenty of signs the place had been abandoned for some time. Broken glass lay everywhere, shattered out of the counter displays and blown in from the windows by the bombing. Daniel squatted in a corner against the walls, then reached out and dragged close a wooden table tipped on its edge. He was hidden from any casual inspection by passers-by and protected from light shrapnel and flying debris. A direct hit on the shop was pointless to guard against. It would destroy the building and kill him with it.

Daniel had time to catch his breath and assess his situation.

The shock started to creep in. He had been shot down behind enemy lines and only two of his crew mates had also bailed out, as far as he knew. They were of little help to him anyway, since he had jumped much earlier, and he had seen their parachutes a distance away. He had no provisions or a weapon of any kind. In this hell of exploding bombs, fires and snow he was definitely on his own. His war was over, as they said, and the future at best was a POW camp. At least, if he was careful about it, this meant Dianne and everyone home in Australia would be told he was alive. The way things seemed to be going, he wouldn't have long to wait before being liberated again anyway.

The thought of meekly surrendering to the nearest German irked Daniel too, and there was also the possibility they might shoot him out of hand just to save themselves the trouble—let alone to avenge the furious destruction of the town. Perhaps there was no need to give in so easily? Daniel was inspired by Billy Cook's escape from the Ardennes forest and the circumstances here were similar. The British army—a Scottish division, Eagleton had said—were supposed to take the town just after the bombing ended. All Daniel had to do was stay low and wait for help to come to him. What was so hard about that?

Another brace of bombs landing somewhere close with a shattering staccato of detonations reminded Daniel he was now a part of the target. Laying low in Kleve wasn't the safest place to hide. The RAF might kill him before the Germans had a chance. What if other things didn't go to plan? What if the Scots division didn't succeed and were beaten back? That would leave Daniel stranded behind German lines for God-knows how long. The Allied armies might even decide to bypass the town altogether if the nut got too tough to crack.

The answer was for Daniel to move south through Kleve as best as he could and get close to the attacking forces. Put himself in the thick of the fighting and somehow join up with friendly troops when he could. Just to make things more daunting, Daniel realised his best chances lay in moving now while the defending Germans were keeping their own heads down and wouldn't see him. Despite what he had seen so far, the town was supposed to be lousy with Jerries and right now, they wouldn't be too well-disposed towards any downed bomber crew.

Daniel allowed himself a sigh at the impossibility of it all. He was tempted just to stay put and take his chances with whoever came through the door first, but he shook that thought away angrily.

He said aloud, though softly, 'Come on, Daniel. At least have a bloody look. You could be back in the pub tomorrow night with a bit of luck.'

That was ambitious, he knew. Encouraging, none the less.

On his hands and knees, he crawled back to the doorway and carefully peered around the edge of the frame into the street. He noticed his back didn't hurt so much and assumed the jerking of the parachute harness may have partially repaired the damage inflicted in the fall.

Things are going my way after all, he thought with a wry, humourless grin.

The road outside was littered with so much wreckage from the bombing that it would have been impassable to anyone except soldiers on their feet. Burning timber, felled trees, piles of rubble from collapsed houses and a succession of destroyed, private vehicles made the street a fiery maze. There were still no signs of life. A steady, rhythmic banging from close by must be an anti-aircraft battery. Daniel decided that wasn't a good thing, because flak guns wouldn't be close to the expected front lines. He was therefore deep inside the town and needed to get going. He remembered that almost three hundred aircraft were taking part in the raid, but he had no idea where S-Sugar had been in the formation. The bombing could last another half an hour, or it might be only five minutes.

Which way was south?

He risked his head outside further and looked up. Daniel was rewarded with a silhouette of a Lancaster flying under the clouds. He knew the bomber stream was approaching from the southwest. Using this, he judged the direction he needed to go.

Towards the anti-aircraft battery.

'Can't be that bad. They'll all be too busy with the lads overhead to notice me,' Daniel murmured to himself with a false bravado. 'I'll just go around it.'

Taking a deep breath, he stepped out into the street and ran in a sideways motion, keeping his back to the nearest wall whenever he could. It wasn't easy because he had to watch where he put his feet, the ground was so covered in debris. An acrid smoke bit at the back of his throat and Daniel noticed a rain of something solid clattering to the pavement the whole time. It was the expended shrapnel from the anti-aircraft shells above. He needed to keep under cover as well. At the end of this street he could see a junction.

What would be around the corner? It might be a whole division of German soldiers who would love to use him for bayonet practice.

It was another road with bombed-out stores and public buildings running at an axis to the way Daniel wanted to go. Nothing indicated what might take him further south, so on a whim he turned left. As he ran past a row of broken windows, a whistling sound warned Daniel that a stick of bombs was going to land close. He threw himself into the nearest building and flattened himself against the floor. It heaved and punched into his face, the wooden boards groaning and splintering as the bombs landed close. A shower of plaster fell on his back.

Daniel raised his head cautiously when he thought it was over—and stared into the open eyes of a corpse on the other side of the room.

Four men had been killed here, all of them civilians. Daniel was sickened by the sight of their twisted corpses. The room itself wasn't so damaged by the bombing, then he saw the bullet marks across the walls and the sprayed blood.

Daniel guessed these men had been forced labour for building the extra defences. At some dreadful point they had outlived their usefulness, or perhaps they had tried to escape when the bombs began to fall and paid the ultimate price. Daniel wanted to just get away from them. Then he was struck by the drab, brown coats each of the bodies wore.

It was likely that many of the residents of the town had fled the coming battle, but some would have stayed, hiding deep in cellars and bomb shelters. Daniel was thinking that any soldiers would think twice about shooting at a scuttling figure in a brown coat, assuming it to be a German civilian. There was a risk—if he was caught, they might call him a spy because he was out of uniform and that was an excuse to execute him on the spot.

Daniel feared they would do that anyway. The Germans were desperate, in retreat and losing the war. No one wanted to be bothered with a prisoner. His best chance at survival now came with a disguise, at least until he was in reach of the Allied troops and needed to be recognised as a friend.

Keeping low he went over to the bodies and inspected them one by one. Each was a nightmare vision of a tormented death and their faces imprinted themselves on Daniel's memory. Only one of the coats was bearable and not too bloodied. Grimacing at the task, Daniel pulled it from the corpse and put it on over his own clothes. He immediately felt the extra warmth and offered a silent thank you to the dead man.

Turning back towards the door, Daniel got a shock.

A young German soldier had come inside and stood trembling with his own fear and surprise, aiming a pistol at Daniel. The noise of the bombardment had masked his entrance.

'Halt!' he nearly screamed, his voice cracking. 'Halt, Amerikana!'

'Steady on,' Daniel said with a calm that surprised himself. His mouth was suddenly dry as sand and he couldn't take his eyes off the black muzzle pointed straight at him.

'Hande hoche! Hande hoche!' The soldier gestured upwards with the gun, making Daniel doubly nervous seeing his finger on the trigger.

'All right, all right, don't get upset.' Daniel half-raised his hands while his heart sank. To have been captured by this teenager made it all the more bitter. In another life, he could have scared him away with a fierce look and loud shout.

The German was probably a Hitler Youth drafted into the defences. He was little more than a schoolboy in a second-hand, ill-fitting uniform that hung from a gaunt frame. That he had only a pistol suggested it was a token weapon given to a boy who wasn't expected to make good use of a rifle when the attack came. Perhaps it wasn't even loaded. His face was smeared with dirt, with darting frightened eyes in hollow sockets. The soldier's helmet looked incongruously large above his wasted features. When he saw that Daniel was surrendering, a thin smile came to him, a quivering expression of doubtful triumph. He spouted a long sentence of unintelligible, guttural gibberish at Daniel that ended in Amerikana again.

'I'm not a bloody Yank, you idiot,' Daniel told him. It got him a shouted tirade that again had the pistol waving dangerously. 'Okay, settle down.' Daniel raised his hands a little to placate the youth.

The German glanced out the doorway, plainly unsure what to do. He must have been keen to take his prize back to his superiors. Maybe he had been sent out scavenging for food or fresh water and returning with an enemy flyer was going to make him a hero. But the streets and falling bombs were hazardous enough for one person to negotiate. Trying to keep a prisoner under control was going to be hard.

'You haven't got a bloody clue what to do, have you?' Daniel murmured.

The German snarled at him in a childish way, then his gaze fell on the dead civilians. He looked back at Daniel, his expression appraising. Daniel knew what he was thinking. Was his captive really worth that much alive? The Englishman might have his pockets filled with escape rations and the German didn't want to share them unless he had to. There was an easy way to find out.

'Don't get any silly ideas,' Daniel said, despairing there was anything he could do other than risk that the pistol had ammunition.

Coming closer, making sure Daniel was aware of the gun, the German reached forward and patted at Daniel's clothing, searching for anything. He found cigarettes in a top pocket and that was enough for the moment, wrenching them out and standing back again quickly as if Daniel might try an attack.

'You stink worse than those poor blokes over there,' Daniel said mildly to hide the insult.

The German answered him with a grunting reprimand and sidled over to the doorway. He ducked his head outside and looked upwards, like a man checking to see if a rain was easing.

In that moment, the first of a stick of bombs landed on the road outside. The rest hit in rapid succession, destroying the opposite buildings. The blast from the first catapulted the German back into the butcher's and sent him sprawling on the floor. He landed badly and the pistol fell out of his hand. It lay just inches from his fingers.

There was a frozen moment in time when they both knew that Daniel was going to make a move. Then the German heaved himself forward desperately. Daniel stepped forward with his boot swinging. The youth got it wrong, thinking Daniel was trying to kick the gun out of his reach and he put all his effort into lunging for the weapon. Instead, Daniel kicked him in the face with all his strength, feeling bone and gristle flatten under the impact. The German howled once, an awful sound, then abruptly curled into a foetal position with his back to Daniel and went still. Only his shoulders heaved. Beyond the door, a roar of collapsing brickwork and the reverberating explosions mocked their private, insignificant war.

Daniel scooped up the pistol and examined it. He recognised it as a Luger, but only because it was such a famous design. How to check the magazine or even the safety catch was a mystery to him. If it was empty and the German recovered, knowing this, he might flee and get help. Then Daniel would be in serious trouble.

'You're a pain in the arse,' he told the huddled figure, deciding to tie the boy up somehow, which he reckoned was a damned sight more charitable than the plans the German had for him.

Daniel went back behind the empty counter, searching for anything that might be of use as rope. He imagined there might be a ball of twine for tying packages, just like back home in Australia. If he used enough of it the youth could be restrained for a while. He searched the lowest shelves, but there was nothing. Daniel stayed crouched down while he considered the corpses. Maybe they had leather belts in the pants? Could he use them?

A scuffling sound made him stand up quickly and he was amazed to see the German staggering for the door. The boy took one terrified glance over his shoulder, showing him a face with missing teeth, a misshapen lump for a nose and all of it covered in blood. Daniel was reminded of Frankston in the last moments before he'd bailed out of S-Sugar.

'No, you bloody don't—stop,' Daniel yelled, pointing the Luger.

The German didn't take any notice. As he reached the street, Daniel pulled the trigger hardly expecting anything to happen. The gun fired, the bullet hitting the youth perfectly between the shoulder blades, pitching him forward again.

This time he lay still with all but his boots out on the pavement. It had all happened in less than a second.

'You stupid, stupid bastard,' Daniel cried, running around the counter. In the short space to the door his self-preservation took over and he kept himself concealed from anyone outside, pressing his back to the wall

Among the noise of the on-going raid he heard no shouts of outrage. No small arms fire aimed at this shop. He dared a look around the door frame and saw the air filled with thick smoke and flames. Without another thought he grasped the soldier's boots and dragged his body back inside. Then Daniel sat back a while, exhausted.

'Stupid bastard,' he croaked again at the German. Remembering, he found the coat pocket where the boy had put his cigarettes and retrieved them, lighting one and taking a deep, shaking lungful of tobacco. 'Now what do I do with you?'

The answer was obvious and came immediately. First, Daniel went to the other corpses and pulled another of the brown coats from one of them. It didn't matter that it was stained and shredded by bullets. Next, he bundled the German's corpse among them, making him a part of the pile, then carefully he draped the second coat over all of them in such a way that none of the boy's uniform showed. He had become one of the executed men. Another of the civilian dead that didn't rate a second look from passing soldiers.

'Time for me to get the hell out of here,' Daniel said to them, shoving the Luger into one of the pockets. 'Wish me luck.'

He left the butcher's and moved as he did before, staying close to what was left of any buildings for protection against falling shrapnel and wreckage hurled by nearby blasts. Daniel didn't think for a second about his chances of a bomb killing him—they were frighteningly high and this rush through the carnage and ruined streets was bloody foolish.

But he didn't want to get captured. Not while he believed that help must be so near at hand.

Through the constant clamour of the explosions and the steady firing of the flak guns someone called to him and Daniel made the mistake of looking around. Several German soldiers were sheltering under an arched granite overpass and one beckoned to Daniel in a friendly way, encouraging him to join them in what they must have thought was a safe haven. Daniel waved back in a non-committal gesture and kept going. He rounded a corner and nearly walked straight amongst a half-dozen soldiers crouched beside a low wall.

Luckily, they were all staring upwards at a Mosquito bomber passing low overhead, a Pathfinder pilot risking falling bombs to check the target. Daniel dived down next to a gutted truck, the first of several wrecks lined up at the curb, the slush on the pavement soaking him all over and making Daniel gasp at the freezing cold. Gritting his teeth, he peered through the shattered cabin at the soldiers. They hadn't noticed him.

Beyond them, Daniel saw the anti-aircraft gun. Its barrel pumped a long tongue of flame upwards every five seconds, the breech fed by five exhausted gun crew. Surprisingly, he felt a grudging admiration, even though the sight embodied one of the true enemy for Daniel over the last four months—a hated flak gun that tried to shoot him down every raid.

While it was fine for the regular soldiers to cower under any protection they could find, the anti-aircraft crew stayed exposed to the hell raining down and stuck to their job. A ring of sandbags would be little use against a direct hit.

He fingered the Luger in his pocket and let a crazy notion play in his imagination for a moment. Was it his duty to try and sabotage the flak gun? If he had five bullets, should he try and kill the gunners? It might save another Lancaster and its entire crew, and wasn't that worth Daniel's life, if he should lose it in the attempt?

'Like hell,' he said grimly.

A grey, running water was creeping over the snow towards him. On a normal, peaceful day the ice would have been thawing slowly, but the hundreds of fires were hastening the melting. The gutter was filling, pushing clods of snow like miniature icebergs towards an already choking drain. While Daniel had to stay close to the ground, he was going to get wetter and dangerously chilled.

He crawled along the burnt-out trucks as far as he could, then made a quick dash into an alleyway. Still no one saw him, but he had to be running out of time. The raid would end, and the defenders would emerge from their hide-outs to face the expected infantry offensive.

After a few minutes of dodging between buildings and through narrow lanes, Daniel arrived at a wide river that was close to breaking its banks. It was full and flowing fast with filthy, icy water laced with floating debris. Daniel couldn't swim across, but he knew that the opposite side was definitely where he needed to be. Between the bomb bursts he could hear the rattle of rifle and machine gun fire coming from that direction.

That meant there was fighting going on. Help was close at hand, if he could reach it.

To his left a stone bridge had a gaping hole in its centre. On Daniel's right was a wooden bridge, complete, but only just. It sagged in the middle, and he could see several pylons were missing.

He had no choice except to try it and he moved that way.

He was on a street bordering the water and the houses had sheer fronts without gardens. Many of them had been hit or suffered heavy damage from near-misses. In each case, Daniel had to climb over a pile of broken bricks and rubble, sometimes the wreckage reaching the water where it impeded the flow like stones in a babbling brook. The melted snow thrashed and swirled around the obstructions.

Daniel groaned aloud with frustration when he saw a machine gun nest at the entrance to the bridge. No one appeared to be manning it, but no doubt the crew were close by with plenty of time to rush out if attackers appeared. Would they bother with one, insane civilian rushing towards the fighting? He hurried towards the intersection, hunching himself over like somebody older and unwell—a local inhabitant who was disorientated and running from the bombs. He didn't have to pretend being scared. Adding to his troubles, he noticed the frequency of the bomb blasts was slowing. The last of the Lancaster stream, the stragglers spread apart at odd intervals, were releasing their loads.

At closer inspection, the one-lane bridge was terrifying enough without the prospect of being shot as he crossed. It bowed in the centre with the weight of the current, curved so much that Daniel couldn't be certain it was still intact beyond what he could see. He didn't wait for his fear to take hold and trotted past the unattended machine gun. Stepping onto the bridge timbers, he felt immediately that they were shifting and trying to break up beneath his feet. It made him stumble and was an alarming sensation.

He was a third of the way across when from behind he heard Germans shouting after him, but there was no gunfire yet, which Daniel took to mean they suspected he was a crazed civilian running the wrong way. He continued on, an awful feeling in the middle of his back where he expected the first round to hit when they started shooting—just like the young German he had killed. The further he got, the worse the bridge's surface became with yawning gaps and missing planks. He could see the churning water below and corpses trapped by the flow against the supports. More floated past like dead leaves in a stream. He was briefly mesmerised by the sight and shook his head, annoyed. It needed all of Daniels' concentration not to lose his footing. If he fell through, he would die.

Once, he glanced up and saw helmeted heads watching him from the far end, poking up cautiously from the rubble. This made Daniel slow down, hesitating. What was the point in escaping one batch of Germans just to run into another?

He looked harder and let out a cry of triumph when he recognised the helmets as having the rounded, brimmed shape of the British army. They were friendly troops waiting on the far side of the river.

'Hey, hey! Don't shoot,' he yelled, waving his arms as he picked up the pace again. No one seemed inclined to wave back and Daniel belatedly remembered the coat. He shrugged it off as he ran, revealing his uniform.

That was good enough for the Germans behind him.

The machine gun opened up and a hail of angry wasps flashed around and past Daniel, smashing at the woodwork.

'Oh shit, you fucking idiot,' he howled at himself and started running flat-out, his steps almost comic as he attempted desperately to tread on secure timbers. He dodged to the right- hand side and here the bowing of the bridge partially protected him as he moved beyond the apex. The German's efforts to shoot him chopped away several beams, and with a loud cracking the whole structure began to slide slowly downstream pivoting on the anchored end that Daniel was striving to reach. Popping noises in front of him frightened him more—the British were shooting at him too.

'Not me, you bloody fools!' he gasped, waving crazily as he ran.

The British troops were firing grenade launchers at the machine gun, in hope more than with any real chance of hitting it at that distance. Tracers from the German side continued to zip through the air.

The last thirty feet of the bridge collapsed under Daniel's boots as scrambled over it, and when his feet hit solid ground, he sprinted headlong for the soldiers crouched behind a pock-marked fountain. They were encouraging him on and Daniel didn't disappoint them, diving spectacularly between their heads to land in a painful heap among their boots and equipment. He was winded and struck his head, leaving him dazed. Strong hands grabbed his collar and hauled Daniel onto his back and against the safety of the fountain. He was surrounded by grimy, suspicious faces.

A thick, Scots brogue asked, 'Is he a Jerry spy, sarge? Should we shoot the prick?'

Another man answered after a dreadful pause during which Daniel was whooping so desperately for breath, he couldn't deny it.

'He bloody might be. Let's see if he can dance. They reckon Germans can't fucking dance.'

Bewildered and panicked, Daniel stared at the sergeant and found himself looking at Michael Connors, the man they befriended at Skegness what seemed like a hundred years before.

Astonished, he managed to croak, 'Bloody hell, Mick. What are you doing here?'

Connors merely grinned. 'I would have thought that's bloody obvious. What about you?'

'The bastards shot us down.'

'Should be more of it,' Connors grunted, jerking his head at the town. 'You fools have destroyed the town so badly we've called off the attack. We can't get in it, because of that—and the bloody flooding. We were just about to scarper when we saw you coming.'

Daniel went weak with relief. 'You mean I'm behind our lines?'

'Only for about the next two minutes, if we don't get a move on.' Connors tapped his wristwatch. 'Can you walk?'

'Shit, what do you reckon after I managed that?' Daniel jabbed his thumb at the remains of the bridge where his running prowess had been on display.

'Funniest thing we've seen for fucking weeks,' someone said dourly.

Twenty-Five.

Daniel was uninjured, so he was unimportant. It took him nearly two weeks to make his way through Belgium and France to the coast, where he eventually got a ride on a troop ship across the Channel to England.

Dianne knew from official notices that he was alive and well. After that, keeping her informed of his progress was impossible. In London, he tried to call her at the airfield to say he was arriving on the next train, but a major raid was underway at Waddington and the best he was allowed was a message to the Operations Rooms. He asked that someone tell Dianne he would meet her at the pub. It was as good as anywhere—better, probably.

He finally got there in the evening just as the first of the airbase personnel started to roll up. Several people recognised him and congratulated Daniel on his return. He got to tell his story several times. The place got crowded as usual to the point where Daniel figured everybody was there except Dianne. He worried that she didn't get his message. And he couldn't help a sneaking fear she had found someone else already.

Then she appeared, pushing through the mob and their eyes met. She came across to stand in front of him.

'Is this what you call coming home?' she asked gently, arching her eyebrows.

'It's where we've spent most of our time together, so it is for me,' he replied evenly, hoping she didn't pick it as well-rehearsed.

They suddenly crushed each other in a hug and kissed hard. Onlookers made good-natured jibes and comments about what would happen next along with suggestions they should take their passion somewhere less public.

Daniel and Dianne slowly drew apart, still holding hands, their faces close.

'Good to see you back,' she said.

'It's good to be back.'

'Come on, let's find a quiet corner.'

He bought drinks and they retreated to a far wall. They exchanged small talk, just enjoying being together again. It was all they needed.

Then Daniel pulled a sad face, 'I haven't been game to ask anyone else. Did any of the others make it? I told them I saw two 'chutes.'

She answered softly, 'Sorry, Daniel, we haven't heard anything. There's still time though.'

'Yes, fingers crossed, I suppose.'

She brightened. 'Cookie's convalescing here now. He's fine except for a few missing toes. They won't let him fly again.'

'Just because of a couple of toes?'

'He's not too happy about it, but Susan is very pleased.'

Daniel raised his eyebrows. 'That sounds serious.'

'Yes, it's serious,' Dianne nodded meaningfully.

'Bloody hell, but he's so short.'

Dianne punched him on the shoulder and he laughed.

She said, 'Don't be mean, be happy for them. Anyway, what about you? What happens now?'

'My proper leave starts tomorrow. Just the seven days.'

'Then you go back in the replacement pool?' Dianne couldn't help the dread in her voice. It seemed so unfair that Daniel should have to start all over again a third time.

He smiled, knowing the answer would please her. 'No, shooting down that bloody doodlebug has come back to haunt me. They're sending me to a training school to teach new chaps my amazing gunnery skills. No one believed me it was sheer luck.'

'Oh, what a shame,' Dianne tried to be sincere. 'I suppose that will keep you out of trouble for a while.'

'Three months minimum,' he grumbled. 'At least it's just down the road. Do I still own a Morris?'

'Slightly borrowed by half the airbase, but yes. It works.'

'I'll be able to see you any time, then?' He sounded nervous, afraid of her answer.

'Just about,' she nodded, then gave him a sly look, well aware of what he was really asking. 'In fact, I've got the next two nights and tomorrow off duty. Why don't we find somewhere to stay where nobody can disturb us?'

It took a moment for Daniel to dare believe what this meant—what Dianne was saying. A slow smile spread over his face and a huge weight lifted from his shoulders.

'That's a good idea—a very good idea. We can have a bath together and I can tell you how much of a hero I've been. You know, for a while I was surrounded by the whole German Army looking for me—'

Dianne cut him off, wearing an amused expression. 'Yes, I'm sure you're due a very big medal from the King himself. Along with everyone else, of course.' She gestured at the room filled with people.

Daniel slowly looked around and turned back to Dianne. With a wan smile he said, 'Nobody thinks we're heroes. I mean, we certainly don't.'

Dianne became serious. 'Actually, you all are. Honestly.'

He touched her glass with his and winked.

'Actually, you're right and we all are—honestly.'

Suddenly the room erupted with laughter as if sharing the joke. The men and women were enjoying themselves, celebrating another day they had survived the war. Tomorrow they would risk their lives again. And again the day following. Until the war was won and everybody could go home.

Still, Danny had spoken the truth. Nobody ever thought they were a hero.

END.

Author's Notes:

As I did with my previous novel And In The Morning, which was set in the First World War, I'd like to explain for those readers who are interested where the facts in this book were stretched, and the occasions when what you'd expect to be fiction are, in fact, the truth.

First of all, this book is meant to provide a snapshot, if you will, of what it was like to be in the RAF Bomber Command between 1942 and 1945. The title, "At The Going Down Of The Sun", a line from the ode that graces thousands of memorials all over the world, is also a reflection that most of the missions carried out by the RAF were flown at night.

The conditions in which the servicemen and women served varied over the years, especially in regards to the equipment and technology they used, and experts in the subject might see some discrepancies about what was available and when, but some things didn't change much at all. For the aircrews, it was a strangely dual existence. At home in England they were given better rations, reasonable pay (without much to spend it on apart from themselves) and a social life like none of the other armed forces enjoyed. I asked Noel Collins, a veteran Lancaster pilot who flew thirty missions only to be shot down on the last—and who has given me many hours of storytelling and personal memories—whether he was "having fun". His answer was yes. Nobody thought too much about the dangers they faced during operations, and between raids they drank and played hard. They had a good time. For a long while they were the only Front Line that Churchill had and the British public revered them for taking the war to the heart of Hitler's Germany even during the worst months.

The opposite side of the coin was the missions they flew and the tremendous risks involved. In busy periods, three and four operations a week wasn't unusual. Beating the odds and not getting shot down must have seemed impossible to men who dared to consider it. In the five months between November 1943 and March 1944, the RAF lost one thousand and forty-seven aircraft, mostly multi-engine bombers like the Lancaster and Wellington, trying to destroy Berlin and other major cities. When you remember this was during the depths of the European winter and missions could hardly have been flown on a daily basis due to poor weather, then the amount of aircrew lost on each raid must have been very disheartening. They continued on even in these bleakest of times.

The daylight raid on Augsberg and the Mann Diesel factory did take place. However, it happened in March 1942 and was planned similar to how it's described in the novel—a long, low-level approach by two groups of six aircraft (and at that time, obviously, there had been no successful D-Day or months of Allied advances yet—so the bombers were over unfriendly territory the moment they passed over the English coast). Desmond Sands, who is the father of Mike Sands, an old friend of mine, was the navigator in one aircraft. (The seed for this book was sown a long time ago). Their formation accidentally flew over a Luftwaffe fighter airbase where the Germans were just landing—not an unexpected anti-aircraft battery—and the subsequent battles from there onwards to the target and back saw Desmond's Lancaster as the only survivor from their flight of six. The pilot, John Nettleton, was awarded the Victoria Cross. Desmond received the next highest medal, the Distinguished Flying Cross, while other members of the crew got awards befitting their lower ranks. Yes, it seems unfair, since they were all in the same aeroplane, but that's how the system worked. Desmond went on to fly forty missions and spend a considerable amount of time as a Station Navigator, before being shot down and taken prisoner in February 1945.

Noel Collins joined up to be a fighter pilot and like many others was diverted to "multi's" and trained to fly Lancasters because of the high casualty rates among bomber crews. It's his personal accounts, cheerfully given over many cups of tea and sandwiches provided by his partner, Rona, that form the backbone of this novel.

The pretty ferry pilot, called Bette in the novel, is real and arrived to confound Noel and his colleagues one day with her display of faultless flying. The only difference being that the Lancaster she delivered was one of the first aircraft to have completely adjustable pitch on the propellers and she literally reversed the bomber onto the dispersal—an amazing sight for Noel and his colleagues.

True, too, was the story of a bomber's rear turret being blown like a billiard ball out of an exploding aircraft, yet the occupant survived. To Noel's knowledge, the gunner never flew again.

Other moments, such as the close calls of being almost bombed out of the sky by an aircraft above them and the 4000lb "cookie" passing the pilot's window all happened to Noel himself, and he was the man who took his Lancaster over a "hot" target three times in his attempts to get rid of a hung-up bomb. Noel was also shot down in February 1945, captured and finally liberated by US forces after enduring an infamous and brutal forced-marched in front of Patton's advancing army (the Germans feared that ex-aircrew POWs, above all others, could return to active service immediately and therefore kept moving them ahead of the Allies).

Daniel's bailing out and escape from Kleve bears no resemblance to either Desmond or Noel's final flights, but the raid on Kleve did take place and the Scottish Division's attack was ultimately foiled by the sheer amount of bomb damage inflicted on the town and flash-flooding from melting snows.

Skegness, as a holiday town, received an almost unreasonable amount of bombing attacks during the war, and one night the renowned bath house and dance hall was destroyed by bombs. Probably the long pier made it too easy to see and tempting for Luftwaffe pilots who had lost their proper targets.

The description of Daniel shooting down a V1 flying bomb comes from an official claim in RAF records. The fact that he toppled it out of the sky, rather than blowing it up, is likely. The RAF had few defences against the V1 at first and found out that only the Hawker Typhoon fighter was fast enough to catch up and fire at the fast-moving doodlebugs. However, this required getting so close that detonating the V1 risked serious damage to the Typhoon as well. Then some enterprising pilot discovered that simply flying alongside the V1 and placing a wingtip close to the bomb was enough to disrupt the V1's delicate flight characteristic and send it tumbling out of control to the ground. As for any turret gunners shooting down a German fighter, as much as I'd like to include such a stirring account, the truth is it was a rare event in the RAF (the USAAF with its daylight raids and constant attacks from Luftwaffe fighters had a slightly different experience—it was still extremely difficult to shoot down the fast-moving fighters). At the most, air-to-air combat in the dark involved fleeting shots at the silhouettes of night-fighters trying to sneak underneath a stricken bomber. Which isn't to belittle the role of the gunners in a large bomber. Their very presence made the Lancasters a risky target.

A complete fabrication of mine were the murders that took place at Waddington in the novel. Serious crime within the services, especially violent and sexual crimes, were practically unknown. But I was intrigued by the concept that a wartime airbase with a high attrition in aircrew was a perfect place to commit such an awful attack. Who could know if the culprit had survived the latest raids? Any police investigation would be made very difficult by this fact, and rumours and speculations inside such a close-knit community would be rife.

After two years of writing and researching this book, I'll admit that the bomber "streaming" tactic used by the RAF during the war is still difficult to imagine in practice. The concept is simple—as most brilliant concepts are—but the reality was a dangerous and frightening manoeuvre in the night skies over a very hostile Germany. All I can suggest is that there are plenty of official websites that can explain it all better than I have, particularly one created by today's RAF to commemorate the 60th anniversary of Bomber Command's inception.

Finally, "At the Going Down of The Sun" tells the story of the crew of D-Delta, young Australian men flying in an Australian bomber squadron. By the end of 1944, there were at least two

Australian squadrons operating out of England, but in reality for most of the war all the RAF bomber crews were made up of Commonwealth volunteers alongside British airmen, and the likelihood of finding any aircraft, in any squadron, crewed exclusively by members of a particular country was remote. Men came from all over the world to join up and were placed in crews wherever they were needed.

Dianne Parker and Susan DeCourt are totally fictitious. I hope they accurately reflect the enormous and courageous effort made by women in the various branches of the air force. Despite blatant discrimination in their wages, conditions and rations they shouldered a huge workload and quietly got on with the job. It was dangerous, too. Many were killed by enemy attacks and even accidents caused by fatigue they couldn't avoid or equipment failure nobody could prevent.

Regardless of how much I've manipulated the facts and figures to suit my story, I'm still confident this book does offer a clear picture of a unique part of military history. The men and women of RAF Bomber Command don't have a memorable epithet like the "Rats of Tobruk" nor do they have any famous victories to commemorate. The night-time air war over Germany tends to be relatively unnoticed, compared to other well-known episodes like the Battle of Britain for example, or the USAAF daylight bombing raids which has been immortalised in movies like Memphis Belle. In fact, for decades following the war, both bombing operations were seldom spoken about because the high civilian casualties caused made them an unpopular topic. However, the RAF's battle lasted four long years without stopping and for some time it was the only one being fought by the Allies.

In their quiet and uncomplaining determination was a truly heroic effort.

Graeme Hague

If you've enjoyed "At the Going Down of the Sun", it will help myself and other readers tremendously if you leave a supportive review on the website where you found this book. I also appreciate any genuine feedback.

I've written many books over the years, some similar to this one, plus in several other genres. One book in particular is "And In The Morning", a novel set in the Great War. Right at this time of releasing this paperback version, And In The Morning is only available as an eBook, but that should be rectified soon and you'll be able to buy a paperback like this one. You can find out more about my writing, music and audiobooks at www.graemehague.com.au. It's also a great place to drop me a line or ask any questions.

And of course, many thanks for reading "At the Going Down of the Sun."

Printed in Great Britain
by Amazon

22588468R00239